Frisian Freedom

Better dead than slave

ACT I – The Last King

Revisited v1.30

A Medieval Fantasy
By Gerd B. Freimuth

This story is a work of fiction and any resemblance to persons living or dead is purely coincidental. Some of the characters are based on historical figures, but ultimately just as freely invented as all the others. They carry the same names, but are never a real life reflection of the actual person. The author may not necessarily agree with everything his characters have to say.

© / Copyright: 2016 Gerd B. Freimuth
First Edition (English)
Cover Design, Illustration: Gerd B. Freimuth
English Translation: Martina Lammers
Publisher / Print: BoD - Books on Demand, Norderstedt

ISBN: 978-3-7412-2590-1

All rights reserved. Any use without the consent of the publisher and the author is prohibited. This is especially true for the electronic or other reproduction, translation, dissemination or public disclosure.

Thanks to everyone who helped me write, correct and improve this book. It may prove useful!

Note: Misspellings at discount prices!

To all those who want to learn more about Altera, myself or Friesenrecht (that is the german title of Frisian Freedom) you can do so on my website (of course most of it is in german):

www.friesenrecht.de / www.worldofgila.de

I hope you have fun with Act 1 Revisited!

Sincerely yours,

Gerd B. Freimuth akaDerAltmeister on 11 June (Brachet) Anno Domini 2016

The World of Altera:

It is the year 1156 according to the Christian calendar. The world of Altera is filled with a multitude of kingdoms, empires, tribes, gods, idols, ancient rites and new ideas fighting each other, uniting or evolving.

The action takes place on the continent of Europe, the so-called Western World, which sees itself competing with the orient. The old Rome has fallen and Constantinople, the city on the Bosporus, is heir to the once mighty empire that embraced nearly all of Europe. After the Barbarian invasions, however, the Western Roman Empire has been captured by various tribes and several cultural power blocs emerge. Among them the island kingdom of the Angles, Western Gaul, the Catalan alliance, the united houses of Burgundy and the East Frankish empire which extends as far as Rome, at least in theory. But in effect the secular king and the ecclesiastical Pope continue fighting for dominance and the appointment of bishops who have been governing parts of the realm since Otto the Great. In addition the realm is interspersed with ancient tribal cultures and partly autonomous provinces that have been able to preserve their independence and cultural identity despite the chaos. One of the groups which managed to elude feudal domination is the tribal alliance of the free Frisians who maintain their own jurisdiction and obstinately defend their coastline on the Western Sea against imperial knights as well as Vikings, looters, wind and tides. They have toiled for generations to claim their fertile marshlands behind the dykes from the sea. But the dykes keep breaking under the onslaught of mighty storms. Those who don't escape to the mounds drown in the merciless waters.

The Frisians who are not wrestling with the ocean are trying to eke out a living on the inland moors and the poor sandy soil of the heathlands, growing buckwheat, peat-cutting and raising livestock. Thus the nobility has no particular incentive to conquer this inhospitable land, poor in natural resources. The Frisians are well known for laying traps in the moors and have drained the wettest regions with canals in order to farm the land. Their preferred weapons are the lance, also used as a pogo stick, and clayballs they fling with their bare hands. These missiles are deadly and even chain mail and gambeson armour afford scant protection.

Despite all their differences, which frequently escalate into minor feuds on misty fields, the Frisians are united by their harsh environment, pride in their own jurisdiction and freedom from arrogant lords, be they secular or ecclesiastical, wanting to extort their tithes. The Church deliberately holds back so as to not unnecessarily provoke the proud and stubborn Frisians, who are renowned for those qualities as well as enthusiastic consumers of their home-made schnapps. They are a rough, but endearing lot.

The freedom they hold so dear also allowed a brotherhood of pirates, former mercenaries in the service of King Albrecht or Queen Margarethe, to find refuge in East Frisia. They call them Likedeeler or Victual Brothers.

These outlaws plunder the vessels of the influential Hanseatic League, an affiliation of merchants with trading posts on the Western Sea and the Baltic whose power extends from Novgorod to London and beyond as far as the coast of Africa and occasionally the Holy Land. Some daring traders have expanded their business via the Silk Road into the mystical kingdom of the sun, even more distant than the Levant. The reckless Likedeeler's swashbuckling pirate life holds great allure for many a young Frisian. One of them in particular, a boy from the vicinity of Esens, has been trying to be accepted into the brotherhood for years. So far without success. But today is another day.

Prologue

Anno Domini 1156, Northwest Coast of the East Frankish Empire, the free East Frisian Territories, tom Brok's jurisdiction, the small town of Marienhafe

The hustle and bustle on the cobblestoned paths clearly indicated the importance of this day. Then there were the numerous banners, the garlands decorating the houses and the dozens of stalls on the market square offering beverages, pastries and roasted meats for little money. Every house owner in Marienhafe was eager to have his property look particularly spruce to acquire and maintain his standing in the community. Befitting the occasion, people weren't clad in their usual working clothes but dressed in their finest, freshly laundered robes. Thus attired they strolled across the well-swept cobblestones, chatting and having a good time. The babble of voices emanating from the vendors, the laughter and the general noise created a relaxed, exuberant atmosphere, not unlike the humming of a busy beehive. The sun was shining through the slender white July clouds and little groups of children twirled and ran around the adults, on the lookout for the jugglers, tricksters and conjurers who tried to earn their living during the festivities. But old men, too, had their fun scaring those willing to listen to their spooky stories. The musicians' simple, joyful songs emphasised the carefree mood. Marienhafe was celebrating the Frisian Freedom. The usually quite sedate little town had a correspondingly small harbour. Normally just one or two ships would moor here every couple of weeks. But today there were four boats anchored at its quay. All of them small, flat-bottomed river boats as none of the high sea cogs with their sharp keels, and certainly no heavy holk, could have berthed here without inflicting serious damage to their hulls. Damage like that would make them easy prey for Frisian warriors exercising their chartered rights to confiscate any goods stranded in their territory. The hazardous journey through the marshy rivers into Frisia, with all its nooks and crannies and ever alert to fresh prey, was actually the reason some crews anchored here. They were pirates; Victual Brothers, as they were sometimes called in the Baltic Sea. Soldiers and mercenaries.

Sellswords and outlaws. Hereabouts they were more commonly referred to as Likedeeler, meaning those who share their spoils equally. They skilfully exploited the shallowness of the Frisian rivers to hide from the heavy Hanseatic vessels, lick their wounds after their raids and to celebrate. Here in Marienhafe and its hinterland they mingled with the Frisians to experience some normality in their otherwise frantic lives. Therefore they laughed and drank excessively, made frequent contact with the locals and often behaved like naughty adolescents. They made the best of each day they could be together because it might all end much too soon. While they were celebrating, panting deckhands unloaded the goods the Likedeeler had captured and brought them to the large warehouse or straight to the market where they were sold for extremely low prices. The Frisians in Marienhafe and elsewhere gladly accepted the merchandise and were none too concerned about its origin.

A young man of sixteen approached the general hubbub in front of the church with firm strides. His well-toned, tall frame supported a head topped by short, dark blond hair and alert, bright blue-grey eyes twinkled in his face. He was dressed in a dark yellow linen tunic, dyed blue breeches, a leather collar and a pair of waders necessary for frequently crossing the mudflats at low tide. His outfit marked him as a descendant of the dyke farmers, who primarily wore this kind of attire. A small leather purse dangled from his belt. So did a Frisian knife, tool and weapon in one, and originally intended for peat cutting. But the youth's actual weapon was a long seax sword in a scabbard slung over his shoulder, the handle of which he was firmly gripping with his right hand. Without a word and a stern expression, he walked towards the Likedeelers' table. The men were being well provided with ale and roast meat by the tavern. Their crude laughter and reverberating burps were unmistakable. These men had fought countless battles and travelled all the known as well as some unchartered waters. They constantly exuded an air of recklessness and the exotic. From the Baltic Sea via the Western Sea up to the Iberian coast and beyond they sailed the world's oceans. But right now they rather resembled a jolly, coarse bunch, craving amusement and scarcely conveying the impression of being living legends. First among them was 21 year old Störtefad, the spitting image of his father, the legendary Likedeeler shipmaster Störtebeker. His unkempt beard, open countenance and the crow's feet lining the corners off his eyes distinguished him as a man who knew how to inspire his crew and make them laugh. He was swilling back a huge tankard of ale while his companions admired him with an eager silence approaching reverence. They never encouraged him in the process. Only once he had successfully drained the vessel did they cheer him all the louder; caterwauling and smashing their tankards. Störtebeker had been renowned for emptying enormous pitchers of beer in a single gulp without pausing once in between. Now Störtefad followed in his footsteps. His first mate, the moustachioed veteran Klaus Schelt, hat been a pirate since way back, since the time in the Baltic Sea, and wielded a heavy cudgel which he used to throw enemy sailors off his ship. He liked himself in the role of hard-hitting sidekick, had no ambition to take command himself, and his invaluable experience was a great asset to Störtefad. On Störtefad's right sat two more famous Likedeeler captains. The one next to him, Master Wigbold, was the one who least enjoyed the rowdy spectacle around him. In his mid-forties, he was regarded as the brotherhood's philosopher, arbiter and brains. He thought strategically and was extremely adept in gaining the advantage over his opponents by predicting their moves. Just like Michels predicted the weather. As a former monk he shied away from battle, but nobody was a match for his intellect. His strength and astuteness weren't the result of powerful muscles or nimble joints, but rather a reflection of his mental agility. His men knew that the master would always do the right thing and despite his general aloofness, he occasionally demonstrated how much he cared about their wellbeing. Nobody ever saw him laugh, but he sometimes grinned when he had one of his ingenious ideas. Untypical for a monk, Master Wigbold was clad in the sophisticated garments of the merchant class - a beret with the Likedeeler emblem, a black silk waistcoat with ornate buttons and a shirt with slit sleeves like the ones worn by the mercenaries. On his right perched the infamous Gödeke Michels holding a tankard of ale, his crossed arms propped up on a big Irish sellsword axe. Unruly, flaxen hair framed his broad, weatherbeaten face, rings adorned his ears and a tricorn with a feather sat on his head. Michel was regarded as a choleric, grim sea dog with an uncanny instinct for navigation; the reason for his men's loyalty. Gödeke Michels always seemed to know the location of foggy patches, which way the wind was blowing and where to find the best booty. In battle friend and foe equally feared and respected him.

The Likedeeler: Gödeke Michels, Master Wigbold, Störtefad, Klaus Schelt

These three were effectively the Likedeeler leaders of the Western Sea region. The other chiefs were either hiding in the remaining hideouts of the Baltic, like the Gulf of Finland, or in remote corners of the Western Sea where they barely scraped a living in splinter groups and small crews. Only the Likedeeler still operated as a complete brotherhood with their own military force and several vessels. The rest were fighting for their very survival. Originally the Victual Brothers had been hired as mercenaries in the battle against Margarethe, the queen of the Jutes. No longer needed, they had been betrayed and declared outlaws because nobody claimed responsibility for their upkeep. The general, cynical attitude was that they should look after themselves. The war was over, their services no longer required and so they did exactly that: they took care of themselves.

The Likedeeler rewarded the Frisians' hospitality by offering them their booty for a song. Occasionally they even gave it away on a whim. Because the Frisian Hauptlinger, the chieftains, had been excluded from the Hanseatic League, they considered it their right to acquire their share of the spoils, in their opinion unlawfully withheld by the moneybags, through piracy. Now and then, and for a fee, the powerful freebooters helped one of the Hauptlinger to strengthen their forces during a feud. In those cases the Likedeeler made sure not to completely devastate or burn the land that provided them with shelter. In fact their efforts contributed to a hitherto rarely known placidity among the feisty and combative Frisians. The reason was simple: nobody fancied a good thrashing from the buccaneers. The Hauptlinger themselves only kept small bands of followers as extremely well armed guards. Their clout was significantly boosted by the Likedeeler. The Marienhafe family of the tom Broks in particular profited by the alliance when their combined forces asserted themselves against the other Frisian Hauptlinger and gained influence inside the Norden, Auerk and Emden triangle.

The young man with the sword, who now joined the festivities, knew all this only too well and had avidly absorbed the many stories about the Likedeeler. He stopped in front of them and at first nobody really took much notice of him. He was just another guest. But then Störtefad put down his tankard with a burp. His men roared in their usual manner and raised their own clay tankards with drunken approval. Störtefad grinned and wiped his mouth. Then he burped heartily again. Even Master Wigbold clapped and said sarcastically: "Well done. That would have woken the Almighty himself were he asleep." He was apparently having a good day. It was Gödeke Michels who finally raised his bushy eyebrows and noticed the boy silently standing there, intently staring at them. "Well, well, what have we here?" he growled eventually. "Isn't that the Frisian urchin who shows up here every year? What was his name again? Timmy, Kimmy, Mimmy?" "Ninny!" one of the men shouted. Everyone snorted with laughter and boisterously hit the tables until they nearly shattered under the impact. A bald-headed guy nearly choked and turned purple. The stout landlady rolled her eyes. She was used to the Likedeeler smashing her furniture, but at least they paid for the damage and the local carpenter and potter were delighted with the additional work. The young man blushed and sulked: "My name is Hinni! Hinnerk to be exact! Hinnerk

Wiards to be even more exact! And you lot would do very well to remember that name because I shall join your crew! Today! Try and stop me if you dare!" Klaus Schelt sneered: "YOU wan to join us? Ha! You can hardly carry that toothpick on your shoulder, you wimp! Go on; run back to your mummy. She's looking for her kitchen knife as we speak." Renewed laughter and the bald guy exclaimed at Hinnerk: "You're killing me!" Now Hinnerk's face contorted into a fierce snarl: "Right, if you're too scared to take me on, just say it and I find some real men who know how to fight!" A giant jumped up and parked himself in front of Hinnerk, towering over the already tall youth. "Pretty lippy, aren't you, lad? You come here uninvited and then you have the cheek to insult us. Allies or not, enough is enough! I should spank your scrawny little arse, you Frisian twit, you..." "Enough, Alrich!" a voice boomed from the direction of the table. It was Störtefad's, who now got up and grinned. "The boy insulted us because we offended him first. He's entitled to defend himself. He's a true Frisian. So relax. We should take the youngster seriously. Sit down, Alrich, drink your beer and have a nap. I'll see what he's made of." Alrich puffed: "Hmpf, okay so. You do that, Störte." Störtefad straightened himself up, cracked his knuckles and tossed back his cape. He casually walked towards Hinnerk with a smile on his face. His shoulders were covered with a leather, rivet-studded armour. He stared at the youth through piercing, bloodshot eyes. Hinnerk stared right back. Störtefad reeked of sweat and alcohol: he had been celebrating right through since the night before.

Suddenly there was a loud slapping noise. Störtefad had unexpectedly tried to hit Hinnerk in the stomach and Hinnerk had blocked the punch just as quickly with his right palm. The force pushed him back a little more and the crowd started to take notice. Some of the Likedeeler whistled with appreciation. "I must admit you've learnt a thing or two since our last meeting, Hinnerk Wiards," Störtefad commented and cocked his head to take a closer look at the boy. Hinnerk grinned, but stayed alert. "Falling for your tricks a second time would have been unforgivable." After a short pause, when he realised that Störtefad wasn't about to attack him again, he continued: "Back then you said that you would accept me if I beat one of you in combat. I didn't succeed the last three years, but this time I'm ready. I've trained for this the whole year and I deserve another chance. I want to become a Likedeeler! I want to see the world and make a name for myself!" Störtefad smirked: "Well, if that's the case we shouldn't waste any more time on chitchat. I'm sure you agree. Any particular preference as to who you want to take on? Master Wigbold perhaps?" Hinnerk shrugged his shoulders. "I don't care. I'll even fight you if I have to." "Aren't you a little hard on yourself? You should actually consider Master Wigbold instead. Fight with the old monk. Why don't you have a praying competition?" The crowd and the Likedeeler laughed cautiously. To everyone's amazement Wigbold replied: "I shall accept the challenge. Right so, you're far too drunk anyway, lad." He got up and came closer. Störtefad and the rest of the Victual Brothers uttered a surprised "Ohhh!" and "Ah!" while Störtefad tried to safe the situation. "Oh, no, Wigbold! It was just a joke. Sit down, old man. Let me take care of it..." Wigbold turned his nose up: "I know you don't think of me as a proper fighter, whatever that may be apart from a sword-swinging madman. But I'm still a member of this mob. And as long as we share the spoils, we also share the work. I'm not one to shirk away, never have been!" "But... but..." "But what? Speak clearly, ale-swiller. Since when do you stutter? Move aside!" Wigbold and Störtefad glared at each other until Störtefad huffed and gave in: "As you wish, veeeenerable Master! If you insist. We're all adults and know what we should and should not do. Have fun and goodnight to you!" Störtefad trudged back to his table, put up his feet and sulked like a little boy. Michels chuckled. Only now did Wigbold turn to Hinnerk. Seen close up the Master had a penetrating, arrogant look in his eyes. The impression was underlined by the way his arms were crossed behind his back. He didn't seem to perceive Hinnerk as a threat. Leaning slightly forward, he gracefully extended his arm towards the market place, reminiscent of a courtly invitation to dance. "Shall we, young Master Wiards?" "We shall," Hinnerk accepted defiantly.

"A fight!" screamed one of the locals excitedly and they now had the crowd's undivided attention. Curious children and young hooligans elbowed their way to the front and placed the first bets. "Make room," Wigbold shouted and indicated a large circle right in the middle of the square. Nobody objected and the people moved back. Wigbold paced the circle and marked it with his foot in the sandy soil. He took his time. Hinnerk couldn't hide his impatience. The ominous tension was nearly tangible. The former monk's calm alarmed the young man more than he was willing to admit to himself. Was Wigbold perhaps not as weak as he suspected? After all, novice monks belonging to the more military oriented orders were instructed in quite a few combat techniques as far as he knew. He had even once witnessed two puny itinerant monks from Helvetia kicking three strong, well-known outlaws so badly that they couldn't get up until the following day. Hinnerk and Wigbold positioned themselves in front of each other and Wigbold enquired: "Would you like to pull your sword out of the scabbard before we start?" The crowd was amused and Hinnerk started to sweat. Why was Wigbold so composed? Apparently he didn't even have a weapon. So how did he intend to fight and fend off his attacks? Hinnerk removed the sword from its scabbard. A murmur went through the crowd when the midday sun illuminated the serrated edge of the blade sparkling in green. The murmurs grew louder. "I know that sword!" "How did the boy lay his hands on it!" "Doesn't it belong to Abbo the Rebel?" "Abbo of the Ghastly Moors?" "That's his sword!" "The sword from Satan's Bog!" "It has to be!" Master Wigbold raised his eyebrows when he caught sight of the jagged, glistening green blade. Hinnerk brandished the sword in a few practice strokes. The blade swished and left traces of greeny trails in the air as if glowing from the inside. Hinnerk proudly explained: "This is Pakhaou, Abbo's sword. I practiced with it for a whole year and I shall beat you with it." "Interesting. A magic blade, I take it?" Wigbold remarked with the scientific interest of an expert. Hinnerk asked curtly: "Aren't you going to draw your own weapon?" He noticed a slight smile on the Likedeeler's lips. "My weapon is always drawn, my friend. Here are the rules: If you hit the dust three times, the fight is over. The same applies if either of us leaves the circle. Should you manage to pin me down even once, you are welcome to join my crew. But it would be your decision whose gang you prefer. Michel values seafaring skills. I prize strategy and cunning. Störtefad..." He looked at Störtefad, who honoured him with a noisy burp. "Well, I guess you can sow your wild oats with him!" "Sounds fair!" Hinnerk accepted the conditions and crouched: "I'm going to attack now!" "Be my guest." Hinnerk stormed forward with his sword. The former monk didn't move, even when the blade came down upon him. And still it struck nothing. The crowd caught its breath and Hinnerk's eye grew as big as saucers when he heard Wigbold right behind him. "You're no killer, son. You hesitate too much." Hinnerk's reflexes made him lash out backwards to hit Wigbold, but again his blade hit nothing. Now Wigbold was standing a few yards from Hinnerk's starting point. Only the swirling dust bore witness to the Master's ludicrous speed and his near silent manoeuvres. Did this really happen or had it been an optical illusion? Hinnerk swallowed hard. These past years he had fought the

Likedeeler's helmsmen, underlings and warriors, but none of them had ever been as fast. "Is it my turn now?" Wigbold asked and Hinnerk prepared himself for the counter-attack. The monk lunged at him with semi-circular movements. Hinnerk responded at the right time, but missed again. Yet he could have sworn that he had hit him. "Round one," he heard Wigbold's voice beside him and tripped over the leg the Master had stretched out. Hinnerk lost his balance and couldn't prop himself up in time. The crowd mumbled and some people clapped when he landed on the ground. Hinnerk jumped back on his feet, his mouth full of sand. He spat it out, shook his head and grinned: "Ok, you're pretty nimble on your feet for a monk!" Wigbold just shrugged his shoulders. "Did you have enough or do we have to continue this spectacle?" Hinnerk smirked: "I'm only starting!" Wigbold nodded: "You're certainly dumb enough to become one of us!" Hinnerk mentally prepared himself for a special move he'd learned from his uncle Abbo. He now realised that the former monk's speed was far superior to his own. The way he effortlessly avoided each strike left Hinnerk no choice but to employ a rather questionable technique which Abbo called the 'Devil's Dance'. He held the weapon behind his back, lurking like a spider in its net, and waited for someone to step close enough to be within reach of his sword, to touch the web, so to speak. This required utmost concentration. He had to be aware of the slightest nuances like vibrations in the soil and the air. Master Wigbold frowned and apparently sensed that the fight had reached a different level. "Alright, you really do have improved. I applaud your tenacity. But that won't help you either." This time Wigbold stormed straight at the boy. Hinnerk didn't move. Kept his eyes closed and concentrated even harder. Then he swirled around his own axis and plunged his sword right behind him; just where Wigbold appeared. This time Hinnerk didn't miss, but hit the Master's chest. But with a move that defied all logic Wigbold still dodged the full impact of the weapon and it only brushed his arm. Then he rolled over, jumped up and re-established the distance between himself and his opponent. He impassively regarded the blood dripping from his arm. "I see. Quite a good plan. What do you call this technique?" "The Devil's Dance." The Master nodded. "A defence manoeuvre? You wait until the enemy is close enough and then strike at the appropriate moment." Wigbold had seen through Hinnerk's strategy far too quickly. Now the boy had to face the intellect of an experienced man who would show him no more mercy. Knowledge and intelligence were not Hinnerk's strong points. He wasn't exactly a halfwit, but he had always preferred action over dull deliberation. "Allow me to try a little experiment!" Wigbold said politely and Hinnerk once again assumed the Devil's Dance position. Wigbold ran towards him like before, but instead of attacking, he kept circling around the boy, always just outside his sword's reach. Being so close to the edge, Hinnerk found it harder and harder to concentrate with each passing second. Wigbold was now effectively staging continuous potential attacks and aggravated Hinnerk's senses to the last. The boy realised that one wrong move could signal the end. His concentration flagged perceptibly under the permanent provocation and irrelevant noises and impressions distracted him. Hinnerk finally lost his patience and took action. One last time he tried to locate Wigbold and when the monk ran past him he forcefully thrust his sword at him. But Wigbold was no longer there. Instead the monk said calmly: "Round two!" Then Hinnerk felt a powerful blow to his neck. Unable to prevent his legs giving way, he fell first onto his knees and then crumbled like a wet sack of rye. Again his mouth was full of sand. His neck was throbbing with pain.

Wigbold stepped up to him and from Hinnerk's angle he looked like a black giant in front of the glaring sun. He inspected the dirt under his fingernails. "How did I beat you?" "N... no idea...!" "Then let me tell you, boy. You might just learn something. I immediately suspected that your strategy was based on concentration. I used to know a similar technique called Spider Bite. Just like a spider in its web you don't move and wait to attack at the opportune moment. It's pretty effective when you're up against a faster opponent like a fly for instance. But people aren't spiders and have to process a lot more information with their senses. Do you follow me? The spider acts instinctively, but we have to consciously concentrate. Because God gave man a brain, but this brain also has its disadvantages. In the end I merely had to stamp my foot and you had become so impatient that you fell for it. Thus the spider becomes its own prey when the fly is aware of the trap." Some people were impressed enough to clap. Hinnerk picked himself up. "Damn it! I guess it won't work if I try again?" "No. The secret is out of the bag. The first time was enough. It's been a while since I've seen my own blood. It's still red. Good to know." He grabbed the boy and pulled him back up on his feet. He even dusted him down a little. "It's basically a good technique, but a bit too complex for your skills. Unsuitable for your... peasant nature..." Hinnerk nodded sheepishly. And forcefully struck Wigbold with Pakhaou. Again, he missed and Hinnerk cursed: "Shit!" The former monk had instantly jumped aside and created a good few feet of distance between him and his opponent. He smiled in amazement: "Oh my! What a crafty move." "The battle isn't over yet, Master! I have one more go." Wigbold nodded: "That was a trifle naive, wouldn't you agree?" Hinnerk's grin seemed a little pained. This fight had been one big embarrassment. Although he had a few more sword strokes up his sleeve, they were all too slow to defeat Wigbold's seemingly superhuman reflexes. Suddenly he had an inspiration. Perhaps it wasn't necessary to strike the Master. He just had to strike everything inside the circle.

Desperate situations called for desperate measures and Hinnerk had an idea how to extend the sword to a radius which would completely cover the battle zone. He had to exploit Pakhaou's special powers even if displaying its magic might badly offend some of the more pious spectators. Fortunately the Inquisition mostly stayed clear of Frisia to honour the official peace. The sword not only possessed magically enhanced strength, it could also change into other types of weapons. The only drawback was the massive pain the fighter had to endure in the process. Pain so extreme, it could make a grown man faint. Only uncle Abbo had mastered it enough for his reaction being no more than a grim gasp. But Hinnerk saw no other way of winning at this stage. He therefore pressed the emblem on the pommel and tightly gripped the hilt with both hands. He collected himself and quietly asked Pakhaou to change into an extra-long broadsword; long enough to cover the radius of the circle. Master Wigbold watched with the interest of a curious scholar. He was blissfully unaware of what was about to happen, and so was the audience. Initially Hinnerk just felt a slight tingling sensation. It intensified until intense pain started throbbing through his arms and then invaded his entire body. His heart was pounding, the little hairs on his neck stood up and he clenched his teeth while he was writhing in the grip of cramps, shrouded in a greeny, nebulous aura. The crowd moved back. "That's witchcraft!" screamed an old woman and crossed herself repeatedly. "Rubbish! That's just Ab.. Ab... Abbos crazy sword!" belched a half-drunk man. Another shouted: "WOW!" The sparkling green weapon changed shape and become longer and longer. Once it had completed its transformation, there was a loud bang and Hinnerk fell onto his knees. Someone else, who was watching from the top of the church tower, took a deep breath. Hinnerk's knees had turned to jelly and beads of sweat were dripping from his nose. Wigbold raised his eyebrows: "You surprise me again, but magic is but a fleeting companion. Nothing but a tool of pretend power. You shouldn't count on it." Hinnerk grinned through the pain and the sweat: "It was a good fight, Master. But now I shall end it." The Likedeeler looked grim: "Seems like it. Here goes!" Hinnerk trudged to the middle and positioned Pakhaou's elongated blade at the edge of the circle. "You better make room!" The crowd didn't need to be told twice and beat a hasty retreat. Hinnerk started to twirl around like a spinning top. He as the centre of the swinging action and Pakhaou as the scythe. Wigbold started running and at first he was as fast as the blade. "A nice little exercise," he observed, apparently not at all challenged or concerned. Some of the spectators grew dizzy at the sight of the ever faster swinging blade when they could no longer recognise either of the fighters. The whirring of the sword became even faster and more piercing and one of the drunken bystanders threw up. Nobody wanted to be close to the deadly weapon. Hinnerk stepped it up another notch and now also moved the blade up and down while still swinging it around. "Faster!" he hissed. The jarring sound was menacing as the speed increased. Gödeke Michels commented calmly: "If the boy lets go of the sword, the force could easily damage the church spire. This could turn ugly." Störtefad agreed: "Either that or it might fly as far as Emden." By now the blade was overtaking Wigbold's shadow, but Hinnerk was exhausted. All the fighting and Pakhaou's transformation had cost him a lot more strength than he had bargained for. This was his last trump card. After that he had nothing left. "It has to work. It just has to! I don't want to wait any longer. I've got to get out of here!" he griped in his thoughts. He felt a jolt travelling through the blade as it hit Wigbold's hazy reflection. Only now did he slow down the speed of the whirling blade and then brought it to a halt. It shrank back to its normal size. Hinnerk's head was spinning more than it had ever before in his life and he nearly missed the crowd breaking into cheers. As if through a veil he saw Master Wigbold's beret lying in the dust. Hinnerk smiled. He had evidently expelled Wigbold from the circle and therefore won the fight. Hinnerk twirled around on one foot and staggered so alarmingly that even one of the very drunk men noticed: "Wha... what's up?" Hinnerk was so elated that his pains virtually vanished and the broad grin wouldn't leave his face.

At last! At last he was a member of the Likedeeler! At last he could go to sea, get away from the boring peasant life and have proper adventures, find treasures and romance. Exploits he would tell his grandchildren gathered around the open fire in his old age. When he contentedly looked back on a rich and full life. He was over the moon. In fact he was so happy that he only vaguely heard the words: "Round three." There was a bang and then everything was shrouded in darkness. But the smile on his face remained. As if there were no more unhappiness on Altera. He had won.

Chapter 1

Stranded Goods

Hinnerk was disappointed and angry. Angry with himself, angry with the Likedeeler, angry with Abbo, Pakhaou, the sword, the dyke he was climbing right now and generally angry with the whole world. Without exception. He had handed the sword back to his uncle right after the embarrassing fight. This gentleman had viewed the whole debacle from the roof of the Marienhafe church. Abbo had treated Hinnerk's aching head with cold compresses and praised his progress effusively, but Hinnerk would have none of it. In his ears it sounded like his uncle was mocking him. Even the Likedeeler's invitation to join them for a drink had done nothing to improve his mood. It had only infuriated him all the more about his defeat. When he pressed him, Wigbold had explained how he had escaped the sword's blade without leaving the circle. Hinnerk's eyes had nearly popped out of his head. The former monk had simply jumped up and had thrown his dagger into Pakhaou's orbit so that Hinnerk thought he had struck him. But Wigbold had never left the circle and had jumped so high that he had only landed back on the ground once Hinnerk had stopped. It seemed incredible, but the Master looked terribly pale and sweat was running down his face. Michels and Störtefad confirmed the story. Abbo, too, had seen it that way. Wigbold declared that it would take him a week to replenish the mental reserves he had exhausted through his superhuman efforts. According to Abbo it was all related to the monks, their prayers and their practice of mixing work with the spirit. Ora et labora.

It was essentially just another form of magic, even if the Master didn't like the description. There were so many questions about his abilities, but Hinnerk only angrily pulled at his hair. He had lost all interest in the festivities or any other diversions. It no longer mattered what happened next. This time he should have won. He desperately wanted to leave East Frisia. Have adventures with the Likedeeler. Not as a sailor or pirate, but as a free man in search of faraway countries, great battles and without concern for boring, mundane worries and duties. He longed to travel the seas and perform heroic deeds as an equal companion of the other free men. Perhaps even with a saucy Irish redhead by his side. Hinnerk chuckled in spite of himself when he sat down on the dyke and gazed at the incoming tide washing over the mudflats. The salty breeze blew into his face. Klütje, his dog, was busy sniffing around and barked when he discovered some voles and chased them off. Life on shore may be enough for all the others, but so terribly boring and tedious even a full stomach couldn't relieve Hinnerk's discontent. Everything felt as flat and drab as the land itself if you disregarded the march which covered vast tracks like a putrid mould. The Frisians' petty territorial feuds were anything but epic, they were childish and stupid. But the sea called Hinnerk with its exotic, magical allure and he wanted to be right in the middle of great adventures as long as he was still young enough. Wanted to fight with the ocean knights and duel with the men of the Hanseatic League, capture rich trading vessels and discover new coasts. Dig up buried treasure and slay monsters. All that and so much more.

But now it would take months again until he'd get another chance to join the Likedeeler. Only the best and toughest men were accepted into their ranks. Störtefad had once explained it like this: "In our crew everyone has to depend on each other, Hinnerk. Everybody has to have a certain degree of fighting ability. Nobody wants a loser who can't cover their backs, right?" Hinnerk understood and that's what annoyed him all the more. Sure, he could have joined any other gang of buccaneers, even the Frisian ones like those of Friedhelm Nordendi or Behrend Attena, which occasionally still sailed towards Jutland or the lands of the Angles for a bit of raiding. Now and again, when the opportunity presented itself, they also attacked Hanseatic ships. But Hinnerk only wanted to sign up with the Likedeeler. He was impressed by the code of honour they practised amongst themselves and even towards the ships they captured and their crews. These men were no dumb robbers, they were much more than that. Besides Nordendi and Attena were too Frisian and set out to sea less and less frequently with advancing age. The era of the Frisian pirates would die with them. The old days were gone. Neither were they adventurers like the Likedeeler. They had no vision and no motto. The Likedeeler, on the other hand weren't just marauders; they were free thinkers, skilled survivors, voyagers with a zest for life.

That afternoon a frustrated Hinnerk reported for duty as dyke warden. This meant sitting on top of the dyke looking out for looters and Norsemen. More than once the latter had invaded Frisia, leaving terror and death in their wake. Although these raids had abated since the Battle of Norden, the Frisians never again wanted to experience such horrors unleashed on their homeland. For this reason, and amongst other precautions, they had founded the modest fleet they called the Frisian Watch. Apart from being duty-bound to build more dykes they had also introduced the Dyke Watch, manned by the younger members of the local families. As soon as they sighted an enemy vessel, they ran to the closest castle, town or village to sound the alarm. So far Hinnerk had not witnessed an enemy approach, but he realised the importance of his task. Today though he wasn't in the mood. He was simply too disappointed and even the loyal Klütje couldn't cheer him up.

Klütje was a calf-high, four-legged predator, as much at home in the water as he was on land. The coast dog could press his four small, muscular legs close to his body in order to move through the water with his wide paddle tail. His head resembled that of an otter; his coat was short and oily and his teeth sharp enough to crack mussels and other shellfish or tear meat apart. Hinnerk threw a chewed up wooden ball down the dyke and Klütje instantly ran after it and brought it back. When he barked he sounded like a small seal. Klütje was a smart and highly active dog and playing with him soothed Hinnerk's frayed nerves. Eventually he sighed and took Klütje's face between his hands, rubbed it until it looked all crumpled. "You're always there for me, aren't you? Yes, you are. And I'll always be there for you, too. You're my little doggy, hey?" Klütje yelped and excitedly chased after some seagulls that were searching for worms. Hinnerk grinned: "You show them!" He gazed at the grey sea again with its white spray breaking against the shell-strewn beach. There wasn't a ship in sight, just the contours of the islands Langeoog, Baltrum and Spiekeroog. Soon the fog would be rising. Hinnerk could feel it in his Frisian bones. And sure enough, the at first thin veils of mists quickly turned into a thick haze approaching the shore and the dyke and gradually swallowed them up. Even the sun was now just a barely visible, shadowy outline. Hinnerk frowned; these conditions were less than ideal for keeping watch. He nervously scratched his arm and noticed that he no longer felt his wounds and exhaustion after the fight with Wigbold. The fresh sea air may have played its part, but his recovery was mainly due to the consecrated water Father Meenhard from the Marienhafe church had made him drink and which was now releasing its healing powers. Meenhard had sold him the blessed liquid at a reduced price because he had felt sorry for the beaten boy. Nights of prayer and chanting had cleansed the holy water and infused it with the essence of God, he claimed. Hinnerk wasn't exactly proud of himself as he now remembered that he hadn't even thanked the priest or his uncle. He pulled at the grass and chewed on a sprig. Then he got up and walked down to the shore with Klütje to have a better view and collect some shells. Travellers on the market in Esens bought them eagerly and certain shells could be worked into a decent mortar substitute and many a healing ointment after a recipe from the Marienkamp monks. It provided a small extra income for the dyke watchers. Flotsam like this was common property and nobody objected. A handful of people were able to earn their living by collecting stranded goods, but they lived mostly on the islands where they claimed everything the ocean washed ashore. The old saying "The sea provides and the sea takes it away" was taken very seriously on the East Frisian Islands along the coast. Farming and animal husbandry was exclusively practised by a very few rich island dwellers. Since time immemorial most of the others had been fishermen and collectors of whatever they found on the beach and the mudflats. Hinnerk leaned forward when he spotted a particularly pretty black shell and shrank back when he noticed the softness of the sand on which it rested. The soil was yielding and warm. It felt like skin.

Then he saw her and jumped up while Klütje growled and went into defence mode. A human being, half covered with sand; legs and arms close to the body. Hinnerk swallowed hard. Never before had he seen a stranded person and here was one of them, right in front of his eyes. He gingerly started to push the sand aside. Now he saw that the creature was a young girl, quite close to his own age. She only wore a skimpy, sleeveless linen tunic and dark, short trousers. Her pretty, even features were framed by purple hair held back with small clips. Eyes closed, she was slowly breathing in rhythm with the waves. Hinnerk instantly found her attractive and the blood rushed to his head.

Red as a lobster, his hands trembling, he turned her face towards him. "Thank God, she's alive!" Hinnerk scanned the shore for help, but there was nobody. Nobody except the three men mooring their sailing boat he had completely overlooked!

The boy got such a shock, he nearly fell on top of the girl. Fortunately he was agile and managed to rise again immediately, propping himself up on her exposed hip. Hinnerk focussed on the newcomers. Their vessel was fast, shallow-draft and nimble, the type preferably used by small traders because it was cheap to buy and maintain. This ship, however, sported an unusual black sail flaunting a stylised, screeching white seagull. There was no doubt. These men were local pirates. The other dyke watchers had told him about them in the tavern in Esens. "That's all I need now," Hinnerk moaned, grabbed Klütje and stuffed him into his pouch filled with salt water. This way he could take the coast dog with him into the dry interior without the animal dehydrating too much or its coat becoming too rough. Like a nightmare he saw the three men approaching through the fog. They made straight for him and their leader was carrying a battle axe on his shoulder. His pockmarked face and nasty grin promised no good. The other two chaps looked just as shifty. One of them was a broad, bald-headed giant, the other thin and lanky with combed back, fair hair.

Hinnerk cursed the fog: "Why now of all times? Shit!" Without it a Frisian guard ship under the command of Admiral Hark would have long discovered the marauders and driven them away. The girl woke up, grabbed Hinnerk's arm in an iron grip and pulled him down to her with unexpected strength. Through salt-incrusted, half open eyes she begged in a weak voice: "Get me away from here. They want to take me with them, but I don't want to. Please!" Hinnerk made a far-reaching decision and drew his dagger. For years now the villains had been terrorising the Frisian coast. They called their leader Driftwood Theo. More vulture than warrior, he was infamous for attacking defenceless merchants and convoys. But his speciality was gathering stranded goods before anyone else could get to them. With the axe on his shoulders he could fell entire masts, if the rumours were true. Theo was wearing a leather helmet, studded around the forehead, and a thick scarf wound around his neck, as well as a dark leather collar. His left shoulder was also protected by a three-pronged armour. Theo's beard was filthy, his broad nose pockmarked, his eyes bloodshot. His eyebrows were close to vertical and two big, ugly scars graced the right half of his face. Hinnerk shouted at the men: "Stay right where you are, Driftwood Theo! This is the dyke watch." Before he knew what was happening, Theo had swung his axe and hit the ground. "Sanddrift!" The sand in front of Hinnerk's eyes exploded, flew into his eyes, nose and mouth and pushed him back like a wall. Hinnerk jumped to the side and shook himself until he saw a dirty grin spreading over Theo's face: "Ha! What have we here? A little Frisian boy, who's playing at being dyke watch, trying to snatch our booty." Theo bend forward with menace in his tiny eyes: "We can't have that, can we now?" He straightened himself and gesticulated with his left hand in a wide, sweeping gesture while his right gripped the axe on his shoulder.

Then he said dramatically: "But I've seen enough blood and death today. I shall therefore graciously forget what I've just heard as long as you surrender the girl. I'd hate having to chop up such a handsome, young lad." Hinnerk frowned and increased his distance: "What happened with the sand?! What kind of move was that?" Theo was clearly amused: "Oh, that? I call it the Sanddrift. Pretty effective, hey? And that was just a small demonstration of my skills as a beachcomber and master butcher." "It was nothing but a sneaky trick!" Hinnerk barked back. All at once Theo became serious: "Listen here now, boy. And listen well. Last night I saw twelve of my men drown in the floods, get it? I toiled across the surf and the mudflats just to get this girl and I will, you hear?" Theo nodded vigorously without taken his eyes off Hinnerk. "I won't be stopped by a snotty-nosed urchin with a death-wish. Is that what you want? Do you want to die, boy? Are you that stupid?"

In hindsight the reply Hinnerk struggled to voice had been just that, a death-wish. He said: "You want the girl? Come and get her, you bastard!" Klütje whimpered in his pouch and Hinnerk slapped him slightly. A sign for the coast dog to stay quiet no matter what. The youth nervously fiddled with his Frisian dagger, a mixture of knife and spade. Theo picked up his axe. "Right, boy. As you wish." Hinnerk countered: "I'm a Frisian. And just like the dyke I won't shrink back from the waves or disreputable scum like you!"

Theo laughed: "Tosh! Useless nonsense. Say your last prayers." The axe flew towards him and the two blades clashed. Hinnerk's arm instantly burned like hell, but Theo was already aiming his next blow. Just in time Hinnerk leaped out of reach and Theo immediately kept up the attack. He was deadly serious now. Without a shield or effective weapon Hinnerk was at a massive disadvantage. He had to fully concentrate on defending himself; attack was out of the question. Theo effortlessly wielded his axe with just one hand while he kept his left arm behind his back. Only his reflexes saved Hinnerk from the deadly blows. Twice the axe scraped him, however, and slashed his skin and shirt. "Not bad," Theo acknowledged. "But take a good look at yourself, boy. You won't survive this fight. Go home and have a glass of milk." Hinnerk forced himself to smirk: "Is this supposed to be a truce?" Theo seemed surprised. "Absolutely not. That was just my conscience talking." "As if you have one!" Theo attacked with renewed vigour. Hinnerk tried to recall what uncle Abbo had taught him about facing an opponent who was armed with an axe. Their blows were staggering but also slow. Axe fighters were attackers with few chances of blocking their opponents which required a shield. But Theo didn't have a shield. Presumably because it was too debilitating in a fight aboard ship where mobility was rather more important. This must be his weak spot. While Theo's blows kept coming, Hinnerk incidentally noticed that his two sidekicks had grabbed the girl and were dragging her to the boat. Hinnerk had to act fast or he would fail just like he had in his battle against Master Wigbold. He growled: "I'm done losing. Enough!" He clutched his dagger so tightly, his knuckles protruded. When Theo raised his axe for another strike, Hinnerk aimed the dagger right at the axe's handle and his arm shot forward like a snake. He struck the handle with the broad part of the dagger. The axe was catapulted back and landed smack-bang in Theo's face. The man wailed and clutched his broken nose. He frantically lashed out so that Hinnerk couldn't deliver the death blow. Instead Hinnerk decided to chase after Theo's cronies who were just about to heave the girl onto the ship. They spotted him too late. Hinnerk flung Klütje's wooden ball full whack at the gangly robber's temple, who slumped down like a sack of potatoes. Then he held the dagger to the bald-headed giant's throat. The baffled man was carrying the girl and couldn't draw his weapon. Hinnerk roared: "Let her go! Right now!" The giant grinned from ear to ear: "Put that little knife away before Theo chains you to the mast and leaves you there to rot with nothing but salt water to drink! You better believe me. It will drive you insane. You'll be so thirsty, you'll swallow anything." Hinnerk pointed the tip of the dagger at the man's eyes. "Let her go! I can repeat what I did to Theo any time. Like right now!" The giant sighed and put the girl down. Up to that moment she hadnt' said a word. But now she opened her eyes. She squinted a few times and caked salt slid from her lashes. "Wh... where am I? What's going on?" Hinnerk pulled her towards him. "I'm getting you out of here. Get off the boat. Come on." The girl nodded slowly and drowsily. The two of them jumped off the deck and hastened towards the dyke. Theo's voice boomed: "Sanddrift reach far!!" Sand shot up from the ground and barred their path. "Just run through it!" Hinnerk told the girl. But the force of the swirling sand was stronger than before and they collided with it as if they'd hit a wall. The girl quickly got back on her feet and tried to help Hinnerk up. She seemed completely awake now. "Get up! Please. We have to get away!" she screamed when the giant and Theo approached. Theo was wiping the blood from his face. The girl couldn't leave Hinnerk on his own. The giant easily scooped her up and put her over his shoulder where she struggled wildly: "Let go of me, you big oaf!" "Oh la la, a fiery little wench, Theo." Theo wheezed: "God help you, if all this isn't worth it..." He grabbed Hinnerk by his collar and yanked him up. "That was an interesting move, boy, to use my own weapon on me. Good idea. Attack is the best form of defence. That's my motto, too. What a shame my irritation has turned into rage and I have to kill you now." Hinnerk tried to free himself from Theo's iron grip, but failed miserably. Theo threw him roughly onto the beach and Hinnerk cursed when he twisted his knee as he hit the ground. He could hear the crunch and saw the pirate coming closer like an executioner with the axe on his shoulder, once again demonstrating the futility of resistance. A whimpering from his pouch reminded Hinnerk of Klütje and he pulled the dog out of the bag. "Off you go. Dive into the sea! Tell Abbo!" Hinnerk whispered. But the animal made no move to escape into the ocean. Instead he wagged his fin and barked encouragingly as if he could help. "Oh," said Theo, "what have we here? I thought I heard something earlier. So that's your pet, hey? A cute little thing." "You so much as lay a finger on him, I swear I'll..." "Swear? You would do better not to swear in your last moments on this earth. Broken promises weigh on the soul and then you won't get to heaven." Theo was very close now and behind him Hinnerk saw the struggling girl being carried away by the giant. When Theo now brandished the axe over the growling Klütje's head, Hinnerk screamed and protectively pulled the coast dog to himself. The girl looked up, saw the situation and suddenly fainted. The giant shouted: "Hey, Theo, there's something wrong with her. Look!" He waved with the girl's limp hand. Theo paused. "Is she dead? What did you do to her, you dumbwit?" "Nothing, I..." The giant's eyes widened in surprise when the girl freed herself with supernatural strength. "Oh, shit!" She faced the giant and pushed his chest with her right hand. Something snapped and the brawny hulk flew through the air like a doll. With a distant splash he landed in the water and the current took him away with a speed that implied it wanted to drown him.

The girl seemed dazed now and staggered along the shore with her eyes closed. Her bare toes clawed into the sand. She turned to Theo and Hinnerk. Those two were so shocked that they forgot their own quarrel. Theo snarled: "Hey there, you bitch! What did you do to him? Get him back here at once!" The girl didn't react. Her eyes opened and were entirely white. The air around her was flickering. Theo muttered angrily: "What the devil is going on?" He noticed Hinnerk's arm pointing to the sea. He spun around just it in time to see a towering, yet quite thin wave heading straight for him.

"Oh, fuck..." were his last words before the water overpowered him and pulled him into the ocean. The wave had been narrow enough to capture just him. Miraculously it hadn't touched Hinnerk and Klütje. The pressure squeezed the air out of Theo's lungs and he lost his orientation in the swirling torrents before he disappeared beneath the water. Another wave approached the villains' boat, embraced the unconscious, lanky pirate and pulled him into the ocean as well. Then, abruptly, everything was calm. Hinnerk and the girl with the white eyes were left standing opposite each other. Only when Klütje nudged him and barked did he snap out of his trance and cuddled the coast dog. "Well? You're still in one piece?" The coast dog shook himself, generously dispersing drops of water all around him. Hinnerk asked the girl: "What is it about you? What happened to your eyes? Did you do that?" Her eyes flickered, then she keeled over and lay on the sand like she was dead. Hinnerk limped over to her and to his relief she was snoring so loudly that he didn't have to fear for her life. "What a day," Hinnerk sighed, got up and carried the girl to the top of the dyke. This is where he would have to stay for the time being, exhausted as he was. All that remained of the pirates was their vessel moored on the shore. The tide had come in.

The girl timidly opened her golden eyes when she woke up beside Hinnerk. They were sitting on the dyke. Hinnerk had wrapped her in a heavy woolen cloak. His leg was more badly wounded than he had thought and he couldn't walk. The pain was visible in his face although he tried to hide how much it hurt. To make up for his friend being incapacitated, Klütje was all the more vigilant watching out for possible perils. There was nothing but a handful of seagulls, however. The girl straightened herself up: "Are they gone? The pirates, I mean." Hinnerk was confused. "Don't you remember?" "Remember what?" Hinnerk gesticulated wildly. "Everything. The waves, Driftwood Theo and his henchmen. The sea swallowed them up! And you did it. At least I think you did. It looked like it. Your eyes were all white and you knocked out the giant. How did you do it?" Hinnerk scratched the back of his head while the girl stared at him totally at a loss. He started to doubt himself. "I did what?" "Well, you... You called the waves and they pulled Theo and his morons into the sea. Slosh! Just like that!" He clapped his hands together. "Really? Wow! That's really something!" She smiled sweetly: "Did I turn into a witch? Without knowing? That's funny." Hinnerk blushed. "N... no idea. I can only tell you what I saw." She fell silent and frowned. Hinnerk cleared his throat, immediately choked and coughed. The girl energetically slapped his back, which didn't really help because she slapped really hard. His eyes watering, Hinnerk said hoarsely: "I'm Hinnerk Wiards, by the way. But everyone just calls me Hinni." The girl pointed at Klütje, who was busy sniffing her over. "And who is that?" She picked him up and petted him in her rough way: "He's sweet." "That's my faithful coast dog, Klütje." "Klüddie?" "Klütje, yes. Some people claim he's just a deformed otter." The girl lifted Klütje up and eyed him from every angle. "He's not deformed at all. Just cute. Is it a boy or a girl?" Hinnerk replied: "He's a boy. He has a..." "Winky?" "Well, yes." "Here comes Klütje, the flying dog." She played with the animal and forgot everything around her. Hinnerk probed: "Sorry, but you are?" The girl blinked. "Um? Oh! I'm Leevke – Leevke Pultjen from Kleene Wacht. Do you know it?" Hinnerk nodded. "The rocky island with the lighthouse." "That's the one. I haven't been on the mainland much. This is the mainland, isn't it?" Hinnerk nodded. "Absolutely, as far as I know. I guess you didn't expect a welcome like that, did you?" Leevke admitted: "Not really." Now that he no longer had to worry about Theo he took a closer look at Leevke. Her neck-length, purple hair was tied into small braids secured by grained, wooden slides. The same kind of slide also held up the short hair at the back of her neck. Her eyes were unusual with their dark golden colour and her irises fanning out like a twelve-spoked wheel. He noticed three slashes on both sides of her neck. "That must have hurt. These wounds are still very fresh." He earned a baffled look and then she laughed: "Wounds? Oh, those! I've always had those. Everybody knows that, silly. I've no idea why they are there. Want to touch them? I don't mind. They're not very deep..." Hinnerk defensively put up his hands: "Oh, no! No! For God's sake! Forget it!" Leevke laughed: "You are funny, Honni." "Hinnerk." "Okay." She shrugged her shoulders and continued playing with Klütje, who was no lying on his back gently snapping at her fingers. She pulled them back in time. Hinnerk accidently glanced at Leevke's firm, young breasts. It could have happened to any young man. She wore just a simple linen tunic and, by the looks of it, nothing underneath. She instinctively noticed Hinnerk's glance and punched his injured leg. Hinnerk howled: "Ouch! What did you do that for?! Ouuuuuch!" Leevke looked surprised. "I don't really know. It was just a reflex." When she realised that Hinnerk was still in pain, she became more gentle. "I'm sorry. Are you okay?" Hinnerk hissed: "It's my damn leg. I bet you the muscle is torn. Or the knee joint slipped out of place. That's why we're still sitting here instead of being on our way to Meppen or God knows where." Leevke sat up. "Right. Let me have a look." Hinnerk winced when she came closer. "Whoa! What are you doing?" "I want to examine your leg." "Are you some kind of a healer? A Deel-Deern?" The girl hummed and hawed: "Don't know. But I once put my hand on my grandpa's cut when he slipped on the rocks. And then it was better again." Hinnerk was quite inclined to believe her after what he had witnessed before. He pulled up his trouser leg and a warm feeling went through him when Leevke placed her hands on his bruised limb. His knee was throbbing. She stopped. "And?" Hinnerk asked eagerly. "Nothing. It wasn't like that time with grandpa." "Well, you tried. Thanks." Her touch alone had already been helpful and invigorating. Leevke pensively rubbed her chin. Wait, there was something else. Yeah! Do you have any water?" "Apart from the ocean over there, there's still some in Klütje's pouch." "Give it to me!" Hinnerk handed her the bag: "Don't drink it. Klütje's moulting at the moment." Unimpressed, Leevke dunked her hands into the pouch and then put them onto Hinnerk's leg. "Aah! It's tingling." Leevke concentrated hard and a faint golden tinge appeared beneath her hands. "Do you feel anything?" "No." "What a pity." Hinnerk laughed out loud: "No! I mean I no longer feel anything. No pain! It's gone!" Leevke beamed with relief. "At last!" Hinnerk couldn't help himself and blushed when he saw her smiling face. The setting sun on the horizon cast its reflection on the ocean. The world was radiant, no longer dull and depressing. Hinnerk asked: "Tell me what happened. How did you get here from Kleene Wacht?" Leevke rolled down his trouser leg again. He loved her strong, determined fingers. She explained dolefully: "It was pretty awful." She pulled up her legs and hugged them before she continued while gazing at the sea: "I live on the island with my grandpa and my nan. It's pretty remote and we only rarely go to Norderney or Norddeich where we sell a few deep-sea fish that you can only catch in the open sea. I've only once been to the harbour in the big town of Emden. That was quite impressive. Especially the church with those tall pillars and the huge organ. But the place was too noisy. And too dry." Hinnerk was mesmerised. "Yesterday Theo and his men came to our island... I didn't really understand what was going on because I was outside and only saw what was happening through the window. All of a sudden it got loud and Theo was pacing up and down and swinging his axe. Then he... he hit nan." Leevke swallowed hard and covered her mouth while tears welled up in her eyes. "She fell down and stopped moving. Grandpa grabbed Theo and hit him right in the face. But it didn't make any difference. Theo was too strong. He just lifted him up with one arm, shook him and struck him. I think my grandpa was bleeding." Leevke wiped her face with her sleeve and sobbed: "That's when grandpa saw me at the window and shouted for me to run away and hide like always. Theo's men stormed out of the house and I ran and ran and jumped into the sea. There was no time to take our boat." Hinnerk asked: "Are you a good swimmer?" Leevke smiled: "I sure am. And I can stay under water for a long time. I wanted to hide behind the cliffs, but the current was too strong and then a storm rose like none I'd ever seen before. The world had gone mad. The sky went very dark and the waves were incredibly high. I kept on swimming and Theo and his men chased me with the two boats. Theirs and ours they had stolen. But ours sank with all his men. His own ship was also hit by the waves and many of his crew were swept overboard. Then the sea gave a mighty roar and everything got dark. I woke up on this beach." She sobbed again. "Where is this actually" "Near Domumersiel. It's part of my watch." Leevke pretended she knew where that was and Hinnerk smiled encouragingly. "It's not far from Norderney." The girl nodded gratefully and leaned forward until she looked right into his eyes: "Can you help me to get there?" "Woah, don't come too close!" Hinnerk panicked. He nearly toppled backwards. But he recovered himself, elegantly jumped up and extended his hand to Leevke: "Of course I'll help you. It's not so bad, hey? Besides, it's my duty as dyke warden. You could say I'm fully authorised. Fully in charge! Anyway, I'm full. Full of knowledge, ha, ha!" She smiled gratefully and he pulled her up. "You are really nice. The nicest land-dweller I know." Klütje barked his approval and started sprinting down the dyke towards the hinterland. Leevke seemed confused: "Aren't we going to swim back?" Hinnerk looked dumbfounded until he realised that she actually considered it a sensible alternative to simply throw herself into the water and swim back to Kleene Wacht. "Um, you might be able to, but I don't have gills. Besides, it's nearly low tide and it's getting dark. You must also be pretty thirsty after swallowing all that salt water." Leevke pressed her index finger against her lips. "I'm a little hungry, actually." Hinnerk nodded and took her by the hand. "I'm sure there'll be something nice to eat at home. My ma's a great cook!"

They walked down the dyke and Leevke cast a last look across the sea: "What about Lisbeth? Are we just going to leave her here?" "Who is Lisbeth?" "Theo's ship. At least that's what they called her." Hinnerk said: "I'll report it to the dyke farmers. They'll take care of her. There's nothing more we can do here. Come on, let's go. It will soon be dark." Fog patches were wafting here and there over the fertile marshland wrestled from the sea, unlike the sparse sandy soil of the heathlands beyond. Here in the marshes the farming folk had planted wheat, rye and other grains which yielded plentiful crops. The heathlands and moors produced little but buckwheat, broad beans and oats. But his family owned several acres of bog which provided them with a good living, Hinnerk proudly explained. Leevke listened attentively and Hinnerk's mood improved with every step. They rambled down a beaten path to the Wiards' holding. To the east of it was the town of Esens, controlled by Behrend Attena, the robber baron. They also called him the bear. He was a rough hulk of a man, rumoured to be of Norse blood, dating back to the brief period of Viking rule under Harald Halfdansson. Esens itself was not far from being a den of thieves itself. To the west of the Wiards' land was the stronghold of Dornum, a fortress in the settlement of the same name. The castle had been built in the modern brick-style in response to the Viking, or ashmen, raids.

Hinnerk and Leevke passed a herd of armoured dyke sheep, guarded by the local shepherd Habbo. They greeted each other and had a quick chat. Habbo knew the Wiards boy well and was a good friend of Hinnerk's father Okko. But Habbo wasn't just a shepherd, he was also an armorsmith. Unlike the usual woolly fleece, his sheep were covered in numerous, fingernail-size, overlapping armour platelets. The armour-wool was forged into especially flexible and lightweight gambeson armour, a sought-after commodity famed well beyond the Frisian borders. However, the armour sheep were a good deal more aggressive than ordinary sheep and one had to be assertive to keep the herd in check. They also constantly needed moor grass so their wool attained the required firmness. Habbo was tough and an experienced lance fighter. He had been one of the legendary Sparrows of Stedingen, a rebel troop that had stood up to the knights in Stedingen until they had been defeated. People said Habbo had headbutted the chief ram to gain the herd's respect. They called him Habbo the Harsh. Hinnerk had frequently fled from the armour sheep. With their thick skulls they could even damage rocks. It was therefore all the more shocking when they saw Leevke vigorously rubbing the head of a fiercely growling sheep: "Coochy, coochy, coo! Aren't you a sweet little thing? Baah, baah! Do you understand that? Baaaaaah!" She energetically shook the animal's head as if it said no. "No? You don't understand?

What a pity." Habbo's mouth was wide open and Hinnerk, too, was terrified.

Habbo said tensely: "Are you mad, girl? Get away from it! But slowly, or..." "What?" Leevke enquired, quickly jumped up and ran towards them. The dyke sheep and its companions pawed the ground with their hoofs and bleated in preparation for a full-scale attack. Hinnerk grabbed Leevke's arm and urged: "Run! Run as fast as you can!" Leevke glanced back to see the large uniform mass of bleating, bad-tempered armour sheep giving chase. The very ground was shaking under the stampede. Habbo cursed and held one of the chief rams back with his crook. "I can't control them all. Run!" "I thought we were supposed to walk slowly?!" Leevke exclaimed and Hinnerk frowned when he realised that he had ignored his own advice. "Damn it! It's too late now." Leevke and Hinnerk sprinted cross-country over fields and meadows, Klütje in front showing them the way. A herd of calmly grazing cattle were unimpressed and unperturbed when the trio raced right through their midst. Only when the sheep came storming forward did they finally move and also ran away from the bleating mob. Now Hinnerk and Leevke were running away from the cattle who were running away from the sheep which were followed by Habbo. Hinnerk was aware of the absurdity of it all. "If this continues we'll soon have the whole hinterland chasing us." Leevke panted: "I can't run much further, Hinni." They had reached a wide and deep brook and Hinnerk shouted: "Jump!" He grabbed her arm and they both jumped together. To land in the brackish water. They hastily scrambled through the nettles until they reached the other side. Drenched through they staggered on and saw the cows behind them plunging into the water. They were speechless when the sheep jumped in after and there was unmitigated chaos between the snorting cattle and the bleating sheep all wildly splashing around. Habbo was out of breath when he caught up. The sheep and cows struggled to climb out of the brook to Habbo's dry comment: "Ah, well, at least I won't have to give them more water today... " Leevke hung her head: "I'm sorry, Mr Habbo. It was all my fault." The shepherd stopped her with a wave of his hand: "Don't worry, child. Just don't make a habit of it. A bit of exercise is alright now and again, but you shouldn't just touch everything you see." "Thank you." "Are you two alright, Hinni?" The young man dusted himself down. "We have a few scratches and nettle stings and we're soaked through. So we're fine." Habbo became serious: "It could have been a different story. The land may be flat and calm, but it has been rumoured that Gobolds have been sighted again in the Ghastly Moors. They like setting nasty traps." "I'll be careful. We're going home now," Hinnerk assured him. Before they were on their way they helped Habbo to shoo the animals out of the water.

Exhausted and filthy Leevke and Hinnerk arrived at the Wiards' farm. Hinnerk's younger siblings soon bustled around them and didn't tire staring at the girl with the purple hair, the slits on her neck and the laughing, golden eyes. "Is she your girlfriend, Hinni?" seven year old Namke wanted to know and touched Leevke's hair. "Absolutely not! Get lost, you lot!" Hinnerk barked and pushed his brothers and sisters, who were ecstatically swarming around Leevke, out of the way. They entered the yard and the big, central barnhouse, passed cows, pigs and chickens before they stepped into the open living area with the stone fire pit in the middle. Hinnerk's mother Hilde, who was kneading bread dough on the large table, greeted the pair. She seemed happy to see Leevke. "You're a very pretty girl. Do you dye your hair?" "No, it's like that," Leevke admitted frankly. Hinnerk cleared his throat: "Excuse me, mother, but can she stay here tonight. Tomorrow we'll have to organise a boat and bring her back to Kleene Wacht." "Excuse me, mother? What happened to hi, ma?" Hinnerk shrugged his shoulders and Hilde smiled: "She can stay as long as she likes."

And so the whole Wiards family and Leevke sat around the table a little later for their supper. Okko, Hinnerk's father, had just been chopping firewood. He was a broad-shouldered man with light brown, closely cropped hair and a moustache. Farming was obviously in his blood. After Okko had said the prayer they started on their meal: bread, light ale and a stew with green beans, roots, herbs and chicken. Hinnerk told everybody what had happened that day and barely got around to eating.

When he was finished, Okko said: "You're lucky you're still alive, Hinni." "True," Hinnerk agreed meekly and Okko nodded knowingly: "Well, I can only hope that they beat all that adventure nonsense out of you. That band of robbers and cutthroats you want to join is dangerous, even for us. Despite all the advantages, sooner or later they will have to pay for their actions. But honest, hard work endures." Hilde took her husband's hand in hers: "Not while we're eating. We have a guest." Hinnerk though wasn't yet done with the subject. "The Likedeeler aren't common thieves, when will you ever understand that? They are courageous, free men who bring us prosperity and gold they've taken from the Hanseatic moneybags, who have more than enough. They are the real robbers! If they were starving in Marienhafe, the Hanse boys would rob the shirts off our backs and sell us mouldy bread at extortionist prices. They are the thieves, not the Likedeeler!" Leevke followed the exchange with confusion while nibbling at her bread. She was also slightly scared because Hinnerk and Okko appeared to be at loggerheads and irritable. She had never witnessed arguments back at home.

Okko banged his fist on the table: "Don't you dare talk to me like that, my friend! You will stay away from that rabble and live a peaceful, sensible life! Do you have any idea what happens out there? Killing and slaughter everywhere. Nobody to help you when you're down. They'll kick you to boot. It may not be terribly exciting hereabouts, but at least you live longer. This is where you belong. Do you get it? How can anyone be so dumb?" Hinnerk crossed his arms over his chest: "I want to see the world and have adventures. Here I just go insane like a caged animal. I have to go hunting." Okko countered: "Even a wolf can be tamed. Just look at Klütje. And that's enough. I don't want to hear another word!" Hinnerk was about to make a stroppy reply, but thought better of it. Hilde sighed: "I'm sorry you had to see that, Leevke. Those two are always at each other. And always about the same thing." Okko said: "I'm not sorry." He furiously took a bite of his bread and Hinnerk followed suit. "Neither am I!" Leevke tried to appease them: "Not to worry. I think deep down they are actually very fond of each other." Hilde laughed: "You may just be right. But they'd never admit it. Men, you know!" Okko's steady and prudent ways naturally clashed with Hinnerk's adolescent thirst for action and rebellious streak. And Leevke's presence did its bit to goad Hinnerk even more into trying to impress her.

Eventually he asked: "Can we take Leevke back to Norddeich tomorrow? She has to go to Kleene Wacht." "Tomorrow we have to get the hay from Nessen's farm, so you can't have the cart. Or the horses." "Does that mean we're supposed to walk all that distance?" "Leevke said: "I wouldn't mind. Really! A little walk..." Okko glanced at her, considered and then sighed: "Right so. I've some business to take care of in Norddeich anyway. Nessen's hay won't run away. We'll be on our way in the morning." Leevke beamed: "Oh, thank you, papa Wiards! That's sooo nice of you." Okko bashfully cleared his throat and addressed Hinnerk: "You'll take good care of her, you hear?" "I will. I promise." The tension lifted. Although they argued a lot there was the occasional moments when Hinnerk was actually glad to have a father like Okko. He could always count on him, if he agreed with him or not.

That night Hinnerk and Leevke were in his room in the loft. Leevke spotted some wooden figures of warriors, chariots and various monsters. "Did you carve those?" Hinnerk smiled. "They're not very good." "I think they're cute. Look at this cow for example." "That's supposed to be a worm..." "Aren't they long and slimy?" Hinnerk frowned. Then he laughed: "No, not an earthworm. It's a lindworm. A large, poisonous lizard, that is." Leevke yawned and they went to bed. Hinnerk fell asleep straight away, but Okko's snoring echoed right through the house and Leevke couldn't sleep. She pulled at Hinnerk's nightgown: "Hey, Hinni?" "Wha... what?" he said drowsily. "I can't sleep." Okko's snoring made the walls tremble. Hinnerk yawned: "Oh, I see. Let's move to the barn. I go there sometimes when everyone here gets on my nerves." They got dressed and walked across the yard in the cool summer breeze. The moon was shining brightly and only an occasional cloud could be seen in a sky dotted with thousands upon thousands of twinkling stars. "How beautiful," Leevke whispered, smiling and dancing in the pale moonlight and giggling when the wet grass tickled her feet. Hinnerk nodded, but thought she was far more beautiful than all the stars and the moon together. In the barn they spread their blankets on the hay and settled down, staring at the bits of grain dangling from the ceiling.

Leevke asked: "Do you think nan and grandpa are okay?" Hinnerk tried to ease her concern: "Of course they are. We'll see them tomorrow." Leevke turned to face him and looked at him lovingly with her golden eyes: "Thank you, Hinni. Without you... Who knows what would have become of me." "It was nothing." "Good night." Hinnerk's throat felt dry. He swallowed. "Good night." Back to back they snuggled into the hay. The boy felt the warmth of her body and listened to her even breathing. How lovely it would be to spend the rest of his life like that. He couldn't help smiling when she started to snore. He didn't mind; he was well used to it.

Coughing and spitting Theo clenched his fists and buried them deep in the pale, wet sand. His throat was parched. It had taken all his remaining strength to reach the small island. The place was hilly and not very big. Theo's eyes were caked with salt and when he opened them they focussed on the large ruins of a castle which must once have been a magnificent sea fortress. The ocean was shrouded in mist; the ruin streaked with fog patches.

There wasn't a living soul to be seen. He didn't even hear the shrieks of seagulls, only the roaring sea and the wind howling through the deserted pile of bricks. The air was cold and damp. Luckily Theo was tough and not easily intimidated. His whole body was covered in scars. His father had delighted in beating him with his leather strap when Theo hadn't done as he was told or whined like a girl. Theo had quickly learned his lesson: you had to be ruthless and hard to protect yourself; everything else was a waste of time. Nowadays he looked back with disdain at his younger self and detested sissies and cry-babies. His strong body and cunning had ensured that he hadn't yet perished like his unfortunate companions.

He knew the currents between the islands of Langeoog and Wangerooge like the back of his hand and was aware that it was useless to waste his strength swimming against the tide. He had survived because he hadn't just made straight for the islands, but waited for the right time. It had still been touch and go. Theo had been scared the whole time, remembering the disturbing rumours about the sea fortress Muddington and a certain grey hunter, an enormous beast able to devour whole ships, assumed to live in these waters. He was under no illusion regarding the fate of his last two henchmen. If they were unlucky they may even have been turned into Draugr, cursed, drowned seafarers condemned to lead a miserable existence on the ocean bed covered in moss and shells for eternity.

Theo got up, dusted himself down and had a look at his surroundings. Algae and moss were stuck to the former stronghold's walls, the gate had long since collapsed, the iron bars rusted. The bricks were black and damp and crawling with tentacled, scrawny-legged creatures in the crevices. Behind the ruined walls towered the highest remaining structure, a wide castle keep which tapered towards the top and ended in a flat, canopied platform, untypically without any battlements. Theo decided to explore the place in detail. Perhaps he would find enough material in the wreckage to build a small raft to get him back to the mainland. He couldn't be far from the coast and he would find a way to get off this island. And to recruit a new crew. Looters and marauders were two a penny. Many a harassed farm hand was only too eager to escape from his hopeless existence. He might even recapture his vessel, the Lisbeth, but that was doubtful. The Frisians didn't easily hand back what they had scavenged on the beach, unless you paid handsomely. The girl was supposed to fetch a ransom, but Theo had had more than enough of her for the time being. But if he should bump into her or that bloody Frisian boy, he would take his time and kill them at his leisure. Nobody messed with Driftwood Theo and Theo prudently didn't mess with anyone he couldn't also punish. He wouldn't underestimate that chit of a girl again.

He had lost his axe and started combing the beach for it, but didn't spot anything useful, not even a heavy stick. He did, however find a little well amongst the rocks to quench his thirst. Theo walked through the ruins, scattering all sorts of wildlife. None of it warm-blooded and everything seemed desolate, grey and deserted. But that didn't necessarily mean anything. This could be the home of an occult ocean cult that still worshipped the ocean gods, dating back to a time when the Frisians had still been pagans. He walked through the remains of the gatehouse and inspected the inner courtyard. Along the walls were the ruins of stables, forges, former living quarters, grain silos and many other stores. He also found a wild herb garden now overgrown with weeds. In its day the island must have been a popular trading post. He searched every building, but found nothing expect rusty nails, shards and rotten planks. Then he came across a trapdoor in the forge when one of the rotten floorboards snapped under his weight. His loud curses echoed far and wide before he opened the trapdoor and saw a chest.

He used a stone to crack the rusty lock and was very pleased when he unwrapped the object he found inside, a finely crafted axe like the one he had lost. "I'll be damned! There we go!" he laughed and tried it out. It balanced well in his hand and he instantly felt better. After having lost his ship and crew he had been pretty depressed, but he took his find as a sign that things were looking up. The axe smashed some old furniture with ease and he left the place a happier man. Perhaps there was more treasure hidden in the tower which he now approached in good spirits.

His mood drastically deteriorated again when he heard the characteristic hissing of sea scorpions. Three of the waist-high, armoured creatures broke out of the ground in front of him, their claws and tails ready to strike. The best way to kill scorpions was to provoke them so they would attack and you could hack off their tail before they'd sting you. Of course they were still dangerous without it, but at least they could no longer daze you with their poison in order to eat you alive. But in the face of not just one, but three of the beasts Theo decided strategic withdrawal would be a wise move and ran to a staircase near the castle walls. The scorpions hissed and crackled in pursuit. Theo grabbed a rock and hurled it at the creatures. The armour of the animal closest to him blocked the stone, but instead it hit the next one. The scorpion screamed when the heavy rock broke its armour. Yellow blood oozed from its body and it died. The other two crawled up the stairs and the first one snapped at Theo's legs with its claws. Theo brought the axe down right between the creature's eyes and immediately jumped back when it still tried to sting him in the throes of death. Two down, one to go, but the axe was stuck in the armour and the last scorpion nearly upon him. Theo growled: "I won't be beaten by a few damned arachnids!" He kicked the brittle wall with all his might and the bricks became loose and forced the scorpion down the staircase where it landed in the yard, thrashing around on its back. Theo extracted the axe from the second scorpion's armour, jumped down and killed the last of them. "Fucking bastards!" he spat and walked towards the big gate with its heavy iron hinges.

For some obscure reason the timbers weren't as rotten and still seemed to be pretty sturdy. Images of Frisian warriors and a one-eyed, four-armed kraken were carved into the wood. Theo threw himself against the door with all the force he could muster and it opened creakily. Pallid sunlight obscured by the mist revealed a dusty entrance hall with faded banners on the wall. There were human skeletons everywhere. He took one of the ancient torches and quickly found some tinder and a fire iron to light it. Visibility was still poor, as if everything was shrouded in a black fog even the torch couldn't dispel. Theo rummaged through the rooms, but only discovered more skeletons, rusty arms, crockery and decayed furniture. Some of the skeletons were slouched over on chairs and benches, others were lying on beds or on the floor as if they had died on the spot. Theo wondered how many people may have perished and why nobody had buried their corpses or at least burned them. He detected the entrance to a tunnel which led to the dungeons underneath the fortress, but the sound of poisonous centipedes prevented him from climbing down for now.

Instead he decided to get an overview and went up the stairs. He passed four levels in all on the winding stone steps. The first level housed the servants' quarters and stores for barrels and sacks, all of them rotten and spilled. The second level was reserved for the soldiers, their armour and weapons. This, too, was littered with dead bodies like a grotesque likeness of a last battle. The third floor had a kitchen, with nothing but mouldy bread and rotten meat, and what he assumed must have been the banqueting hall. On the fourth floor, apart from a number of offices, he came across a heavy iron door he couldn't open and which emanated an unpleasant chill. The pagan runes did the rest to deter him from simply breaking it down. But in the other rooms he found a handful of old coins engraved with the picture of a one-eyed kraken, some useful tools and timber still good enough to build a raft. He picked up a piece of cloth and stored all his finds in his makeshift bag.

Finally he climbed up the small steps leading to the observation platform at the top of the keep where he was greeted by a stiff breeze. Amidst the tattered banners wafting in the wind stood a throne with a mummified man wearing a crown and faded clothing slumping on it. He was surrounded by corpses in rusted armour, armed with spears, swords and shields. The wind was howling noisily and Theo thought he could hear human voices in it. He took a closer look at the well-preserved remains of the king.

Although the mummy's eyes were closed, Theo couldn't shake the feeling that something was wrong. The corpse had flowing, grey-white hair; the skin was wizened and shrivelled. But Theo was mostly fascinated with the ornate and richly decorated silver crown inlaid with rubies which adorned the man's head. He wore several beautiful rings on his fingers and a well-preserved robe. The sword behind the throne was just as well-preserved. Theo had no scruples robbing the dead. If he didn't, somebody else would. He reached out to snatch the crown, but just as his fingers touched it, two strong, bony hands grabbed his arms and held them in an iron grip. A clear, thunderous voice boomed from the mummy: "Who dares to steal from the King of all Frisians?!" Theo's eyes widened in horror when the corpse stood up, seized his throat, his eyes still closed, and effortlessly lifted him up. His attempts to break free were futile. The mummy's eyes opened and Theo looked into milky-white eyes with silver irises. The undead king snarled: "Who are you? Did you come to kill me? Did the Franks send you? The Pope?! Talk!" Theo coughed. "Who?! I don't know what you are talking about? Who are you?" The undead king glared at him. "I? I am Radbod, King of all the Frisians! Nobody will kill me as long as there are Frisians! As long as their thirst for independence boils in their veins, I shall not be moved!" With those words Radbod hurled Theo right across the platform. Theo lost his makeshift bag and all the goods he had gathered scattered everywhere. He slithered precariously close to the edge and just about managed to hold on instead of falling off the tower.

The fall would have killed him. Radbod approached with heavy steps. "A looter! A common thief! Theo panicked. "Forgive me, Si... Si... Sire. Please! I didn't know it was you. Please, spare my life. I can be of use to you." Radbod looked down at Theo and considered. The strong wind was howling and Theo desperately clung to the edge. "Shit!" he whined. "Please, Radbod, your Majesty, Lord of the Frisians. Help me and I shall help you!" "Tosh! You want to help me? What could you possibly have to offer?" Theo saw the skeleton knights getting up and reaching for their weapons. Tiny red lights gleamed in their hollow eye sockets as they came closer to stand by their undead king. "I know of a power that could help you! Help you to become king again!" "I AM the king, you worm!" Theo tried to smile: "Here you are, but not on land. You may own this isle, but Frisia is governed by the Hauptlinger and the Church. I don't know anyone who has sworn fealty to you!" Radbod growled and stared at the mists. "That's because those fools have forgotten. Forgotten that I am still their rightful king. It was beaten out of them." "I agree, Sire, but I know how you can show them that you still exist. How to remind them that Radbod is still their true sovereign and nobody else!" Those were Theo's last words before he lost his grip and started plunging to his death. Radbod's arm darted forward and effortlessly pulled him back up with Herculean strength. "What kind of magic might that be, looter?" "My name is Theo, Sire. There is a girl, your Majesty. She is versed in spells!" "What kind of spells?" "It's somehow connected to the water. To the sea!" Theo sighed with relief when the bony hands flung him back onto the platform. His relief was short-lived when he saw the king's piercing eyes: "Tell me everything..." Theo was surrounded by the undead and had no choice but to accept his fate. At least for now.

Chapter 2

Mud & Silt

The Wiards' cart made its way down the path at a leisurely pace. On their left was a young forest with the Ghastly Moors behind it and to their right was the dyke. Seagulls, scouting for food, were circling above them. Okko was holding the reins attached to the old plough horse pulling their wagon and Hinnerk and Leevke were dozing in the back amidst sacks and crates. Hinnerk's arms were folded behind his head. He was chewing on a chicken bone. Klütje was curled up on Leevke's lap, snoring just as loudly as she had during the night. "You've never actually been on the mainland, have you?" Hinnerk eventually observed and shifted the bone in his mouth. "Is it that obvious?" "Well, let's put it this way: if you haven't learned not to pet armoured dyke sheep at your age..." "I thought they were placid creatures. All covered in wool, you know..." Hinnerk put on a posh accent: "Impressions can be deceptive, your ladyship." "Really?" "Really, trust me. Just think of the Fenna. They look like nice little old ladies, but they'd tear you to pieces if you don't look out." "Fenna? Who or what is that supposed to be?" Hinnerk sighed and was about to break into a long-winded explanation. Okko saved him the bother: "The Fenna, Leevke, are creatures who haunt the moors and fields at night when it's foggy. They are scrawny like twigs, rickety like skeletons. They stalk through the fields on their claw-feet and whisper to you. Anyone who doesn't answer them in a firm voice becomes their next victim. They can smell weakness and fear. They rush towards you and if you don't die of fright at the sight of them, they'll kill you with their claw-hands. Not many have survived their attacks. The Fenna rarely face you in open combat. They are hunters." Hinnerk und Leevke now popped up either side of Okko's head. Leevke was impressed. "It's really creepy here on the mainland." Hinnerk's father cleared his throat: "You just have to be careful. Stay away from the moors and open fields at night and if not than never walk them alone or without a torch. There are other creatures, too, which terrorise people in these parts. Most of them can be kept at bay with fire."

Hinnerk theatrically beat his chest: "Don't worry. I'll protect you, Leevke. I'll take on a dragon, if needs be." Leevke's eyes sparkled: "Ohhh! You would really do that?" Hinnerk tried to look heroic, whipped out his Frisian dagger and waved it about: "I'm a champion, trained by a crusader, by a master in combat. I know a trick or two!" Okko rolled his eyes: "Tricks that make you foolhardy and take unnecessary risks, like fighting against Theo." "Are you saying I should have abandoned her?" "No, you should have gone for help. That's your duty as a dyke warden." Hinnerk huffed, crossed his arms over his chest and demonstratively stared at the back of the cart. Leevke nudged him with her foot: "Hey," and he relaxed a little. At noon they approached the gates of Norddeich, a town under the control of the Häuptlinger Friedhelm Nordendi. Norddeich was a popular trading post for the local farmers and also for some bold merchants from the Hansatic League who came here to do business with the Frisians they frowned upon.

They took advantage of the fact that the Likedeeler sold their wares cheaply to the townsfolk and bought them for a song to sell them on at a respectable profit. The dyke watch kept one of their outposts here. The collectively organised institution resembled the assemblies of the delegates of the regional Frisian communes and the men in charge were armed and fed by the indigenous population. Hinnerk's dyke watch was part of the Frisian coast defence system. The town was busy and the crews of two somewhat older, flat-bottomed merchant cogs from West Frisia were unloading their goods and replacing them with sheepskins, cloth and even horses. They were anchored in the purpose-build pit in front of the dyke which still carried sufficient water at low tide so that the ships wouldn't run aground. But they still had to wait for the next tide before setting sail again. For this reason the Frisians preferred using flat-bottomed vessels. It was said that the Frisians had invented the cog, but the ashmen had used ships like that before them, the wide, open knarr for instance. The town was located on a mound and consisted of several cottages arranged more or less in a half moon shape with its opening pointing to the harbour. The warehouses where the traders stored their goods were built on stilts and close to the harbour so the merchandise could quickly be sold when the opportunity presented itself. Some armed sentries were patrolling the place to prevent looters from plundering. On another mound, not far from the cottages of Norddeich was the fortified stronghold of the local dyke watch. Okko stopped the cart right outside the gates where they were welcomed by two guards with spears. "Here we are," Okko said and helped Hinnerk and Leevke off the wagon. "I shall tell the dykemaster that they can tow Theo's ship away. If it isn't gone already. Attena usually doesn't waste any time when there's something to be grabbed. I'm going to buy some provisions and then stay the night here. You two can walk to Kleene Wacht." "Walk?" Leevke echoed and Hinnerk said: "Oh, no!" "Oh, yes," Okko replied with a mischievous grin. "The tide's nearly out." Leevke clapped her hands and excitedly jumped up and down. "Great! Does that mean we'll be hiking through the mudflats?" "I don't know what's so great about that," Hinnerk grumbled. "Why? I love feeling the soft ground under my feet. And there are all those cute animals everywhere!" "Cute?" The place is teeming with dangerous crabs and if you're not careful you drown in the mud." Leevke smiled roguishly: "It can hardly be more dangerous than one of your dragons, can it now?" Hinnerk thought about it and said: "Let's go." "Oi! Hinni!" Okko called him and threw a small pouch at him. "Here is some money for a guide. Don't go on your own." "But we can..." "No! You take a guide and that's it! Do you hear me?" "Yeah, yeah." "What was that?" Okko held his hand to his ear and pretended to listen hard. "Yes, father." "That's better. Off you go now. Good luck, Leevke. Say hello to your grandparents from us." "I will, Mr Wiards. Thanks very much for all your help again. And don't worry, I'll keep an eye on Hinni!" She took Hinnerk's hand and pulled him with her. "Come on!" Hinnerk sighed and followed her to the market where they bought some food for on the way. Their brief enquiries led them to a young guide called Muddy Joost, who was in the process of preparing fish soup outside his cottage. His weatherproof clothes were filthy from the mudflats, his bearded face inviting and his eyes a sparkling light blue. He wore a red bobble hat over his shoulder-length hair and leaned on an on iron lance which looked more like a shovel. The concept was similar to that of Hinnerk's Frisian dagger, a combination of weapon and tool.

Joost greeted them affably: "Morning, ladies and gentlemen. Fancy a romantic walk on the mudflats?" Hinnerk blushed and muttered: "There's nothing romantic about that." Joost smiled while he poured the soup into a wooden bowl: "An experience like that can bring two people closer together, you know." "What? With you there as well?" Joost laughed. "You got me there!" "We need to get to Kleene Wacht," Hinnerk informed him. The guide pulled at his moustache: "You look fit enough, alright. I can take you as far as Norderney. From there you'll have to hire a boat to bring you to Kleene Wacht. I can organise that for you. Do we have a deal?" Hinnerk shook hands with him. Meanwhile Leevke had started to follow a crab which had strayed from the beach and imitated its sideways walk. "She's not from around here, is she?" Joost observed. Hinnerk sighed: "She's from the islands." Muddy Joe replied with a serious face that he was also from the islands. Hinnerk blushed again, but Joost laughed: "That was a joke! I'm from around here. But it doesn't matter anyway. It's all the same to the sea and the mudflats. Right! Are you ready?" "Are you?" "I just have to finish my soup. You two can help me if you like."

Together they emptied the pot and also ate the bread Hinnerk shared out. Joost got up to put on his boots and turned to Leevke: "You better put your boots on, too, girl. Because of the toebiters. They're stubborn little buggers." Leevke was baffled. "I don't like shoes. They make me feel as if my feet suffocate. And they get all sweaty. Yuk!" Hinnerk asked: "How about sandals?" "They aren't too bad," Leevke conceded. Hinnerk called Klütje back from chasing a sandpiper and they headed off to the mudflats. Unlike other dogs, Klütje managed the slippery ground with ease. The mudflats were a haven for small animals, including a variety of worms, crabs and shellfish. The dyke farmers' fertile clay soil had once been part of the mudflats before they had dammed it up, drained and reclaimed it. But here, too, lived dangerous creatures like giant mud shrimps, swarms of spider-eyed peckergulls, toebiter clams and the enormous, but fortunately rare, sandworms. Hinnerk had no desire to encounter any of them, but he enjoyed imagining heroically defending Leevke against them. She would kiss him gratefully and then they would retire to a secluded spot in a tight embrace... "Are you okay?" the object of his dreams enquired when Hinnerk started to drool. He quickly wiped his mouth: "Me? No. I'm fine." "I guess you're still hungry. The soup was good, but back at my place we'll get something really tasty." In good spirits they skipped across the slushy mudflats and kept bombarding Muddy Joe with questions. Questions about the clicking sounds of the mud shrimps, the habitat of the sandworms and all the other creatures in the biotope. Joost answered them all at length and with obvious love and respect for his environment. Hinnerk knew most of the things Joost told them about already. He had often hiked to Baltrum or Langeoog on errands for the farm and to visit friends with his family. Slowly but surely they were approaching Norderney, famous for its large mussel beds. Although the island seemed quite close, it was actually still a few hours' walk away; an optical illusion which many a heedless traveller had paid for with his life. Those who took their time ran the risk of being taken by the flood and pulled into the sea. Hinnerk contributed one of his uncle Abbo's stories: "Long ago, the Romans in league with the Chauci between the Ems and the Elbe didn't know anything about the tides and were too arrogant to hire a guide. Half their legion was washed away!" Leevke was impressed. "Wow, you sure know a lot of stuff. I don't know anything like that." "You do now." Leevke grinned sheepishly and wanted to link arms with Hinnerk when Muddy Joost abruptly stopped. Every syllable in his voice signalled danger: "Don't move! DON'T!" Leevke took his words literally and stood there balancing on one foot. Even Klütje stayed where he was with one of his paws raised and his tail standing up. "What is it?" Hinnerk whispered. Joost pointed his lance at two or three large mounds which were rapidly moving towards them. Nobody had noticed them before. They were churning up the mudflats and pushing the piles of sand forward. At the same time the ubiquitous clicking and clacking in the air assumed ear-shattering proportions. The wandering mounds came very close and Hinnerk grabbed his dagger. Joost confirmed his suspicion: "They're giant mud shrimps." Ordinary mud shrimps posed no threat to humans or anything really except plankton. They were small enough to fit on a fingernail. But these specimens were bigger than fully grown oxen and sometimes even attacked stranded humans and fishing boats with their claws before devouring their prey between their fangs. At low tide they reacted to tremors in the mudflats and were thus able to correctly identify the location of the noise. Only by moving extremely carefully could one avoid being detected by these creatures. Hinnerk flexed his muscles when the two wandering mounds collided shortly before reaching them. Mud and sludge exploded as the two shrimp leaped out of the mudflats. Leevke screamed and Hinnerk protectively jumped in front of her. Klütje barked, but the coast dog quickly realised that he was powerless against the chitin shells while they were being bombarded with chunks of mud. "We have to attack!" Hinnerk roared at Joost, but the guide was amazingly calm and shouted back: "Don't even think about it! Don't move!" Now Hinnerk saw that the mud shrimps were fighting each other. The slightly larger one on the left had dug his claw into the shell of the younger one on the right. Dark yellow blood, the consistency of oatmeal gruel, was oozing out of the wound. The two giant shrimps kept churning up the mudflats around them and Hinnerk, Leevke, Joost and Klütje were completely covered in mud when the younger beast retreated and buried itself into the sludge again. The bigger one raised his claws and noisily beat them together; presumably as a sign of its victory. Klütje whimpered. Satisfied with its performance, the triumphant shrimp dived under; leaving a baffled group of people behind.

Joost was the first to shake off some of the dirt. "That's not something you see too often. And I'm glad," he chuckled. "I don't think that was funny," Hinnerk grumbled while he also tried to clean himself up a bit. "Are you okay, Leevke?" he enquired, but only heard an unintelligible mumbling and they saw that the girl was covered in mud from head to toe. "Oh, dear! Come and give me a hand, Joost!" Together they freed Leevke from the mud. She gasped for air. Hinnerk was concerned: "Are you alright?" Leevke replied fitfully: "That... Was... Incredible!" "Wasn't it just?" Joost agreed enthusiastically. "It's not often you see a fight between two shrimps as big as that. Two real beauties. What a story I'll have to tell them at the guide meeting next Wednesday." Leevke nodded: "But I thought it was sad that the smaller one was bleeding. That must have hurt a lot." Joost shrugged his shoulders. "That's nature, girl. The stronger one wins. But I think the other shrimp will survive. They were fighting for their territory; the usual." Hinnerk was dumbfounded: "I don't believe it! You two actually seem to think that was funny!" Leevke and Joost looked at him as if they had no idea what he meant. "Forget it!" Hinnerk said, picked up the filthy Klütje and washed some of the dirt off him. The coast dog was delighted and enthusiastically wagged his tail. "Well, Klütje and I thought it was very dangerous, isn't that right Klütje?" The dog barked as if to confirm his master's sentiment. Leevke asked: "Are you alright, Hinni?" "I'm fine. Our wise and evidently mad guide is back in charge." "Weren't you scared?" "No," Hinnerk lied. Leevke understood: "I knew that they wouldn't harm us. I heard them." "Are you saying you can talk with animals?" Leevke smiled: "I'm not sure. Maybe." Hinnerk held Klütje up to her: "Let's see. Say something, Klütje!" Klütje barked. "So, what did he say?" Leevke frowned: "Hello, I think?" "That's it?" Hinnerk put the dog down again and Leevke laughed: "What is he supposed to say, Hinni? You're funny." Joost called back to them: "Come on or do you want to wait until the tide comes in?"

They reached the yellow shore of Norderney without further incidents. The only tavern on the island was in a small fishing village on top of a hill. Here Hinnerk treated them all to fish soup and bread after they had properly washed themselves. Joost thanked him and went in search of a fisherman to take them to Kleene Wacht. Meanwhile Hinnerk, Leevke and Klütje warmed themselves in front of the fireplace. It was still just before noon and the tavern was deserted apart from the innkeeper and his wife. Hinnerk asked Leevke: "Why do you live with your grandparents?" Leevke looked glum and explained: "My parents aren't around anymore." Hinnerk realised that he had touched on a sensitive subject and instantly regretted his curiosity. He fell silent, but Leevke continued: "I don't even really remember my parents. I only know that we were surrounded by water and every time I'm by the sea I remember. It's like being homesick. I must have been happy there. That's what it feels like." Hinnerk cleared his throat: "What happened?" Leevke shook her head: "I don't know. Grandpa and nan told me that my parents drowned in a storm and I survived in a wicker basket. I was lucky." Hinnerk nodded: "That's just like the story of Moses. He was also found in a wicker basket." "Mossy? Don't know him. Anyway, they brought me to my grandparents on Kleene Wacht. I've been there for as long as I can remember." Leevke paused for a few seconds, then she asked anxiously: "Do you think grandpa and nan are okay? I'm scared that Theo hurt them after I had gone." Hinnerk reassured her: Your grandparents are fine." "But what if they aren't?" She glared at the sizzling flames, worry written all over her face and couldn't really get warm despite the fire. Hinnerk considered offering her to stay on the Wiards' farm if it became necessary, but then decided against it. He didn't want to crush the girl's hopes. But he was far from convinced that the old people were okay. How could he be? For all he knew they were already dead. The idea didn't sit easy on his shoulders and he wondered how he could comfort her. Klütje also sensed Leevke's grief. He jumped onto her lap and let her pet and cradle him. Leevke tried to smile and wiped a tear from her eyes. Hinnerk was reminded of a mother holding her child. He was about to tell her when Joost returned. "That's sorted, children. Gerd the Grumbler will take you." They gathered their belongings and walked to the northern side of the island where the boat was anchored.

Radbod had sat down on his throne and Theo was kneeling before him, surrounded by the armour-clad undead and their rusty spears. The King of the Frisians repeated his question: "So, you're telling me that this girl has the power to control the water? The ocean and the tides?" The ice-cold wind was howling so mercilessly, Theo was shivering. He was kneeling with his head on the cold stones in front of an undead king.

Many a man would have conceived this as a deep shame and humiliation, but in Theo's view he had no choice if he didn't want to needlessly jeopardize his health. "Yes, your Majesty, that's the truth of it. It was the reason I was trying to catch her." The undead soldiers' bones were creaking and were only held together by an unholy spell, not by muscle and flesh. From up here Radbod could see anything and anyone approaching his tower. Once the Frisian kings had ruled the Seven Sealands, but they had been killed in battle against Frankish invaders, converted by missionaries or send into exile. Radbod was the last of the free Frisian kings and had been extremely popular in his day. He was a fanatical opponent of anything Christian and had every church and chapel burned to the ground and their monks and priests slaughtered. The Church itself he regarded as nothing but a control tool of the Franks he tried to subdue through a Frisian alliance. Just like the Cheruski under Arminius had put an abrupt end to the advancing Roman armies long ago. But Radbod hadn't achieved the success he desired. He was true to the old gods, which eventually also contributed to his downfall. It all escalated in an inter-Frisian war where Radbod's followers were marginally defeated in Utrecht in their battle against the Christian Frisians under the command of the holy missionary Liudger. Radbod and his faithful men barely managed to escape. For some time he still maintained a base in Esens and the adjacent islands until the Christians finally defeated him after violent fighting in the moors and forests of Eastern Friesland. Badly wounded Radbod was forced to retreat to the rocky island of Bant where he stayed with his last remaining retinue. From here it was that he implored the ghosts of the long sunken land-bridge between Frisia and the land of the Angles and the ocean gods to give him the strength to reconquer his realm. The gods promised him the power in exchange for his and his men's souls. But a mighty prayer by the missionary Liudger, who had spotted Radbod's intentions in time, condemned the king to be a prisoner on the island, never being able to leave it. All his pagan power no longer served the king and he and his men were trapped on the island of Bant forever. Liudger sacrificed his life to this end. Ever since Bant had been cursed, hidden behind unnatural mists and nobody in their right mind dared to venture anywhere near it. Theo only now remembered having heard the story as a child. It was known all over the Western Sea. Unfortunately he had let himself be blinded by his greed and not given a second's thought about entering the lion's den. And the fact that the lion was still in residence. For the first time Theo damned his recklessness which had served him so well until now. The king of the Frisians announced: "You will deliver this girl to us, looter." Theo looked up: "You intend to let me go?" Theo started hoping that he could simply abscond once he was on the mainland. Radbod nodded: "Yes, you will go to the mainland for us, Theo. Are you ready, my love?" A woman's voice sounded from behind the pirate: "Always, my beloved king." It belonged to a tall, well-proportioned, pretty woman whose arms and skin were covered with suction pads like those of an octopus. Her pupils were elongated and a live kraken crouched on her head, its tentacles framing her head like ringlets. She supported herself with a scythe-shaped staff carved with numerous runes. Radbod got up and turned his back to Theo. "We shall need some insurance that you won't betray us, looter." Theo was sweating. "What do you mean, Sire? What's going on?" The kraken lady was dancing around him and giggled: "He's strong enough, alright. He'll survive, hehehe." "Survive what? What is this?" Theo jumped up and wanted to flee, but the undead army held him back just before the sharp blade of the scythe flashed right beside him. The woman chuckled: "Not so hasty, my friend. We haven't even started yet, hehehe." Radbod growled: "Do it, Ursula." "Alright! For once there's somebody else to talk to..." Before Theo could react, Ursula wielded her scythe and spoke some pagan words; conjured up some arcane magic. Theo's heart stopped beating. It was a strange feeling. As if time and the world had ceased to exist. Everything was silent, dull and dead. He found it increasingly hard to think and a dark veil cloaked his soul like a shroud. He heard Radbod's voice like it emanated from a tunnel. It drowned out everything around: "Welcome to my army, Theo!" All of a sudden he was catapulted back to life. He gasped for air like a fish out of water and screamed loud enough to be heard on the neighbouring islands. Ursula giggled: "He sounds like a newborn. Which would be quite fitting." Theo felt something twitching under his shirt and he yanked it up. "What?! What is that?!" A dark red, throbbing creature with a human eye in the middle was stuck above his heart. Its eight tentacles were clawed into Theo's flesh, right into his rips. He felt the kraken sucking at his heart and pumping the blood through his veins instead of his own heart.

He wanted to tear it out and remove the parasite, but Ursula rested her head on his shoulder and said: "I wouldn't do that if I were you, Theo dear. You'd bleed to death. That little guy is your heart from now on, hehehe." Theo looked at Radbod: "What did you do to me? What the fuck is going on?" The king of the Frisians turned around and pointed his finger at him. Contorted with pain, Theo's knees gave way from under him. "You now carry a soulkraken in you breast. Through the grace of Njord it is connected to me and beats and exists through nothing but my will, just as you do now. Whenever I want to end your live, a thought of mine will suffice. That is my safeguard." Theo needed a few seconds to grasp the situation, but he caught on quick enough: "If I bring you the girl who can control the sea you'll remove it again?" Radbod nodded patronisingly: "Then you will have paid your debt to me. Perhaps I can even admit you into my ranks, if you so desire. I always reward loyalty very generously. Take a look at my men. They are still serving me beyond death. That wasn't Liudger's so-called God, but unshakable loyalty." Theo seemed to understand and Ursula pulled his shirt down again. "Don't worry about your little companion. He's very tough and not easy to destroy. Just stay away from Christian symbols and consecrated ground. It could stop your heart or make it explode. Just some friendly advice." Theo cleared his throat: "I shall need a boat to get back to the mainland." He suddenly felt quiet a bit stronger and more courageous. Was that the influence of the soulkraken? Was he even still master of his own thoughts and words or was it Radbod? Radbod explained: "A boat won't be much good to you. It would sink because no timbers from this island float. Nothing from here can cross the sea. You have no choice but to walk." "Walk? On water? I'm hardly the Christ." Ursula pointed downwards with her index finger: "Not on, under." Theo surprised himself by instantly understanding what she meant: "I can breathe under water?" The kraken witch stretched her limbs: "Yes, you can, you brainiac. You are now kind of halfdead. You no longer have to breathe, but you can. You are also stronger and more resilient. But don't expose yourself to direct sunlight. It weakens the arcane forces." Theo instinctively knew that she was speaking the truth. There was a brief red flash in his eyes. Radbod told him: "Take this gold for any expenses you might have." A skeleton in rags handed him a bag. The King of the Frisians continued: "Bring me the girl." "Yes, your Majesty. As you command." Theo didn't hesitate and jumped off the tower. The wind was howling around his ears as he shot down towards the courtyard. Sand and stones scattered everywhere when he landed on the ground. He got up without a problem and walked through the gatehouse towards the sea, feeling invincible while the waves were lashing against the shoreline. He waded into the water and made for the next island. His lungs didn't hurt; the kraken was breathing for him. With a bit of luck he would find a boat on the island to sail to the mainland. Despite his new abilities, he saw no reason not to avail of a more comfortable mode of transport.

The broad-shouldered Gerd the Grumbler spat into the water and mumbled something into his non-existent beard. Hinnerk guessed why the nickname had been bestowed on the man in his mid-forties. Joost heartily shook his hand despite Gerd's grumpiness. Then he turned to Hinnerk and Leevke: "Well, my two lovebirds. Look after yourselves. This is where I have to leave you." Leevke smiled: "Pity, really. We had a lot of fun together!" Joost took his leave:" You're in capable hands. Good luck." The grumbler muttered: "Onto the boat with you then." They climbed aboard. The vessel was full of fishing gear and smelt accordingly. The fisherman from Norderney wasn't exactly talkative. Puffing, he pushed the boat into the sea, set the sail and took the rudder. Leevke already knew him and cheerfully quizzed him about his last catch, the past few days and the weather. The grumbler answered readily enough, but his expression remained just as sour. "You two know each other?" the slightly jealous Hinnerk wanted to know although Gerd was old enough to be Leevke's father. Leevke grinned: Gerd often visits us to sell the things we can't get otherwise. Bread, apples, pears, blackberry jam, timber, stones, bitumen, linnen, wool, carrots, nails, sausages..." The girl stopped and asked the fisherman: "Do you know if grandpa and nan are okay?" Gerd the Grumbler tilted his head while he considered: "You know there was that strange storm yesterday. Came out of nowhere. Very unusual. So I really don't know, little one." He paused, then asked her: "What were you actually doing on Norderney, Leevke?" Leevke told him about everything that had happened and Hinnerk filled in the gaps. The fisherman snarled. With determination written in his face he asked Hinnerk to take over the sail while he pulled out two long oars. He sat down and advised them: "Hold on tight. It's going to get rough!" The two youngsters held on to the side of the ship and the ropes. Straining the oars to breaking point, Gerd the Grumbler manoeuvred his boat through the waves with tremendous force. The water was splashing everywhere and soon they were soaked to the bone. Hinnerk was now desperately clinging to the ropes in fear of being flung into the ocean. Leevke, however, was enjoying the showers and laughed out loud whenever they tore through a wave. Klütje was cowering at the stern, clinging to Hinnerk's trousers with his teeth. At their rate of progress they soon sighted Kleene Wacht, a small, rugged and rocky island with a more level southern aspect and a small, ascending wooden jetty hewn ito the rock. Between the grass and occasional trees on top of the island towered the lighthouse which guided ships through storms and fog. Beside the building stood a small cottage and a shed for storage.

Goats and chickens were left to roam freely; they couldn't escape anyway. As they came closer to the island Leevke suddenly shouted: "There's grandpa! He's alive! And nan, too!" Tears of joy rolled down her cheeks and she hugged Hinnerk who could have held her like that forever.

Her grandparents had already spotted Gerd's boat from a long way off. Leevke's granddad was armed with a lance and shield; a necessary precaution after yesterday's events, Hinnerk thought. Gerd was wheezing heavily when they arrived. "Here we are, kids." He moored the boat at the pier. Leevke climbed up the rocky path with lighting speed; even Hinnerk found it hard to keep up with her. "For a girl who's spent all her life by the sea, she can climb amazingly well..." Leevke threw herself into her grandparents' arms. They were just as relieved to have their granddaughter back. Her grandmother held her tight: "We were so worried about you, little one." Hinnerk and Klütje joined the happily reunited family and Leevke laughed: "You're smothering me, nan! Hey, Hinnerk, this is my nan, Hampke. She's really strong. And that's Enno, my grandpa." Hampke stroked Leevke's hair: "Did Driftwood Theo and his men hurt you, sweetie?" "No, thanks to Hinni! And you? How are you?" Enno said: "As soon as they realised that you had disappeared into the sea, they rushed straight back to their ship. Then the storm came and we feared the worst for you. I've been trying to contact Norderney for hours, but my signal horn can't be heard far enough." There were tears in his eyes and Leevke hugged him as well. "Don't be sad, grandpa!" Enno laughed: "Sad? I'm delighted to have you back! Now you better introduce us. We know the Grumbler, of course, but who is this handsome young man?" Klütje was starting to jump around grandma Hampke when Enno spotted him, too. "That's Klütje. He belongs to my rescuer, Hinnerk Wiards. But everyone calls him Hinni." Hinnerk self-consciously scratched his head: "True, but it was nothing. I mean I was on dyke watch anyway and there she was washed up on the shore and then..." Enno had stepped up to him. "You saved our child, my boy. For that we shall be forever grateful." With those words he embraced Hinnerk and heartily slapped his shoulder. "It warms my old heart to know you land-dwellers still know how to stand up for yourselves. That calls for a celebration, I think You must be exhausted after your adventures. I know I am. But I am old."

"Oh, grandpa," Leevke interjected. "Hinni can't stay very long. He has to go home. Or do you, Hinni? What did your pa say?" Hinnerk thought about it while his stomach decided to rumble at an unprecedented noise level. Everybody was suddenly very quiet and listened. Enno laughed: "How can he possibly go home hungry as he is? Come on, Hampke will cook us something yummy. Or do you really have to leave already, young Wiards?" "No, no. I can stay the night, if that's okay." Hampke smiled: "Of course it is." Enno also invited Gerd, but the fisherman declined. "Can't. Got to get home in time or the wife will tear the rest of her hair out. You know what she's like, Enno..." "I do," Enno confirmed, but didn't comment any further. Gerd said to Hinnerk: "Well, boy, I'll be back sometime tomorrow morning to collect you. I'm also glad that everything's alright here. Hinnerk nodded and they said their goodbyes. The rest of the group walked over to the little cottage with its smoking chimney. Leevke cheerfully ushered Hinnerk inside. "Come on in, Hinni. And you, too, Klütje. We're having lobscouse and seaweed salad!" She made it sound like a delicacy, but Hinnerk wasn't fussy. For some inexplicable reason his heart was pounding like mad. Even more than during the rapid crossing or the encounter with the giant mud shrimp. The simple wattle and daub cottage consisted of a passage leading to the main room with its hearth and cooking area, table and chairs and shelves. The walls were hung with nets, harpoons, shark yaw skeletons and a tapestry depicting the Battle of Norden. Left and right off the passage were two further rooms. One a bedroom with a double bed, wardrobe and chest. The other housed a washtub, shelves and soap as well as a rainwater barrel and another bed with various wooden and stone toys, all of them a little worn by salt water. There were shells on the windowsill and a starfish mobile dangled from the ceiling. This must be Leevke's room. All in all the place was very humble, but warm, cosy and well-built to withstand the strong winds. By comparison Hinnerk's tall barnhouse seemed like a mansion to him.

Soon the food was sizzling on the fire. Leevke scurried back and forth, prepared the vegetables and was altogether pretty excited. Hinnerk, sitting at the table, watched her every move while Enno filled his pipe and puffed away. Leevke was chopping the carrots so vigorously, lots of bits were flying through the air and Klütje was quick to eat them. Hinnerk had quite a job trying to stop him. Enno was royally entertained: "What a lively little chap. He's a coast dog, isn't he?" "He is, Mr Pultjen." "Call me grandpa. Or Enno. I didn't know that coast dogs could be kept as pets. "Hinnerk lifted Klütje and intently stared into his eyes. The animal became calmer and then really tame. Hinnerk explained: "It wasn't easy. Coast dogs are actually predators. It takes a lot of patience to tame them. But then they are extremely loyal and sometimes really clever." Hampke smiled at him over her cooking: "I'd say most of all it takes a lot of love, what do you think?" Hinnerk agreed: "True. It helps..." He felt slightly awkward and didn't quite know what was expected of him. His thoughts darkened. Once he was back home he may not ever see Leevke again. He may bump into her on Norderney now and again, but how often did he ever get there? He felt responsible for her and wanted to look after her. Should all this end before it had even begun? He would end up becoming a farmer like his dad. The adventure was over all too soon and he hated his prospects of a settled life.

Finally the meal was ready. Enno even produced a bottle of Burgundy and Hinnerk didn't say no. "A Flemish sailor gave me that after I had fished him out of the water. His ship had been attacked by a seamonster with countless tentacles. The beast is terrorising the cost along here and it is rumoured that it is commanded by King Radbod the Indomitable, the last free king of the Frisians." Grandma Hampke shot him a reproachful look. "I wish you'd stop with your old horror stories. Don't invoke the wrath of the sea. We only just had our share of drama. That's enough for me!" "Never mind. Let's eat," Enno appeased her and tucked into his food. Hinnerk tried Leevke's seaweed salad, but didn't really like it. Leevke though shovelled the stuff into her as if she couldn't get enough of it. She chomped away at an alarming rate. "Hampke said: "Slow down, Leevke." To Hinnerk she said: "Our girl loves seafood." Leevke slurped the last bit of seaweed from her wooden bowl, sighed contentedly and burped loudly: "Ahhhh!" Hampke turned purple: "What happened to your table manners?!" Erno grinned: "She never had any. Let her burp. Today I don't care, Hampke." His wife took a deep breath and smiled: "You are right. Just for once." They eventually finished their meal and Hinnerk thanked them for the food. The sun was setting and Enno suggested that Hinnerk could sleep in the lighthouse.

He relit his pipe and then said in an unusually serious voice: "But there's something we have to discuss first. It's about the attack yesterday and about Leevke..." The girl looked up: "About me?" Enno nodded slowly and Hampke took her granddaughters hand. The two old people sadly looked at each other and reached a silent agreement. Enno started: "There's something we couldn't tell you before, but I guess now we don't have a choice. And it would be unfair to you to keep it from you any longer." "We always wanted to protect you," Hampke added. "Ummm..." Hinnerk voiced. "Should I be here? If this is something private, I..." In reality Hinnerk was just as concerned about Leevke's fate as everyone else in the room, except Klütje who was snoring in front of the fire. Leevke defiantly pushed out her chin. "Hinni should know. He's my friend!" She glanced at him with a serious expression in her eyes and he looked back, his head as red as a beetroot. He was her friend.

And so Enno and Hampke told them about the fateful day on Kleene Wacht when they had weathered an almighty storm together which had threatened to devour the island. It had been like a tempest from the old legends with thunder and lightning, gigantic waves reaching skyhigh and embracing the land as if to bury it underneath the floods. It had been like the end of the world and the lighthouse itself had been trembling when the waves lashed against its walls. Hampke and Enno hid at the top of the lighthouse and feared the worst. At last the storm abated enough around midnight for it to be safe to step outside. The moon and the stars clearly illuminated the foaming sea. The wind was bitterly cold. While Enno investigated the damage to their cottage and shed, Hampke searched the cliffs for objects and food the storm had washed away from their home. In the moonlight she saw a glistening block of ice wedged between the rocks. She called out for Enno, who grabbed a torch, ran down to join her and took a closer look at the block of ice. To his amazement he discovered a naked girl inside it; perhaps fourteen years old, huddled up with her legs close to her body and her eyes closed. She had no hair and resembled a newborn although she was already the age of a young woman. Together they heaved the block of ice to the lighthouse and gradually melted it at the fireplace. When it finally released the girl, she was barely breathing. They warmed her as well as they could, but the strange child was more dead than alive and couldn't open her eyes. Hampke fed her small bits of food, but the girl could barely keep any of it down. Enno prayed fervently and the following day asked Gerd the Grumbler to provide them with herbs that would aid the healing process. A month later, when they put her into a bath of warm water to wash her, she fully opened her golden eyes for the first time and instantly smiled at Hampke after briefly examining her. Hampke cried with relief and Enno did the same soon after. From then on the girl behaved as if she had completely lost her memory. She didn't even know a language or her own name and initially couldn't walk properly without falling and scraping her knees. But she could swim better than anyone after even years of practice. It soon became apparent that the sea was her element.

The fear that the ice could have inflicted mental damage soon vanished when it became clear how fast Leevke, as they called the lovable, clumsy girl, learned the Frisian language and everything important for day-to-day life. It only took two years until Leevke's mental age equalled her physical one and only her inexperience in mundane matters distinguished her from ordinary girls. This she compensated for with her frank, inquisitive manner which would see no evil in any creature. To everyone's amazement, the girl made the thoroughly obnoxious Grumbler come out of his shell and even laugh again for the first time in years. All because Leevke had been straight and sensitive with him. Her outgoing nature made her quickly form friendships although mostly among the younger children. Adolescents on Norderney and Kleene Wacht thought her too childish and simple. Over time she developed a head of purple-blue hair, which she tied back with clips she made herself from shells. Her hair grew down to her neck, but never any longer, which Hampke in particular found sad. In her view a girl should have the traditional free-flowing long hair. But when Leevke objected that Hampke herself hid her blonde mane twisted into a pigtail secured to the top of her head, she had no reply. Leevke's innocent way of questioning things endeared her so much to the old people that they had no problem accepting her as their own. Their first-born son had died on a trading expedition to West Francia and their daughter hadn't survived him for more than a year. Enno and Hampke had grieved too much to start another family and withdrew to Kleene Wacht by mutual agreement where they had resigned themselves to their humdrum existence when Leevke had miraculously been washed ashore. They never questioned the gills on her neck or the colour of her eyes and hair and made the the girl feel she was no different to anyone else.

Leevke's love of the sea increasingly came to the fore and she often swam around the island to explore her underwater-world. Sometimes she stayed there for hours. She neither had to come up for breath nor did her skin get shrivelled. Diving was her forte and she frequently salvaged objects from the ocean bed Enno and Hampke had long written off. Occasionally she found treasure in the form of gold coins and thus supplemented the household with a little luxury. Apparently Leevke didn't remember what had happened and why she had been drifting in a block of ice in the Western Sea. Once, when she enquired about her past, her adopted grandparents had invented the story about her parents perishing in an accident. They thought this kind of fate sad but not uncommon and believed their story would at least preserve the appearance of a normal identity for the time being. Now and again, however, it was obvious that the girl was something special. It wasn't just her ease in the ocean. By touch and a little concentration alone, for example, she could confer a golden, honey-like glow onto the water which gave it healing properties. And the sea creatures she talked to seemed to follow her every word.

She always took great delight in the crabs, which she would have parading up and down in front of her. Sometimes she just sat on the beach for hours and played with the water which she could shape into spheres which floated like soap bubbles and then burst. Enno and Hampke soon realised that the girl's gifts could lead to problems if the Church got wind of them. Even the people of Norderney wouldn't approve outright of such powers or keep their mouths shut indefinitely. Someone would inevitably talk.

The Church didn't tolerate supernatural abilities.

Leevke was unaware that she was different and took it for granted that she was so in tune with the ocean. Her grandparents tried to hide her talents from the world, but eventually a tipsy sailor in a tavern on Norderney talked too much and the word was out. Driftwood Theo had quizzed him explicitly about the "Seawitch of Norderney". It wasn't hard to guess the pirate's motivation. He wasn't interested in magic, but the gold that somebody was offering for her head. Wherever Leevke had come from originally, her past had now caught up with her. Although they had successfully dealt with Theo they could confidently assume that they would soon have to face other bounty hunters who wouldn't be as easy to shake off.

Enno ended his tale: "Of course we will protect you, but I'm afraid this place is no longer safe for you, sweetie." Leevke was silent while she gradually digested what she'd just been told. Hinnerk swallowed hard. It was all a lot to take in. Finally Leevke looked up: "So you aren't my grandparents?" Tears were welling up in her eyes and Hampke immediately reassured her: "But of course we are. And we always will be!" Both Enno and Hinnerk didn't know what to say and tried to find a solution. Eventually Leevke stated with determination: "I don't want those powers. Where can I give them back?" Hampke smiled: "I don't think it's as easy as that..." "Why not? You don't have them! Perhaps it would have been better if I had gone with Theo." "The hell it would!" Enno shouted indignantly. "My child will not bow to some common scoundrels who threaten us with violence! I'm always open to discussion, but I won't tolerate their vile methods. Fearmongering, I call it! You agree, don't you Hinni?" Hinnerk nodded: "Without a doubt. They're up to no good." Enno continued: "You are a Frisian, Leevke. It doesn't matter where you came from, you're one of us now. A Frisian bows to no man, only to the Emperor or God. And even that only because it is necessary and just." Hinnerk added: "It also doesn't bear thinking about how those criminals intend to do use your powers. I saw the tidal wave that washed Theo and his men away. Powers like that in the wrong hands can do a lot of damage." "Hear, hear!" Enno backed him. Leevke sighed and dried her tears. "But what am I supposed to do? Where can I go?" She had just uttered the most important question of the evening. "If you really want it, we have to get rid of your magic," Hinnerk suggested. "I don't know how yet, but there must be a way. We should really consult someone who knows about those things." Hampke cradled Leevke in her arms: "Do you have someone in mind, my boy?" Hinnerk crossed his arms over his chest and closed his eyes. "A priest? A wizard? A real witch? Not some wannabes like the Harugari. The Deel-Deerns perhaps? No, they know even less... Oh!" He opened his eyes: "We could ask my master, uncle Abbo!" Enno frowned: "Don't they call him Abbo the Rebel?" Hinnerk became enthusiastic: "He is a good man who fought for our freedom in Stedingen. And he fought the Saracens in Iberia! A crusader and a local hero. He will know what do to. He's been around." Leevke seemed undecided. "I don't know. That means I have to leave here, doesn't it?" Enno and Hampke encouraged her to try at least after assuring her that she could also stay with them. But Leevke didn't want to stay because her presence would endanger them. The grandparents offered to go with her, but that, too, Leevke refused. "No, you have to look after the lighthouse. Besides, you're too old to travel..." Everyone smiled as Leevke had once again voiced the obvious nobody had wanted to admit. Enno turned to Hinnerk: "I know it's asking a lot and you have your own duties to attend to, but would you take our child with you to Norderney?" Hinnerk beat his chest: "I won't just bring her to Norderney, I will also help her solve her problems. And I'm the only one who knows where to find Master Abbo. Sooner or later you would have had to ask me anyway." Hampke took his hand: "What a brave young lad. A bit like you in your day, Enno." "Yes, nearly." Enno's concession had been so dry, they all burst into laughter. Leevke was her old self again: "Can Hinnerk and I sleep in the lighthouse tonight? Please?" Hampke grinned: "Sure. Takes as much time as you need to get ready. We'll keep watch." Granddad Enno escorted them to the lighthouse and up the winding stairs. On the first floor were two simple beds, a table with a stool and writing materials and a single, high window with heavy wooden shutters. The timber floor crunched under their feet. "Make yourselves comfortable. I have to go and light the fires," Enno told them and trudged up the steps. Klütje was busy sniffing around when Leevke gave Hinnerk a big hug. "Thank you for helping me. I don't know what I would do without you. Everything's happening so fast." Hinnerk reassured her with a moronic grin: "Hey, it's no problem. Hehehe!" and felt extremely oafish. She looked up at him. A hand's width shorter than he, she was still quite tall for a girl. "Is there anything I can do for you in return?" she asked. The spontaneous, massive lump in his throat made it difficult for Hinnerk to reply. "No... no ne... " "None? Oh, I see, no need! " Hinnerk nodded: "That's what I meant. No need. I don't want anything, hehehe." Leevke eyed him suspiciously and Hinnerk staggered over to the window: "I'm doing this for the adventure. Finally I've got a reason to explore the world and see its wonders. This is great!" "I hope we won't have to travel too far away from home. I love being here right by the sea. I don't really want to leave." Hinnerk realised that he sounded as if he just wanted to use Leevke to satisfy his need to for adventure. "I didn't mean it like that. I just need to get away from home, you know. Can you understand that?" Leevke plunged down on one of the beds. "Not really, but maybe we're going to have some fun after all," she giggled. "Hinnerk pulled out his dagger and twirled it around in his hand. "Of course I shall shield you from all harm." "You're starting to sound like a true knight." Hinnerk sat down opposite her and grinned: "Have you ever seen one? A real knight, I mean. Not just one of those underlings in chainmail. No, one in plate armor and with a broad-sword?" Leevke shrugged: "I guess there was one in the Tavern on Nordeney once. He was boasting about his life in Burgundy in his strange accent and somehow ended up losing everything. All he was left with was his armour." Hinnerk nodded: "A suit of armour like that is worth as much as fifty estates. Nothing can penetrate it." He smiled: "Tomorrow we shall go to Norderney and then back to the Wiards' farm to fill in my people and to meet Abbo. "That's fine," Leevke endorsed his plan. Hinnerk doubted if she'd actually understood it all. She pulled up her legs and rolled back and forth on the bed. "What are you doing?" Hinnerk murmured and Leevke simply replied: "Just rolling over and back. You should try it sometime. It helps falling asleep." Hinnerk took off his boots and followed her example.

When Enno came back down the stairs he saw two youngsters laughing and rolling around on their beds. When they spotted him, Hinnerk jumped up and stuttered. But Enno waved him off: "I've relit the fires and I'm going back to the cottage. If you need anything, don't be too shy to wake us, okay?" Leevke said: "Thank you, granpa. Do I get a goodnight kiss?" "Good night, sweetie. Good night, Hinnerk. You are now the man in charge." Hinnerk saluted unnecessarily and a little over the top: "At your service, sir!" Once Enno had departed, Leevke rolled back and forth again. "I think he likes you." she laughed. When they had finally settled down, Leevke peered at him from under her blankets. She looked at him through her half-open, golden-coloured eyes with an intensity that made Hinnerk gasp. "Good night, Hinni. Sleep well. "Goo... good night," Hinnerk stuttered and turned over on his side. Shortly after he could hear Leevke's even and enthusiastic snoring. Hinnerk loved and treasured the sound as he had never treasured anyone else's snores before. He had no idea how anyone could even achieve a feat like that. He gazed at the timber ceiling and listened to Leevke and the sound of the sea splashing against the cliffs of Kleene Wacht. Klütje, also fast asleep, was stretched out by his side. The combined efffect was hypnotic and Hinnerk fell asleep before he knew it. He had so wanted to stay awake to watch over Leevke. But the days' events had taken their toll. He needed to rest.

Chapter 3

Moor Thiefs

The following morning, after Hampke had woken them with a substantial breakfast of bread, sausage and cheese, Enno showed them the view from the top of the lighthouse. In the strong wind they could see past Norderney, Langeoog and Baltrum as far as the mainland. Towards noon Gerd the Grumbler showed up to take them back to Norddeich on the tide, aided by a favourable northeasterly wind. Leevke's grandparents said their goodbyes to their grandchild and everybody exchanged heartfelt hugs. Enno took Hinnerk aside: "I nearly forgot. I've got something for you. Wait here." He went to the stable and returned with a round shield wrapped in cloth. He handed it to Hinnerk: "This is an old heirloom of the Pultjen family. I have my own shield and rarely used this one. But my father used it in his lifetime to ward of the fog spirits and to guide the ships before the lighthouse was built." The shield was decorated with a lighthouse radiating beams of light. Enno explained: "The shield is called Lux Maris, the light of the seas. It has a name just like swords do." Enno leaned forward: "It is supposed to be steeped in old magic." "Really? Pagan magic?" "I believe so. But make sure that none of the priests get their hands on it. They are only too keen to confiscate artefacts like this one. Lux Maris can dispel the darkness and the densest fog. But I've forgotten the spell. It's been too long. But never mind. A shield is a shield and this one is made from good iron and reinforced with steel rivets on the back. Even crossbow arrows will bounce off it. I had intended to pass it on to my son, as is the family tradition. But he died before I could give it to him. He wasn't really all that fond of fighting in any case... Take it Hinni. Protect yourself and Leevke with it." Hinnerk swallowed hard: "But it is a family heirloom. What if it breaks?" Enno said: "It's only metal, my boy. So what if it breaks? Still better than either of you getting hurt. In the end it is nothing but a lifeless object. Use its power when you can. I'm afraid that's all I can do for you." Hinnerk accepted the shield and lifted it by its handle. Despite its heavy construction it was remarkably light. Hinnerk had quite often practiced with a shield and uncle Abbo's wooden ones were still heavier than Lux Maris. It had obviously been forged by a master blacksmith. Hinnerk acknowledged the gift gratefully: "I am honoured." Enno smiled: "Perhaps I was wrong about Abbo the Rebel. I always took him to be a warmonger. People say a lot of stupid things. But if you are his friend then all those rumours are just nonsense." "They are," Hinnerk confirmed. Enno embraced him. "You will hold your ground. We shall wait for your return." Hinnerk felt slightly embarrassed: "I... I will do my best. I swear it on my life." Hampke and her granddaughter had packed a bag with Leevke's things which she tied around her waist. Hinnerk stepped up to her: "Are you alright?" "Yes. I hope we'll find a way to make me normal." "You... you ARE normal." Leevke stared at the ground. "Do you really think so?" Hinnerk hesitated and that was enough of an answer for Leevke: "So you also believe I'm not normal." Hinnerk composed himself; her question had taken him by surprise: "Normal? It means nothing. Normal is boring. Who wants to be normal? Not me! Compared to all those weird creatures out there we're even far too normal. It's about time we go mad." Leevke chuckled as Hinnerk got more and more muddled: "You're far more normal than Muddy Joost! For sure. He and his giant shrimp. And you're more normal than my family! Take my brother Willi. He fell off the roof once because he wanted to catch a cloud! Those people are nuts. You're boring by comparison. I... I don't mean... in a negative way. Normal, you know... um... shit." Leevke laughed out loud: "Okay, okay. I know what you mean, hi, hi. Who knows where I'd be without you! Thank you." Stop thanking me all the time. I haven't done anything yet. You can thank me once I've clobbered a dragon or spanked a troll's bottom..."

The Grumbler shouted: "Are you ready? We have to leave if we don't want to run aground." They climbed onto the boat and waved back at Enno and Hampke. Kleene Wacht became smaller and smaller until it disappeared from view altogether.

The journey back was eventless. Thanks to the tide, Gerd brought them straight to Norddeich where they enquired after Okko's whereabouts and were directed to one of the taverns. His cart and the old horse were parked in the adjoining stable. They found Okko at a table with a few other men; drinking beer from Hamburg and playing dice.

"There you are, son." Then Okko frowned: "Why's Leevke still with you? Could you not get a passage? Was there a storm? What happened?" Hinnerk said: "I don't know if I can tell you. It's all a bit... complicated. You understand? But basically everything's fine. We were with Leevke's grandparents. They are okay and so is Leevke. She'll be staying with me for the time being." Okko wasn't usually fobbed off that easily, but apparently he didn't want to create a scene in front of his drinking buddies and simply said: "No problem. Is that the truth, Leevke?" She smiled: "Absolutely." Soon after they left the inn, harnessed the horse to the cart and were on their way along the dyke back to the Wiards' farm. In the meantime there had been a light rain and the ground was soggy, the air damp. They had hardly left Norddeich behind when they couldn't contain themselves any longer and told Okko the real story. He listened patiently and then assured them: "Don't worry. I won't tell a soul. Apart from your mother, perhaps. She always wants to know everything and she'll notice immediately if I'm holding something back from her." Leevke smiled: "That's fine. I trust you just like I trust Hinni." Okko mused: "So you want to see Abbo? He may actually know a thing or two. I for one would ask the priests. I doubt they would think you a witch. And even if, here in Frisia you are pretty safe. The Church doesn't have the same power here it has in other parts of the realm. Just one word from me is enough and all the dykers will chase them off. This is our land. We've worked hard for our rights." They arrived at a confusing turn on the road. To the south of them stretched a forest behind which the Ghastly Moors began, a place where many a careless wanderer had lost his life. Only the bravest peat cutters or moor rangers, dared to go there. This was where Abbo lived, not all that far from the Wiards' farm. Every time Hinnerk wanted to practice his fighting skills with him, he had to whistle a certain melody and soon after his uncle emerged from the moors to take him back to his modest, remote hut. Hinnerk could only guess why Abbo lived so secluded from civilisation. He had always been a solitary loner and hunted furry moor creatures with bow and arrow to sell their pelts to Okko. Only rarely did he venture as far as Esens or Dornum to buy provisions the moor itself couldn't provide. He also kept the predatory Gobolds at bay which frequently ransacked the nearby farms.

The cart came to an abrupt halt. The mare did her best, but couldn't pull it any further.

Okko cursed: "Damn it. A pothole. I'm afraid we'll have to push." They sound of a misshapen horn made Leevke exclaim: "Perhaps they will help us!" They watched as a ten-strong band of Gobolds rose from under the shrubs and stormed at them wielding their weapons. "It's a trap!" Okko growled. Gobolds were small, scrawny creatures with tiny, piercing-yellow eyes, crooked fangs, overlong arms and short legs who always walked with a stoop. They wore rusty weapons, primitive cudgels and rags made from rabbit- and wolfskin or roughly woven fabric. Those of them who had learned the language of the humans, employed it to go about their business as smugglers or black marketers. They were generally no threat to a full-grown man and relied on strength in numbers and ambushes like this one. They had been responsible for digging the hole. Okko shouted: "We have to fight! Hinni!" He extracted his sword from under the seat. The Gobolds were already upon them and Hinnerk jumped off the cart armed with shield and dagger. Klütje snarled and attacked one of the creatures. Hinnerk's shield proved useful in fending off the Gobolds' pointed sticks while he stabbed them with his dagger. With an ugly squeal the first of them went down. Leevke sobbed and couldn't watch. Okko, too, had already defeated his second opponent. From one moment to the next the peaceful path had turned into the scene of a bloody massacre. Hinnerk was chasing three of the Gobolds when he realised that Okko had also been lured away from the cart. The Gobolds were after their provisions!

The bewildered Leevke stood on the cart and saw with horror how a second band of five Gobolds climbed onto it. The first attack had only been a diversion. Leevke jumped back when the creatures started throwing crates and sacks at Okko and Hinnerk. One of them struck Leevke's head with his cudgel and knocked her unconscious. Swiftly two more of them snatched the girl and dragged her off. Hinnerk and Okko hastened to her rescue, but by now they were surrounded by Gobolds on all sides throwing stones at them while Leevke was carried into the forest. The horn sounded again and the Gobolds withdrew, some of them still grabbing what they could get. Hinnerk managed to catch one of them because the creature was completely overloaded with crates and didn't want to let go. Okko cited the old saying: "A Gobold treasures his loot above his own skin." Klütje yelped indignantly. Apart from a bloody snout, he seemed alright although he was limping. "Hang in there, buddy," Hinnerk whispered to him while he gently picked him up and put him in his pouch. The water inside it had lost its golden glow, but Klütje seemed to feel better as soon as he was immersed in it. He even wagged his tail. Relieved Hinnerk turned to his father: "Are you alright, pa?" Okko nodded: "Yes, and you?" Hinnerk wiped his mouth. "I've got to go after them. I can still catch them!" "Don't be stupid, Hinnerk. They went into the moors and who knows what other traps they have set. They won't kill Leevke. When Gobolds kidnap people they do it for the ransom. They've done it before..." Hinnerk nagged: "And if not? Look after Klütje! I have to follow them!" He put down the pouch with the coast dog and ran into the forest. "Damn it, Hinni! Come back!" Okko cursed and found himself in the precarious situation of leaving Klütje and the cart unguarded or following Hinnerk. In all likelihood some of the Gobolds were still watching, hoping for a second chance to plunder the cart after all. "Curse the boy! Why can't he think before he acts?!" He grabbed the pouch with Klütje and ran after his son.

Hinnerk raced through the forest past prickly blackberry bushes and now and then thought he could see the Gobolds in the distance. He was glad Abbo had taught him how to control his breathing to sprint faster and more efficiently. The Gobolds were also pretty nifty on their feet, especially when on the run. Hinnerk started to catch up and spotted them through the trees. They'd already left the small forest behind and had reached a field with the Ghastly Moors behind. The Gobolds noticed their tracker and Hinnerk found himself confronted by two of them who barred the way with their spears. Hinnerk held the shield in front of him and simply broke through the barricade, flinging the creatures aside. The fog was rising from the moors and as he stepped into the brackish water he instinctively slowed down. Although the ground was only slightly slushy, he soon no longer knew where it was save to step. The waist-high grass made it hard to discern a path. He followed the broken reeds, but the rising mists made this increasingly difficult as well. He saw the Gobolds carrying Leevke through the rushes and pursued them. One of them fired an arrow at him, but he blocked it with his shield. The fog intensified and, scared to lose sight of the Gobolds, Hinnerk remembered the magic powers the shield held according to Enno. He tried various spells to activate them. "Darkness be gone! Mistus disappearus! Lux maximus!" Not knowing any Latin, he kept improvising: "Darknum minimum! Pathus appearus! Lux beamus! Come on, you bugger." He finally gave up: "Oh, Kiss my arse!" A split second later a beam of light as wide and round as the shield itself shot through the fog and provided him with perfect vision through a tunnel of light. Not too far away he saw the Gobolds and Leevke. They had noticed the light and were jabbering with excitement while speeding up. "Stop!" Hinnerk shouted and chased after them. He trudged through the moor and had nearly caught up with them when one of his feet got stuck. The more he tried to pull his boot out of the ground the deeper it was pulled into the swamp. The Gobolds briefly cheered and quickly disappeared into the fog.

Hinnerk had stepped into a bog hole. In his panic he started sweating, his stomach felt queasy, his legs were trembling and he suddenly felt dizzy. He pulled at his feet, but nearly toppled into the swamp. There was no safe ground in sight; he had strayed too far into the pit. Hinnerk actually knew everything about bog holes, but in his haste he had fallen right into the trap. He slowly turned around while the quagmire clung to him and he sank even deeper. There was no sign of the Gobolds. They were gone. There was nobody to help him. All on his own he would perish in the moors. He screamed: "Hey! Is anybody there?! Heeeelp!" He tried to dig himself out of the swamp with the shield and pull himself up by the reeds. But he could neither dig as fast as the brown sludge kept refilling what he had just emptied, nor were the surrounding rushes strong enough to carry his weight. Soon he was immersed up to his waist and he gave up. His brain throbbed with the numb realisation that he was going to die. Only the croaking of toads and the beastly hums of gnats filled the air, He tried to fight them, but tears of regret filled his eyes. His life hadn't even started yet. He shouted for his father, anybody. But the moors swallowed each scream for help. He couldn't escape. Only face the inevitability of death.

Hinnerk would become a bog mummy. They were created when the deceased still had business in the mortal world. He would be a revenant, one of the living dead. "I don't want to die!" Hinnerk finally cried and felt drained when the sludge covered his chest. He sobbed and his throat felt parched and hoarse. The more he struggled, the worse it got. Hinnerk started to pray and implored God to help him. But God wasn't coming to his rescue either, regardless of how fervently he clutched his hands together, how often he cried amen. God didn't listen to his entreaties. Perhaps his prayers didn't penetrate the dense fog and not even the Lord could see and hear him. Hinnerk screwed up his face when he saw how Enno's shield was still glowing through the mists. And then he remembered. With his last remaining strength Hinnerk swung the shield around. Perhaps somebody would see the light, a moor ranger maybe. But it was far more likely that the light would be mistaken for a will-o'-the-wisp and ignored. It often happened, as he well knew. Hinnerk had a last, desperate idea. Will-o'-the'-wisps shone steadily and confused wanderers with their constant, hypnotic glow and thus led them off the path. But they didn't blink! "Kiss my arse!" he said and the shield stopped shining. "Kiss my arse!" and the light came back on again. Hinnerk kept repeating the spell over and over while the sludge had already reached his shoulders. When it came up to his chin, he started crying and his voice failed him. "It's a male voice," were the last words he heard before the mud went into his ears. "Hello? I could swear I heard something! Hello?!" Somebody was walking through the reeds. Hinnerk cried with relief and he wanted to shout, but his voice still wouldn't do his bidding. The man moved away again and his words started to fade: "Hello? Was I mistaken? Didn't I see a light?" Hinnerk realised that his last spell had turned Lux Maris's light off. He gathered all his reserves and suddenly exploded: "Here! Here! Please! Here! Help!" Then he collapsed and sobbed as the sludge invaded his nostrils and he swallowed some of it. The mud gushed into his windpipe, but he couldn't cough. He fainted. Why hadn't he listened to his pa?

A smouldering pot was suspended above the open fire in front of the small clay hut. Abbo had been cooking when he noticed the strange light in the distance. Initially he had believed it to be a will-o'-the'-wisp, a common occurrence in the Ghastly Moors. But when it had started to flash, he got up to investigate and also heard some vague and faint cries. The light abruptly disappeared and he was no longer sure of its original direction. Besides, he had to be careful not to lose his footing. He shouted a few more times and was about to turn back when he heard Hinnerk's distraught cries. Abbo turned Pakhaou into a lance and with all his strength and Pakhaous' help he lifted the boy from the quagmire which reluctantly released him with a squelch. Abbo's arms were on fire, but he didn't stop until he had saved his nephew. He cleaned the boy's nose and mouth and ensured that he was still breathing. Then he carried him to his hut, put the still unconscious lad onto his bed and took off his filthy clothes. He fetched a bucket of water and washed him thoroughly with a sponge and a little carbolic soap before gently covering him with a blanket. He washed Hinnerk's clothes and took them outside to dry them by the fire. Then he stirred the stew to let it simmer until Hinnerk would wake up. Two hours later the boy slowly opened his eyes.

Everything seemed surreal. He was clean and lying warm and snug in a bed in a one roomed hut he identified as his uncles when he saw some of Abbo's weapons. He looked towards the door when Abbo entered. Hinnerk sat up and Abbo laughed: "Behold, young Hinni has risen from the dead!" Hinnerk couldn't help grinning: "So I'm not dead?" Abbo sat down beside him on the bed and handed him a bowl of steaming hot stew and morels: "That was a close shave. You don't owe me anything but an explanation perhaps. If you feel strong enough, that is. Otherwise take your time. A good warrior knows when to preserve his strength..."

Suddenly Hinnerk remembered the events of the past few hours and reached for Abbo's arm: "We have to go after the Gobolds, uncle Abbo! They've got Leevke! We have to leave! Right now, before they're gone!" Abbo took Hinnerk's hand. "Calm down, boy. You've only just escaped from certain death. Take your time and eat something first. I know how precious everything is after an experience like that. Food never tasted better to me than after a battle. Apart from all that, I won't let you storm off into the moors again. What would have happened if I hadn't accidentally spotted your shield glowing? Your father would never forgive me." Hinnerk shook his head: "We have to help her! I gave her my promise!" Abbo considered for a while and when he saw Hinnerk's determined expression he said: "Alright. Tell me everything from the start. I need to know what happened. And who is this Leevke girl? Your girlfriend? Since when?" Hinnerk blushed, but told him his story as well as he could. When he had finished Abbo said: "I know that some of the Gobolds have a camp in the South. They're getting bolder all the time seeing that they dared to come this far..." "Will you help me, Master Abbo?" Hinnerk didn't admit it, but he was scared to death to venture into the

moors again by himself. The thought alone made him tremble. Abbo agreed to help and smiled cynically: "That's going to be fun! But now eat something."
Hinnerk tried the stew and pulled a face. Abbo couldn't fail to notice: "I'm still a lousy cook, I guess." Hinnerk shook his head and Abbo nudged him in the side: "The lad's unbelievable. The scrapes you get yourself into!" "Not on purpose, uncle!" The warm food helped to calm Hinnerk's nerves a little, but he was still shocked by his recent narrow escape. He nearly felt tempted to go home and never set foot in the moors again. But when he saw Abbo, he knew that he would get over it, and rather sooner than later. Hinnerk had no intention to let the experience ruin his life.

When they had finished their meal, Hinnerk put on his knee-length linen shirt, his dark breeches, boots and leather collar, secured Lux Maris to his shoulder strap, checked the dagger in his belt and nodded at Abbo. His uncle was carrying Pakhaou and a leather covered round shield and wore a riveted armour worked from leather and iron: "Let's go and rescue your sexy girlfriend!" Hinnerk blushed again while the grinning Abbo marched ahead into the Ghastly Moors. Discounting the moor rangers, the peat cutters, he knew the place better than anyone else. The fog was still sitting heavy on the moors and clung to their skin. They didn't use Lux Maris's power to illuminate their way so as not to alert the Gobolds. Abbo frequently paused to listen to the sounds of the moor, warned Hinnerk when the path became treacherous and shook him awake whenever he threatened to succumb to a will-o'-the-wisp. It was a difficult and cumbersome journey. A knight or legionnaire in all his heavy armour wouldn't have stood a chance in the mud. Suddenly Abbo crouched down and Hinnerk followed suit. Abbo pointed through the reeds and whispered: "I guess we found them. Take a closer look." Spread before them was the Gobolds' fenced-in cluster of wooden shacks. Hinnerk wasn't sure if the place was supposed to be a village or a fortress or a mixture of both. Two of the thieving Gobolds, armed with bow and arrow, were standing guard in front of a half-heartedly patched together gate, busily picking their noses. "Do you recognise them?" Abbo asked quietly and Hinnerk growled: "One of them looks as ugly as the next." Inside the fence the Gobolds were scurrying about and screaming at each other. They were obviously having an argument which wasn't surprising. Loyalty and friendship were not included in the species' vocabulary. "Dishonourable as a Gobold" was therefore a common insult if you wanted to infuriate someone. The Gobolds valued control and the resulting need to accumulate more and more possessions, if they needed them or not. They buried their treasures like dogs buried their bones and believed they endowed them with mystical "powers". Abbo and Hinnerk retreated after they had watched the camp for a while. Abbo suggested: "We can wait until it's dark or until they go raiding to surprise them." Hinnerk thought about it: "Perhaps we should talk to them. What if they hurt Leevke?" "We have to use the element of surprise. There are too many of them." When he noticed the boy's scepticism, he relented: "Maybe I spent too much time fighting the Saracens... Alright then. Gobolds only roam the land in search of prey, mostly meat and treasure. They avoid a fight if they aren't absolutely certain they'll win. Look confident and don't reveal any weakness or insecurity. Gobold are seasoned liars. That's why they quickly spot if someone's not telling the truth." "I'm not scared of them." "Good. By the way, I wouldn't step any further if I were you." "Why?" Hinnerk looked down and was horrified. Abbo pulled him back just in time. "A Moorfang. You would have lost your leg if you had walked into it." Only a foot away from Hinnerk there was a gaping hole in the ground lined with sharp fangs on top of a deep, dark jaw. There was no movement, but that was a fatal illusion. Moorfangs were creatures who waited motionless until somebody stepped into them when they snapped their jaws together with a force capable of breaking bones and even steel. They weren't invincible, but people had always had to abandon their attempts to dig them out. Once they had been unearthed up to a certain height the Moorfangs disappeared into the unknown depths of the moors. Their hunters would give up, throw flaming torches into the hole and fill it up again. Some of the peat cutters believed in the existence of an underground colony; others assumed they were the servants of a pagan moor deity that dwelt in unfathomable underground chambers of a long forgotten age. Hinnerk took a deep breath.

They left the rushes, Abbo walking ahead. The two startled sentries frantically blew their bugles. Abbo raised his hands when he saw a number of Gobolds perched on the stockades aiming their shortbows at them. "We come to trade!" "Are you alone?!" one of the Gobolds screeched. "We are. Look around you. It's just me and my friend here."

"What do you have to offer?" I don't have my goods with me. Nobody can pull carts like that through the moors, if you know what I mean." The Gobold seemed unwilling when another one pompously cackled: "I am prepared to do business with you. But you have to trade with me exclusively!" The first one bickered: "Oh, no! The deal is mine, you prat." "Take that back, you moron!" "Never! Prat! Prat! Prat!" They two Gobolds starting hitting each other with their clawhands. Abbo sighed: "Gobolds..." Another bugle sounded and a garishly bejewelled Gobold, an ostentatious feather in his cap, along with his well-armed entourage quickly restored the peace with his shortsword. He appeared to be the leader, judging by the way the rest of them cringed and cowered in front of him. The chief made them open the gates and signalled Abbo to enter. "Come! Trade!" All eyes were on them. Hinnerk felt extremely tense and winced when somebody coughed. "They are trying to cheat us!" one of them screamed instantly and within seconds the two humans were surrounded by non-humans wielding their weapons at them. Hinnerk and Abbo defended themselves well and injured many a Gobold, who quickly withdrew again.

The chief stepped forward and continued as if the skirmish had been nothing, just one of those usual interruptions. "Me Tipnek. Biggest here. What you want, human? You come our camp with boy and say you have goods. Goods good. We do trade." The Gobold straightened himself a little to look taller. Abbo wasn't impressed. "Sounds alright to me, Tipnek. You seem to have the lads well under control, hey." Tipnek nodded: "Was much worse before. Now very quiet. Your cart? Where is?" Abbo smiled and took a step towards Tipnek. "That's the funny part, you see..." Before the Gobolds could react, he had drawn Pakhaou and pointed it at the chief's chest. "Somebody robbed me." The Gobolds howled: "No trade! Betrayal! Ohhhh! For the love of Wlop-Klop!" "Shut up! It's your own fault if you forget all caution with all that fighting and greed! Besides, it's true. You lot robbed our cart. The boy here was there!" Tipnek bared his crooked teeth, screwed up his nose and commented calmly. "Know nothing about that." Abbo pushed the sword a little harder: "Then I know nothing about a promise to let Tipnek live."

Abbo's determined expression made Tipnek nervous: "Argh! Okay. Wretched, noisy manpup! Today can't trust no one!" Abbo agreed: "Trust has to be earned, so talk: where did you hide what you stole?" Hinnerk exploded: "Where is the girl, you swine?" Tipnek grinned. "Oh, I see. Don't know about girl." Abbo's eyes narrowed to slits: "Don't play games with me, Tipnek. Yours is the only Gobold settlement for miles." "That no proof we guilty. You see kidnapper here?" Hinnerk glared at the sea of sickly green faces around him and didn't recognise any of the earlier attackers. But they might have been hiding in their hovels. "I recognise them all!" he boldly declared and the Gobolds collectively burst into laughter. Tipnek smirked: "Bad liar. You not know. No proof." Abbo got more threatening and every one of the Gobolds listened carefully: "Where is she? I won't ask twice!" Tipnek realised that the game was up. Abbo was prepared to ransack their entire village and even Hinnerk started to be scared by him. Tipnek explained: "She gone." "Gone where?" "Man came. Offered much money if we bring girl with purple hair and gold eyes. Man said to look everywhere. All the land." "Who was that man?" Abbo quizzed him. "Tipnek not know name. Man didn't say. But man smelled of fish. Was fisherman, yeah. My people follow a bit. Man took girl to Esens. Tipnek know no more. Poor Tipnek all empty in head." Abbo lowered the sword. "It will have to do. Esens, hey? That's Attena's town." Tipnek grinned broadly: "You pay now, yes?!" "Your payment is that I didn't kill you!" "That not much." "Do you think so? Don't get greedy. My friend here would dearly love to kill every one of you, wouldn't you, Hinni?" Hinnerk menacingly raised his sword. Tipnek knew when he was beaten: "Tipnek understand. You go now?" Abbo and Hinnerk left through the gates with their swords at the ready and only relaxed once they were well clear of the settlement and had been swallowed by the mists. Abbo now walked in a north-easterly direction towards the Wiards' farm and Esens. Hinnerk rested Lux Maris on his shoulders and asked: "Why didn't we kill them? You can't actually think they've learned their lesson. The only way to stop their dirty work is to destroy them." Abbo took a deep breath. "Many a noble knight in Iberia expressed the same sentiment. And then you are facing a trembling mother with her two children and you have no idea if she is Christian, Saracen or God knows what..." "I get your point, but they are Gobolds! Not humans. Nobody is going to miss them." "You didn't look very closely then. I saw women and children in those huts. Gobolds may be a nuisance, but they also want to live. I don't want to destroy them. I've seen enough killing in my day. We and our enemies alike were followed by grief and blind hatred. There were no more differences, regardless if people followed the cross or the crescent moon. It was all just an excuse for perpetrating atrocities." Hinnerk let the matter rest. More than once before Abbo had indicated that the crusades against the Iberian Berbers hadn't been as glorious and heroic as a lot of the crippled veterans proclaimed in the taverns. Abbo cheered up again: "We did well to use their internal bickering to our advantage. Tipnek will have his hands full now that his ability to lead the tribe is in doubt. That will occupy the Gobolds for quite some time and they'll leave us alone for a while." "Did you learn that during the crusades as well, uncle Abbo? How to set people against each other?" Abbo nodded. There was always some infighting on both the Muslim and the Christian sides and the other side would use it to their advantage. Remember the old saying: the tighter you hold the reins, the more the horse wants to break free. The Gobolds aren't all that different to us." Hinnerk shrugged: "I still wouldn't miss them." Abbo flashed him a tired smile while the moved through the Ghastly Moors, always watching their backs while also being careful not to step into a Moorfang.

First the two of them went back to the forest where Okko and Klütje were waiting for them, both of them covered in dirt and looking exhausted. Abbo and Hinnerk rushed over and handed them the waterbag. "What happened, Okko?" Okko cursed: "Chased after Hinni. Lost his trail. Then I found bog mummies, four of them. I guess the Gobolds must have roused them." Abbo sympathetically cleaned Okko's wounds. "Shit!" "Only too right! I couldn't kill them, but I couldn't go any further either. Their aura took all my strength away." Okko looked at Hinnerk, who was gazing at his father through terribly worried eyes, and grinned: "Well, what do you know. There he is." "Pa, I didn't mean to..." "I know. How can I give out to you for wanting to save a girl? It just didn't work out. But your mother will throw a fit." Hinnerk gave his dad a huge hug and Abbo smiled. "Don't worry, Hinni. Your old man is tough. He was tough in Stedingen and got even more resilient over the years, isn't that right, Okko?" "Stop it, Abbo. We're no longer as young as we used to be. In those days we were the masters of the moors and not those bastards. But what about Leevke?" Hinnerk wiped the tears from his eyes. "We were too late. She was already gone. We think a fisherman from Esens had her kidnapped." Okko raised his eyebrows: "Had her kidnapped? That sounds pretty weird. Who would have that kind of interest in her? Who knows about her?" Hinnerk thought, then said: "Driftwood Theo! But he's dead." Okko considered: "Theo is known far and wide in these parts. He's wanted everywhere. There's a reward of 210 guilders for his capture. If he had survived they would have found him and tied him to a pole until he'd drown in high tide. So even if he should still be alive, he wouldn't want to run the risk of being discovered." Abbo and Hinnerk helped Okko onto the cart and climbed on themselves. Hinnerk stroked Klütje and cursed: "Damn it! It's already starting!" "What do you mean?" Abbo asked. "That people are hunting Leevke because of her powers." Abbo said: "Our fisherman friend can't have too much of a headstart on us. Let's take Okko back to the farm and then have a look around Esens. But it's already getting dark and..." Okko stopped him: "I know what you were going to say, but I believe in you Abbo. I trust that you bring the boy back unharmed." Abbo smiled and tousled Hinnerk's hair. "I watched this rascal grow up. Don't think for a minute I would let anyone hurt him. Neither on the moors nor anywhere else." Hinnerk sighed and then a big grin spread over his face. He would never have admitted it, but he was jolly glad that he wasn't alone.

They said goodbye to Okko at the turnoff to the Wiards' farm. "You two are lucky. You don't have to listen to Hilde's nagging," Okko grumbled and Abbo replied: "There's many a man who'd envy you. Good luck." "To you, too. I pray you'll find Leevke. Be careful, these are dark times." Hinnerk, Klütje and Abbo continued their journey until their cart reached Esens towards the evening. The small town in the Harlingerland on the North Sea coast of East Frisia was known for its adherence to the ancient Frisian traditions and its proximity to the Chauci tribes in the Wangerland to the east which had control of the islands Wangeroog and Spiekeroog. Esens was governed by the Frisian brigand Behrend Attena. His brutish figure and violent rages were attributed to his Norman blood. Esens was a place where people preferred a good fist fight to a debate. Hinnerk and Abbo enquired if people had seen anyone suspicious lately, but nobody had and their hopes of quickly finding the culprit vanished just as quickly. They entered a seedy alehouse and ordered Pilsener beer from Jever, the seat of the Häuptlinger Edo Wiemken. "We won't learn any more tonight, so let's take a room and continue tomorrow," Abbo said. "Perhaps the innkeeper or the guests know something." In the taproom some of the local farmers, artisans and other townspeople were drinking their beer, throwing dice and playing cards. Not a few of them eyed them sceptically. "Good idea to stay the night," the innkeeper remarked when he served them their food. "Why? What's going on?" Abbo probed. The publican sighed and sounded as if he had a lot to moan about in his life. "The Fenna are on the prowl again." "Here in Esens?" Hinnerk asked as the innkeeper joined them at their table. "You better believe it. Only last week they took old farmer Wiedekamp. He must have forgotten how late it was when he was picking blackberries. They crawled out of their holes and that was the last anyone saw of him." Abbo nodded: "I've had the dubious pleasure myself. Apparently my greeting wasn't convincing enough for them..." The innkeeper was impressed: "You survived the Fenna? I take my hat off to you!" "It was a close shave. Wouldn't like to repeat the experience." Could you get rid of them? It pays 200 pieces of silver. Perhaps you could smoke their nest out." Abbo waved him off: "I'm sorry, but I have other fish to fry. Why don't you assemble a troop and set fire to their caves when its daylight? There must be enough brave lads in Esens." The innkeeper looked sheepish: "They're all Attena's men and they'll want more silver than we can offer." Hinnerk piped up:"I may help you, but first we have to find our friend. Somebody kidnapped her! A fisherman who came here to Esens." The innkeeper considered: "There are fishermen down in Bensersiel." "Shit! What if he's already left on a boat?" Hinnerk cursed. Abbo brooded: "That's unlikely. He couldn't have got back until low tide and no ship will sail at night unless he tried to force the crew. And that wouldn't have gone unnoticed." Somebody who had overheard their discussion sat down beside them and said: "All they have at Bensersiel are rowing boats and two small sailing ships, not strong enough to go far. And there's a strong north-westerly breeze. No, the man you're chasing is still there. If he went to Bensersiel, that is." Abbo proffered his hand. "Thank you. I'm Abbo, by the way, and this is my friend Hinni Wiards." "Oh! Abbo the Rebel, I take it? My name is Petzl. I'm originally from

Greetsiel, but I often go to Benersiel to buy in more goods. Can I interest you in a barrel of herrings? Top quality!" Abbo grinned: "Not right now." "I understand," Petzl said. "I shall gladly take you to Bensersiel, if you like. I know just about everyone in that place and perhaps we can find out more together." Hinnerk laughed: "That would be great! Wait a minute... is this a trap?!" Petzel laughed. "The boy's smart, ha, ha! A wise move in a town governed by the Bear. And he's right, I'm not all that altruistic. I'm counting on you folk advertising Petzl and his delicious fish. I can cook you an eel right here and now, so you won't have to tell lies. What do you say?" Abbo and Hinnerk agreed and the innkeeper let the fisherman fry three eels. Everyone in the tavern had their share and the atmosphere improved dramatically. Eventually Hinnerk and Abbo decided to go with Pretzl the next day and stayed the night at the inn. But Hinnerk couldn't sleep. He missed Leevke snoring beside him and no fish, no matter how delicious, would ever be able to replace that.

Early the following morning the three of them were on their way and soon reached the fishing village Benersiel consisting of a dozen or so fishermen's huts built on top of a mound. A few boats were moored at the wooden pier. Everywhere the fishermen's wives were busy mending nets and the smell of fish was overpowering. A group of men around a fire were cooking some plaice with wild garlic and turnips. "Morning, lads!" Petzl greeted them. They sat down beside the men and quizzed them about anyone suspicious they may have seen. "The only one suspicious around here is Malle Pugnose," an elderly fisherman told them glumly while turning over the sizzling fish in the pan. "Kept everyone away from his cottage and then ran to Esens with a hood over his head. Came back sometime in the middle of the night. There's been no sign of his missus or his brood since. And we can't get a word out of him. He's gone mad if you ask me." Petzl probed: "Where is he now?" The man pointed to a hut close to the dyke where a flock of sheep was grazing at the slope. Hinnerk, Abbo and Petzl walked over and Petzl knocked at the heavy oak door: "Morning! Malle Pugnose? It's me, Petzl. I'd like to have a word. Do you have a moment?" An oppressive silence was the only reply. Abbo providently whipped out his sword, ready to kick in the door. Hinnerk took up position beside him. Eventually Malle Pugnose cautiously peeped through the entrance. He was in his mid-thirties, with a big crooked nose in his pale, unshaven face. "What do you want, Petzl?! Hey, I don't know those two. Get lost!" He tried to close the door again, but Abbo was too quick for the man and pushed him back into the room. Malle brandished his own sword. A woman was cowering in the corner with three screaming children. Malle started to attack, but Abbo easily disarmed him, dragged him outside and flung him to the ground. Petzl yelled: "Shit, Abbo! What do you think you are doing?!" He had pulled out his knife, prepared to defend Pugnose whom he had known far longer than the two strangers. Abbo put his sword back in its scabbard and motioned Hinnerk to do the same: "Something's wrong here." "You can say that again!" Petzl grumbled. Hinnerk roared at Malle: "Where is Leevke?! Where is she?!" Malle binked his eyes and crawled back: "I... I don't know what you're talking about. Who are you?! What do you want from me?" To Hinnerk's chagrin Abbo handed Malle back his weapon. "Forgive us for attacking you like this, Mr Pugnose. It wasn't right." Hinnerk glared at him; "To hell it was right. He abducted Leevke!" The woman came out of the house with her children in tow. "Please don't hurt him! We'll do anything you say." Abbo took a deep breath. "Nobody is going to hurt anyone. My name is Abbo and this is Hinnerk Wiards. You know Petzl." He offered Pugnose his hand and helped him back on his feet. "We are looking for a friend of ours and thought you might be able to help us." Pugnose stared at him through wide open eyes: "So you are... Oh, no! I had no choice. He forced me! He took everything we owned. I had to use all our savings." "Calm down, please." Malle was shaking like a leaf. He was deeply distressed. Abbo was only too familiar with the fisherman's reaction. It was the shock of a man who had hitherto led an honest existence and had suddenly been faced with a violent and stressful situation he couldn't cope with.

Petzl said: "Stop worrying, Malle. Nobody's going to harm you. You're fine." "I'm not fine. I'm a criminal. I don't know how I..." Abbo understood: "You had no choice. They threatened your family, right?" "Y... yes!" "They made you find and catch a girl with purple hair and golden eyes." The fisherman looked at Abbo as if he'd seen a ghost:" How do you know?" "It wouldn't be the first time somebody used blackmail to get someone else to do their dirty work. Who was it?" Pugnose fell silent and Abbo leaned forward: "Did he forbid you to talk about it? Because then he would come back and kill all of you?" Malle nodded silently and Hinnerk said: "Whoever it was, he will not harm you any more. I give you my promise." Abbo agreed: "You will never find peace if you don't talk about it, Malle. The sooner, the better or everything will suffer, not just your nerves." Abbo gestured to the family that they could join the father. The children immediately clung to him and sobbed heart-rendingly. Petzl shook his head: "None of it makes sense. What good is it to use somebody who's totally unfit for crime?" Abbo thought differently: "On the other hand, who would suspect Pugnose to do something wrong? A loving father who is friends with everyone. He can come and go as he pleases and nobody would notice until it is too late. You went straight to the Gobolds, didn't you, Malle?" "I did. They were the only ones I could approach without leaving any traces. Nobody would believe a Gobold." Abbo smiled. "That was smart. What else do you know?" "Well, the girl was not to be hurt, that was of utmost importance. The man waited here with my family as hostages. Until I brought the girl back. That was last night. Then he went away with the girl. I don't know where to. I was terribly scared and stayed in the cottage, trying to get back to normal. The place feels strange since he was here." Hinnerk asked: "What did he look like?" and Malle's wife told him: "He had two scars on the right half of his face. He was wearing three leather collars, shoulder armour and a leather and steel helmet. He was threatening us with an axe. His clothes looked quite wet, as if he'd just been in the water. He didn't eat anything the whole time, but his stomach didn't even growl. At times he seemed like... like a corpse." Hinnerk exclaimed: "Theo! He survived after all!" Abbo looked bleak: "We can't be sure yet. Perhaps it was a Draugr?" Petzl disagreed: "Draugr don't talk and they're incapable of complex plans. Perhaps he did survive." "It's not impossible. Could he have escaped by boat?" Petzl suggested: "Let's ask the fishermen. Come with us, Malle. Perhaps your own boat is gone!" Pugnose forced himself to calm down: "Okay, you are right. I have to make things right again." Abbo put his hand on Malle's shoulder: "You are a brave man." "Far from it, Mr Abbo. I'm not brave at all." He turned to his wife: "Let the children play outside, Miemke. We can't let fear dictate our lives and stay cooped up inside forever." The woman tried to smile behind her tears: "You're right. Petzl?" "Don't worry, Miemke. I'll bring him back in one piece, the old charmer, hey?" Malle even smiled a little and together they went back to the village. The fishermen had finished their meal by now and were preparing to go back to sea. Abbo asked them if any of their boats had been stolen lately. Malle's own boat was still moored in its usual place. One of the fishermen replied: "Erwin's boat was missing a while ago. But it had just drifted away and he found it again in a bay not far from here. But apart from that... not that I know of." "Shit!" was Hinnerk's frustrated comment. Petzl said: "He may have stolen one somewhere else. Doesn't have to be from here." "Great. That means we'd have to search the whole coast. Theo'll be well gone by then." Pugnose volunteered: "The islands! He could have taken a boat from one of the islands." Hinnerk thought about it: "He could have been stranded on one of them. It's possible. But which one? He was washed away to the north of Dornum's coast." Petzl explained: "The current should have taken him towards Langeoog!" Abbo rubbed his chin: "Or beyond it perhaps? Past Langeoog and Spiekeroog?" "It's possible, but what exactly do you mean, Mr Abbo?" Malle wanted to know. "Oh, nothing. T'was just a thought." Hinnerk straightened himself: "Right! How do we get there?" Petzl pointed to his small vessel: "It's full of fish, but I can make room for two." "Am I not going?" Malle enquired timidly and Hinnerk waved him off: "No, you stay with your family and friends in case Theo should come back after all. You are stronger as a group. Use your nets and hooks if needs be." Malle heaved a sigh of relief: "I hope you'll find the girl. It would make me feel infinitely better." They said their farewells and Petzl took them to Langeoog. Abbo showed Hinnerk how to sail. The boy was quick to learn and managed the last third of the journey on his own. The salty north-westerly breeze temporarily dispersed the smells of Petzl's fish barrels.

Chapter 4

The Stranded Merchant

They reached the harbour of Langeoog and secured their vessel. Petzl saw them off with the words: "I'm sorry, but I still have work to do. All this fish still needs pickling. I hope you understand." Abbo smiled: "Of course. Our thanks for your help. I shall tell people nothing but good about you." Hinnerk added: "And so shall I!" Petzl laughed: "That's wonderful. Good luck! I shall be in Greetsiel, if you are looking for me. The best fish in all of Frisia from all of Frisia!" The fisherman put out to sea again and Hinnerk, Abbo and Klütje walked along the beach and onto the islands green interior where the islanders had settled. At a tavern they asked the landlord if anyone was missing a boat. "None of us do, but you should ask that fellow back there. He's been sitting there for two days looking miserable." The man in question, the only other guest, was sitting at a table, his head propped up on his hand, and gloomily stared through the window.

Spread in front of him were various writing implements and documents with lists and hastily scrawled and crossed out numbers. His garments were of rich quality, similar to those of Master Wigbold. On his head perched a black beret with a coin embroidered into it. He wore a dark silk coat with slitted sleeves and a grey-white shirt beneath it. His legs were encased in wide breeches with numerous pockets and his feet rested in brown bucket top boots. Blue-green eyes under light blond hair flashed in a thin face dominated by a long nose. The three-day stubble seemed somewhat contrived. His lean, gangly body was tall, going on six foot two. All in all he looked like a typical merchant. "Good morning to you," Abbo greeted him. "Do you have any objection to two travellers sharing your table?" The man briefly glanced at them, rolled his eyes and then gestured them to sit down. When nobody said anything he asked: "Well?"

Abbo delicately cleared his throat: "Forgive me. How rude of me. My name is Abbo and this is my friend Hinnerk Wiards. We have some questions we would like to ask you." "Jens Janssen. Widely known and widely esteemed. Tradesman from Eilsum or Greetsiel, take your pick." His eyes sparkled: "May you be interested in eight fardels of beans?!" "Beans?" "Yes, sure!" Jens Janssen jumped up and gesticulated wildly: "A wonderful vegetable. Especially with bits of bacon! Yum! A delicacy of the pure finest. Keeps you young and sprightly. Makes granddad run to the whores and then bed grandma! They can be eaten any time, are easy to store and the rats leave them alone because they are poisonous when they aren't cooked! Or did you every see rats cooking? Well I haven't. Ha, ha! They're marvellous. Simply marvellous. Well, what do you say? I could do you a sample." "Um..." was Abbo's reaction and the man became visibly sceptical. "Wait a minute. What do you actually want from me? I... I always pay my taxes, I think..." Only now did he notice that Hinnerk and Abbo were armed. "Damn it! You're not from Hamburg, are you? Did I forget something?" Abbo reassuringly lifted his hands: "Not that I know of. We're neither from Hamburg nor do we mean you any harm." Jens reluctantly sat down. "And neither do you intend to buy anything, I take it." Abbo smiled: "Not right now, thank you. We're looking for a girl who's been kidnapped." "I see." "Yes, we have reason to believe that she was abducted in a boat that was taken from here." "I see, interesting... I assume you two are from the dyke watch?" Abbo shook his head again: "No, we're just two people looking for our friend." "Right," said Jens and the distrust in his eyes became so apparent that it looked comical to Hinnerk. He found in somewhat difficult to take the man seriously. The merchant adjusted his clothes, pulled at his sleeves and cleared his throat: "I havn't seen your girl. I was too busy getting pissed and praying that the sea would take me because I can't make up for the losses I incurred." Hinnerk asked: "Why? Did you miscalculate?"Jens' grin was grim: "No, my impudent friend. My vessel was taken. Stolen. A proud little boat by the name of Lobscouse. All I'm left with is a lot of beans that nobody wants on this island..." The innkeeeper interjected: "I've already bought half your load!" "Well, apart from that." Abbo leaned forward and ordered a round of beer which Janssen gratefully accepted. He continued: "I was in the middle of mooring the boat when this weird guy climbed out of the water. I thought I was seeing things. He threatened me with this axe and said he was taking my ship but I could keep the beans and threw them overboard. There's apparently no end to people's audacity these days. Everybody's on edge. It doesn't bode well... And now I'm stranded here on this island with a load of beans nobody wants and without a ship. And me being a tradesman. Are you sure you don't want any beans? Beans are very nutritious and they keep. If you store them properly, that is. I've got a little family recipe I'm willing to throw it in for free depending on the quantity you buy!" Jens extended his hand to them in turn, but Abbo declined. "We didn't come here to buy beans!" "Okay, okay. No need to get all worked up. Somebody else who's on edge," Jens huffed.

Abbo closed his eyes and massaged his nose: "Don't get me wrong, Mr Janssen, but I have a problem when people are trying to fob stuff off on me. It's a long story. But one no should be enough, wouldn't you agree?" Jens tried to redeem himself: "Of course. You are absolutely right. I apologise." Abbo asked: "Did the man who stole your boat happen to have two scars on his right cheek? Did he have a scruffy beard and act like a beachcomber?" Jens crossed his arms over his chest and thought intensely: "Well, I don't know if he acted like a beachcomber. I usually stay clear of riffraff like that, but he certainly behaved like a robber, if that's any help to you. Apart from that, your description fits the man. Is he an acquaintance of yours?" "You could call it that. Does the name Driftwood Theo ring a bell?" The merchant moaned: "Ah, that's who it was. Now that you say it..." Hinnerk probed: "Do you know where he came from or where he went?" "As I said, he came out of the water like a Draugr and he stirred my boat towards the mainland." "So he just climbed out of the water?" Abbo felt the merchant was trying to deceive him, but Jens said: "Yes, damn it! The man must have been protected by some spell that stopped him from drowning. What do I know? I'm just the guy who sells the BEANS around here." "Take it easy," Abbo calmed him down and Hinnerk had to stop himself from laughing. Jens continued unperturbed in a businesslike manner: "Right, you want your girl back and I want my ship back. Perhaps we could come to an arrangement. What do you think? You look like two strong fellows to me and you could benefit from my talents as a linguistically gifted trader and man of the world. Everything in life is governed by commerce and bargaining, be it beans, ships, armour, houses, land or even emotions like love, don't you agree, boy?" Hinnerk sniffled, tears in his eyes: "What? Sure..." "So, you see, everything boils down to business!" Abbo warned: "It could be dangerous." Jens demonstratively put his stylish merchant's dagger down on the table. "I can take care of myself." "But how can Theo walk under water?" Hinnerk wanted to know. Abbo's face clouded over: "I'm afraid that only strengthens my suspicions. There's a small island between Langeoog and Spiekeroog. An island nobody likes to talk about. And for good reason."

The first thing Leevke noticed when she came to were the drops of water splashing into her face. She jerked and jumped up. It was dark and damp and something was rustling in the corners. She was in a dungeon and only some weak, bluish light penetrated through the small cracks in the door. Her golden eyes were slow to adjust to the darkness. All she discerned were rough outlines and twitching shapes. But there wasn't much more to see anyway. She was sitting on a rotten plank anchored to the stone wall with two chains. When she explored what felt like straw on the ground, some many-legged creature frantically crawled over her hand. She yelled out, pulled up her legs and cowered on the make-shift bed. Quietly she asked: "H... Hello? Is there anyone here?" Nobody answered and she was actually glad. She took a deep breath. The air was foul.

She remembered the Gobolds overpowering her. By the looks of it she had been kidnapped, but she seemed okay and wasn't hurting anywhere and she hoped that Hinnerk, Okko, Klütje and the horse were also unharmed. Leevke shivered and tears welled up in her eyes when she considered all sorts of terrible possibilities her vivid imagination so willingly supplied. Eventually she took heart and decided to find out what had happened. She walked to the door on her bare feet and hit it with her fists. The hinges squeaked wretchedly when Leevke shouted: "Hey!? Anyone there? Let me out, please!" No reply. The door had a little hatch, but it could only be opened from the outside. Leevke could sense the proximity of the sea. Centipedes scurried over her feet and something bit her heel. She screamed and repeatedly threw herself against the door in growing desperation. The rusty hinges groaned with a ghastly echo. Several unsuccessful attempts later she gave up and leaned against the door. Which promptly opened.

With a loud bang Leevke and the door crushed onto a long corridor illuminated in blue. The girl quickly got up and noticed a blue torch affixed to the wall. The stone walls glistened with damp and were crawling with insects. The corridor extended into an obscure, dim distance in both directions. Above the howling wind she heard scraping noises approaching her from the right, amplified and distorted by the stone. She concentrated hard and saw two glowing red eyes in the darkness. Her own eyes widened in panic when she recognised the contours of a white, very thin man. Nothing but scraps of former clothes and putrid, leathery flesh hung from his skeletal body. The creature stopped just a few feet away from her and stared at her through red dots peeking through black sockets as if he perceived her only now. Leevke stopped breathing. The skeleton slowly raised his right arm, pointed trembling, bony fingers at Leevke and emitted a blood-curdling scream. The scream resounded from the walls and

Leevke winced. Now completely overcome by panic, she stumbled away from the screeching undead, tripped and fell down. She briefly glanced back and saw the shrieking skeleton coming closer, grotesquely limping and scuffling. Blinded with fear she bumped against a spiral staircase. The weak light from above made it possible for her to see the steps. She ran up until she reached another rotten door while the undead was still trailing her. She threw herself against the timber and her heart missed a beat when the door opened without resistance and she found herself in a large entrance hall. She hastily closed the door and jammed it with a chair. The screeching stopped instantly and Leekve got a chance to take a deep breath and calm her pounding heart. Two blue torches lit up the decayed room. To her terror three more skeletons in ragged chainmail now got up and also pointed their fingers at her. Leevke threw up her hands in despair and whimpered: "Oh, no! No more screeching!" A female voice whispered: "Get's on one's nerves, doesn't it? Don't fear, little mackerel. I'll turn them off. They won't hurt you." Leevke cautiously opened her eyes: "He... Hello?" The woman's voice came from behind the three skeletons which now lowered their arms and fell onto their knees. "I'm sorry they scared you. These undead are our ever faithful servants. They won't harm you. They are a little ancient, hehehe." "Where are you?" "I'm up here." One of the skeletons indicated that he was going to lead Leevke. "Follow him. He'll take you to me." Leevke pursed her lips. She didn't trust any of it. "Why am I here? Where are my friends?" "We can find that out together. But I can't help you if you don't let me." Leevke peered at the heavy double doors. The disembodied woman noticed. "I won't lie to you. You're our prisoner for the time being. But I'm not half as bad as you may think." The skeleton put his hands on his hips and pranced over to her. It looked ridiculous enough to make Leevke laugh. "What's your name?" "Call me Ursula. And you?" "Leevke... Pultjen." "Ah! Interesting. Come on. You'll see it's not so bad!" Leevke took a deep breath before she followed the skeleton up the stairs.

At the top of the tower she got a shock when she spotted the decrepit Radbod sitting on his throne, fixing his dull eyes at her. She wailed when she recognised an old acquantance kneeling beside him: "Theo?!" The pirate grinned: "There she is! She woke up. Don't worry, little one, I'm done with you. But let me introduce you to the king of all the Frisians, Radbod the Indomitable." He leaned over to Radbod? "Now, about my heart..." The king brusquely waved him off: "You shall be released once I have received what you so grandiosely promised. Not a second sooner!" Theo tried to force a smile: "Certainly, your Majesty. As you wish and command." Leevke swallowed: "Whe... where is Ursula?" The skeleton who had escorted her remained resolutely silent.

Radbod got up and approached her: "No need to be afraid, girl. I shall take you to her presently. I just need you to answer one question before we go. Can you do that?" Leevke shrugged her shoulders. "I doubt I have a choice." Radbod grinned: "Everybody has a choice. Any time." The king now eyed her from top to bottom. Embarrassed and defiant Leevke turned her head away. Radbod chuckled: "I don't desire you, girl. I am interested in your abilities. Tell me, can you command the sea? Yes or no?" Leevke glanced at Theo: "Does his life depend on it?" Before Theo could react, Radbod stated curtly: "It does." Leevke nodded and said quietly: "I don't know. It's really just small things I can influence. Sometimes something big happens, but it just erupts from inside me. Afterwards I can't remember anything." Radbod angrily spun around: "What is the meaning of this, Theo? What's she talking about? Didn't you say she can control the sea?!" The king of the Frisians placed his finger on Theo's chest and the soulkraken inside it clenched up, making the pirate cringe with pain. He immediately sank onto his knees and gasped: "Damn it! She did and she can! I'm not lying, Sire. How she does it, I don't know... Please! My heart! I'm dying!" Leevke was shocked. It was one thing getting Theo back for what he had done to her, but watching a person suffer so much that he turned red and contorted with agony was a different matter entirely. Radbod thundered: "Where did you get your knowledge?! Who told you?" Theo panted: "I was in Bergen to get rid of some stolen goods. It was there I overheard a conversation between a tradesman and some creature in a robe..." "What kind of creature?" "No idea. I couldn't see its face, but it had fingers like string and offered a lot of gold and gems for the capture of the girl with the powers. I'd heard rumours about her before back in Frisia. So I grabbed the opportunity before someone else could get there before me..." Radbod released Theo from his stranglehold and the pirate coughed. "A remarkable story. Does it mean anything to you, girl?" Leevke shook her head and Radbod bared his teeth. "I don't care who was looking for her. What is important is that somebody did. That means she is of special value." Theo cleared his throat: "Perhaps she is as yet inexperienced with regards to her powers, your Majesty. She may not be fully aware of her true potential." "Are you trying to tell me that she needs training?" Theo shrugged his shoulders: "She is still but a child, my king." Radbod growled, cursed in Old Frisian and gazed across the tower into the mists. "Alright. Follow me, girl."

Leevke was shaking, and not just because of the cold wind. "Wait! What happened to Hinni and Okko?" she asked Theo. "Who? The little shithead on the beach?" "Leevke nodded and Theo just said: "I've no idea." Leevke looked crestfallen and followed Radbod, who led her to the heavy, stone door with the occult pagan symbols. They stepped into a large semicircular room with a stone altar in the middle, carved with regular pagan runes. The walls were lined with shelves holding books, chemicals, bottles and tools that resembled torture instruments. There was also a hearth, chairs and table and a soft double bed with a woman who stretched her limbs and sat up with a yawn: "Ah, finally! Hello, little one. I am Ursula." The tall, athletic woman with the generous bosom was wearing a dress which pointedly emphasised her curves. Her arms and legs were covered with suction pads and her long, very thin light brown hair glistened with fish oil. Unlike the undead surrounding her, she seemed relatively normal although her pupils were horizontal like those of an octopus. She got up, walked over to a small basin, took out a kraken and placed it on her head. Its tentacles framed her face like hair as she smiled at Leevke: "The latest in Njord's fashion. Helps me to stay close to my little creatures. She went to the altar, extracted a scythe-like wand and danced over to Leevke. "You are a cute little thing. Come here."

Radbod screwed up his nose: "She's not here for your entertainment, Ursula." The woman moaned: "Of course not. Can't remember the last time we had some fun. You're such an old grouch!" "Save your comments, kraken witch. We've wasted enough time. No more jokes. This girl has the potential to control the oceans. I hardly have to tell you what that could mean for us." Ursula rolled her eyes. "Yes, yes, I understand. That's all you've been talking about." Radbod straightened himself up and wheezed: "Don't go too far, missy. Düll already thinks that I'm leaving you too much freedom." "Freedom? Rotting away with you on this island you call freedom? Interesting." "Enough! We've had this discussion too many times. Just do your work." Ursula huffed: "Yes, your Majesty. I shall transform this girl for you. A dream comes true!" The king of the Frisians stormed out of the room and Ursula let the stone door bang shut behind him. Inside she was seething with resentment and Leevke didn't dare move. She even held her breath until her gills started to flare. Ursula noticed her turning purple and reassured her: "We always go on like that, little one. Hey!" She snapped her fingers: "Don't forget to breathe!" Leevke gasped for air with tears in her eyes. Ursula walked over to her, smiled, lifted her up and sat her down on the altar. She was remarkably strong for a woman, her muscles bulging beneath her skin. She pushed some stray hairs from Leevke's face: "Nice hair colour. Unusual." "Your hair is special, too," Leevke observed. Ursula touched the kraken. "The little fellow helps me to concentrate. Besides, around here one's grateful for any kind of company. "She pointed at the door. "In the old days Raddi was a different man. But he's always been a leader and a born king. It's in his blood. He doesn't mean to be rude, but he used to be much nicer and more attentive. Not as grumpy as he is now." The kraken witch sighed: "Sometimes I just don't know anymore... I miss the old days, you know. It hurts to see him like that: obstinate and lonely. And yet, I'm still always there for him." Leevke smiled: "You lo... love him, don't you?" Ursula broke out in a grin: "Every woman loves somebody. I'm sure you do as well, don't you?" Leevke was a lousy liar: "N... no." "Not even the boy you enquired after? Well? I heard you. I hear everything. Except what the Tentacleman blubbers about in his cave down there..." "Tentacleman?" Captain Düll. A close friend of the king's from the past. Unlike the rest of his stalwarts he hasn't yet decayed. Njord's pagan magic keeps him alive. Here, underneath Bant, there is a cave, the source of his power. It provides a link to the otherworld, the realm of gods and ghosts." Ursula leaned back: "But that's it as far as celebrities are concerned hereabouts. My friends are my kraken. The one on my head, the one in Theo's chest and the big one keeping watch beneath Bant." Suddenly Leevke sobbed: "I want to go home." Ursula handed her a cup of green tea and spoke to her soothingly: "So do I, little one, I also want to go home. We all do. And the sooner you help me, the sooner that will happen. Don't cry. Nobody wants to hurt you. We are all desperate here... You are somebody really special, I heard?" Leevke defiantly stuck out her chin: "I don't want to be special." Ursula briefly paused, then smiled: "Oh dear, we have a lot more in common than you think. You are afraid of your powers and they get you into trouble, true?" Leevke nodded slowly. "Let's make a deal," Ursula suggested. "You help me get away from this island and I help you get back home and teach you how to manage your powers. They don't call me a witch for nothing." "Aren't witches bad?" Ursula shrugged her shoulders: "There we go again. Good old Christian propaganda. It still hasn't changed after all those years." She started pacing up and down. "There was a time when witches were esteemed and respected, Leevke. They were the wise women of the Frisians and of other tribes, too. Wise women! Nowadays there are only the Harugari of the Chauci or the Deel-Deerns with their severely limted knowledge about herbs. But back then, when the old gods were still venerated, witches still had real power! Bestowed by the gods and channelled by themselves. They used them to protect their loved-ones and take care of day-to-day problems. If that's evil, then I must be as well." Leevke smiled and took a sip of green tea. He golden eyes beamed with delight: "Is that seaweed?" "It's about all we have here." "It's delicious!" "Ha, ha! You are the first one on Bant to have ever said that. You're so cute!" Leevke had started to calm down. Ursula's room was spacious, open and the windows, small as they were, let in more light than elsewhere in the fortress. For the moment she felt safe and decided to give Ursula a chance. Perhaps everything wasn't actually as bad as it had seemed: "Okay, I'll take a chance." "Thank you," said Ursula and clapped.

Pure disbelief was written all over Jens Janssen's face, but Abbo didn't budge: "Yes, I believe we should pay Bant a visit, Mr Janssen." Jens looked grim: "And I believe we should do no such thing. Bant is cursed. Just mentioning it could make you slip and break your neck! Or your backside!" Abbo and Hinnerk stared at him: "We thought you wanted your ship back?" "Not that badly." The merchant drummed his fingers on the table, stopped and sighed: "Well, actually I do. My whole life depends on that ship. Do you understand?" Abbo nodded: "I guess I do. Like the craftsman depends on his tools. Don't worry. I can defend the both of us, if needs be. You have my word." "Glad to hear it. I'm not particularly battle-proof, if you know what I mean. It's actually been a while since I've used my dagger." Abbo grinned: "Everybody has their talents. I, for one, am a miserable salesman. Just thinking about lying turns my stomach." Jens chuckled: "Lying is such a harsh word. I prefer to call it perspective displacement." "Ha, ha! Abbo laughed. "I'd have never thought of that, you see. Pers... what?" Jens was flattered: "Stop it. It's all just words whereas your cause is far more honourable." Hinnerk agreed: "Exactly! Don't compare a ship to a girl!" "Never, my excitable young friend," Jens winked at him. "But I'm not just good at waffling, I also know how to organise a thing or two. Do you have any idea how we shall get to Bant?" "Seeing that we can't walk on water, we'll have to get a boat," Abbo briefly summarised their options. Jens raised his hands and dropped them again: "Right, let's be off on our suicide mission!"

Together they started searching for a fisherman who'd ferry them over. North of Langeoog's main gates they found a group of them, some of them still bobbing up and down on their boats along the coast, hunting the salty deep-sea fish Petzl sold with harpoons, rods and nets. Jens Janssen approached them openly and kindly, but no sooner did he mention Bant, the men thought them full-blown weirdoes who were wasting their time. One of the fishermen was even convinced that Bant didn't exist at all and had only been the fantasy of a drunken monk's overactive imagination. But a younger, more broad-minded man referred them to a veteran fisherman who might be able to help: "That's some undertaking you're planning. Nobody here wants to know about Bant. But old Melf Kapsoch might be able to help you. They say he wasn't even christened... But he's quite alright, is old Melf. Showed me a trick or two. Try him. Tell him Lüdde Tiel sends you." They thanked him and found Melf Kapsoch further east, apart from the others.

The rather small, bearded fisherman was standing by the water casting his fishing rod. Jens greeted him and explained their dilemma. Melf sniggered knowingly: "Nobody goes to Bant, because nobody ever returns..." Jens asked: "Because of the current?" "No, because of the curse. You youngsters don't know anything anymore. St. Liudger cursed Bant in the old days. The whole island and everyone who was there with Radbod. All the pagans had to stay or convert. So they stayed. And they're still there." Jens grinned: "As Christians we won't have to worry that we'll be stuck there so, or?" Kapsoch waded out of the water and reeled in his rod. He scrutinised the strangers intently: "Follow me." The old fisherman led them across the dunes and the grass-covered dyke while he told them: "Radbod hated the Church with a passion. For him it was a symbol of oppression and to this day he's sore that his tribal kinsmen and women let themselves be fooled." Abbo frowned: "You sound as if you agree with him." Kapsoch brought them to a small hut where the fishermen stored their gear during a storm. This was also where they laid out their nets to dry. "I see it the way it is. I've lived long enough to recognise the recurring patterns a mile away. The Church is only interested in power and does everything to secure it. She owns land, people, gold and influence. It's a business. Radbod has always known that. He heard the Church preach about love, but knew what she really said: bow down to us! Give us your land, your sons and daughters to do our bidding. We will brainwash them so they shall turn against you and your ancestors. That is the hidden message of all those wanting to attain power. Sometimes they do it with honey, other times they try to fool the people with reason. It's always the same old bullshit. And has been for generations. Right. Enough of all that. Here we are." They were looking at an old boat. Kapsoch commented: "She's small and poxy, but she still does her job, even if it's been half a year since I took her out." Klütje barked and jumped right in to claim the vessel for himself. Hinnerk, Abbo and Jens's enthusiasm was limited. The boat was worm-eaten and close to falling apart. A simple rowing boat, without mast, and shells clinging to its bottom. Melf said: "I'll make you a present of it." "V... very generous," Jens stuttered, but Hinnerk couldn't help himself: "It's a pile of crap!" Melf laughed out loud: "You're right there, boy. I nearly thought I had you fooled, but before I turn her into firewood..." Abbo was more practical. "We'll take her. We shall need pitch, nails and a few planks. I'll give you some money to buy the necessary, Mr Janssen. In the meantime Hinnerk and I will inspect it more closely." Jens took himself off to the village and Hinnerk asked: "Was that a good idea? He could do a runner with your money." Abbo replied: "Don't always be so sceptical, Hinni. Trust often pays off. Besides, he seemed like an honest soul to me. But perhaps you're right to be cautious." Only a little later Jens returned with a wheelbarrow load of materials and some food. It took half a day to make the vessel seaworthy. Then the merchant cooked his beans and some fish from Kapsoch, which tasted surprisingly good after their work. Jens belched loudly: "BURP!" I still can't believe we're really doing this. Can't we hire someone to take us to Bant?" Hinnerk muttered: "And how do you intend to pay for that? With your beans?" "What a charming boy," was Jens's sarcastic comment. They launched the boat in the late afternoon and said goodbye to Kapsoch who wished them luck and pointed them in the general direction of Bant: "If in doubt, just follow the densest fog."

They took turns at the oars and soon encountered a misty region which promptly swallowed them up. Langeoog and the East Frisian coast disappeared behind a white wall. Now the water became calmer, nearly flat. Abbo broke the silence: "Bant has to be somewhere here, like Kapsoch told us. It is said that the island is surrounded by a fog to shield the inhabitants from the sun. Jens nervously quipped: "That's why the undead don't get sunburn, ha, ha, ha." Hinnerk loudly screamed: "Boo!" and Jens nearly fell overboard with fright. The ensuing laughter relaxed even Klütje, who was keeping watch at the prow, his tail up in the air.

Ursula took Leevke outside the castle, through the disintegrating gatehouse down to the beach where they walked barefoot in the sand. Ursula explained: "When you use magic and sorcery it is always important to stay in control and to concentrate with the aid of an object. Preferably something with a natural connection to the arcane sphere like my wand which was carved from a tree from Albheim. Don't you have something similar?" Leevke shook her head. Possessions meant nothing to her. Apart from her shell hair clips, she carried absolutely nothing. The two of them strolled a little further into the sea and the cool water softly washed around their ankles. The kraken witch smiled: "It doesn't matter. Perhaps you don't need any props. It worked without any so far, hasn't it?" "Yes, if without my knowledge..." Ursula stretched herself: "Good, but first you have to stop all internal chatter and only soak up the external impressions. Feel the breath of the omnipresent force. Reflect. Listen to the ocean, the sound of the waves and try to connect your soul to it. Become one. Try to predict its movements as if the sea is a part of you..." Leevke gladly followed the instructions and closed her eyes. She intently listened to all the sounds of the ocean; its depth and its surface. Slowly she started breathing in rhythm with the sea swirling around her legs. Then she saw something. Sensed something inside her crawling to the back of her conscious awareness. It felt like a floodgate had been opened. As if the pent-up water was erupting. It stormed at Leevke, embraced her like a gigantic, hungry beast – and wanted to devour her entirely.

When she opened her eyes, she was somewhere else, right in the middle of the ocean. She glanced back and beheld an enormous black abyss; a deep, cavernous hole deep down where all the water in the world vanished, never to be seen again. This enormous hole was the end which could never be escaped. An ever devouring, ever hungry monster in the shape of a gigantic tube. She sensed that it was only waiting for her to give up and suck it down. It pulled her with all its might, but Leevke didn't want to go under; definitely not. She looked ahead again and saw a huge floodgate with a deluge of water shooting out of it. The sky-high, massive gate was made from the finest white marble and full of symbols Leevke didn't comprehend. It took all of her strength to swim forward, but, after the current's final attempt to grab her, she managed to struggle through the gate, away from the yawning abyss.

It took all she'd got to force herself through the invisible barrier. Then everything was silent. The roar of the thundering ocean had suddenly ceased. She looked back and saw the water still gushing towards the vortex, like a herd of cattle plunging from a cliff. But behind the gate everything was calm. The vast, clear sea embracing her seemed endless and only way, way up could she detect a glimmer of the sparkling surface. Everything else was without life; no sea creatures, no plants. She swam outside the floodgate's range, but as soon as she found herself outside it, something tugged at her and tried to pull her down. What she saw below her was terrifying: there was no ground and no end; nothing but complete darkness and cold. Again she panicked and frantically tried to swim to the surface until her muscles were burning with exertion. Something from the depths reached out to her with icy fingers, wanting to drag her down. It was as strong as the vortex, yet different. With superhuman strokes, she finally made it to the surface and breathed in the fresh, clear air. The suction from below stopped instantly. She surveyed her surroundings. Behind her roared the gigantic flood gates with the whirlpool beyond, but up closer she saw a small yellow island with a crimson crystal and a single palm tree. She swam towards it. It promised escape and badly needed rest. She swam for her life, away from the abyss, and reached the shore. Dragged herself on land with her last remaining resources before the cold owerpowered her.

Drenched in sweat Leevke opened her eyes and fell backwards. She crawled away from the sea as if it were a monster. Ursula was immediately beside her and hugged her: "What happened. You were totally spaced out. For a whole hour! I couldn't wake you and the sea... The sea contracted, became all hazy and formed strange images... Wow! I've never seen anything like it, and that means something!" Ursula laughed while Leevke trembled and tried to shake off the drowsiness. "It was terrible. A nightmare." Ursula understood: "When I first experienced magic, little one, I screamed so loud that even Holger Danske heard me in his dungeon. This was your first contact with a force which has so far raged uncontrolled inside you. What you saw was a mirror of your thoughts and your potential power." "It was scary." "It's always shocking to realise what one is actually capable of," Ursula observed. Leevke was still trying to digest what she'd been through. It had seemed so real, yet it had only been a dream, a vision. Ursula challenged her: "Try it again. Consciously. I'll be here to look after you." Leevke hesitantly stretched her hand towards the water. She wanted it to rise and shape a simple column. She concentrated and squinted her eyes. "It's working!" Ursula exclaimed and clapped. Leevke opened her eyes and was amazed to see a pillar of water swaying back and forth like a celestial, unstable water worm. At that moment of elation Leevke was simultaneously overtaken by a kind of tiredness that made it hard to keep the pillar upright and the fear returned. An angry, growling beast appeared from out of the depths wanting to tear her apart, to destroy her. In a panic Leevke let the pillar collapse and at the same time the beast of her thoughts snarled and retreated. Leevke swallowed hard: "Something doesn't want me to do that..." Ursula sighed, then smiled: "That was pretty impressive considering that you're only starting. Better than I had hoped for. Congratulations!" Leevke got up on her shaking legs. She felt dizzy and nauseous. "You're quite pale, little one. How about a scrumptious plate of fish entrails, crabs' eyes and eel heads? What do you say?" Leevke threw up while Ursula sighed and rubbed her back. "Not to everyone's taste, I guess. Haven't been among people for a long time. She led the girl back to her room in the tower where she tucked the exhausted Leevke into her bed and purred: "I'll be back in a minute." Meanwhile Leevke stared at the ceiling and tried not to think. Her internal world scared her. What was all that inside her head and why her? There were so many questions.

Ursula hastened to Radbod who was standing at the edge of his viewing platform, gazing south towards the mainland. "Raddi! I've got news for you, my virile king. Radbod was far too engrossed in his own thoughts to turn around to her. "The people over there have no idea of the danger they're in, Ursel..." The woman forgot about her glee and listened: "All the so-called free Frisians don't even begin to suspect the immense lies they've fallen for; the conniving way their souls have been perverted. They still meet regularly to debate how to protect their lands, but the Church has long infected their society. Their endless talks make them weaker and more gullible with each generation. Soon there shall be no more pride in their hearts, only the struggle for survival and the fear of God." He panted: "I have to free them from the yoke of the bishops and the parsons. I shall burn down their churches with the fires of hell and lead my people back to the old gods. The gods who have stood by us for so long and who are the link to our ancestors. The forefathers whose abandoned souls accuse all of us: 'Why have you forsaken us? Why do you worship a dead cross more than us, your own blood?' Why do the children desert their parents in such a cruel way? For what? Do you understand it? Do you understand why I am the way I am, Ursel?" Ursela nodded loyally: "Of course, my king. I understand more than anyone..." She embraced his back: "I would hardly still be here if I didn't have the same objectives as you, great destroyer of Charles Martel's might." "That was a long time ago." "But it happened. With Njord's help we will reconquer the coasts and Magna Frisia will rise again from the ashes of the burned Christian cities. We shall call on the fertile floods for the sake of all free men and women from Flanders to Jutland." Radbod was satisfied and kissed her hand. "Is it any wonder I love you. So, you have news, I gather. Did Theo lie to me about the girl?" "Not at all. She's more suitable than anything else has been in the past centuries. No sacrifices, no invocations, not even Njord's personal support could be as useful to us as this little bundle of magic. She has enormous, primaeval strength. Her powers are beyond me. The potential is endless and completely free from Liudger's curse. With it we could even liberate the coasts of Greenland, Asia and Africa if we wanted to! We could go from victory to victory. Unstoppable like the storm tides! You and I!" Ursula danced around Radbod while untold possibilities unfolded in her mind. "As husband and wife we shall protect them all, like one big family! Strict, loving and just!" Radbod looked at her: "Justice and freedom should be our biggest allies. Then all the free peoples of this world will join us. Pepin's heirs won't believe what's happening when all their men desert them. That will be the moment when their whips will fail them. Heligoland and Dornum's disgrace shall be erased. We will plant oak trees again, so the people will gather and openly decide how they want to live. Under the protection of their forefathers' spirits. With respect! I swear, I Radbod, last king of Magna Frisia. I curse the Church and the Franks!" Ursula was grinning from ear to ear. "The little one may not see it that way. But I have an idea..."

Jens didn't hide the fact that he was afraid and tried to calm himself with his incessant chatter: "Perhaps we should turn back, my friends. As much as I appreciate your endeavours, I don't see why we should have to deal with creatures that don't even have goods to trade. Hey? I mean, what's the point?" Hinnerk grinned while he was holding the rudder. "How do you know that the undead have no goods? Radbod was a king after all and Bant is bound to still have some treasures. Old gold coins and the like." Jens rubbed his chin: "I hadn't thought of that. Well... Do you think Radbod may be interested in beans?" Abbo shrugged his shoulders: "Don't know, but it must be a while since he had any. At least 300 years." Jens briefly considered. "Never mind, but the thing about the old coins could be promising. Perhaps he would be into a barrel of wine? Or furs?" Suddenly Klütje started barking, his tail up in the air. Hinnerk exclaimed: "Land Ahoy!" Fog patches slowly drifted past and allowed them a glimpse of Bant, the cursed rocky island. Menacingly and defiantly the dark castle keep with its crumbling, mist-enshrouded fortifications towered above the island. They rowed to the shore and climbed on land, except Jens who was still desperately clinging to the boat. "This is the wrong place. Where is my ship? I don't see it!" Abbo heartily stretched his limbs: "She could be moored at the other side of the island or she may be in the inner harbour." "Inner harbour? I've never heard of such a thing!" Abbo explained: "It's a place inside the fortress to keep their vessels in case of a siege. A rocky island like this lends itself well to the purpose." Hinnerk asked: "Did you learn that on the crusades, uncle Abbo?" "I saw something like it at a coastal town, yes. At times of danger the ships were taken into the castle to make a sally or to escape during the night – whatever made more sense." Jens whimpered: "So my pour Lobscouse is inside that dreadful fortress?" "It's possible. You can stay here, but it would be foolish, Mr Janssen. First of all you are unprotected and secondly I can't guarantee that we shall return with your vessel. If something goes wrong, you'd be on your own." Jens immediately climbed out of the boat: "A convincing argument, Mr Abbo! Don't you have a surname, by the way?" "Abbo will do. My friends call me uncle." "Right, but don't expect any heroics from me. Mercury knows I'm just a trader!" Hinnerk rolled his eyes: "I think we got that by now!" Abbo gestured for the two of them to be quiet. Nobody was guarding the gatehouse; everywhere appeared to be deserted. And still Hinnerk felt as if they were being watched when they crept into the bailey, taking cover wherever they could. Close up the tower looked even more massive and the boy felt as if countless eyes kept monitoring their every move through the crenels. They selected a ruined smaller tower to the west of the main keep as their hideout and only spoke in whispers so as not to wake the undead. Jens was trembling and hyperventilating. Hinnerk took pity on him and firmly grabbed his arm: "Steady. Take a deep breath. In... that's right, and now out again. Feel better?" Jens smiled: "Thank you, my boy. You're more courageous than I am. Somewhat embarrassing that." "Let's see what happens. I may not be as courageous as all that." Jens said: "I have no objections if it stays as calm as this." Hinnerk chuckled. He liked the merchant. He wasn't as stiff as the other grownups. More like someone his own age, who wasn't the world's greatest fighter, but had brains instead. Besides he made it easier for Hinnerk to be brave because the boy wasn't prepared to admit to his own fear in front of him. It was actually quite helpful that somebody else was afraid instead of him. That way he wasn't too tense and liable to make mistakes. Although Hinnerk wasn't scared of Gobolds and giant shrimps, the undead were a different story entirely. Their very existence was utterly wrong. Their movements seemed surreal – as if they were the result of a nightmare – and yet real. Hinnerk knew the tales about moor mummies and revenants only too well; about the terror they inspired in the living with their unnatural, grotesque imitation of real life.

Abbo's expression became more serious and harder. Secretly he felt transported back to the times as a crusader in enemy territory. Even Hinnerk didn't really know that side of him. Something was wrong. After surveying their surroundings Abbo explained emphatically: "Listen carefully. Judging by the construction of this castle, all the main rooms are inside the keep. I suspect the Lobscouse is stored behind it, in that stone building right beside the wall bordering the sea. All the other buildings in the inner courtyard are just ruins and nobody lives in them apart from sea-scorpions perhaps." "Great," was Jens's sarcastic comment. "Ultra-large, poisonous, armour-reinforced, spider-like creatures with claws are much better than sword-wielding skeletons." Abbo ignored him. "I'm going to see if my hunch is correct and swim to the harbour. You lot stay here and keep an eye on the main gate. Absolutely don't do anything without my approval. Particularly you, Hinni! Got that?" But what if they bring Leevke outside? Shouldn't I grasp the opportunity and...?" Abbo brusquely cut him off: "No! We will get her together. No solo efforts! You hear me! Jens and I don't want to end up having to rescue the two of you from Radbod's dungeon." Jens agreed and Hinnerk finally accepted Abbo's decision. "Right," Abbo said, "I'll be back soon." He made sure that Pakhaou was safely dangling from his side and inched along the remains of the outer walls, past the also decayed north-west tower to the back of the keep. The inside was completely collapsed and the wind howled through the open structure. Hinnerk and Jens took up their positions in the ruins and peeked at the entrance through the stones and ivy. Jens whispered: "Abbo knows what he's doing." Hinnerk nodded quietly while Jens kept on blabbering: "How's that mutt of yours doing? I'm surprised he's so calm. And you speak his language? Dog-talk?" Hinnerk sighed: "We have a sign language. His name is Klütje and he is a coast dog, not a mutt." "My apologies." "We've known each other for seven years and a hand signal from me is enough for him to be quiet until I tell him otherwise. He's very obedient." "That's fascinating," Jens said, glad to be able to talk about something trivial. "So, it's a kind of magic." "It's not. I trained him for ages." Hinnerk stopped and admitted: "It can get pretty boring on the dyke sometimes, you know?" Jens shivered and massaged his arms. "Boredom is underrated, if you ask me. I wouldn't mind being bored. Brrr. It's freezing." While they were waiting Hinnerk spotted some strange, blue and green flashing lights in the tower's upper storeys. Jens forcefully pulled him back: "Don't look at them! That's bound to be black magic! Who knows what it will do to your eyes or, even worse, to your head?!" "It's only lights," Hinnerk replied, but he noticed how he already felt dizzy. "I only hope Leevke will be alright or I shall personally sink this whole damn island." Nothing happened for a long time and the two of them became restles again. "What's taking him so long?" Hinnerk muttered and Jens said: "I don't want to be a prophet of doom..." "Then don't."

Chapter 5

Coast Dog on a Secret Mission

Abbo climbed down the slippery stones to the back gate. The harbour building was connected to the main tower by a tunnel, so one could get to the boathouse without being seen. On the outer wall he detected a small set of stone steps, hardly visible from the front, which led through the water to the shelter's heavy bronze double doors. In all likelihood Jens Janssen's ship was stored inside it. He took a stouthearted plunge into the cold water to search the surface for an opening to get into the inside of the boathouse, but all he found were a couple of holes beneath the water's surface needed to supply the inside of the boathouse with water. Getting through those wouldn't have been possible without immense effort and noise. So Abbo climbed back up and rejoined his friends. They were relieved to see him back safe and sound.

After Abbo told him about the construction of the boathouse, Hinnerk had an idea: "How thick are the outlet valves?" "About twice the size of my upper arm. Why?" "Because Klütje could easily slip through them!" Abbo laughed: "And then? Will he open the gate from the inside with his snout?" Hinnerk shot him a reproachful look while Jens listened attentively. He was only too glad that he didn't have to do anything dangerous and he wasn't going to jeopardize his luck by saying anything stupid. Hinnerk elaborated: "At least we have more of a chance than marching through the main gate and slay hordes of undead and Radbod." Jens agreed: "You've got something there, young man." "Besides," Hinnerk continued, "Klütje is only meant to find Leevke. He has a good nose. We need him to bring her to the boathouse. He is very well trained." Abbo conceded: "That's all very well, but only if he finds the doors unlocked. And what are they supposed to do next? We still won't be able to open the gates." "Leevke will do it somehow. With all that water in the basin she'll find a way to break through the gates. She does have her powers, you know." Jens contributed: "We could also try to prise the gates open with something, couldn't we?" Abbo was concerned: "Are you not worried about Klütje, Hinni?" "Only if the undead attack animals." Jens looked baffled while Abbo voiced his thoughts: "Not as far as I know. Their hatred was always directed towards people... but I can't be sure..." "So we'll do it. Are you ready, Klütje?" The coast dog wagged his tail and they went to the boathouse. Hinnerk stepped into the ice-cold sea and let Klütje splash about to the dog's delight. Like a dart he shot through the icy-cold sea to wet his parched fur. Hinnerk picked him up and kept talking to him. The boy furtively extracted a sock from under his leather collar and let the dog sniff at it. He released Klütje and the animal instantly made for one of the valves and vanished. Abbo asked: "Was that one of Leevke's socks?" Hinnerk blushed and Abbo grinned: "Did she give it to you?" Hinnerk blushed even more and Abbo's grin broadened. "You nicked it, didn't you?" "Just stop it, will you? It's only a stupid sock. I found it in her room on Kleene Wacht. Of course I wanted to give it back to her, but isn't it just as well that I forgot? Now Klütje can follow her scent!" Abbo smiled: "I thought she had an aversion to anything on her feet?" "I think that only applied to shoes, not to socks... "Jens finally got what this was all about. "I see! Don't worry, boy, we've all been through it. Oh, yes, the sock phase, the stocking phase, the sweaty shirt phase..." Hinnerk growled: "May be you did, but I didn't. Weren't we going to hide until Klütje comes back?" They retreated to the crumbling north-west tower and took turns watching the castle's entrance. For a moment Jens actually forgot about the mist, the icy cold water and the undead. Instead he thought about Taalke, his girlfriend back home and it warmed him more than any blanket could ever have done.

The interior of the boathouse was dimly illuminated by a torch. Just one little boat with a canopy at the stern was silently bobbing up and down. Without making a sound, Klütje slithered through the gate and onto the access ramp. He immediately started sniffing the ground for the scent of Leevke's feet. He bumped against the leg of a skeleton and jumped back into the water with the fright. The skeleton with spear and shield didn't move. Its red, weakly glimmering eyes were gazing in his direction, but it didn't do anything. Klütje warily approached it, but still no reaction. The coast dog barked and jumped right back into the pool. That's when the skeleton finally moved. But not towards Klütje; it marched right around the pool instead. Klütje used the chance and ran through the boathouse into another corridor, but soon a locked door barred his way.

He patiently waited until a skeleton opened it, quickly slipped through it and found himself in the entrance hall. He sniffed until he found Leevke's scent. Running up the stairs a few more skeletons passing by took no notice of him. On the fourth level he was met by another locked door and a strong smell of octopus. Leevke's trail ended here and the coast dog started scratching at the door and yelping. Somebody came closer on the other side. "Who is it?" enquired a female voice. The door opened...

The tide was rising, the mists were getting denser and Jens was getting impatient. "The dog is taking his time..." Hinnerk assured him: "He'll be back. I know him well." "You make him sound human, the way you talk about him." The boy got upset: "He's more human than a lot of people who simply look human!" Jens apologised: "I'm sorry. I blab too much, I know. But I'm cold and wet and we're surrounded by the soulless undead and below us are all sorts of deep-sea monsters who can't wait to gobble us up. It's also dark and the fog doesn't exactly improve things. "Okay, okay, Jens," Abbo indulged him: "But we have to pull ourselves together if we want to get out of here alive. Can we count on you?" In response to Abbo's words the merchant stopped shaking so much. "I'll be there when I'm needed. If that will do any good is another question, but I WILL be there." Hinnerk grinned: "With or without beans?" "For your information, Mr Country Bumpkin, those beans are of a special variety and possess magic powers which can ease many an ailment. They also enhance one's virility." "Really?" "Really!" Hinnerk wasn't sure if Jens was sarcastic or serious. "Well, why can't you sell them then?" Abbo stopped them. "That's enough, you two. This is not a game." It worked and they remembered the immediate danger they were facing. If Radbod should find them and they didn't have a seaworthy vessel by then, escape would be difficult, if at all possible. Jens voiced his concerns: "Shouldn't we have hidden our boat?" Abbo growled: "It's too late for that now," while Hinnerk kept rubbing his hands: "Come on, Klütje!"

Ursula picked up Klütje: "Aren't you a cute little seal?!" The coast dog sensed that there was something wrong with this woman with the kraken on her head who was anxiously staring at him. Coast dogs occasionally chase small octopuses in the water. They are part of their menu. "How did you get here? I think we have a few gaps in our donjon. But skeletons are known for their shoddy workmanship and they certainly can't cook. Absolutely no taste, poor fellows. No tongues left. Right, we shall put you into this cage for now. Who knows when I might need seal eyes again, hehehe! It's been a while," Ursula chirped. Klütje barked in protest, but Ursula raised her finger: "I wouldn't annoy me if I were you, my friend, or I'll have to seal your snout with snail slime." Considering the threat, Klütje thought it wiser to stop barking. Ursula went over to Leevke who was sitting at the the table with a bowl of soup in front of her. She had watched with great interest. "How are you feeling now, sweety pie? Have you recovered?" "A little. This mussel chowder is really good." "I'm glad to hear it. I think I'm the only one on this island who still has taste buds. Radbod eats hardly anything and Düll feeds on nothing but slime." She joined Leevke at the table, propped her head up on her hands and smiled broadly at the girl: "You are a pretty little thing. A bit chubby and rustic, but quite presentable." "I'm not chubby." "Only compared to these scrawny carcasses around here. I meant it as a compliment." Ursula leaned back: "We could do with your help, little one." "With what?" "Oh, nothing special. Let's say there have been a few misunderstandings between the Church and my king and it all ended in us wrongly being banned to this island. A bad old man called Liudger imprisoned us here way back and we've been suffering every since. Year after year. We can no longer cross the sea, you understand? We need somebody who can bring us over to the mainland. No ship can carry us." "Is that why you abducted me?" Ursula stretched her limbs: "I'm afraid so. We are desperate. Look at it as your chance to finally take up the position that is rightly yours. With your powers you would soon be the most powerful person here and everywhere else. You could do and have whatever you like. There are no limits. Your potential is enormous. Radbod and I will protect you and help you. Together we will avert all the dangers that threaten Frisia and establish our own realm where nobody has to suffer. And where you are free again." Leevke pursed her lips: "I don't know..." "They won't resist much when they see your and our power. There would be but few casualties. In the end everyone would profit. Right now most people are moaning under the taxes and oppression by the self-proclaimed kings. But you and I, all of us, we can put a stop to it and restore order and justice. You shall be revered and esteemed. You will be loved. All you have to do is to put your powers at our disposal and we look after the rest." Ursula extended her hands: "Take your time and think about it. I will have to leave for some time anyway. There are certain arrangements to take care of. But remember: you are special and it would be a shame, a crime even, if you wouldn't use your powers for the good of mankind!" With those words Ursula walked out of the altar room, leaving a bewildered and confused Leevke behind. "This soup's really quite good," she mumbled to herself when Klütje whimpered. "Hey, Klütje! I nearly forgot about you. Come, let me get you out of that cage. I didn't say anything because I didn't want her to see that we know each other. What are you doing here?" Klütje barked a few times and Leevke tilted her head: "I don't quite understand. Can you repeat that?" The girl concentrated on what the dog had to tell her. She more or less sensed what he had to convey. Klütje repeated his message and Leevke had to grin when she understood: "Hinnerk is here, isn't he? You want me to follow you?" Klütje wagged his tail. Leevke felt immensely relieved and tightly hugged the dog to her chest. Ursula's words still echoed in her head. Even if her intentions should turn out to be genuine, Leevke didn't want to become the tool of a king who certainly wasn't stranded on this island for nothing and who surrounded himself with the undead and outlaws like Theo. Perhaps she would change her mind, but only of her own free will and not because they held her captive and she had no choice. Before she would decide anything, she wanted to see Hinnerk and talk to him. Talk to him and hug him...

Radbod was climbing down a slimy and threadbare spiral staircase hewn from rough stone. He was on his way to the lowest point of the island, a small cave below sea level, dating back to the time before the castle had been built and whose walls had been worked from the stone of an ancient pagan place of worship. It was damp and an abundance of woodlice and centipedes lived in the niches. This was Bant's shrine. A square room dedicated to Njord, the Norse god of the ocean and the storms. Embedded in the north wall was a well adorned with runes with a tar-like black substance bubbling inside. This was the source of some of Radbod's and Ursula's strength and also kept most of his liegemen alive. There were only few of them left.

Many a foolish hero, wanting to liberate Bant, having sworn an oath after a few tankards of ale too many, underestimated the bone-soldiers in Radbod's retinue. On the surface they were nothing but the remains of the warriors they had once been, but inside their bones still slumbered the memories of battles against the Franks and the Christians. Arrows and stab wounds basically didn't harm them at all. Only blunt weapons like clubs or cudgels presented a problem for them and could damage the magical net that preserved them. Their biggest asset, however, was their tirelessness and their fearlessness. Skeletons needed neither rest nor sleep. They could fight forever without becoming fatigued and as long as they weren't buried in consecrated ground, a skilled necromancer could order them back to battle at any time. It was the terror of the invincible and everlasting the undead used to defeat their living opponents. The well was black because it contained a gateway to the gloom of Njord's depths. Beyond the black surface was a pressure that would instantly kill any human being. In addition it was a portal into the otherworld: the realm of ghosts and gods.

Radbod was kneeling in front of the well and dunked his right hand into the water. "Come on, old friend. The time has come. Once again I need your help in the battle against the cursed cross." At first the water hardly moved and only small concentric waves emanated from its middle where Radbod had immersed his hand. Then the surface formed ever more frantic bubbles and green light lit the entire cave. Radbod pulled his hand back and regarded it without moving. He was one of Njord's creatures himself and had nothing to fear when the lights started to pulsate more violently and the pressure reached his ears. Two tentacles, thick as arms, shot out of the boiling water and wildly bashed about the room before holding on to the edge of the well and heaving out the rest of the massive body. The two tentacles constituted the right arm of the armoured humanoid being which now stood up, its right hand covered in a gauntlet made from iron. The body was draped in slime-dripping platemail and the head hidden behind a helmet with three vertical slits. The creature's voice slurred: "Ah, Radbod, my friend and king! It's been a long time..." Radbod nodded and opened his arms. "And so it has, Düll. But Ursula has finally found a way to get away from Bant. Inform Njord and call the cursed of the sea to our side. Those drowned souls under his spell..." Düll indicated a curtsey: "I shall not disappoint you, friend. This time nobody will stop us. To the old gods!" Radbod shook his hand: "To our peoples' freedom. Hail our ancestors! Hail the young who follow them!" Düll reciprocated the handshake with his tentacles before disappearing back into the darkness of the well, into a place beyond reality. Radbod would never forget how only Düll had stayed true to him when his greedy relatives, full of lies, had hypocritically kissed the cross and wanted to slyly murder him to crush the pagan rebellion. Side by side Radbod and Düll had fought against the assassins whose highest god preached love to his followers. What a mockery. What hypocrisy! The ensuing war Radbod had had to wage against his own family permanently weakened the Frisians and cost them their freedom. The success that had been denied the Frankish soldiers, had been achieved by the parsons' empty words, believed by idiots in their naiveté or their blind greed to attain higher positions in the Church's new power structure. In the end Radbod had to give up and retreat from Western Frisia with his remaining entourage. But Düll had stood by him, related by blood or not. They were brothers in spirit, in their desire for revenge. Ursula had always disliked the rough Frisian warrior, but nobody had ever questioned his loyalty. Even now that he had become the chosen one, Radbod didn't doubt his friendship. They were standing side by side once again. But this time they would be the ones to attack unexpectedly. Radbod left the cave.

Radbod and Düll – side by side and back to back

Leevke was slowly opening the door when Theo brutally yanked it open and pushed her back. Klütje growled and the pirate hissed: "Hey! What do you think you are doing? Having a little stroll, you brat?" Leevke squinted her eyes. "None of your business." Theo brooded, then he started to grin: "Hey, wait a minute. Don't I know that mutt from somewhere? Doesn't it belong to the boy?" "No!" "Oh, yes it does. It's his. So the boy is here. To save you? That means he must have a boat!" Leevke shook her head, but the pirate had smelled a rat. She moved back from him. "I could help you, girl. Let's put the past behind us and be realistic, right? The fact is that I want to get away from here and so do you. Together we can do it. Otherwise we'll never get off this damned island and I will tell Ursula about your little friends." Leevke was completely taken by surprise: "Please don't!" Theo laughed: "I knew it. You just admitted it. You've got a lot to learn, sweetheart." Leevke looked grim and Theo said: "I like it when you get angry. And you have every reason to. But I'm also peeved.

They've planted this thing inside me. Have a look!" He lifted his shirt and Leevke was shocked when she saw the one-eyed kraken which had bored itself into Theo's chest, throbbing to the rhythm of his heart. "I've got to get rid of it." "Does it hurt a lot?" Theo looked surprised as if he hadn't anticipated the question. "I've had worse injuries. But the undead here accept me as one of their own. What's your plan?" "Klütje wants to take me away from here." "What? That mutt? I've got a better idea. One that shall protect us from Radbod's prying eyes. There is a boathouse on the northside of the fortress where I left the boat of those fools from Langeoog. We'll use it to get away." Leevke didn't know how to contradict him. "You know that Hinni isn't exactly your biggest fan right now?" Theo shrugged his shoulders: "Who is? Come one. Before the witch gets back." He grabbed her hand and dragged her with him. "Let's get out of here." Theo and Leevke with Klütje taking the lead sprinted through the castle. Soon some of the skeletons challenged them with their rusty swords. Theo told them: "Don't worry. I'm one of you." The undead screeched and pointed to Leevke: "Not sheeeeeee!" Theo sighed, brandished his axe and attacked. Rattling and screaming loudly the skeletons collapsed and there was nothing left but a heap of bones and smouldering metal. The spectacle was repeated several times during their flight until they reached the ground floor. Klütje led them to the boathouse where Theo took care of another of the undead who had been posted as a sentry. "We sure have their attention now! Run! I open the gate and you set the sails." Leevke dashed off and Theo worked the windlass that slowly opened the iron gate. The ancient hinges and chains squeaked and yowled deafeningly and could be heard all over the island. In the meantime Leevke jumped on board and whispered to Klütje: "Run, Klütje! Get Hinnerk!" The coast dog leapt off the vessel and dived outside through the opening. Theo had to use all his strength because it usually took two men to open the gates. He used the shaft of his axe as a lever while Leevke loosened the ropes. At that moment she spotted Hinnerk who was hanging onto the gate and winked at her before plunging into the water. "You okay?" Leevke laughed and was glad to see him. "Here I am!" Eventually the gate was open enough to guide the ship through it. "We're ready!" Leevke shouted to Theo who quickly planted a wedge in the windlass so the gate stayed open. He tried to jump aboard the Lobscouse, but barely managed to hold onto the railing while he threatened to slip. "Shit! Help me!" But Leevke stalled. Theo was a robber, blackmailer and kidnapper who was only concerned about himself. On the other hand Leevke wasn't heartless enough to leave him behind on the island, especially considering that the soulkraken in his chest really looked very painful, so she dragged him onboard. "For a moment I actually thought you were going to leave me here." Leevke nodded: "So did I." Theo laughed as if that had been a joke. "Never mind, let's get out of here!" He kicked the Lobscouse away from the quay. Shortly after the boat was on its way and Hinnerk, Jens and Abbo jumped onboard. Jens kissed the mast: "There you are, my poor little Lobscouse. Did they hurt you? You are a loyal vessel, a great battle ship..." Leevke embraced Hinnerk in a fierce hug while Abbo frowned when he saw Theo: "Well, well, if it isn't the famous Driftwood Theo." Hinnerk said: "We should leave him here with the rest of those vermin." Leevke shook her head: "He helped me. I wouldn't have made it without him. Sorry..." Theo provocatively whielded his axe: "Of course I'm aware of my precarious situation, but perhaps we should discuss this in peace once we've left this island behind, okay?" Radbod's voice abruptly sounded from above where he was standing on the roof of the boathouse, his cape blowing in the wind. Behind him stood twenty skeletons in chainmail and rusty helmets. "Nobody is going to leave here without my permission!" Jens clung to the mast: "Oh, really? Great timing!" Radbod ignored him and addressed Theo instead: "I have obviously been too trusting when I believed that you had adequately covered your tracks, beachcomber. So you're trying to sneak away. You disappoint me. You have lost my favour, worm!" "It's not what it looks like! I've apprehended them for you, great king. Look, I..." Radbod stretched out his chin and reached for Theo's chest. The pirate opened his mouth in a silent scream, his eyes wide with pain and terror. The soulkraken strengthened its hold on his heart; made it stop with a fierce grip of its tentacles and pumped poison into the pirate's veins. Theo collapsed onto the deck like a dead man.

Radbod straightened himself up: "Now to you, intruders! This girl is of paramount importance for my plans for a free Frisia. I shall triumphantly return as king for the good of all free men. You would be well advised to humour me and relinquish the girl into my keeping." Abbo resolutely stepped forward: "Your time is over, Radbod. Everyone knows that. The world has changed." Radbod's eyes narrowed to slits: "Who are you, man? I recognise the sword at your side! That's Pakhaou, isn't it? It once belonged to the Frisians in the east, but was lost in the Devil's Moors, as I was told." "That's where I found it and now it serves me." You shall let us go, Radbod!" "I am your rightful sovereign! The king of the last free Frisians! All of you forgot that. They made you forget!" "You are not my king. None of us swore you fealty." Jens quietly interjected: "Which doesn't mean that we won't, or does it?" Abbo continued: "We are living in a hard-earned peace. Nobody is interested in rekindling the old feuds." Radbod was beside himself with rage: "Peace?! A life as the sheep of those traitors? You call that peace?! I can't rest while you blindly accept your situation. While you forget your mothers and fathers and piss against the monuments erected in their honour!" Jens sarcastically addressed Abbo: "Well done, you prince of diplomacy. I might still have been able to negotiate a deal, but thanks to your verbal inadequacies we'll all find a premature end here on Bant! Bravo! Words fail me!" Abbo snarled: "So you want this sword, Radbod? And the girl? Then I challenge you to a duel! If I win, we leave the island unharmed, all of us. If not, you get everything!" Radbord considered: "Alright. I accept your conditions, warrior Abbo. Let fate decide." Hinnerk whispered to his uncle: "Are you mad, Abbo? If at all then we shall fight him together. He has his skeleton army!" Abbo pulled Hinnerk closer and whispered back: "Listen well. I shall hold him back while you escape on the boat. Leevke can help with that. Once you're out of range, I'll also make my getaway. Radbod can't cross the ocean, but I'm a good swimmer. His pride is his weak point. He will fight me on his own. I know…" Hinnerk nodded slowly, but he was still worried about Abbo although the man was the best fighter he knew. Abbo jumped up the stairs to take up position opposite Radbod, who lifted his right hand so the skeletons would form a circle. Both men drew their weapons, in Radbod's case an immaculate Frisian seax by the name of Durjawer. They circled each other like wolves while Hinnerk quietly asked Leevke: "Can you make the water push the boat out? Away from the enemies' arrows?!" Leevke seemed determined but a little uncertain. She hadn't forgotten what had happened to her the last time. "I can try, but I can't guarantee it will work." Klütje buried his head under his paws and cowered whimpering in a corner of the vessel. Jens was hugging the mast so tightly as if it were his last moral support. Leevke closed her eyes and concentrated.

The water around the Lobscouse started to billow and shook the boat. Jens shouted: "A seaquake! Or what is this?" Hinnerk was holding on to the railing: "Not a seaquake! It's Leevke. She'll get us out of here!" "Very good!" Leevke turned around to face the island, bent both her arms back and then quickly made them dart forward. The mass of water at the stern swelled up like a balloon.

At that moment a black kraken tentacle shot out of the ocean, grabbed Leevke and took her away. The balloon collapsed in on itself and the girl screamed while she was being dragged through the air. Jens shouted: "Is that part of the plan?!" They hastened to the railing and Jens crossed himself when he beheld the monster beside them. "Holy cow!" An enormous deep-sea kraken had risen up and was now swinging Leevke through the air. Jens and Hinnerk looked at the north-west tower where they saw Ursula standing in the breeze with her scythe pointing at the ship: "You're leaving already? Without saying hello to my friends?"

Meanwhile Abbo attacked Radbod and a violent fight ensued. The king grinned: "You're not playing fair, Frisian!" "That coming from someone like you..." Radbod smiled sardonically: "You have spunk. I like that!" Radbod threw Abbo back. Their fight was pretty even and Abbo managed to strike the king a few times. Normally this wouldn't have made much difference to the undead, but Pakhaou was a magic weapon and Radbod could feel the pain. His lifeless eyes were now filled with undisguised hatred and Abbo enraged him even more: "Looks like I have the upper hand. If that's the best you can do, old king, the free men of the islands and the mainland will cast you back faster than you can land!" Radbod broke into mad laughter: "Bwahahaha! Do you honestly believe that's all I've got? It is time to demonstrate my true strength: the force of the god of the storms and the waves, the immortal Vanr Njord! Ursula, send in the Ghost of the Mists!" Now Abbo also spotted the kraken witch on the crumbling north-west tower. "Won't be a minute!" Ursula shouted back. The wind was tugging at her garments and made her appear like a ghastly figure from much older, wilder times; more ethereal then real. She raised her scythe-wand and screamed her invocations in long-forgotten languages. It had already been cloudy, but now bolts of lightning flashed through the sky, only barely missing the witch. She didn't mind, apparently even enjoyed the electrifying danger. Then she swung the scythe around and diverted one of the bolts from her to Radbod. It hit him and electric snakes climbed up on him. Abbo saw how Radbod's shape changed. The king literally evaporated to be replaced by a dense fog until only his crown, his eyes and Durjawer were still visible. Abbo cursed: "What kind of scorcery is that?" Radbod's sword moved as if wielded by a ghostly hand and suddenly lunged out. It was unbelievably quick and Abbo had a hard time predicting its moves as he couldn't see the arms that swung it. Durjawer could change its position with lighting speed. They were still surrounded by the inert, eerie skeletons. Ursula giggled and commanded the kraken: "Listen, my old friend. Grab the others from the boat. Today we shall capture some exceedingly promising booty, hehehe!" The kraken now stretched out his other tentacles to snatch Hinnerk, Jens and Klütje from the Lobscouse. Jens picked up an oar and beat at the slimy arms while nimbly escaping from their reach. Klütje heroically sank his teeth into another tentacle and Hinnerk managed to stab it a few times with his knife. Black, stinking blood oozed out of the creature's wounds. The kraken was holding Leevke close to its heads and stared at her through its single spider-like eye. Her voice was trembling when she asked: "Why are you attacking us? Please, let us go!" Ursula was fascinated: "Nice try, but he serves me, and me alone. I raised him." The witch mumbled some kind of spell as the kraken put Leevke down on the tower in front of her feet. "You were very naughty, little one," Ursula said smugly, then ordered two of the skeletons: "Take her back to my room. I shall deal with her later." "I will never help you!" Leevke exclaimed defiantly, but Ursula only grinned: "Even if your friends are in danger?" Leevke swallowed: "You are mean!" "Well, it goes with the profession." Leevke glanced over to the boat where Hinnerk, Jens and Klütje were fighting for their lives and tore herself away from the skeletons. Jumped over the battlements right into the sea below. But before she plunged into the water, she was grabbed by a tentacle that squeezed her so hard, she nearly fainted. Then the kraken deposited her back on the tower. Ursula smiled: "Feisty, aren't we? I like it. But you shall do as we bid or your friends will be fed to the fishes." To the kraken she shouted to bring her the others. The creature obeyed and openly attacked the Lobscouse. Leevke dragged herself up and with her last remaining strength created a huge water balloon behind the ship which propelled it forward with a loud bang. Only with extreme difficulty did Hinnerk, Jens and Klütje manage not to go overboard. Leevke smiled and shouted: "Flee!" before she collapsed. Ursula cursed: "Follow them!" and the kraken tailed the boat under water.

Radbod's shadowy movements were unpredictable and a few times Abbo couldn't avoid being hit. Radbod's spectral voice mocked him from all directions: "I warned you! But you preferred not to listen. Now you'll pay for your folly." He broke Abbo's defences and Durjawer pierced through one of the few weak points in Abbo's scale armour. Abbo spit out some blood and sank to the ground. The fog became denser again and Radbod returned to his former shape. "You fought honourably, but it was futile. Like every type of resistance against the inevitable. I have the power of our ancestors on my side." "You may have your ancestors, but I have friends!" Abbo retorted. "We shall see! As I've lost Theo I shall need a new liegeman. One who knows a little about leading an army..." Abbo looked grim and held his bleeding chest: "I'd rather die than serve you!" "What you want makes no difference. You shall be the first to follow me onto the mainland. As my general and liegeman. Time will convert you to our side. It always does." Abbo still tried to escape to the boathouse, but the skeletons held him back and forced him to the ground. His wound was too serious and he realised that he would bleed to death.

Jens roared: "We've got to get out of here!" But Hinnerk hit one of the kraken's tentacles and roared back: "We are not going to desert her!" "And how, may I ask, do you intend to do that? They have an army of skeletons, a king made of fog, a witch and a colossal kraken thrown in for good measure! We can't win and we will die if we stay!" Hinnerk's eyes sparkled with rage: "Just shut up!" Jens hit one of the tentacles with his oar: "We will come back, but for the moment we're beaten. Your obstinacy will be the death of the last bit of hope we still have!" Hinnerk sensed that Jens was right. There were only two of them, three if you counted Klütje, so how could they defeat such superior numbers? He was devastated when he saw Abbo being beaten and dragged away. His uncle's last words were: "Get away! Keep watch!" Hinnerk understood. His throat was parched. "Set sail, Jens." "Finally, phew!" Jens agreed. Hinnerk and Klütje fended off the kraken's tentacles while the beast kept rocking the boat and Jens saw to the sail. Crates and barrels were flung everywhere and some of them ended up in the water. The kraken's blood covered the deck. It was grimy and black and reminded Hinnerk of the consistency of the candles made from wax and pitch at home. He asked Jens: "Do you have a torch?" "I do if they haven't looted my boat." "Get it! It could save us. I hold the fort!" "Aye-aye, Sir!" Jens dived into the vessel's hold, accompanied by the alarming creaking of the planks. Inside the low hold he had to crouch amidst an array of goods; many of them long since rotted or undisturbed for years. Jens firmly believed that everything would come in handy at some stage. He frantically searched for the torch. In the meantime the kraken had lifted the boat right out of the water with its eight tentacles and was shaking it like a tree. Hinnerk grabbed Klütje and held on to one of the ropes. Amidst the general mayhem it seemed like a miracle when Jens emerged from the hold with a torch and tinder. "A... are we floating?" Hinnerk just nodded and Jens accepted it with the stoical composure of a man who had made his peace with the world. Hinnerk said: "All we need now is something to light it." "Get it!" "No, you get it!" "Where am I to find something to light it with? I'm not a chandler am I? Oh, wait, I am!" The kraken was rocking the boat more violently. Jens was hanging on to the mast. "Damn it! I never meant to touch it again, but it seems I have no choice. Shit!" Jens disappeared again into the general disarray of the hold and returned with a book. "What is that?" Hinnerk asked. "Are you going to read me a story?" "Certainly not. This book belonged to a genuine wizard!" Jens asserted and frantically leafed through the pages. "Fire... fire." "Hurry up!" "I can't find anything to do with fire! It's not even Latin! What kind of scrawl is this? Oh, I see a picture with a torch." Jens grabbed the implement and panted: "I can't guarantee anything!" Hinnerk roared: "Just do it!" The kraken squashed the boat, bending the planks with ugly growns while rivets shot like missiles out of their brackets. Jens's fingers scanned the lines of the book. His index finger started to glow and little magic sparks covered his skin. He grimaced with the hot tingling in his hand. Then he took his hand away, closed the book with his other one and clenched his fist. The red glow invaded it and he shook it like a dice player. "Take cover, Hinni! Ive' no idea what's going to happen now!" "As long as something happens!" Hinnerk screamed back when the kraken got bored and was about to tear the ship into the depths; into its wide open jaws.

Jens and Hinnerk clung to the mast, the kraken squirming underneath. The fact that something as big as that was lurking for them in the depths of the ocean was nerve-shattering enough. But Jens's nerves were already shot, so all of it had a rather calming effect on him. He kept shaking his fist, not knowing what the magic in his hand may trigger. Anything could happen. Whatever he was about to unleash would definitely far surpass his ability to control it. He felt a pulling sensation in his head, his chest, his entire soul. He stretched out his glowing hot hand and screamed: "BEANS ARE DELICIOUS, START BEING VICIOUS!" The magic in his hand had no idea what was expected of it. It needed direction Jens couldn't supply. So it got angry, in keeping with its fiery nature. And produced sparks within the fabric of its reality. The torch ignited, but that wasn't enough to satisfy it. It wanted to break beyond a smouldering piece of timber, make an impact! The magic's fire penetrated the depths, enveloped the kraken. The deep sea monster yelled as the fire hit its wounds, set it on fire. Its tentacles aimlessly lashed out through the ocean and released the Lobscouse with a bang. The impact of the water nearly swept them overboard. The kraken was wreathing in agony. To escape from the fire, the beast dived under, but even there the fire continued to seethe. The water hissed and steamed as if it were boiling. Jens gasped: "Now or never!" They set sail and the emerging eastern wind provided them with the required force to get away from Bant. Hinnerk still saw the kraken disappear into the ocean like a nightmare shadow that had become reality. "Is it dead?" he asked and Jens commented: "Let's hope so, but knowing our luck, I doubt it very much." Hinnerk helped him set the sail and get rid of the worst mess while they made for Langeoog, past Bant. They boy thoroughly checked Klütje to make sure he was okay. To his relief he found that the coast dog was doing fine, only the kraken flesh stuck between his teeth made him retch a little. Hinnerk sat down beside Jens at the rudder: "Are you a real wizard now?" "Not at all. I'm a bastard sorcerer at best. I bought the book for half nothing from a weird old geezer. I thought it was a good deal. Books are worth a lot. In the evening, when I sat down to read it, I leafed through the pages and this glow appeared. I shook the book and cursed and then it happened..." "What happened?" "The magic! It just did whatever it felt like. All of a sudden my loaf of bread came alive. Have you ever been attacked by a snappy loaf of bread? What a fight! There were bits of bread everywhere. It all ended in the pigsty." Hinnerk squinted: "You were attacked by your own loaf of bread?" Jens nodded: "You can't control magic. I've learned my lesson and try to leave it alone before I end up as pig swill myself." Hinnerk stroked Klütje's back. "I am returning to our farm and tell my father what happened. Then we can inform the dyke watch together. Perhaps Attena will join our forces, or even Nordendi." Jens agreed: "Good plan." "In the meantime you go to the abbey and ask the monks for their help. I'm sure we'll need some divine assistance to combat those pagans." Jens sighed: "Do I have to? I'd really rather go home. I'm being expected." He noticed Hinnerk's reproachful look. "Alright. I'll see what I can do. Talking to the monks can't be as difficult as handling magic, but I can't deny that I've never been as scared." Hinnerk understood: "You weren't the only one. I was scared as well. At least a little bit. Abbo... Leevke..." Jens cleared his throat: "Don't worry too much, my boy. Abbo and Leevke aren't lost. They gave me back my Lobscouse. I'm in their debt and I intend to repay them." Hinnerk smiled gratefully: "Well, Mr Janssen. Off to new adventures, hey?" They shook hands. "Just call me Jens, boy." "Just call me Hinni." Jens looked past him and wondered: "What are we going to do with him?" Hinnerk followed his gaze and his eyes settled on Theo's corpse between some barrels. "Let's feed him to the kraken," said Hinnerk, walked over and kicked the pirate. The man didn't move. Together they heaved him overboard. Just before the pirate landed in the water, they heard him coughing. "Is he still alive?" Hinnerk and Jens asked in one voice and Theo's head emerged from the waves. "Help! Get me out of here!" Jens turned the boat and they pulled Theo back onboard. Hinnerk pointed his dagger at him: "One wrong move and I feed you to the fishes again! Is that clear?" Theo was vomiting blood and water. He smirked grimly: "What a warm welcome! Will this ever stop?" "We thought you were dead!" Jens informed him. Theo nodded: "I was. I am... Oh, I don't know, but it's shit!" He lifted up his shirt to expose the soul-kraken still sucking at his chest. "Still there, the bastard." Jens said: "I don't get it. Didn't Radbod kill you?" Theo had to think. "I don't know. Something is different... That damned soul-kraken is still there, but the strength it gave me is gone... Radbod can't control me any longer. He must have stopped it himself. My heart can beat on its own again, but fuck, I have some headache!" Hinnerk glared at him: "That should be the least of your worries. You'll have to pay for your crimes!" They tied him up and the pirate made no attempts to escape. He was too weak and he'd lost his axe in the ocean. Jens asked him: "So you were under Radbod's spell? Could he also try that with Leevke and Abbo?" Theo shrugged his shoulders: "It's possible, at least as far as the man is concerned. That dreadful woman Ursula, the kraken witch, is somehow in charge of the girl." Hinnerk paced up and down the deck: "How can we rescue Abbo?" Theo said: "Only Radbod can release him, but you saw how that went with me. And I was lucky I didn't drown." Jens thought for a minute. "There has to be a way to cut off the connection. To remove the kraken." The pirate pretended to be moved and grinned: "You would do that for me?" Hinnerk aimed a kick at him, but Jens observed: "May not be such a bad idea to have a trial run, what do you think, Hinni? The Benedictine monks at Esens may know what to do. I'll take him with me." Hinnerk shook his head: "You're not taking him on your own. I'll go with you. Our friend Malle Pugnose can alert the dyke watch. Everybody knows him and he's also been involved in this whole thing." Theo grimaced: "You really want to wage war against Radbod? Good luck with that, is all I can say. He's already made contact with his allies. Just thought I let you know." Hinnerk probed: "What allies?" "He went right to the bottom of the castle. I guess to ask his old gods to support the invasion he's planning. He also talked to somebody from the tower. It was as if the wind carried his words. And the witch is also doing her bit. There were sparks in her room. Judging by the dialect, it seemed as if he was talking to the Vikings." Jens was aghast: "The ashmen with the longboats? Nordendi only recently managed to fend them off near Norden." Theo looked glum: "That's what it looks like, Frisian. They are still pagans, so an alliance would make sense."

Hinnerk's determination grew with each word. "All the more reason to warn our people. We have to stop Radbod before it's too late and he can gain a foothold! And, of course, we have to rescue Abbo and Leevke!" No doubt there would be a war. The Frisians had to flock together to avert the threat. Their responsibilities weighed hard on Hinnerk's and Jens's shoulders. So far their fellow Frisians were unaware of what they were about to face. Hinnerk desperately missed Leevke. Knowing that she was held captive in that disgusting tower, against her will, and that he had been unable to protect her made him mad with rage.

Now it seemed like a dream that they had only met each other a few days ago. It couldn't have been a coincidence. Hinnerk had been chosen to look after her. He had to be there for her, hold her when she fell, comfort her when she was sad. He filled his lungs with the fresh Western Sea breeze. It was time to put things right and he was not alone. The Frisians would follow his call. Defending their land had been their right since ancient times, before and after Radbod.

Chapter 6

Of Monks and Falcons

Abbot Wynfried gazed absentmindedly out the window and pulled at his long, curly chestnut-brown beard. Subdued sunlight illuminated the small chamber, sparsely furnished with a bed and the table at which he was brooding over some manuscripts. Above the door hung a plain silver cross until it crashed to the floor when a hysterical novice tore the door open and stumbled into the room.

The abbot turned around: "Do we no longer knock here at Marienkamp, Brother Witzelt?" The novice blinked and opened his mouth, but was unable to produce a sound. Brother Witzelt was the youngest novice and had only recently joined the monastery. Eighteen years old, the young man from Schortens wasn't a particularly bright scholar, but his strong and clear singing voice infused new life into the monks' otherwise not very enthusiastic chants. He was also considerate and always obliging. His youth and nature often made him act impetuously, but he did his best to one day be accepted as a fully-fledged monk into the religious community of Marienkamp.

Now he looked miserable and nervously scratched his hand while he tried to remember the important message he was supposed to deliver. Abbot Wynfried had frequently noticed that the boy had problems concentrating; that his mind went blank whenever his nerves got the better of him. The abbot sighed and put his quill aside. Then he smiled: "Relax, Brother Witzelt. Take your time or come back when you've calmed down." Witzelt gulped: "I... it's alright, Abbot. But it's hard to explain. If you would please follow me and see for yourself. It's urgent." "So be it," replied the comparatively young abbot – he was only 36. He got up and followed the novice through the austere, freshly swept cloister walk to the inner courtyard with its pond and herb garden. A lot of the monks had already gathered and were whispering in little groups. On seeing Abbot Wynfried, they rushed over to him and told him about three men outside the monastery who asked leave to be admitted on important business. The strangers had told fantastic tales of the old Frisian king Radbod, who was planning his return, and of an unavoidable, impending war. Now the Frisians were pleading for the support of the Church and the abbey. Panic and excitement were written in the monks'

faces.

Wynfried raised his hands: "Collect yourselves, brothers! We shall listen to what the men have to say and then discuss it in a civilised manner, as always. We are monks, not fishwives. Let them enter." The monks calmed down. Brother Witzelt operated the rope winch and pulled up the iron gate to admit Hinnerk, Jens, Theo and Klütje. Wynfried greeted them with a bow: "God be with you, brothers, and welcome. What can we do for you?" Jens also bowed and introduced himself and the others before he said: "Be thanked for receiving us, worthy Abbot. I am aware that I should frequent mass more frequently, but my line of profession doesn't always allow it, hehehe..." Hinnerk nudged him: "Tell him why we're here!" Jens nudged him back. "I was just getting around to that, you impudent urchin!" Wynfried smiled: "I believe you have a serious request?" The inquisitive monks came closer, their arms crossed, to listen. Jens straightened his garments: "That is indeed the case, worthy Abbot. We have just returned from the island of Bant. You know it?" "I've heard of it..." "Anyway, that's where the old king Radbod is planning his attack on the mainland. We strongly suspect that he will avail of pagan sorcery; there is a witch among his following. In the name of all Frisians of the coast we therefore ask you for your support in our fight against the threat to Christianity. People say the monks of Marienkamp are wise and shrewd when it comes to defeating God's enemies." The abbot pensively tugged at his beard while the monks whispered even more animatedly amongst themselves. "Your claims seem rather remarkable, Mr Janssen. I find it hard to believe them..." Theo pushed himself forward: "Then you may believe this!" He gestured to Hinnerk to pull up his shirt. The shocked monks drew back from the soulkraken slimily rooted to his chest and crossed themselves: "Holy Calvary!"

Jens immediately apologised: "Forgive us! Forgive us, worthy brothers! We should have been more cultured..." Wynfried frowned: "This creature... it is enwrought with magic. I can feel it." He pointed to the monks' assembly hall: "Alright so. Come with me and tell me what happened from the beginning. And you, Brother Witzelt, close the gate again!"

The monks ushered them into a high-ceilinged hall with several long tables and chairs. The walls were hung with wood carvings of saints and the previous abbots of the

Marienkamp friary. The guests sat down opposite the monks who nearly tripped over their own feet in their desire to know more. Jens, Hinnerk and Theo related their adventures and the monks' expressions darkened with each word. Eventually Abbot Wynfried called on the elderly, half-blind friar Tennus: "Brother Tennus has studied Radbod's history. Please, Brother, tell us what you know. It will be beneficial to understand and recall the history before we make a decision." Brother Tennus nodded: "Thank you, Brother Abbot, for your trust in me. Now then, knoweth: in his day, St. Liudger imprisoned the old Frisian king and his remaining followers on the rocky island of Bant, an ancient pagan place of worship. The thus cursed can not cross the sea. That is the exact wording in Liudger's chronicle, and I beg you to take this into consideration when exploring the issue." Brother Tennus cleared his throat and Witzelt handed him a goblet of wine. "Thank you, my boy... Where was I! Oh, yes! Do you really believe that this protective spell no longer has any power? The spell for which Liudger gave his life and for which he was sainted as a martyr? I don't think so. Is it not far more likely that Radbod found a way to elude the curse? With help from the outside? That is my preliminary theory." Jens glanced at Hinnerk, who stated: "That he found another way is a certainty. He has access to powers that let him command the sea itself." The monks gasped and Brother Tennus coughed: "Impossible, boy! Only God can divide the sea... Not even at the height of their powers were the sorcerers able to work such a miracle. The ocean bows to nobody but God himself. Everything else is blasphemy!" Abbot Wynfried called the agitated monks to order and folded his hands in prayer. The friars calmed down again.

After a minute of silence he finally spoke: "I don't detect any lies in their words, Brother Tennus, so kindly forgive the harsh words, Mr Janssen and Mr Wiards." Jens stopped him with a wave of his hand: "Don't worry. I can hardly believe it myself." Wynfried's smile was weary: "My brothers and I are deeply aggrieved that the old evil can reveal itself again. We thought it was all over and done with. But evil never dies if one doesn't vanquish it completely. I sense that you aren't telling us everything you know. But do I also sense that you have valid reason not to?"

Hinnerk swallowed and said: "We do." Abbo Wynfried continued: "Well, so be it. We Benedictine Brothers of Marienkamp shall help the people of this land in any way we can, as God has decreed is our task. In commemoration of St. Boniface and St. Liudger who should be our role models in our battle against the pagan witchcraft. May the Lord be with us." The monks nodded obediently. None of them were keen, but each was convinced that they weren't alone against such work of the devil. That God would guide them. Brother Tennus got up: "We shall need a lot of holy salt and holy water. It is also important that we rehearse the liturgies of battle to disperse the pagan chants and magic with our voices and our unshakeable faith." "Very well, let's get to work, brothers. Strengthen your souls and prepare yourself in prayer." Thus Abbot Wynfried ended the meeting and ordered food and drink for the guest – fish braised with herbs and slightly sour wine.

Meanwhile the monastery became a hive of activity. Marienkamp's previous sedate peace had abruptly vanished, as if somebody had roused a busy beehive. Their meal finished, Jens and the others went to the inner courtyard, where Wynfried was mobilising his troops, and asked him: "Do you know of a way to remove the soulkraken that's torturing this man?" For the first time Theo looked interested again. "We need to know if there is a chance of healing because a valued friend of ours is very probably also afflicted with such a creature. We would like to help him before it all ends in his demise." The abbot understood: "I'm impressed that you're concerned about your friend. Very Christian of you. You'd be best advised to consult our Brother Saltpeter in this matter. He has extensive knowledge of pagan witchcraft and its alchemical components. I'm sure he'll also be able to prepare a mixture for you. You will find him in the herbarium. Brother Witzelt will escort you there." Wynfried had such an aura of authority, strength and tremendous knowledge, it surprised nobody that he had been elected as abbot at an extremely young age.

The novice took them to the remote herbarium where the old monk Saltpeter was crouched on a stool in a room chock-a-block with shelves, bottles, dried herbs, mortars and pestles. In his mid-fifties, his grey, shaggy hair formed a semi-circle around the back of his otherwise bald head. His left eye was blind; its pupil white. Before anyone could ask, he explained in a croaky voice: "It was a seagull. We were arguing over a bundle of glasswort. In the ensuing fight I nearly lost my eyesight, but the seagull starved to death, ha, ha..." He turned around and gazed at the strangers through his remaining eye: "What is your concern? What did I hear about Radbod? Everyone here is suddenly talking about all that ancient history." Jens explained the situation while Brother Wizelt at the door was waiting and silently chanting to himself. Brother Saltpeter patiently listened to their story before examining Theo's soulkraken with his experienced hands. "You managed to acquire a particularly nasty specimen, young man." "Can you remove it, monk?" Theo growled. "We shall see, lad! Who knows? First I shall have to find some writings about it. Nothing like this has happened for hundreds of years. A rat may have shat on the appropriate page and the leaves may have decayed." They anxiously waited in the stuffy chamber while Brother Saltpeter combed his shelves and rummaged through pages of ancient scripts. Jens felt a bit queasy, but surprisingly alright. At last the quirky monk deposited a dusty folio on the worm-eaten table: "This should be it!" While they were waiting Hinnerk and Jens looked at each other and grinned. The air was imbued with narcotic substances.

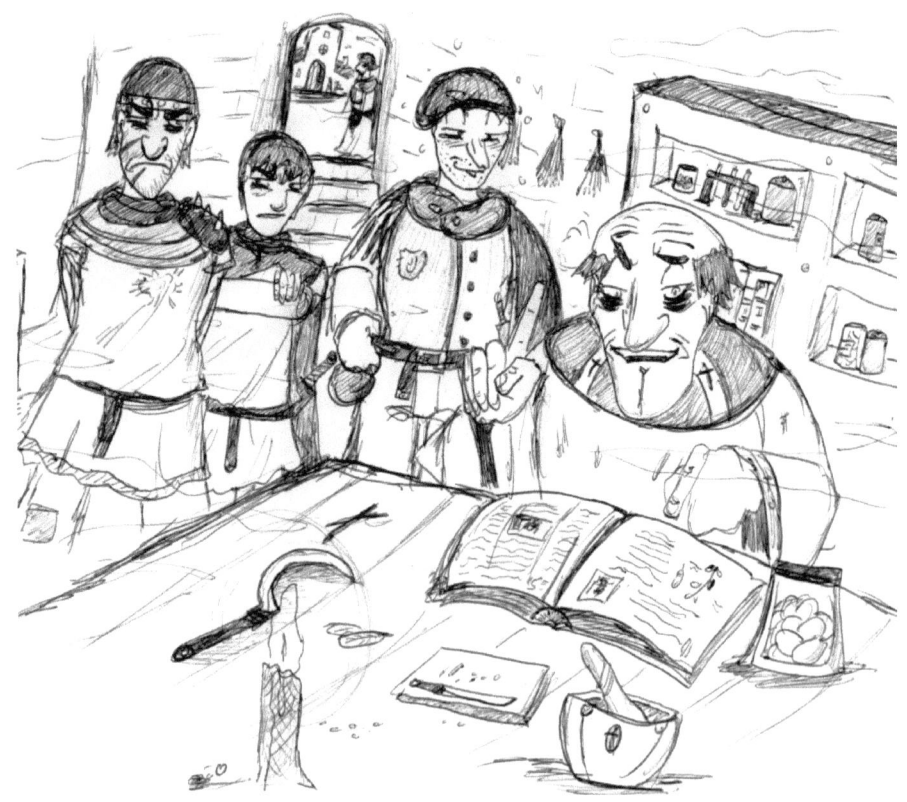

"Aha!" said the monk finally and clapped his hands, waking his audience from its semi-slumber. "There's something written here!" "What?" Hinnerk asked excitedly through watery eyes. "What does it say?" "The recipe for giving you the runs! Works extremely well if you're constipated. Your trousers won't ever be the same after. Marvellous! I've been looking for that. It also makes a good addition to stink bombs. Throw one of those behind the enemy's line and see how they scatter!" Theo rolled his eyes and pointed to the kraken: "That's just great, but how do I get rid of this, old man?!" "Of course, sure! Annoying little creatures, aren't they? Attached right to the heart... It can only be shaken off through inner strength. It's the only way." Hinnerk asked: "Don't you have a holy blade or something like it, so we can simply cut it away?" "That would also tear out his heart, his rips and his lungs. No, no! If we use force, the creature will get its teeth in even deeper. Furthermore, the connection to Radbod can be reactivated at any time..." Hinnerk whipped out his dagger and stepped back from Theo: "Shit!" Jens was still grinning woozily: "Could be worse, Hiiinni, could beee worse." Saltpeter's chuckle revealed several gaps in his teeth: "That shocked you, hey? Ha, ha! If there really still was a connection, he would have gone up in flames the minute he stepped on monastery grounds." Theo was aghast: "Now you tell me?!" The friar shrugged his shoulder: "Consecrated ground is denied to the undead. This applies even more so to the pagan undead! But we can safely guess that Radbod is too far away to re-establish contact. Did you know that soulkraken are parasites that attach themselves to the organs of large whales to feed themselves? But they also attack other animals and with humans they usually cling to the heart. Must taste particularly good, I guess. During the absorption process they produce a metaphasic field which is used by pagan scholars to manipulate the victim's mind. It's like the kraken becomes part in a chain of command." Jens was trying to digest what he had just heard. It took him a moment while neither Hinnerk nor Theo had understood any of it. Jens slurred "Um... um... does that mean youuuu could also use the kraaaaken? To control Theo?!" "In theory, yes. Master Beanpole. But the Church forbids such practices. Especially since the animals are hard to catch and the side effects are too great. To this day, however, some pagan sorcerers use it to impress people. But the masters of this kind of mind control were and are the Norse priests and their gods. The old Vanr Njord, in particular, has a soft spot for such tricks. They say that the Draugr were solely his creation." Hinnerk put his dagger away: "Be that as it may, but what can we actually do if we can't chop the creature off?" Brother Saltpeter moaned: "Give them patience, Lord! One doesn't achieve great things with great force, you doubters! It's occasionally enough to just give things a little nudge to start the ball rolling. The rest will take care of itself." Theo nodded: "Nudge me, so. I'm ready. As long as I get rid of the damned thing." The monk grabbed a few leaves of silver ragwort and other ingredients, shredded them, ground them in a mortar, boiled them and ended up with a glimmering, green, distilled liquid.

"We better go outside. It's always quite a spectacle..." They followed Saltpeter into the yard. Some monks, who were busily storing their equipment on donkey carts, eyed them with interest. Saltpeter placed Theo at a safe distance from everyone else and the pirate asked: "Should I be worried?" The friar shrugged his shoulders: "Only if you are not a true believer in Christ. But you are, aren't you?" Theo growled: "Is there... no other way?" Saltpeter didn't honour him with an answer. Instead he held Theo's nose closed. "Open your mouth!" The pirate had no choice and the monk poured the liquid down his throat. Theo coughed and spat: "What a disgusting, bitter brew!" As fast as he could Brother Saltpeter ran over to the others and shouted back: "What's bitter to the palate is good for the stomach!"

Theo clicked his tongue to get rid of the taste: "Oh, yuk! Well, I don't feel a thing... Are you sure that...?!" Suddenly a blaze of light blinded all those present and a passing peasant who just happened to glance at the monastery tripped and landed in his own pigsty. The bang was so loud and violent, it made all the bystanders lose their balance and the abbey's bells started to ring. At the same time, Theo roared with pain as if somebody had removed the abundant hair on his butt with hot wax. The blast subsided again and he stood there with smoke fuming from his mouth. Then he keeled over. Everyone ran up to him, lifted his shirt and the soulkraken did actually loosen the grip of its tentacles one by one until it dropped off – dead. Saltpeter quickly stuffed the corpse into a receptacle: "I'll have to take a closer look later. It's not something you see every day." Jens commented: "It's all yours. Is Theo... dead?" The pirate was no longer moving, but Saltpeter explained: "He isn't. Had he been a heathen, he would have burst. Somebody must have thrown him into the baptismal font when he was little and mumbled something about God. That's what saved him. But his reaction was still more intense than expected. The man must have sinned a lot and forgotten to go to confession for quite a while."

Jens's head slowly started to clear: "Did you cleanse him from his sins? What kind of a concoction was that exactly?" Brother Saltpeter explained: "It was an elixir of purifying substances. The bitter parts activate the body's natural decomposition juices aided by the holy salt and holy water. Personally I like to add a little blessed ash of martyrs. The process is commonly referred to as purification; a cleansing of the soul." Hinnerk asked "Does that mean his body rebelled from the inside?" "That is what happened. Not just his body, but his soul, too, rid itself from the kraken's poisonous influence. Now he is free of all his evil, sinful thoughts." Jens frowned: "That's easy. Why don't you give your concoction to every villain and they automatically turn good?" Brother Saltpeter lifted his cane and hit Jens on the head: "You oaf! This specimen here won't change from Saul to Paul through having imbibed the brew! The effect is only transient. It does purify, but after a while the filth in body and soul accumulates again. Look at it as a new start. It's up to the individual to use it wisely. But most immediately revert to their old ways. Apart from this, the potion is difficult to prepare and the ingredients very costly..." Hinnerk understood: "Not everyone can afford it, right?" Saltpeter nodded: "Absolutely, lad. But in situations like this, I deem it appropriate. Usually only wealthy nobles buy it to alleviate their guilty conscience. A massive waste, if you ask me. It doesn't really change anything in the long run." Jens pondered: "A potable confession? Well, I never..." Saltpeter corrected him: "It's no substitute for a confession. In their dreams! I'm not going to charge you and you can keep the rest of the stuff for your loyal friend. It should work on him as well. Provided he has been christened." Hinnerk pointed to Theo: "That's great! You can keep him in exchange. Let him do the donkey work like cleaning the privies or whatever." Abbot Wynfried joined them: "You have been successful, as I can see. Well done, Brother Saltpeter. And don't worry about Driftwood Theo. We'll find plenty for him to do. He won't get away from paying for his crimes that easily."

Hinnerk stowed the vial away in his belt bag and Klütje yapped. "We should make for Esens now," Hinnerk suggested, "Pugnose may have already returned." Abbot Wynfried blinked and pensively pulled at his beard: "I know that name well." Hinnerk confirmed: "Yes, Malle Pugnose. He's a fisherman from Esens. We asked him to inform the Frisians of Radbod's plan and to prepare for battle." Wynfried agreed: "A wise decision. The more men we can muster, the fewer casualties there will be. But there's somebody else you could ask to come to our aid. People who don't dwell far from here, but who are not our biggest fans. I'm referring to the Arians, the last remaining Chauci. The Falcon Warriors from the settlements around Werdum." Hinnerk knew about them.

The Chauci occasionally came to the market at Esens. They were Arians and believed in the Christ of the Cross, but not in the trinity of the Father, the Son and the Holy Ghost. Originally the Catholic Church under the Pope had wanted to ban their faith and persecute their adherents. But the result was a bloody war in the name of the Lord. To maintain the peace in the realm, the emperor at the time issued a decree whereby the Arians were allowed to keep their religious convictions as long as they acknowledged the Emperor as their supreme sovereign, the way the Frisians had done. Of course, this was based on power politics as the Arians recognised the emperor, but not the Pope, who couldn't excommunicate them. As such the emperor always had the Arians on his side in case of feuds with the Church. These were not infrequent, especially under the reign of the Hofenstaufern emperor Frederick the First, called Redbeard.

The Arians were composed of the remaining Germanic tribes which were official allies of the realm, but had stayed independent from the Church. Amongst others these tribes were the Chauci, the Langobards and the Franks as well as the Early Saxons, the Bavarians, the Engers, Westphalians, Thuringians and Hessians. Just like their forefathers they lived in villages and communities, in open holdings and loose federations. The monks of Marienkamp were in no position to win them over as allies.

The Chauci only just about tolerated them and had a justified aversion to the Church because it kept trying to find reasons to convert the independent Arians to true Christianity, and not always by fair means. Abbot Wynfried was only too well aware of the fact when he finally said: "You should go to them. Their Hauptlinger Tjarko is a reasonable man. I wish we could have a better relationship, but politics dictated by the hierarchy make it difficult. We are lucky that the bishop in Emden thinks along similar lines. It assured us many years of peace." Hinnerk and Jens were ready to try their luck and said their farewells to the monks.

After having left the abbey, a visibly exhausted Okko was riding towards them on his horse: "There you are! Malle Pugnose told us everything and I rushed over as quickly as I could. Why didn't you come to us right away? Are you okay, Hinni?" Hinnerk nodded: "I'm fine but there was something else we had to take care of first. It could save uncle Abbo's life." Okko turned to Jens: "You must be Mr Janssen. I am Okko Wiards." They shook hands and Jens smiled. "Good morning, Mr Wiards. I'm Jens Janssen, merchant from Greetsiel and somehow involved in this whole affair." "Just like the rest of us," Hinnerk explained. "We still have to visit the Chauci to win them over as our allies." Okko took a deep breath: "Your mother is sick with worry. The Gobold attack upset her more than any of us. You are coming home with me now. Abbo's already lost and I won't allow my eldest to throw himself into one act of madness after the next. You've done your bit. Let others take over now." Okko grabbed the boy's arm and was about to pull him onto the horse.

But Hinnerk shook him off. "How dare you defy your father?!" Okko flared up. Tears in his eyes, Hinnerk roared at him: "Abbo is not dead! He's alive! And so is Leevke! I'm not going to sit around at home waiting for something even worse to happen! I am a Frisian, just like you!" Okko didn't know how to react. The ensuing awkward silence was disrupted by Jens: "Forgive me, Mr Okko, for barging in, but this young man and the good Master Abbo have helped me to get my ship back. I couldn't have done it without them. I have experienced the dangers at first hand and I understand your concern about your son. But I feel duty-bound to do everything within my power to avert the threatening disaster. If you insist, I shall pledge my life to guarantee Hinnerk's safety. At least as far as the Chauci are concerned." Jens intimated a bow and Okko finally released the boy to shake the merchant's hand: "Very well then, Mr Janssen. Please take good care of him. I'm counting on you... You know the way, Hinni; we've been to Werdum before." "I do, father." Okko continued: "The Chauci are a different breed of people and quick to draw their weapons if they feel disrespected. But Tjarko is pretty reasonable." Hinnerk wiped a tear from his face and Okko said: "But come straight back if you don't succeed with your mission. Nothing is worth risking your life for, Hinnerk. Nothing! Not even Abbo, as much as I hope that he's still alive."

Jens suggested: "Why don't you come with us, Mr Wiards?" "I don't have the time. I'm now in charge of our defence and everybody trusts what I tell them. The story about Radbod is actually true, Hinnerk, is it?" "Oh, yes, it is. He will come, I'm sure of it." Hinnerk's father turned his horse: "You know one doesn't call the dyke watch for no good reason. How many soldiers should we expect do you think?" Jens explained: "They're not soldiers. It's more like an undead army of Radbod's old followers. We can't give you any numbers." "Hm, he will hardly come alone. Very well. We shall meet in Esens, at Attena's place two days from now. Farewell until then and I wish you luck!" Okko rode away in the direction of Esens while Jens and Hinnerk went east towards Werdum.

Jens sighed: "Off to the next shemozzle, hey?" Hinnerk was already striding ahead. "Hey, wait for me!" Hinnerk stopped: "Thank you for speaking up for me..." "A purely egotistical move. I didn't want to face the Chauci on my own." Hinnerk slapped him on the back. "You are alright. Come on." They were on their way.

At first their journey led them through the fertile marshlands, with their swaying golden fields of rye, followed by a bleak forest. Hinnerk knew that the main Chauci settlement of Werdum was located right behind it. The path was getting progressively worse the closer they got to the forest. The afternoon sun shone above them through the trees' rustling abundance of leaves and cast fluttering shadows on the two wanderers. Twigs noisily broke under their boots. Jens talked incessantly to calm himself: "The woods always have something creepy about them, what do you think, my boy?" Hinnerk agreed without turning around: "True. It's creepy alright. A lot of creatures may be hidden here: Gobolds, Pyrks, Fenna, lindworms, boars..." "Li... lindworms as well?" Jens asked, starting to panic. A bead of perspiration was trickling down his face and he smiled nervously: "Do you mean those poisonous worms with claws and scaly skin thick as chain mail? Please tell me they don't exist around here." Hinnerk elaborated: "Don't be too sure. Just two weeks ago a group of three adventurers passed through here. From Nuremberg they were, judging by their accents." "That's quite far away." "Adventurers, as I said. Anyway, they went into the woods to hunt the wolves that had torn Habbo's sheep apart. There was a reward for their pelts. But none of them was ever seen again." Jens gulped: "Well...?" "Well, that wasn't strictly true. One of them still made it as far as Esens. Covered in blood and pale as a ghost, he was. He dragged himself up to the bar and wheezed: "Its claws tore my friends to shreds! It was a Wyrm. It puked poison all over me and then..." With those words the man keeled over and died on the spot, foaming from his mouth. Ever since people avoid the woods and rather go the long way around. That's the story." He looked at Jens: "You look a bit pale, Mr Janssen." "Are you surprised after all those horror stories you're concocting. Mind you, the path is really not that pleasant. Perhaps we should..." Hinnerk peered behind Jens, panic written in his eyes: Oh, fuck! Don't move!" The boy slowly drew his dagger and took the shield from behind his back. Jens was petrified, not daring to breathe. The loud roar of a beast startled him and he cowered whimpering on the ground. Something stung him in the back "Oh! I've been hit! I'm dying!" He was rolling from side to side when Hinnerk's broadly grinning face appeared above him. Jens squinted his eyes a few times before he realised that Hinnerk had just royally taken the piss. He jumped up: "You... you miserable little snotbag! That wasn't funny. I could have had a heart attack. Unbelievable!" He frantically looked around. There was nothing; only Klütje happily barking and wagging his tail. Jens accusingly lifted his finger: "You just made it up, didn't you? All that stuff about lindworms." Hinnerk crossed his arms behind his head and laughed "Maybe... Ha, ha, ha... But a good few people have actually disappeared in these parts and something is definitely lurking around here. Perhaps a fanghound or a shaderunner, who knows? But they only come out at night and avoid the paths. Ha, ha, it's really easy to scare you, Master Janssen." Jens brushed himself down and turned up his nose: "Master is the keyword here, young man. I'm supposed to mind you, and I could do without that kind of carry-on. Phew! Oh, dear! I think I'm going to faint. My heart! It's all too much. Too many pirates. Too many undead. Too many Radbods. And too many kraken. And tentacles. Too much!"

Hinnerk continued walking: "I don't believe it! I just had a little fun to disperse all that gloom and then I have to listen to your nagging!" "Nagging, he calls that! I'm slowly starting to understand your father. You could badly do with some discipline!" "Ha! Why don't you join forces? But I'm not going to change, no matter what! You're like an old fishwife. You just have to blabber all day long!" "F... fishwife? Who, may I ask, did the blabbering about lindworms and the like, hey?" The two of them were too engrossed in their quarrel to notice that they were being watched. Two pairs of dark eyes had spotted them and followed them while hiding behind the bushes. Only Klütje sniffed, his tail alert, and raised his paw. But Hinnerk hadn't noticed the dog's warning signals in time when suddenly a man with a bird's head barred their way with a feathered lance. Jens grabbed his heart: "Ohdearohdear. Raven men?! Fantastic!" Hinnerk screwed up his eyes: "You're wrong. They are Chauci. Their symbol is the falcon, not the raven." "I'm not really all that familiar with..." Hinnerk's hand instinctively went for his dagger, but Jens quickly stopped him: "Don't. Let's not provoke them unnecessarily!" The merchant gasped when he turned around to see another bird-man with a seax sword, ready to strike, right behind him. "Speak," said the man in front in a young, muted voice: "What is your business in the land of the Chauci, travellers? We don't know you." Hinnerk was about to answer him, but Jens quickly took the initiative and stepped forward. He sensed that a little charm and good manners might serve them well. His trader's instinct had taken over: "We apologise for our unannounced arrival, valued Chauci gentlemen. My humble name is Jens Janssen, merchant from Greetsiel. And the boy over there is Hinnerk Wiards, son of Okko. We extend our greetings to the valiant Chauci and we come in friendship and with honourable intentions. We are here to talk to your Hauptlinger as representatives of the Frisians. Our cause is of paramount importance and concerns us all, you too." "What cause?" the young bird-man asked. Jens sighed. "The old Frisian king Radbod wants to return." "He's long gone. And dead." "That's what we also thought until recently. But I saw him with my own eyes. He wants to come back and we very much doubt that he will bow to the Chauci. To avert the danger facing all of us, we have to work together. We therefore humbly request an audience." Hinnerk nudged him: "You didn't have to say humbly." "Quiet!" The two bird-men retreated to confer. At some stage the one with the lance stretched out his arm for a falcon to land on it. The young Chauci fed him something and then placed him on his right shoulder. Hinnerk whispered to Jens: "Still, well done. I wouldn't have been able to express myself that elegantly." The bird-man with the lance and the falcon on his shoulder took off his mask to reveal a youngster about Hinnerk's age. He had vivid, grey eyes and dark blond, shoulder-length hair combed to the side over his ear. "I know Okko Wiards well. My name is Hauke, son of Tjarko. Follow us. We shall take you to Werdum." So they did and Hinnerk murmured: "So that's Hauke. I know him from way back. A stuck-up twit, he is." Jens instantly got it: "I take it you share a previous history." Hinnerk screwed up his nose: "Let's say we've had dealings before." Jens left it at that. He only hoped that whatever had happened between the boys in the past wouldn't have a negative effect on their negotiations. The Chauci seemed a pretty tense kind of people if they already felt threatened by innocent travellers. Previously he had only heard of them when he had been detained by a storm on the Chauci island of Wangeroog. It was said that the islanders there were governed by a *dune queen*.

Ursula was brooding over Leevke's unconscious body lying on the altar. Eight steadily burning candles were symmetrically correct arranged around the girl and kept her in a twilight sleep. A purple gleaming magical bubble created by Ursula protected Leevke from outside stimuli that could have woken her. Ursula knew that the girl, if fully conscious, could no longer be relied upon to help after what had happened. It made just as little sense to implant Leevke with a soulkraken as she had done to Theo. That way she would be able to control the girl's body, but even Ursula herself had only minimal abilities to adequately direct Leevke's powers. It was as if trying to recognise colours with the help of a blind person. The kraken-witch felt the enormous power inherent in the young girl and the possibilities and sheer force made her shudder. The potential to flood entire regions and drown them in the sea. Somehow she had to milk that potential. Make it serve her like a magic well.

To that end Ursula performed a ritual while Leevke, enshrouded by the bubble and the candles, was unaware of what was taking place. The energy required for the sphere was supplied by Ursula's own strength. She controlled every movement inside it, as well as each physical or supernatural pull. The room was abuzz with pagan powers. The tower itself was trembling right into the depths of the ocean. When she had finished, she picked up her scythe-wand and walked through the bubble without touching the girl. Thus the wand gathered some of Leevke's strength and darted through Ursula's fingers straight into her body and mind. A current like that produced by an electric eel made her fall to her knees. Her legs felt like jelly and her breathing was shallow. Bathed in sweat, her eyes were torn wide open like those of a startled animal. She felt like a weightless ghost and giggled while gripping her wand as she had never before. Her skin was covered in goose-bumps: "That was incredible. The power! And it was only a fraction, I guess. Wow!" Still slightly dazed, she got back on her feet and left the chamber to join Radbod on the platform. Surrounded by his armoured skeletons, he was gazing south at the mainland. She stood beside him and extended her hand towards the mist-covered sea around Bant. Radbod watched her in silence. A huge water-tentacle emerged from the ocean, rose higher and higher until it bent down in front of Radbod's face. Ursula laughed as the tentacle burst and drenched Radbod in seawater. She chuckled: "Ups, sorry... But it's working! I can tap into her! At last we shall be able to return. To feel solid ground beneath my feet! I missed it so much..." Radbod nodded grimly: "Very good, Ursula. Once we've ousted the Church and slain her disciples, the Frisians will revert to their old faith. Proud and brave they will reclaim their lands, as has been their right from time immemorial. People everywhere will be inflamed and cast off the shackles imposed by Church and kings. From Frisia the fire will spread to all the oceans and from the coasts it will reach inland. Until all of Altera is free." "The gods are with us," Ursula said dreamily and longed for a touch or at least some attention from the man she loved. But Radbod's gaze was firmly directed at the mainland; his mind purely focused on the still distant goal. A skeleton came up from down below and shuffled over to them. In a clipped voice with a hollow, ghostly echo it said: "Shippps arrrrived. Wanttt to talkkk to my kkking." Radbod replied: "Thank you, old friend. That will be the reinforcements. They will fight side by side with us or perish." Ursula asked: "And what's happening with Theo? Can you still see him in the distance?" Radbod narrowed his eyes and listened inward. Eventually he said: "No. I've lost contact with him. I guess he's bitten the dust by now. No great loss. We've found a far better replacement. A real Frisian." Ursula felt a long forgotten thrill of anticipation rising inside her. She had never regretted having committed herself to Radbod. It had been the best decision she had made in her life. Back then she had been demonised as a witch and nearly killed by a crazy missionary if it hadn't been for Radbod, who had rescued her. She had never forgotten and she still loved him, despite all the hardships she had endured. And that for more than 300 years. Even the undead around her, Düll or the signs of the time could not change that. Radbod carried an air of the heroic and victorious. There was good reason that the Frisians hadn't forgotten him. For them he was a symbol of resistance against oppression and slavery even long after his banishment. Defying all the abuse and ridicule of the Church that discredited him and aimed to malign him as a pagan butcher. People respected his integrity and belief in more in-depth, ancient rights with which he fought all injustice. He was as much of a hero to his people as Charlemagne was for the Franks or Widukind for the Saxons. Radbod still had sympathisers among the Frisians, particularly in rural areas where the old rites and traditions had prevailed the longest. He was glad that they still governed themselves and were not the subjects of feudal lords. But the fact that they had surrendered to the Church was the beginning of the end in his eyes. He saw the insidious decay of just those virtues that for him represented everything Frisian: big-hearted kindness rooted in freedom. Without that freedom there was no strength and therefore no kindness or a united people. Those who were left were distrustful schemers, liars, confidence tricksters and hypocrites. Nobody regretted having to fight against his own people more than Radbod. His grimness was nothing but deep-seated worry and anger about the bitter necessity. The Chauci, too, were Frisians, even if they didn't call themselves that or considered themselves to be. Aeons ago they had voluntarily converted to Christianity. Radbod could only attribute it to the Arian faith not imposing any fat bishops or the Pope on them. They were left to worship this Jesus person without anyone being able to exert their power over them. That's why Radbod had tolerated the Arian faith in the old days. It didn't interfere with his own beliefs and didn't challenge the Frisian Freedom. But now he thought differently. The harmless Arian faith was the foothold the Church used for its violent entry into Frisia where it spoiled everything that was good and just. Furthermore there was the incessant whiney and cowardly twaddle about original sin and eternal damnation which had always grated on Radbod's nerves. It was pathetic and only encouraged the mentality of future slaves instead of free, upright men who lived, fought and died for home, family and comrades. The Nordic gods were more honest, had their flaws and were more human overall. They could be just a cruel as they could be benevolent, expressing their displeasure or approval through storms or plentiful harvests. But they didn't demand total submission, just mutual respect. And if they made mistakes, they were also punished for them. There was no perfection. But the god on the cross wasn't accessible. He was distant and arrogant. His moral superiority was aped by his priests who emitted the same putrid, insincere stench. Obsessed with power and psychotic, this god was even effective in his excesses against the Egyptians whose defenceless, first-born children he had massacred instead of fighting openly and honestly.

Radbod knew these tales of horror and could only laugh when the priests told him about God's love and mercy. What derision, what a two-faced, hypocritical brood of vipers who shamelessly paraded as his friends when they were actually his enemies. It was never very long before those frauds, shamming love, advanced with force to put the "arrogant Frisian" in his place who openly revealed their lies and exposed them for what they were. The Franks were the Church's willing troops and conquerors. Their example made Radbod realise what could become of a once honourable and proud tribe. At this stage the Franks were no more than slaves whose inner Christian perversity now directed itself against women, old people and children with incredible cruelty. And while their missionaries slew the Oaks of Peace and preached about God's mercy, their henchmen raped young girls, tortured children and jeered while they kicked the elders and their wisdom into the dust. They destroyed the farms and the next day promised better roads and a great economic upswing. A golden age feasting on innocent blood. The Frankish traders were immediately granted special privileges to attach themselves to Frisian soil like festering sores. Hereafter their guilds mercilessly condemned every local artisan to poverty unless he joined them voluntarily. It was irrelevant if his work was of a higher quality, in fact that was even rather disadvantageous to preserving the peace within the guild. The Frisians were promised that their rights, the Frisian Freedom, would be respected, but ultimately it was the feudal lord who made the decisions at his own discretion and according to his mood. The court hearings were a farce. Only intended to preserve appearances; reminiscent of a lifeless ghost.

The incredible privileges of these people, so deeply anchored in their black hearts, were repulsive beyond measure. Even without a war raging and all they had to worry about was re-educating their new children, they had to instil their poison into them. Ursula had witnessed such educational methods first hand and still wept when she recalled all the terrible suffering inflicted on the children in the name of freedom and the Church. Each minute sign of self-reliance and healthy insubordination – so typical of children – was beaten out of their heads with the scourging reminder of God's love until they were silent and numb to the daily miracles around them. Just as vacant as their parents, their young lives sacrificed to a distant, cruel god. It was a system of destruction.

Ursula had often asked herself what kind of people were capable of such cruelty. Her only explanation for such perfidy was a deep-seated self-loathing of their own wretchedness which manifested in atrocities towards other people who weren't as cruel. They had to be slain like rabid dogs. They were beyond rescuing. Those people wouldn't rest until the whole world would resemble their disturbed psyche. Would be a desert of desolation; a virtual hell on earth. No more joy and all justified rage stifled into resigned monotony over the years, until everyone was numb and only felt alive when they turned the violence against themselves. These people did exactly what they pretended to prevent.

The Frisians weren't aware of any of this; they believed themselves strong enough to resist the Church. But this was a deadly fallacy; the poison was spreading with each day. The Frisians didn't think about the long term while the disease spread, weakening their healthy bodies unnoticed until their bones were sucked dry and any serious exertion would break them.

Radbod said: "I shall welcome our guests. Be ready, as we discussed." He went down to the eastern part of Bant's beach on his own to see two armed men coming ashore. They jumped from a longboat adorned with a viper's head and several round shields. The taller of the two was in his mid-twenties and bald-headed with only a tuft of hair left on his forehead and two braids of hair each dangling from his temples. His face was clean shaven apart from a moustache. Beside him stood a stocky, muscular, scar-faced warrior, carrying a drinking horn as well as an axe and a shield. On his head he wore a simple iron helmet with leather covering and his broad face was also adorned with a bushy moustache.

The younger Norseman nodded at Radbod: "I am Rörik Klaksson and this is my servant Karl Ole Brand. I am the leader of three longboats and two knarrs with a total of 142 men. The other ships are anchored by Heligoland so they won't be detected by the Frisians." Radbod replied: "I am Radbod of Bant, king of the free Frisians. You have received my message, as I can see?" Ole Brand smirked. The aura of death surrounding Bant didn't seem to perturb him and he just growled: "We were anchored at a fjord in one of those boring swamps when the campfire started to talk and we heard the voice of a wanton wench telling us to come here. We thought the mead had gone off, but apparently that wasn't the case. I lost the bet." Rörik Klaksson took a bow: "We offer you our support, King Radbod, as you requested." "What do you demand in return?" "Well, on the one hand we would be delighted to fall in battle, so the Valkyries can take us to Valhalla as true warriors. On the other, however, we still have to attain glory here on earth which shall endure for a while, if you know what I mean." Radbod understood instantly: "You want land." Rörik confimed: "You say it. Less than thirty years ago my father was given this land as a fiefdom, but the Frisians unlawfully chased him away. We now demand this very fiefdom as a reward for our services." Radbod narrowed his eyes: "You misunderstand my intentions, Jute. Frisia will retain its freedom and nobody will have feudal tenure!" "Rörik looked grim: "In that case we won't come to an agreement." Radbod held him back: "Nevertheless, I could do with some help recapturing my domain. There would be new posts assigned to abolish the remnants of ecclesiastical and secular power. At least for the time being." Ole Brand hissed: "Secular power? Isn't that what you represent? As king of the Frisians? Where's the difference?" Radbod gripped his seax more tightly while the wind was rising. "I am the king who was elected to save the realm from its doom. I don't attribute my reign to some god or bloodline like all the others of your bastard kings who enslave the people. In my Frisia nobody will dare to elevate himself above others. As soon as the old order has been restored, I shall be able to abdicate and die in peace." Rörik und Ole Brand withdrew to consult. When Rörik came back, he said: "I am risking my man for a precarious venture. What concrete power do you possess, Frisian King, who isn't actually a king?" Radbod smiled grimly and his voice echoed far: "Ursula! Show them! Show them what power we have." With a seething sound the ocean itself rose and lifted the longship into the air. Two strong kraken tentacles whipped out of the water and grabbed Rörik and Brand, tossed them about like toys before they could reach for their weapons. The rest of the kraken's body was now partly revealed while an army of skeletons jumped from the keep and the walls and arranged themselves in perfect rank and file. No less than five hundred soldiers filled the beach. Radbod announced: "These are my loyal followers. I can raise three times as many and more warriors from the depths of the ocean, impervious to arrows and spears. The sea god Njord is on my side with his champion Düll!" The slimy knight landed beside him on the sand, unharmed after having jumped from the very top of the tower. Radbod grinned: "I need you less than you need me, Rörik Klaksson." Rörik cried: "Okay, okay – we have an agreement!" The kraken released the two ashmen, who plummeted onto the sand, and retreated to his place beneath the island after gently replacing the longship on the water. Radbod and Rörik shook hands and the latter seemed extremely shaken: "Give us the sign and we shall go into battle with you! My fleet is at your command, King Radbod." "Good. I intend to use you on a special mission. You shall be able to prove your expertise in looting the hinterland. Just make sure to have a constant fire going on your vessel so Ursula can keep you informed. That's it." Rörik gulped: "As you wish, King Radbod." The Vikings went back to their longboat and rowed back out to sea – perhaps a little more frantic that usual. Radbod couldn't help chuckling and returned to the old fortress with Düll.

The village of the Chauci was located on a mound surrounded by a sparse forest. In the days of the Frisian king the coastal strips and the islands had been the last bastions where those who sympathised with the pagan faith still found allies. The people of Esens were believed to be the heirs of the ancient Frisians who had lived here before the great migrations, before the dykes had been built. They preferred to keep to themselves and were regarded as eccentric and reclusive, headstrong and with a coarse sense of humour. The Chauci themselves still practiced the Arian, early Christian faith and were solely accepted and protected by the emperor in whose view they were as much citizens of the realm as anyone else, as long as they paid their tributes and rendered their services to the Crown. Of course, the Catholic Church only tolerated all this with reluctance and kept trying to missionise the Arians to accept the Holy Trinity. They had never succeeded. Because the Church itself owned holdings and was entitled to the lands they were trying to convert to its faith, they also had a major economic interest. The old tribes were therefore valuable allies for the emperor and, steeped in their bellicose Germanic traditions, also strong warriors who he could count on as brothers in arms. Should the emperor be excommunicated again someday, the Arians would care just as little as if the same fate befell themselves. They would stand by the emperor because the pope had no authority over them whatsoever and the emperor protected their special status. But from time to time many a militant bishop was infuriated by this open rebellion against the ruling forces, as had happened in Stedingen. It was a kind of mutual assurance against revolts and enemy alliances.

The Chauci inhabited the Wangerland and parts of Östringen and were distantly related to Edo Wiemken, the Hauptlinger of Jever. The small island-kingdoms of Wangeroog and Spiekeroog also belonged to their sphere of influence. The Chauci adorned themselves with falcon feathers and their shields and helmets were trimmed with the birds' beaks, wings and claws. Each one of their warriors kept his own falcon as a hunting companion he could also employ in battle. The tradition originated back to the times when they still hunted swamp creatures in the marshy coastal regions. Although the Chauci deferred to the general laws of the dyke, they still built their settlements on top of the actually obsolete mounds. However, since the dykes were liable to break, the time-honoured method of erecting their dwellings served them better than the Frisians who thought such precautions excessive because they fully trusted the dykes. Even in Roman times the Chauci had been regarded as a reclusive, peace-loving people engaged in trade and livestock breeding, especially horses. Like all coast dwellers, who had to move across fenlands and marshes, they were well trained in the use of slingshots and notably various pole weapons such as spears and lances. Therefore the Frisians also referred to these spear warriors as porcupines.

Hinnerk and Jens were escorted to the village square and the people greeted Hauke with enthusiasm, but were met with nothing but aloofness on his part. He acted as if this were a precarious, deadly-serious affair whereas Jens clearly noticed that the Chauci of Werdum were not remotely as unfriendly or distrustful as people said. Their girls giggled when they saw Hinnerk and the old men chuckled through their curly beards and silently welcomed them with a nod. Hauke stopped outside Werdum's central warehouse. "Wait here!" Jens and Hinnerk stayed were they were with the other Chauci warriors until the chieftain's son re-emerged; slightly embarrassed, judging by his demeanour. "Come in..." Inside the house, behind a central fireplace sat the strong, broad-shouldered Hauptlinger Tjarko in an armchair. His bulbous nose and shoulder-length hair conveyed the impression of a military yet kind man. Hauke took up position to his left and fed his falcon while on his right a woman in her mid-twenties with a pointed nose and short hair with red stripes from her forehead to her neck bobbed up and down with a smile on her face.

The Chauci of Werdum: Hauke, Tjarko and Kea, a.k.a. Woodpecker

Tjarko indicated for Jens and Hinnerk to come closer: "Step forward, Frisians. Hauke has told me about you." Hauke said "Pay proper homage to the lord of Werdum!" The sharp-nosed woman rolled her eyes and mumbled: "Sensitive as a grumpy Pyrk Tze!" "You stay out of this, Kea," Hauke hissed at her. Jens smiled and was about to kneel down, but Hinnerk's refusal made him hesitate: "I bow to nobody! I am here as a free man. Or am I a prisoner?" Hauke erupted: "This is Hinnerk Wiards, father. He'll only cause trouble. I know him. Always ready for a fight, he is, the..." Tjarko's thundering voice shut him up: "QUIET!!" A general silence ensued before he continued: "I believe we should introduce ourselves before we go for each other's throats like a pair of fornicating lindworms, okay?" Tjarko got up and circled the central fireplace. After sternly eyeing Hinnerk and Jens he said: "Hi, I'm Tjarko, Hauptlinger of Werdum and leader of the Wangerland Chauci. And I'm not a king who needs to be bowed to. I am the one who does what needs to be done to protect his people. If that deserves homage, I do not know and don't want to know either." He smiled and pointed to his two counsellors: "This is my rather hot-headed son Hauke, whom you have met already. Forgive him his brusque manner; he is a sceptical fellow. As he has to be. The lady beside him in the feather dress is Kea. She is our Harugari. Most people call her Woodpecker." The woman indicated a curtsey: "You may call me that, too." She grinned at Hauke who shamefacedly avoided her gaze. "So you are Okko's boy, Hinni?" Tjarko mused. "And who is your tall friend here?" "Jens Janssen, Master. Pleased to meet you." Tjarko shook their hands in turn: "You are not my prisoners, young Wiards! You are my guests. Heda! Bring us food and drink. Soon after Hinnerk and Jens were seated and handed plates of stew with bread and small ale. Tjarko asked: "You say that Radbod has returned?" Jens swallowed a bite: "That's right. I saw him with my own eyes." Hauke huffed: "Radbod can't come back. Every child knows that!" "But now he has the means to do so, don't you understand?" Hinnerk retorted. Hauke exclaimed: "Where is your proof? I bet this is one of tom Brok's schemes to distract us, father. Edo warned us this might happen." Hinnerk replied: "Proof? What proof do you need? An army of undead soldiers? A kraken flying into your house?" "Nothing but empty words!" "Not empty words. This is about a devious bastard like Radbod who nobody expects!" "You are lying!" "Ha! You wish!" Jens nudged Hinnerk and Tjarko pulled Hauke back. The merchant sighed: "It appears these two have some unfinished business?" The Harugari Woodpecker smirked: "Oh, it's nothing much worth mentioning. It only concerned the Princess of Wangeroog: Mayla. A good-looking girl, I admit." Jens looked at Hinnerk: "I see! That was your problem. Interesting. A girl, hey? I wonder what Leevke would have to say about that..." Hinnerk turned as red as a beetroot. So did Hauke, who said: "Th... that was a long time ago and has nothing got to do with now!" Woodpecker shrugged and chewed on a piece of pear: "Of course not." "It's true!" Tjarko rubbed his nose with exasperation and smiled: "That's what I have to listen to all day long, Mr Janssen. Woodpecker teases and Hauke reacts." He laughed out loud: "Strangely enough, it kept my spirits up all those years, their stupid bickering! Ha, ha, ha!" Jens enquired: "Are you going to help us, so? The monks from Marienkamp will also be there, if that's a problem..." Tjarko waved him off: "Let them. As long as they don't try to convert us, I can live with their presence. Radbod...Ummm... I still think we should consult our Harugari before going to war. It is our custom and who am I to break with it?" Kea wiped her hands on her breeches and smacked her lips: "Shall I prepare everything for a little presentation of my skills?" The Chauci Hauptlinger nodded: "Please do, Kea." The woman jumped up, held her back with a moan and then skipped out of the room. Jens frowned: "Is she slightly confused...?" Tjarko smiled indulgently: "She sometimes gives that impression, but no. She is special and not just because she is a Harugari." "What exactly is a Halli-Galli? Is it something like a Deel-Deern?" Hinnerk wanted to know. Hauke was patronising: "How ignorant you are!" "Enough, Hauke, you'll see the Princess Mayla again soon enough," his father stopped him. The young Chauci shut up and Tjarko explained: "The Deel-Deern are only the leftovers of the old Frisians' Harugari. They are maidens and women who look after the community's spiritual wellbeing, act as midwives, introduce young men to the arts of love and make herbal potions and remedies. All these tasks have evolved from the Harugari. They are the last remnants of magical powers in our ranks, of ancient pagan tribal rituals and the conjuring magic of our ancestors..."

They waited until the whole Chauci village had assembled in the great hall and a large cauldron had been hung over the fire pit. Soon the hot water inside it was bubbling away. Kea re-entered the hall with firm steps, completely wrapped in her feather-coat. For a while she stared into the fire in the middle of the room and quietly hummed an old melody. Everyone watched her spellbound and huddled closely together. Kea produced a bag of herbs and added the contents with elegant, elaborate gestures to the cauldron while circling it. She threw back her hood and moved her head from side to side. The atmosphere had become silent and reverent - even the children were quiet, their eyes wide open – so Jens's murmur could clearly be heard to his instant regret: "Oh my, that beak is huge..." He was referring to Kea's pointed nose he hadn't noticed before. All eyes were abruptly on him and Kea also lifted her head, squinted in his direction and accusingly raised her finger: "That's rich, coming from someone with like a schnoz like yours!" Now it was Jens who blushed amid the general giggling. An old woman beside him commented kindly: "That's why we all call her Woodpecker. She's got her nose in everything." The Harugari was now kneeling in front of the cauldron and had scooped some of the brew into a wooden bowl. She slurped it down with her eyes closed. The flames crackled while everybody was eagerly waiting for her proclamation. Kea mumbled something nobody understood. The old woman resumed her explanations: "That is the language of the dead. She is now talking to the spirits of our ancestors." Jens and Hinnerk winced as the flame changed to blue and bathed the hall in an eerie light, casting wild shadows.

The Harugari opened her eyes, but only the white was visible. The Hauptlinger regarded her through the blue flame and she spoke with a deep, echoing voice that didn't match her effervescent behaviour at all. "The Frisians tell the truth – The king is returning – The army of the kraken strangles the stone bear – No prayer can tame the sea – The falcons have to fly – Itching skin penetrates the shield – The ocean is restless and raging..." The Woodpecker's voice got louder and she gasped: "The ocean is raging! It is raging! The sea is rising. Higher than all mountains and walls! Screaming! Frozen in the ice! Coming from the beyond! Older than any graves! The screams break the dykes! Devour the mounds! Thousands of corpses drifting in the still waters, their faces turned down! Contorted in a scream!!" She slumped down with a cry and sank to the ground. Hauke came to her rescue and pulled her back up on her feet. Nobody dared to say a word. Some had tears in their eyes. Kea's slowly came to, sweating, trembling and breathing heavily. "I'm alright." Leaning on Hauke she pointed to Hinnerk: "You have to save the girl from the ice, boy. Only you can do it." Hinnerk stared at her and rose: "I shall save her. I already promised..." Tjarko was also supporting the Harugari: "What did you see, Kea?" She shook her head: "There was a flood our dykes couldn't withstand... Radbod comes and the dead are floating on the water." A murmur went through the crowd: "The storm tides." Tjarko handed the Woodpecker a goblet with elderberry juice. She grimaced: "He is determined to destroy all those who carry the cross. Including us. His patience is at an end; his revenge hotter than any fire." Tjarko pensively lowered his head: "Rest now, Kea." He turned to the congregation: "Our forefathers gave us these visions to warn us, but also to encourage us. We have to take up our spears and shields to face the enemy even if it means our doom. Mounds of earth alone won't deter him, as little as it held back the Red Terror or Klak. If we now hesitate and wait there will be another bloodbath. I won't let it come to that. Long enough we've been hiding in the hope that this cup will pass us. But it never happened. So we shall face this enemy! Call all the soldiers to arms and only leave a handful here to protect our village from looters and wild beasts. Hauke, you shall lead the defence of Werdum in my absence. This also includes the other settlements under my protection. No arguments! It's a great responsibility and I'm counting on you. Should we fail, it will be up to you to save what can be saved." The young man nodded grimly although it was plain to see that he would prefer to follow his father into battle.

Tjarko whipped out his seax and held it into the flame: "Let's fly, my falcons, with sharpened claws on broad wings! We are nobody's slaves and kick anyone's arse who thinks he can lord it over us. If humans, spirits, ghosts or demons, yes, even the world itself, we shall rather die than kiss the feet of those who threaten our children with chains. But we shall be victorious!" The people roared their approval at Tjarko who affirmed: "A hunting we shall go, friends. God gives us his blessing." The Chauci men departed to get prepared. Tjarko went over to Hinnerk and Jens: "Well, you two, convey this message to the Frisian contingent: the Chauci shall join the alliance against Radbod and fight at their side. For all our freedom!" Jens couldn't keep the sarcastic undertone out of his voice: "Great news! War! Just what I've always wished for." He didn't cherish the thought of the impending carnage. He toyed with the idea of following his mercantile instincts and simply abscond with his Lobscouse. He was already far too involved in other people's issues. It was never good for business not having any control over what was happening. Jens was a coward and not someone to wield his sword against the enemy. The thought of battle alone made him go weak in the knees. He had promised Okko, but he may have been a little too hasty. Woodpecker joined them, still pale: "Oh, it's the nose-woman. Are you okay again?" Hinnerk grinned. She grinned right back: "A man's nose is a sign of his pecker, little schnozzle." Hinnerk stuttered: "What a lot of nonsense. Ha! In that case you'd have a gigantic you-know-what!" She pointed at Jens: "Why don't you compare yours with your friend's to test my theory?" Jens intervened: "We're not here to compare sizes, Miss Woodpecker!" The Harugari cleared her throat: "You can't take a joke, can you? Never mind. Hinni, was that your name? What's they story about the girl on the ice?" Hinnerk didn't have to think twice. She must mean Leevke: "We haven't told anyone about her. How...?" "A little birdie told me... What's her secret?" Jens explained: "She's in Radbod's hands, that's all you need to know." Kea nagged: "Really? That's all I need to know?! If you are withholding information from me that is vital to the survival of the Chauci, people I helped into this world, then...!" Hinnerk reached a decision: "She can influence the sea. She has the power. Is that enough for you?!" The Woodpecker looked right into his eyes and smiled: "Really? No wonder you want to keep that to yourself. But don't worry; your secret is safe with me, hehehe." She winked at him: "Little schnozzle." "I don't have a little schnozzle!" Kea ignored him: "I know what I'm talking about. I saw one growing up, right, Hauke?" The young man, who was talking to his father, looked up: "Is she talking rubbish again?" This time Woodpecker winked at Hauke: "I love this boy. Watched every step of his growing up. But you, young man," she addressed Hinnerk, "have slightly bigger nostrils – which is a sign of another characteristic..." Jens interjected cheekily: "The subject seems to fascinate you, madam." Woodpecked cleared her throat and continued in a more serious fashion: "If Radbod has found a way of using the girl's power, she may have to be eliminated..." Hinnerk growled: "Never! I'd rather eliminate you!" "It's only a figure of speech, calm down. All I'm trying to say is that everything hinges on her. I know a little about pagan witchcraft and I'm aware that they had the means of extracting the life force from their victims through a magic bubble and to use it. Unless the girl voluntarily...?" "Never!!" "Then you have to burst the bubble to rescue her." Jens asked: "How are we supposed to do that? Burst it with a spear?" "Not quite. It has to be the wand of the sorcerer who created it." Hinnerk clenched his fists: "I shall take care of it." Woodpecker pursed her lips: "Let's hope so, boy. Here, have some of this soup." Jens glanced at the cauldron that had facilitated Kea's vision: "You can eat that?" "It will bring you closer to the spirit world and make you more resilient against their influence. Everybody here eats it." She gave Jens and Hinnerk a bowl each of the concoction. It tasted very bitter. The Woodpecker laughed: "Hauke used to pull a face just like yours, hehehe!" Hinnerk, Jens and Klütje took their leave from Tjarko, his son, the Woodpecker and the villagers and returned to Esens. Time was of the essence and they weren't even sure that the Frisians would send their contingent. They may end up marching against the undead with just the Chauci and the monks...

Ursula had grown up as an only child in the little riverside village of Tjølling on the southern coast of Norway. People had noticed very early on that she possessed a talent for pagan sorcery and could communicate with the dangerous trolls who frequently pestered the surrounding homesteads. Turida, the local woman adept at interpreting the runes, soon took it upon herself to instruct Ursula in her skills and direct her talents in constructive ways. Ursula herself was a rather thin and pale girl with dry lips, greasy hair and tired blue eyes. Like so many other villagers, her father was a whaler. Blubber, oils, whale meat, timber from the dense forests as well as the rare ambergris had made the village reasonably wealthy and its inhabitants saw little reason to jeopardise their sales outlets in the land of the Angles or the southern realms of the continent through raids the way other Norsemen did. Although she had been spared the condemnation of the Church, Ursula never had access to her peers. The boys found her quite interesting, but mystical, while the girls were jealous of her special station and bitched about her behind her back. At some stage all of them – even the boys – called her greasenoodle and sweathead because of her constantly greasy hair, which even the rune-sayer with all her herbs couldn't cure. But because none of the parents wanted to fall out of favour with the old pagan powers, they punished their offspring for blaspheming the soothsayer or her disciple. But this only aggravated the animosity and made Ursula even more unpopular although she always endeavoured to please everybody and fit in. She hadn't chosen her gifts and she only did as she was bid. Reviled by her peers, she felt more and more drawn to the animals whose benefits and therapeutic fluids she had to learn about from scratch. The sensitive Ursula didn't have the heart to kill the animals. Although she could gut their carcasses and cut them up, the killing itself held such horror for her, it made her blood boil and she had to throw up. The old witch often gave out to her, but even when Ursula could get over herself, she spat on the entrails, thus rendering them useless. Of all people her father, the whale hunter, showed some understanding for her reservations. For him she would always be his little girl and somewhat more sensitive than other children. Alas, he was rarely at home.

Ursula's mother, however, placed great value on her family's reputation within the village community of Tjølling and urged Ursula to integrate herself more in order to consolidate their standing in the society. It was good to have a future rune-sayer in the family. The village had unwritten hierarchies and to be held in high regard was of some importance even if every Norseman called himself free and independent. Someone with a tainted reputation was avoided by the others, effectively shunned, and didn't profit from the many advantages the community could offer, be it favours or presents. Whoever evaded the rules wouldn't survive for long. At least not at the standard of living the village enjoyed. The acquired prosperity needed to be maintained and enlarged against the surrounding settlements. The Norsemen had always considered themselves to be industrious traders and even sailed up the Dnieper as far as Constantinople and along the African coasts. They also kept slaves and serfs, called thralls, and their raids of the coastal regions of the Western Sea and the Baltic continuously provided them with new supplies. So Ursula eventually found herself not only helping people with their daily minor ailments, but also brewed the berserker potions that made the warriors wild and temporarily unbeatable in battle, carved runes onto the serfs' bodies that lent them greater stamina and crafted necklaces made from bone that could be sold as lucky charms. She also learnt to perform rituals to ensure fertility and a plentiful harvest. The old rune-sayer Turida consigned an increasing amount of responsibilities to her and at some stage Ursula no longer dared to contradict the grim woman. She silently endured the growing demands on her and her heart beat more frantically at night. When she was less than thirteen years old, she increasingly dozed off. Dark circles appeared under her eyes, but nobody noticed. Everybody was far too engrossed in their own problems to recognise her silent suffering. Quite the opposite in fact. Because Ursula mastered everything asked of her and never complained, it was alright to exact ever more of her. Everybody had to make sacrifices; there were no privileges.

When her father returned from a successful trading expedition to the land of the Rus and brought back finely woven cloth for her thirteenth birthday, it slipped through his hands when he beheld how sickly and tired Ursula looked. At the next open-air council, against his wife's advice, he loudly voiced his disapproval about everyone having taken advantage of the girl. The air was rife with indignation as Ursula's father ranted and raved and most of the villagers wouldn't put up with the accusations. Despite the common affluence, the atmosphere had become increasingly rough as the weeks progressed.

It all escalated in a wild brawl on the market square where Ursula's father was severely beaten up. Witnessing what was happening, something inside Ursula exploded and her delicate body convulsed in spasms. With an angry scream she violently unleashed her magic power. Turida tried to stop her, but was also sucked into the vortex of timber and objects. In the ensuing tornado in the middle of the village the rune-sayer was also hit by a plank which shattered her head and arcane energies spread everywhere like bolts of lightning. When Ursula had calmed down again, Tjølling had been reduced to rubble. A lot of the villagers were injured, many a child among them. Ursula's father picked up his daughter, ran with her to the pier and urged her to leave the village in order to save herself. He wouldn't be able to raise enough money to pay the wergild imposed under Norse law for the damages. Ursula therefore had no choice but to flee in a small fishing vessel with some meagre provisions. She was meant to sail to friends in Aalborg and, thanks to the favourable winds, actually got there. Unfortunately a bloody feud was raging at the time she arrived. A band of strand warriors tried to drag her off the boat and take her for their pleasure when her screeching conjured up a young kraken creature that saved her, killed the men and henceforth never left her side. Scared to the bone she travelled down the west coast of Jutland and found shelter in foggy East Frisia where she aimlessly roamed about and supported herself through petty theft while her kraken hid away in one of the many small streams. She ventured as far as the settlement of Auerk, not knowing that she had thereby crossed an invisible border and entered the Christian part of Frisia. When she was caught thieving, she used her magic powers in her panic to defend herself. Blue sparks flung the sentry high up through the air and he died. Cornered and hungry, she threatened the onlookers with the same fate unless they would feed her. And out of fear of Ursula's powers, the people did. Ursula herself withdrew to the Ghastly Moors where her kraken was also hiding; a place where the Frisians didn't dare to venture because it was said that a shark-like creature was on the prowl. Ursula did, however, spy a few wild Gobolds, but they immediately took to their heels after she had lit a ritual bonfire. From then on she was supplied with food offerings every week and it would be a lie to say that Ursula didn't enjoy the comfort. For the first time in her life she was aware of her personal power and intended to use it solely for her own aims from now on and never let herself be exploited to other people's advantage again. She fed the kraken and it kept growing under her care. A Frisian Harugari once approached her to offer her help, but Ursula declined. She no longer wanted to "function" for others. She'd had enough of that. The Harugari left again.

A year later a Christian missionary called Keil of Aachen travelled through the country to spread his Christian faith. The people gathered around him and promised to convert if he got rid of the "Witch of the Moors". Keil was a forceful missionary, his eyes flaming with rage, who felt nothing but contempt for the pagan deities; shrugged them off as superstitious phantoms and condemned them stridently. Keil had cut down many a Holy Oak and knew how to entice believers away from their faith. Radbod was still the official king of the Frisians and watched the Church's activities in his lands with growing suspicion. He would never convert to Catholicism himself, but let everyone make up their own minds. He saw more and more churches and monasteries sprouting up everywhere and steadily gaining power while the old order crumbled. Eventually Radbod also heard that a witch was terrorising Auerk and so the king went to the town to clear up the matter and face the missionary as the earthly representative of the old gods. The people held out great hope for Keil, who blessed every one of them before setting out to the forest with his entourage to catch Ursula. Ursula was blissfully unaware of what was happening until they surprised her in her hideout. She tried using her powers, but Keil warded them off with a prayer to break the spell. "Do you see?" This is where the evil is hiding! Inside the body of a filthy and mad young girl! It's the devil's work. The force that holds the whole land in its deadly stranglehold! Crazy, scruffy, poor and contaminated!" Ursula's powers had never before deserted her and she panicked, fled, but tripped and was captured. Keil's men shackled her and exhibited her on the market in Auerk. Meanwhile Radbod had arrived and demanded to see the girl Keil so venomously accused with such eloquence to expose Satan's slyness behind the veil of her innocent appearance. The villagers did nothing to stop him.

Radbod approached the fiercely trembling Ursula: "What's your name, girl?" Ursula blinked: "My name?" "You're not from around here, are you?" "No..." "I can hear by the way you speak Tedeschi. You're from Jutland, am I right?" Ursula gulped: "Norsk... Will I die now?" Radbod looked at her: "Do you believe you deserve to die?" Ursula shrugged her shoulders: "I think so. I'm not made for this world... Everything is full of hatred and I just can't go on. I'm exhausted; only want to sleep. Is that wrong?" Radbod took a deep breath. He placed his strong hands on her face and stroked the greasy, thin hair from her tired eyes. "No, that's not wrong. You shall sleep as long as you like. You can lie down at my place and when you're rested enough, you can still kill yourself if you want." He smiled and Ursula stared at him. She was crying. Radbod unshackled her and took her hand to the consternation of the onlookers. "I shall take responsibility for the witch child. I shall settle all her debts including the wergild for the dead watchman in accordance with the old custom. Nobody has to die around here anymore." Keil of Aachen roared: "How dare you scorn the victims of this pagan fury by paying wergild?! You're going too far, Radbod. You're incurring the wrath of God and the Church if you continue taking the side of the heretics!" "Heretic?! You're calling me a heretic, you foul-smelling windbag? You cross-lovers come to my country, threaten me and my people with hell, suffering and death and spit on our old laws!" "We offer you salvation from evil!" "You are the only evil one around here, nobody else!!" Radod was furious and reached for his sword. The crowd backed off. Keil grabbed his missionary staff and his eyes narrowed to slits: "You raise your hand against me and there shall be a war that will destroy you." Radod wielded his seax: "Let there be war so!" With those words he thrust his sword through Keil of Aachen's chest, who bled to death on the square. Radbod had made enough concessions. Now it was time to separate the wheat from the chaff. He angrily declared open warfare on the Church and its proponents from then on and was sick and tired of the continuous back and forth between the fronts. He forced all those newly baptised to beg their ancestors for forgiveness and to scrub the baptism off with local soil. He also had their churches and monasteries burned to the ground and their valuables melted down. Ursula followed him wherever he went.

From then on she was constantly at Radbod's side and became his personal advisor, healer, soothsayer and lover. The once so apathetic girl literally blossomed and fully embraced her new role because finally somebody was taking care of her. Radod didn't force her to do anything against her will, let her choose for herself, something she had never experienced before. It was this open love, that didn't smother her with duties, which made her stay with him.

Radbod also longed for true feelings. He was fed up with the hypocrisy and lies of this world that had cost him so dearly. They confided in each other how much the betrayal of their families and alleged friends hurt them and held each other close while they wept in private. Gave each other support in a world that plotted against them. Outcasts, each in their own way. Ursula had her kraken brought from East Frisia to Dokkum and with its help Radbod was able to fend off a menacing fleet of crusaders from Gaul. The king was mighty proud of his little witch and together with the Frisian warrior Düll they fought the Church wherever they encountered it. At first they were quite victorious and dispersed the Church's heralds. For many years Frisia breathed easily and Radbod invoked the Magna Frisia, the Frisian Kingdom, the alliance of all free coast dwellers, at the Upstaalsboom. He had never been happier than in those days and Ursula had never felt as satisfied.

But the peace wasn't to last for long because Radbod's ruthless approach had been too late in some cases. Many a Frisian had fallen prey to the Church's doctrines and they conspired against him and the Magna Frisia in the hope of attaining salvation, economic clout and new landholdings. The Franks increasingly believed that Radbod's uprising had been the last rebellion of a once great predator whose time was up. Furthermore there was the new missionary Liudger, a wise, powerful, eloquent and most of all congenial monk. Where Radbod and Ursula incited the people against the Church, Liudger promised them peace and calm if they surrendered to Christ. He never exerted any pressure, instead he simply presented a friendly, nonbinding proposition. People started viewing Radbod as a warmonger with a personal vendetta against the Church who wasn't open to reason. He was, after all, together with a pagan sorceress. The incident with Keil had only been the last straw to break the camel's back. But those facts soon faded into insignificance because although Radbod had initially planned to renounce the rights the open-air council had bestowed on him, he now felt forced to keep them in the face of the Christians' imminent insurrection in his realm. He didn't want to risk and lose everything again. His enemies exploited his actions to portray him as a power-obsessed tyrant, thus triggering the inter-Frisian civil war. To begin with the Christian side was the weaker one, but they received massive military and financial support from the Franks. Because there had been a peace treaty, Radbod officially accused them of a breach of contract, alas none of his complaints reached its destination or was shrugged off as ridiculous and disappeared. Therefore Radbod couldn't really build on his earlier success and bit by bit lost control over the Magna Frisia which eventually completely collapsed in West Friesland.

Dokkum was burned to the ground and his family was scattered to the four winds. The missionary Liudger also pursued him in East Frisia and the holy man led the Christian army to Esens where Radbod had allied himself with the Chauci and was preparing for the last, all decisive battle. Ursula's magic was crushed by the power of the Christian god and when she fainted with exertion and Düll was mortally wounded, Radbod had to retreat with his ships to continue the battle from the islands which he thankfully still commanded thanks to the kraken. He sailed to Bant where a large fortress had been built from an ancient shrine. The Chauci had to surrender, but were allowed to keep their Arian faith. Liudger put a curse on Radbod and his followers so they could never again cross the sea and sacrificed his life to the spell of excommunication.

Without their leader the Frisian pagans' resistance collapsed albeit their traditions are preserved to this day. There was another Frisian king after Radbod, called Poppo or Bubo, but he was no more than a Frankish puppet to maintain the appearance of the Frisians' indepedence; not their last true king. When Poppo realised what was happening, that the Church and the Franks simply laughed at him, he drummed up the last remaining pagan resistance fighters and led them to the hopeless battle of the Boarn where they were defeated and the Magna Frisia was effectively wiped out. West Frisia was given to the Franks and East Frisia was regarded as barren swampland which was left to its own devices for the time being until they surrendered to the emperor later on in exchange for their independence and autonomy.

During all the time that followed Radbod and Ursula had looked for a way to get back to the mainland. Year after year the king had paced the shores of Bant, always with his glance directed towards his homeland. It was due to Ursula that they survived while Düll turned all his attention towards the sea god Njord in the hope he could carry them across the ocean. But apart from heathen magic and relative immortality, he was unable to aid them. Radbod's entourage didn't survive, but pledged their eternal loyalty beyond death itself. Deep inside their undead souls there still lived a vestige of their former glory.

Ursula sighed contentedly when she saw how the skeletons set the magic bubble holding Leevke into the ball bracket buckled onto the waist-high nomcrab. These crabs with their steely shells were placid planktivores Ursula found easy to control. The creatures fed on algae and sea moss and retreated into their shells when threatened. Despite their size, they were shy and were hunted for their meat and their shells. Because she couldn't take her altar with her, she had carved the necessary runes onto the nomcrab's shell so that it now functioned as a substitute mobile altar. This way the kraken witch could use Leevke's power everywhere she went, but not to its full extent – that would have killed her. A quick cut with her scythe-wand through the bubble sufficed for her to absorb enough energy to subject the sea to her will for a short while. No heathen magic Ursula had tried in all those decades had been able to break through Liudger's barrier. Leevke's power, however, was not of a pagan nature, but originated from realms utterly unfamiliar to Ursula.

Radbod felt confident when he had his undead troops marching up and down Bant's shoreline in perfect formation. From the sand itself emerged those who had been sacrificed to the old gods aeons ago and whose restless souls Ursula was giving new form especially for this occasion to fight again for their freedom. Their bones were shaped from vitrified sand and their empty eye sockets stared vacantly at the ocean. Soon the faint rattling of a thousand bony soldiers filled the air and escalated in a loud, nerve-shattering crescendo like the clattering of the giant mud shrimps in the tidal flats. The wind whistled harshly through their fleshless bodies, tore at tattered, washed-out robes and long faded clothes. Captain Düll distributed blades of stone and bronze, presents from Njord. Ursula couldn't help herself; just the sight of him made her shudder. Although he was Njord's champion and an ally, he was no longer the man he used to be. Back in his day he had been Radbod's right hand man, a feared, great warrior, hard-drinking, direct, rough and ready. Loud and crude, but rock-solid and honest. But since he had dedicated his life to Njord to become his voice and receive his divine strength, he had more and more withdrawn to the caves beneath Bant. Not even Ursula could see what happened beyond the black pool and Düll never talked about it. Radbod saw no reason to doubt his friend's loyalty; none whatsoever. The only thing one could criticise about him was that he wasn't as talkative as he used to be or no longer showed any human emotions. But if Ursula was honest with herself, the same applied to Radbod and even herself.

The years on Bant had taken their toll despite the mutual foresight with which they observed what was taking place in East Frisia. For years now Düll had been surrounded by a slimy aura and water was permanently dripping from under his helmet. Neither were his eyes still visible under his helmet, only a bubbling darkness. "How are the preparations progressing?" he asked Ursula, smacking his lips as he pronounced each word. Ursula smiled self-consciously but politely: "Very well, Dülly. I've loaded everything." Düll nodded slowly: "Very good. I have asked Njord for support. He will lend us some of his warriors." Again Ursula was glad to have Düll and Njord on their side. She nearly felt sorry for the Frisians on the mainland who had no idea what they were about to face – a war of liberation, the recapture of the old religious sites, the rise of the ancestral gods and their powerful following with the blessing of all their forefathers who had been forgotten, but would be remembered again. They were on their way. Radbod gave the signal and Ursula wielded her scythe.

Chapter 7

Better dead than slave

Hinni, Jens and Klütje returned to Esens to inform the Frisians who had gathered there by now that the Chauci and the monks were joining them. The town watch at Esen's palisade walls gruffly demanded gate money which Jens willingly paid before Hinnerk would lose his rag. The place was full of coarse men, laughter, drunkards and the sound of wrought iron being hammered. Jens was pleased: "It appears Attena will help our cause judging by all the activity here." Hinnerk turned up his nose as they made their way through the narrow alleyways. "That doesn't necessarily mean anything. Attena always prepares for battle. He's a pirate, a brigand and always organises raids into other territories. Not many do anymore, but he does." Jens surveyed his surroundings and perceived the scarred roughnecks, some of them toothless, who eyed them with extraordinary interest. He quickened his pace and checked his merchant's dagger just in case. They reached Attena's stronghold and were admitted after Hinnerk had informed them that he was Okko's son. They were led into the hall on the motte where Okko Wiards, Behrend Attena, Abbot Wynfried of Marienkamp, Friedhelm Nordendi of Norden and many others had gathered in the meantime; all elected leaders from the adjacent villages and most of them quite wealthy. They were assembled around a table, deeply engrossed in a discussion. Pugnose was also present and purposefully approached Hinnerk and Jens: "Thank heavens that you've come! It wasn't easy to convince these people, but luckily your father came to our aid. They didn't want to believe me at first. Laughed at me, the swine..." Jens said: "Greetings, Master Pugnose. Radbod won't simply disappear if he's being ignored. Believe me, I tried!" Pugnose forced a tired smile: "Well, Mr Janssen, that's what people are like. They can't imagine that a terror like that can happen on their own doorstep and pretend everything is alright until it's too late. Until a man with an axe kicks your door in and you can't protect your family anymore because there's nobody else around... I've seen it." Hinnerk snorted derisively: "I thought we Frisians would always face any danger without hesitation!" Jens scratched his ear: "We're not dealing with a raid by the people from Oldenburg or Hamburg or the ashmen. I can kind of understand that people here have their doubts..." Hinnerk shouted through the room: "But it's true! Radbod is coming! We have to fight! Now!" The crowd fell silent and made room for them to come forward. Okko nodded at Hinnerk while Behrend Attena's thundering voice roared: "I hope he is coming, for your sake, young Wiards!!" Suddenly Hinnerk felt quite queasy. Behrend was a giant of a man with massive shoulders, bursting with strength he found hard to control. Just a small blow of his could break a jawbone with ease. He was extraordinarily hot-tempered and not very well liked, even among the Frisians. It had been due to Okko that Attena desisted from looting the farms close to Esens. He respected Okko's achievements against the people of Oldenburg in Stedingen and had once had a scuffle with him. Since then a fragile peace prevailed and Attena restricted himself to attacking only hanseatic cogs and occasionally sailing to the land of the Angles to raid them in the Norsemen fashion. There had been several attempts to remove him, but nobody was able to capture his castle, particularly when Behrend had manned the battlements and flung huge boulders that crushed everything in sight, men and objects alike. Nobody in the whole of Frisia was able to compete with his brutish strength and tenacity. His thundering voice continued: "This funny abbot here confirms the story of Malle Pugnose and this boy here. I presume that means that God's on our side, or some such hogwash, am I right?!" Wynfried smiled sardonically: "That is exactly the kind of hogwash it is. And we shall face the enemy." Attena swallowed the mead from his tankard and smashed the vessel on the ground: "Aaaah!! Get me more! What about you, Friedhelm? What do you make of all this crap?!" The slight, shabby looking man in his mid-thirties with the short, grey-white hair, the grinning skull on his chest and the three-day beard smiled: "Well, if those Holy Joes are prepared to go to war, I guess we have no choice." Attena laughed out loud: "It's about time to smash your face in again, grinning death!" Now Nordendi also laughed: "Just you try it, Bear of Schmeer! May you get sucked into one of my bogs and beg for mercy!" Okko cleared his throat: "You'd better wait with all that until we've dealt with Radbod. Hauptlinger tom Brok will not send any reinforcements, at least that's what Keno tom Brok told me. As it happens Armin Harger and Edzard Allena are also feuding right now. Fockena is only interested in how he might profit and Lütje Lübben of Auerk prefers to reinforce his own fortress..." Pugnose asked: "How about the islands? Will they send help?" Okko ran his fingers through his hair: "They're too scared of being attacked to leave the islands unprotected. I fear we're on our own." The way Attena grinned now made Hinnerk feel uneasy. It was the face of a man who was looking forward to what lay ahead instead of being afraid. "All the more for us so!" Attena enthused. "I hear Radbod has tons of treasure!" Nordendi chuckled: "Do you actually believe he'll bring it with him?" "He'd better or I'll beat it out of him. Hahaha!" Jens leaned over to Hinnerk and whispered: "Can it be that they're both pretty crazy?" Now Attena also made everyone else laugh: "Let's find out if I can defeat Radbod with a couple of strokes!" Even Abbot Wynfired had to chuckle and Hinnerk smiled: "These are the best fighters in all of Frisia. Nordendi expelled the ashmen single-handedly and Attena is a law unto himself."

Hinnerk was glad to meet his father on the market square of Esens after the conference. Everyone was talking, drinking and laughing; presumably to disguise the general tension. Others, however, seemed as relaxed as could be, downright overjoyed even, as if they'd only been waiting for a chance to marsh into battle again. Okko exclaimed: "I'm relieved to see the two of you back again. And Klütje." Sniffling, the coast dog scampered around his feet. "I shall remain here to stave off any possible attacks to the hinterland." Hinnerk couldn't believe it: "You're not going to fight Radbod with us?" Okko nodded: "I am not. This is not easy for me seeing that I helped rounding up this bunch. But I have reason to suspect that Radbod is planning something treacherous. Abbo told me about Radbod's raids against the Franks and if we aren't careful he'll flank us and break through our defences. I want to support the main army from here and provide cover." He sighed deeply: "I presume you want to take part in the battle?" Hinnerk confirmed his fears: "We've got something to save Abbo and Leevke cannot stay even a second longer in the clutches of that kraken witch!" "Alright then. You're well able to take care of yourself. But should the battle take a bad turn, you run and mobilise the other Hauptlinger. Don't try to be a hero. That wouldn't serve anyone!" Okko put his arms around his son and hugged him tightly.

The sound of drumbeats and bugles echoed through the town. Okko observed: "It's starting. Attena and Nordendi don't waste time. Hey there, Mr Janssen!" Jens was in the process of trying to sell his beans to a group of oafish people from Esens whose demeanour implied they hadn't a penny to their name. He stopped and joined the group: "Yes, Master Wiards?" "I thank you for having taking care of my son." Jens stopped him with a wave of his hand: "Don't mention it." Hinnerk nudged him: "You're a chicken, but quite okay." Jens nudged him back: "And you're a nuisance, but quite okay."

He clapped his hands. "Well, I think that's it then for me. I'd be more of a hindrance than a help in the battle, ha, ha! I don't have to go to my Lobscouse in Bensersiel yet, so I shall stay here for a while and wait until it's over..." Hinnerk objected: "Don't you think that your magic book could be of use to us?" "That's on my boat... Oh, give me a second..." He fumbled with his belt and grimaced: "No, I brought it so that Radbod wouldn't get it... Damn!" Hinnerk patted him on the back with a smile: "Don't worry, you don't have to fight, but you may be able to contribute the decisive breakthrough when everything hangs in the balance." Jens commented sarcastically: "Either that or seal our fate forever when I make the skeletons a hundred feet high. Magic is like a Gobold on mushrooms: unpredictable and destructive." "You are not from here, Mr Janssen," Okko said. Nobody would blame you if you go home." Jens replied with a heartfelt sigh: "Just don't expect me to be a hero. I belong at the very back of the troops." Okko shook his head: "It's sometimes enough just to be there. I shall coordinate the defence from Ochtersum. That's where you'll find me if you need help. It will be our assembly point for any scattered troops should Radbod break through our ranks." They took their leave from each other and Jens and Hinnerk retired to a well-frequented tavern where Jens ordered two tankards of expensive ale. Hinnerk said: "Hey, Jens, if you find magic too unpredictable, why don't you acquire something safer?" "Like what? Do you want me to bore Radbod to death with my ramblings? The fellow strikes me as someone acting from conviction. I doubt negotiating with him would be successful." Jens noticed the friars from Marienkamp shyly huddled together in small groups as they faced the strongly armed men. Abbot Wynfried, however, knew no such timidity and was drinking with the rough and ready lads. Brother Saltpeter, a broad grin on his face, was chatting with the local Deel-Deern, a buxom lass in her mid-twenties with short brunette tresses. Hinnerk clinked tankards with Jens who asked him: "Have you ever lain with a woman, Hinni?" The boy nearly choked on his beer. "Wh... what?!" "That ale was expensive... Anyway, I just wondered, you know, if we aren't victorious it would be a shame never having had that experience." He pointed to the Deel-Dern; her broad smiled paired with her casual, affable nature enchanted any man longing for warmth and intimacy. But she was no competition for the local harlots because she only invited those men to her bed who for some reason or other were unable to overcome their inhibitions. The Deel-Derns were extrovert woman and young girls surrounded by an unsurpassed air of freedom, warmth and jauntiness. Every village had their Deel-Derns who were regarded as big or little sisters by the inhabitants, even by the women who looked at them as their friends with whom they could talk about everything. They were spiritual advisors, herbalists, midwives and guardians of ancient traditions. Hinnerk stared into his tankard and admitted sheepishly: "Dad... Okko already gave me the same advice. Not directly, but he hinted." Jens smiled and leaned forward "But now you have Leevke, don't you?" Hinnerk gave him a reproachful look: "I don't have her. She..." "...is just a friend, I know." Jens clicked his tongue and toppled over on his stool. He pulled himself up again amidst the general laughter. "For once I'm trying to be casual and then...!" Unmoved, Hinnerk enquired: "What about you, Jens?" "I have... well, a girlfriend." The boy couldn't quite believe it: "Really?" "So what? Is it that unusual for a grown man of my age?" "It's not. Is she pretty? Or..." "Pretty is relative. In my eyes she is more beautiful than anyone else. Her name is Taalke and she makes my life infinitely richer. I would love to go back to her and hold her in my arms. That's pretty enough for me." Jens dreamily leaned on the table: "With her I never discuss profit and loss, you know, don't argue about petty domestic matters and the neighbours' nagging... We've got an unspoken agreement, that feeling of profound harmony. I've seen tons of couple who constantly argue and never understood why. They either work towards achieving that same harmony or they can't stand each other. They may also not be the problem at all, but it's something that comes from the outside. If you're seriously looking for a row, you may just as well coat yourself in honey and run screaming into a bear's cave. It's faster." Hinnerk shrugged his shoulders: "A little spat now and again keeps romance alive, am I right?" "Sure." Jens set upright. "It's no different with Taalke. She can be just as stubborn as me. But there is a time for everything. A time to be angry. A time to be sad. A time to love, but also a time to laugh in the face of convention..." "Con... what? Hinnerk shrugged: "Jens clinked tankards again: "I know I'm waffling on. Must be that I'm scared. But don't worry. I'll think of something. Okay so, no Deel Dern for you then I take it?" Hinnerk lowered his gaze: "No, not now." Jens understood and patted his shoulder: "Not for me either lad." They finished their drinks and Jens joined the monks while Hinnerk took a deep breath and took out Saltpeter's green vial once again and looked at it. He held it in a firm grip: "Hang on there, uncle Abbo. I'll come to rescue you. Both you and Leevke!" He had sworn a solemn oath. Klütje beside him barked and jumped onto the bench. "Hey, little mate, I nearly forgot about you! You have to stay here and keep watch. Go back to the farm and mind the others. You'd only be trampled down in the thick of the fight."Klütje whimpered and Hinnerk held him close: "We'll meet again. I promise you!" The sound of a loud bugle from Attena's tower echoed through the alleyways and the army started moving towards the beach of Osterbense.

Bunting and flags in the Frisians' blue and white colours were fluttering in the wind making Hinnerk feel immensely proud. The Frisians had positioned themselves behind a wall of shields on the sloping dyke. Radbod would have to face the soldiers in an uphill battle. Though few in numbers, the well trained Chauci, under the command of their Hauptlinger Tjarko, secured the right flank with their falcon warriors while Friedhelm Nordendi and his cunning followers were positioned on the left flank armed with clay pellets as missiles. Between them stood Behrend Attena with his main force of belligerent soldiers. Abbot Wynfried and his monks blessed the warriors and stayed in the background to support them with their prayers and attend to the wounded.
The soldiers' wives helped the monks preparing herbs and poultices. Meanwhile the Frisians were waiting for Radbod's arrival on the beaches between Langeoog and Wangeroog. The weather, which had so far been quite pleasant, turned more stormy and threatening clouds now gradually covered the entire skyline like a shroud. The icy wind was howling from the northeast. It was quite a damp day and fog patches glided

eerily across the ocean, creeping forward like ghosts. Attena swore: "Curse that damned mist!" He impatiently fiddled with his heavy, rivet-studded club. Hinnerk, Malle Pugnose and Jens stood close to Abbot Wynfried. Malle had firmly grasped his net with both hands in stoical silence. Hinnerk was waiting for his chance to rescue Abbo and Leevke and Jens wasn't just trembling because of the freezing temperature. They had unceremoniously equipped him with a shield, helmet and lance so he could feel a little more prepared, but it only made him even more nervous instead. Every nerve inside him urged him to flee, but he was surrounded by men with grim determination. For the umpteenth time he checked if he really had the magic book with him. He intended to only use it in a dire emergency. Hinnerk had left Klütje behind in Esens, pampered by some pretty maidens who thought he was incredibly cute and never stopped petting him, because he didn't want the dog to distract him. Radod had defeated Abbo, so he couldn't take the slightest risk. Should the same fate as Theo's have befallen Abbo, the purification offered a fair chance of saving him. Hinnerk had wrapped the vial in a heavy cloth to prevent it from accidentally breaking in the thick of the fray. The plan simply had to work. But for now they could do nothing but wait. The men in the harbour started to quieten down now as thousands of eyes scanned the horizon for changes.

Finally, after torturous long hours, two reconnaissance vessels sent out to spy on Radbod returned with the incoming tide. The crew included a trembling Malle Pugnose who had volunteered for the mission. He and his fisherman pals were beside themselves and greedily drank from the water bags Attena handed them. "He's dividing the ocean! Radbod is dividing the ocean. He's not coming by boat, he's marching through the water!" The news spread like wildfire among the troops. Abbot Wynfried screwed up his eyes: "So it is true! The king has found a way to evade Liudger's curse. He couldn't cross the sea, but he can cross the dry ground beneath it. He just had to get rid of the water..." Attena roared: "Just get rid of the water?! Why didn't he run over during low tide then, hey?! Then it's also not an ocean! Only mudflats!" Wynfried shook his head: "Bant is located outside the mudflats on the Dogger Bank, Attena. The low tide is no use to him out there. Besides, he would never reach the mainland with his army before the high tide returns." Attena hissed: "Whatever. Let him get his arse into gear and come. We shall see that he gets a fitting welcome. I can't wait to taste blood again! BWAHAHA!" His men joined in his caterwauling which also spurred on Nordendi's and Tjarko's followers. They joined in as well, banged swords and lances against their shields and a deafening noise echoed across the sea. The high tide had swallowed the mudflats and broke against the shore. Between Langeoog and Wangeroog they could see a rift in the ocean slowly coming closer.

The Hauptlinger Tjarko, Attena and Nordendi

Radbod heard the jeering and howling of the Frisians and couldn't suppress a grin. His Frisians were apparently still game for a good old battle despite the namby-pamby teachings of the crossbearer. To his left and right the waters of the Western Sea rose like a wall and gave way wherever he stepped. Behind him, in perfect rank and file as usual, his undead soldiers marched in silence, led by Abbo with vacant eyes. The soulkraken had finally managed to break his will after all. The clatter and rattling of his three thousand men strong army was muffled by the roaring mass of water surrounding them. Ursula was riding on her kraken through the water around the rows of undead and repeatedly cut into Leevke's protective bubble with her scythe to feed on the girl's strength. The nomcrab marched beside the soldiers with the girl on his back in the magic cover. When the mainland eventually reached his field of vision Radbod was overcome by a longing and love for his native country he didn't realise he still possessed. "Home at last!" Before they had even climbed out of the ocean he could already see the army that had set its mind on challenging him. "Make room for me, Ursula!" Radbod shouted into the waves. Her voice answered him from every angle as if she herself were the sea: "As you wish, my king!" She sounded far more cheerful than she had for ages. Radbod walked forwards and smiled with his eyes wide open: "Forward and onwards! On to take a stand. On to free our land!" He held the pommel of his stainless Frisian seax Durjawer in an iron grip. They traversed the sea and Radbod positioned his army on the beach in a formation facing the Frisian/Chauci contingent on the dyke after Ursula had widened the aisle through the water and the undead had swarmed on land. From a distance one could have still mistaken the skeletons for ordinary, if extremely scrawny people, but every living man here sensed that this was not true, just an optical illusion. The fact that there was no sound, no noise emitting from the undead, conveyed the impression that they weren't breathing or had any other needs of living creatures. It was an army of ghosts. Abbod Wynfried, his monks and the priests who had rushed over to join them intoned prayers and their liturgical chants to assure the Frisians of God's protection and instil them with courage. Radbod looked grim when he heard them: "There they are already, hiding behind Frisian blood and mocking us, cowards that they are." Düll stood beside him: "Present them with our offer. We still have honour and propriety." Radbod took a deep breath and walked forward on his own, without cover or fear. The Frisians, who were ready with their missiles, hesitated and eventually Attena, Nordendi and Tjarko emerged from the troops to face him, keeping a respectful distance. Behrend Attena roared: "What do you want here?!" Radbod replied: "Isn't that obvious, Bear? I am here to liberate you."

Nordendi exclaimed: "Looks more like an invasion. We've had enough of those." "I'm well aware of that. I saw the ashmen and the Red Terror. But you are blind and don't realise the dangers threatening you from inside. The Church will be your downfall." Tjarko countered: "We stand by God and the Church is no concern of ours." Radbod nodded: "Typical Arians. It's to your honour that you managed to survive. But you, too, are mistaken. As soon as you show a moment of weakness, the Church will destroy you, Pope or no Pope. It's in its nature. All they know is misery and the cross. They pray to the god of suffering. They have lost their joy. Their whole existence is based on wretchedness and sorrow. It's sick. And everyone who follows their corrupt beliefs will end up just as miserable." Radbod pounded his chest and shouted: "Listen to me, Frisians! Free yourself from the yoke of oppression, from the lust for suffering! Together we can reclaim everything that's been taken from us and breathe freely again!" Attena leaned on his heavy sword, burped and said: "We've got the Church under control, Raddiboy." Radbod laughed:" "Ha! That's exactly what they want you to believe. But they infect your children, make them forget everything that makes us who we are until nothing is left but an empty shell and then nothing at all! They get into your very bones! You are struck with blindness. I can see the difference to the old days. Your Tedeschi already sounds watered-down; your dialect infested with Frankish tripe and phrases. It creeps up on you because you don't have the foresight, but I can see it clearly. I have the power to overthrow their god of suffering!" Behind him the sea rose to a wave twice the height of the dyke itself, a wave on which Ursula rode on the kraken, her scythe sword raised before she disappeared into the water again while the monster was wildly whipping the waters with its tentacles. The onlookers were immensely impressed and Radbod grinned: "You can't win!" Nordendi smiled: "Tohohoho – let's wait and see," and Tjarko contributed grimly: "We shall neither betray our God nor our people! We are one. Until the bitter end." Radbod concluded: "It's decided so. We are now at war!" Negotiations having failed, the leaders returned to their respective armies.

Meanwhile Hinnerk was on the lookout and shouted: "I can see Abbo, Jens! He's on their right-hand flank, which means on our left. It seems they really have implanted him with a soulkraken..." Abbo was in command of Radbod's troops' right flank while the left flank was headed by a slimy-green knight covered in ferns and algae. Radbod turned towards the dyke and gave the silent signal to attack. The croaking of three thousand souls and the sound of long rotted bugles made everyone's skin crawl. The dead army hadn't started to move yet. Instead another huge flood wave rose up and this time washed over the dyke. Like the jaws of a giant beast it threatened to rip a massive hole in the midst of the Frisian troops. The wave wasn't wide enough to engulf the entire army; Ursula's reach didn't stretch that far. It was a tremenduous pre-emptive strike and Brother Tennus was the first to realise: "That's no heathen magic! We can't stop them!" Behrend Attena was quick to react: "Build an embankment!" The thunderous tidal wave devoured them all. Without mercy the men were whirled around and dragged into the sea. Radbod slayed one of the Frisians floating past him and his skeletons followed his example. The corpses drifted out to sea. When the water receded from the dykes it was obvious that most of Attena's forces were still standing.

Only a few of them had been swept away because all the other men had grabbed onto each others' arms. Attena's and Nordendi's men as well as the Chauci, like a human web. The Frisians had frequently had to fight the tides in the past and knew that they could only survive if they stuck together. To this end they rammed their feet and spears firmly into the ground and held tightly onto each other so they wouldn't succumb to the tide. This ancient tactic the coast dwellers had perfected through centuries of floods, had once again saved them from certain death. Attena released Abbot Wynfried and spewed water: "Next time you better tell us in advance when you can't protect us, get it? That was too close!!" Wynfried himself was shocked: "Th... that's not normal. Where did Radbod get his strange powers" Attena growled: "He's got them. That's enough! Nobody else shall be flushed away next time, is that clear?!! But they are kind enough to grant us a little reprieve before it really starts, right? Right?!" The men's shouts endorsed him even more. Whatever people made of Attena, he certainly was no coward.

Jens, Pugnose and Hinnerk were also holding onto each other, but luckily they were on the safe left flank. Nonetheless Jens in particular was clinging onto the other two for dear life. Pugnose asked: "Are you okay, Mr Janssen? You are very pale." "I'm just a little scared of the water, that's all..."

Radbod was impressed: "We won't beat them that way, so. They're grabbing each other. Right, let's do it the traditional way. Abbo? Düll? Prepare to advance. I'll take the middle." At a hand-signal from their king the skeleton army marched rattling and clanking through the wet sand, their three generals at the front. Jens was trembling even more now: "I have a certain respect for the sea, lads. Well, actually I'm scared shitless. What just happened didn't exactly contribute to calming me down..." Hinnerk stretched his neck and hopped up and down to loosen up: "You're afraid of the sea, yet you sail on it with an old boat like the Lobscouse? That's funny." Jens said: "I love danger?" Hinnerk laughed: "You're my hero." He nudged Malle Pugnose who was ready with his harpoon and net: "This is what we do: I go and get Abbo and you keep ready in case I need you. Alright?" Pugnose nodded. They heard Nordendi's raucous laugh and his men brandishing their clay balls. "Tohohohoho! Break their bones, my friends! It's time for a massive bombardment again! Let it rain!"

Collectively the Frisians and the Chauci fired their missiles – powerful projectiles that smashed bones and skulls and were therefore highly effective against Radbod's undead. Some of them raised their shields to block the missiles which dropped onto the sand with a dull thud. Behrend Attena was in his element and effortlessly flung chunks of boulders from Esens with primeval strength at the ranks of the undead, crushing and breaking their bones. The skeletons screeched shrilly when they perished and emitted blue sparks. Ursula was close to the coast on the back of her kraken and caught the soul fragments with her scythe wand. With those fragments she immediately created new skeletons from the sand which picked up the old weapons and rejoined the battle as if nothing had happened. Soon the air was filled with the crackling and screeching of the undead. A surreal howling that pierced you to the bone.

Hinnerk ran towards Abbo who was leading the undead. Armed with the magic shield and his Frisian dagger Hinnerk took a last deep breath before he stormed through the battle line down to the shore. Friedhelm Nordendi cursed: "Hey! What's gotten into the boy? Stop throwing!!" Abbo didn't display any kind of emotion when he spotted Hinnerk. Instead he wielded Pakhaou. Hinnerk was able to fend off the first blow with Lux Maris. Abbo was fighting as well as ever and his blows were even stronger than before. In no time Hinnerk's arms were burning with overstrain. "It's me, uncle Abbo!

Hinni! Don't you recognise me?!" Abbo just grunted with a mad fire in his eyes and attacked more forcefully. Hinnerk received two further blows while Lux Maris vibrated like a bell.

Meanwhile the undead skeletons army approached the dyke. At least Hinnerk had succeeded in enticing Abbo away from the host. His uncle showed no signs of exhaustion and fought with the unfailing determination and stamina of the undead. The soulkraken multiplied his already great strength immensely.

Effortlessly Radbod dispelled the missiles aimed at him in mid-air with his seax. Even when Attena threw a rock at him, he split it with a single stroke and the two halves crashed to the ground. One of the Frisians murmured with admiration: "That's a true king..." Attena rewarded him with a heartfelt slap in the face. "Why don't you join him then and lick his arse, you loser?!" He gripped his cudgel with both hands and wheezed: "Right, let's find out how tough you really are, bonerattlers!!" The skeletons didn't storm forward the way a living army would have done. Unperturbed they maintained their steady marching stride even as the first hits of Attena's club send them flying through the air and scattered their limbs to the winds. The Frisian spears turned out to be mostly useless and the men quickly reverted to batons such as bludgeons. Now the familiar bashing, pushing and stabbing started. The undeads' movements were abrupt and seemed jerky as if their joints hadn't been greased. And yet they had the strength of grown men and their clipped movements irritated the Frisians as much as their silence which only ended in their piercing, nerve-shattering screams once they had been destroyed. Radbod effortlessly killed two Frisian warriors who attacked him. Their blood splattered everywhere and hit some of the skeletons who didn't even mind the warm blood in their eye sockets. Attena pushed himself forward: "Out of my way, you sons of whores! That clown is mine! Keep your hands off him!" With a roar he heaved his cudgel above his head and flung it at Radbod: "Let's have some royal stew!" The impact made the ground tremble. Clods of earth and grass rained like hailstones onto the battlefield. Radbod had dodged just in time and was now stoically standing a few yards away. Attena grinned: "The fucker's fast, isn't he?" Then the Bear ran forth and struck anew with full force. Radbod dodged him again, but this time by moving towards his enemy. Attena blinked with surprise when he saw the blade in his chest. Spitting blood, he laughed: "Bwahahaha! Well, well, well!" He lunged out with his right hand and slapped the king right in his face. Radbod stumbled back while dark blood trickled from his mouth. Attena pulled the seax out of his chest and threw it at Radobd: "Go on! Bwahaha! Keep on fighting! I haven't even warmed up yet! Let that red shit continue to squirt! BWAHA!" Radbod eyed him with the respect of a true warrior. It was good to see that there was still real strength amongst the Frisians and their blood hadn't yet been completely corrupted. It was wonderful!

The Frisians yelled loudly in view of the turn of events, seeing that some of them had believed that the Bear had been killed. They had lost their fear of the skeletons and threw themselves into the battle with renewed strength. Their losses weren't large; however, the undead army didn't seem to diminish as Urusla constantly renewed it. Attena forcefully kicked Radbod and the king fell down. Attena's cudgel quickly did its work. There was a loud shattering sound, the sand swirled up and obscured the vision. Once it had settled, Behrend Attena saw dozens of smashed skeletons in their battered armour who had protectively thrown themselves over their king. Radbod got up unharmed.

The Chaucis' right-hand flank was being attacked by Captain Düll and he proved to be just as skilled in battle. He swung his axe with his right while his left tentacle arm strangled his opponents to death. .His plate armour as well as his slimy cover protected him from the attacks which didn't affect him in the least. Although some of the clay balls dented his armour this didn't seem to deter him at all. The Chauci proved to be even better fighers than the Frisians on average. Especially the elite-soldiers with the falcon masks broke through the undead ranks and made the most progress. Ursula was no longer able to keep up. Tjarko tackeld Düll with his sturdy winged spear and wounded his kraken tentacle. Stinking black blood oozed out of the wound and the slimy knight mumbled through his helmet: "I could never stand you Chauci." Tjarko contentiously slapped his chest: "And that's not going to change any time soon. I promise!"

Düll versus Tjarko

Hinnerk lured Abbo to the top of the dyke and shouted: "Now!" Pugnose jumped out from behind his cover and threw his fishing net right over Abbo who got entangled and tried to chop his way out. Hinnerk jumped at him with a roar and toppled him over. Together they rolled down the dyke down to the beach. Hinnerk had to use all of his strength to keep up with Abbo. "I can't do it!" Hinnerk called out to Pugnose as Abbo reared up beneath him. Hinnerk felt his muscles being torn apart when two sets of arms grabbed the possessed Frisian. They belonged to Pugnose and Jens who now shouted: "Make him drink it!" Hinnerk grabbed Abbo's mouth in a stern grip and opened it. But his uncle roared like a wild beast, flung Pugnose and Jens aside and directed his sword at Hinnerk. The boy still managed to pry Abbo's mouth open and to ram the vial down his throat while he rolled to the side at the last moment. Abbo's sword missed him. "Get away from him!" Pugnose and Jens didn't need to be told twice. Abbo puffed and coughed and cut through the net. He took a step towards Hinnerk. Then he exploded in a blaze of light.

The blast made them all fall over as it had done during Theo's purification. Jen's face was covered with sand when he got up: "Gosh! Couldn't it be a little less dramatic for a change?" Abbo was lying on his back, his limbs stretched out and smoke fuming from his mouth. Hinnerk cautiously approached him to check his pulse. "He's alive..." Malle and Jens heaved a sigh of relief, laughed and brushed themselves off. Hinnerk wiped a tear from his eyes: "Thank you for coming to my rescue, Jens." The knight in shining armour waved him off: "There was nothing I could have done back there anyway. I was just standing around, shitting myself. I'm no soldier, so I thought I do what I do best: blindly bump into other people..." Hinnerk smiled: "Can you take him somewhere safe? I'm not done here yet." Jens nodded: "Leave it to Pugnose and me. What do you say, Malle?" The fisherman agreed eagerly and together they carried the unconscious Abbo behind the dyke to the baggage train.

Hinnerk put his dagger away and picked up Pakhaou. Just holding the sword from Satan's Bog again filled him with renewed confidence. He swung it around. The battle was well underway. Endless ranks of undead fighting the Frisian army of the living. Hinnerk searched the beach to find Leevke and discovered a small commando of skeletons in the shallow water. They weren't moving forward; instead they were guarding a heavy nomcrab with an opalescent sphere embedded in its shell. Ursula rode her kraken over on a wave and cut the bubble with her scythe. "Leevke must be inside it," Hinnerk thought and ran towards the crab, bypassing the battle and rows of undead. The closer he got, the more obvious it was – it really was Leevke floating inside the sphere, all huddled up, the way he had found her the first time...

The main army of undead was engaged in a constant back and forth of attack and defence with the Frisians and the Chauci. After having delivered Abbo, Jens stayed with the baggage train for a while. His work was done. Malle had rejoined the battle although it was no longer his war. But these men were also defending his freedom, even if he lived a bit further away on the western coat of East Frisia. Jens scratched his head: weren't they actually fighting for everyone in this country, for their families and friends and loved ones? Wasn't it everyone's duty to defend these important people? Or was all that talk about freedom only an excuse to protect one's own, less honourable interests: market shares, property and holdings. Not all the Frisians had shown up, so why should he care? He was just a merchant and all this was money-losing business. Jens clenched his fists. There it was again, that unbearable feeling of helplessness, being at everyone's mercy and ice-cold calculating. Would he ever be able to be the master of his own faith? Could anyone actually ever do that? Or was he like a piece of driftwood tossed around by the tides to amuse the higher powers? His rational mind advised him to abscond and the feeling in his bones and trembling knees endorsed the idea.

Tears welled up in his eyes as he silently removed himself from the baggage train and the scene of the battle. Each step felt harder and yet lighter at the same time. He hated himself for running away, but he was a coward through and through. So far this attitude had served to preserve his life the same way a woodlouse preserved its existence. A blood-spattered envoy rode past him and entered the baggage train. Shortly after he heard the sound of great lamentation. Jens hurried towards it and even from afar he heard the cursed word that unleashed fear and terror in all the coastal regions: "Ashmen! It's the ashmen!" The herald shouted: "They are attacking from two sides, trying to close in on us. It seems there are two groups; one went to Ochtersum, the other to Thunum!" The women wept and sobbed at the news. Frisian as well as Chauci mothers, daughters and sisters who would return to burned down homesteads and those they had left behind believing they were safe. Jens realised that the situation was worse than he had thought and that he now had to make up his mind. Did he want to help the father or the son? His mind was doing summersaults while escape tempted him with a syrupy grin. The chaos and burgeoning panic of the people paralysed his brain and he closed his eyes; suppressed the terrifying images and considered what to do next in the business-like way his uncle Ulrich had taught him. He made a mental inventory of his options and skills. There must be something he knew that might help. When he opened his eyes again a few seconds later he actually had a plan. He ran over to the monks, Brother Saltpeter, his target, among them. The friar had casually mentioned something before, but Jens realised it had been important...

Armed with the magic shield and sword, Hinnerk charged at the skeletons guarding Leevke. The nomcrab carrying her nervously scurried on its clawfeet as if it was going to make a run for it. Hinnerk's first blow met its target and severed the head of one of the armoured skeletons at the cervical spine from its torso which landed in the shallow water with a splash. Only now did the undead react and brandish their swords. Hinnerk was snowed under by a barrage of strokes he hadn't anticipated. One of the blows was even violent enough to make the edge of his own shield bash against his head. He instantly leapt back, spitting blood. "That must be their elite," Hinnerk thought. And indeed beneath their torn cloaks, the skeletons were draped in chain mail and ancient scale armour the likes of it hadn't been seen for 300 years. Their blades were just as rust-free and immaculate as Radbod's sword. Hinnerk threw sand into their grinning, bony faces, but they didn't react. Then he tried to entice the slower of the undead away, but the skeletons only followed him to a certain spot and couldn't be entrapped like Abbo. Hinnerk raised Lux Maris and shouted: "Kiss my arse!" A glaring beam of light shone onto the undead who screamed piercingly and scattered like somebody had upset an anthill. But still they kept bashing at Hinnerk who rolled aside to escape their onslaught. Apparently the undead were allergic to light and reacted with increased aggressiveness. Meanwhile the waves lashed higher and the sky was nearly black with heavy clouds obstructing the horizon. Hinnerk had also learned the art of wrestling from Abbo, a fighting technique using no weapons taught to every aspiring knight and page. Although he was no expert himself, Hinnerk at least knew how to use his weight to his advantage. Protectively holding the shield before him, he now stormed forward right into the first armoured skeleton knight. The impact knocked the warrior down and flung him into another skeleton which also toppled over. Hinnerk snarled: "You need to eat more, you scrawny lowlifes, or should I say nolifes?" For Hinnerk it was mostly muscle mass that lent him the added force. Although the undead possessed stamina, strength and even skill, they did not have weight. They only consisted of bones and some armour. Hinnerk also managed to defeat the other three undead. His force smashed their arms and skulls and they immediately tried to reassemble themselves. But Hinnerk wouldn't let them and severed their heads with Pakhaou. Finally he turned his attention to Leevke and the nervously shaking nomcrab. Hinnerk jumped onto its shell while the crab receded into it. He was hit by a jolt when he touched the magic shield. "Leevke! Wake up! It's me, Hinni! Wake up!" Leevke didn't react to his entreaties and simply kept on sleeping. Inside the sphere there were no sounds apart from a bubbling, deafening din comparable to being inside the womb. Hinnerk pounded at the sphere with his fists, but that only elicited further jolts each time. He aimed his sword and struck, but missed. The ground disappeared from under his feet. A thick tentacle arm embraced his legs and violently yanked him up. He heard amused, female laughter. Held in a water bubble through Leevke's power, the kraken floated across the sand. Even in the water this creature looked fearsome, but now it was fully visible in all its terrifying glory while it whipped its eight gigantic tentacles through the air. Dangling by his feet, Hinnerk saw the kraken-witch perching on her kraken with a complacent expression, her head propped up by her hands: "How cute. Has our little Leevke found a friend after all?" Hinnerk threatened: "Let her go, you bitch!" Ursula grinned even more; not the reaction he had hoped for. "You defeated Radbod's bodyguards. Respect! Used your weight, didn't you? Quite clever. As scary as they look, they are just not the same anymore. But, you see, they'll always get up again. They're committed." Ursula pointed her wand at the slain skeleton sentries. The bones twitched and tried to reassemble themselves, but Ursula had to give up with a moan. Hinnerk laughed: "It's not really working, is it?!" The kraken witch screwed up her nose: "So you have the magic sword, Pakhaou. There I was thinking we were on the same side, and than that!" Hinnerk was still dangling: "Ha! We shall defeat you!" Ursula smiled: "I don't think so..." Hinnerk tried to free himself, but the kraken intensified its grip and nearly strangled him. He was still holding Pakhaou but couldn't move his arms at all. "Don't bother, boy," Ursula remarked sardonically," there's nothing you can do to stop us. Unlike you lot, we know what we're doing..."

Abbot Wynfried flung another prayer at the lines of the undead by folding his hands, turning forward and shouting: "De Nihilo Nilis!" One of the skeletons collapsed and didn't get up again. Wynfried crossed himself, beads of perspiration dripping from his forehead. His fellow brothers were also giving it their best. Brother Brutalus wielded a consecrated mace at the enemy in close combat. But the sand skeletons were soon upon him, pulled him down by his habit and stabbed him to death with their rusty blades. Wynfried crossed himself again while Behrend Attena – covered in wounds – fought Radbod roaring and laughing as if he was having the time of his life. The abbot had to admit to himself that he had misjudged the Bear from Esems. The man may not be a particularly great friend of the Church and had also repeatedly have the parson of Esens thrown out of the chapel because he had disagreed with his sermons, but now the Hauptlinger's pugnaciousness proved to be a gift from the heavens. There he was now, bleeding and huge like a bear; his fierce eyes beneath the bushy brows terrifying any man and making him fear that the end was nigh. Attena was a nightmare for any ordinary mortal, yet the undead Radbod still had the edge.

At this stage the king of the Frisians was more or less just playing with the Bear whose countless wounds slowed him down and weakend him more and more. Wynfried assumed that Radbod was still trying to win him over to his cause. The only other great warriors here were Friedhelm Nordendi and the Chauci chief Tjarko. Friedhelm was practised in fighting the ashmen and considered to be a cunning tactician. His people were still holding the defences of the shield wall while his stone throwers broke rank and bombarded the undead with their clay missiles from their right-hand flank. His distinctive laugh kept echoing aross the dyke, no less manic than Attena's himself. Hauptlinger Tjarko and his Chauci also did well. It even looked as if his falcon soldiers would now completely penetrate the right-hand flank and decide the outcome of the battle. The skeletons collapsed into themselves like puppets whose strings had been cut. Now the Chauci pushed towards the centre and Hauptlinger Tjarko beat the tentacle-armed knight Düll down the hillside. The Chauci flanked the middle section of Radbod's troops to the joyous sound of cheering, mocking and bugles.

The enemy drew back, the end in sight. Wynfried, however, didn't share the confidence of certain victory and the very next moment two things happened that would radically turn the tide again. A terrifying, many-armed creature was approaching from the beach in front of Nordendi's clay missile skirmishers: a five-eyed kraken floating on a bed of water above the undead, holding a young man. Its eight tentacles were lashing around, searching for victims to kill. His arms grabbed individual skirmishers; lifted them up to send them flying across the dyke so that they landed with a crash, breaking all their bones in the process. On the Chauci side, too, humanoid creatures trudged out of the water. Düll exclaimed: "Ahhh! At last! The sea god is sending reinforcements! Look! The Draugr. The Draugr have arrived!" Tjarko briefly released the captain and yelled his commands at the Chauci to adjust to the new threat. But his men were still so euphoric about their victory that they couldn't react right away. Only the falcon warriors instantly followed his orders. From a distance the Draugr looked like humans. They were dressed like mariners, but their garments were decayed and coated in algae and moss. Crawling with clams and crabs, their slimy green clothes had grown onto their skin and their heads were entirely covered by seaweed and algae. Their noses, eyes and ears were either also covered or bulged out unnaturally from beneath. Their teeth had become arranged in a circle reminiscent of a lamprey; their eyes round, protruding and black as coal. Under the algae all of them were hideously deformed. Drowned seafarers they were, half dead. Like the skeletons they scuffled over the sandy soil, howling and wailing. Abbot Wynfried recognised them: "Draugr! The condemned of the sea. God help us!" Roughly 500 of them now scaled the dyke and attacked the Chauci's disorganised right-hand flank. A handful of Chauci managed to draw their bows and shoot them at the slow advance of attackers. The Draugr's flesh was rotten and the arrows had no effect. The creatures were just as immune as Radbod's skeletons. Düll called them: "Come! Come you condemned! Come and unleash your wrath!"

Advance of the Draugr

The middle section was now in dire straits and Radbod slashed Attena's chest one last time. The Bear fell onto his knees: "Fucking bastard..." Radbod ignored the bleeding man and unimpeded butchered everyone brave enough to obstruct him. No sword fighter managed to exchange more than two strokes with him. No shield provided adequate cover against his onslaught. No spear harmed him. It felt like they were jinxed.

For the first time abbot Wynfried felt overwhelmed by fear: "God help us against this madness..." Up to now he had always been sheltered and protected behind the thick monastery walls. Now he saw himself personally confronted with the Church's ancient, bloody enemies and did not know if he had the strength to defeat them. The abbot gulped, produced his oak-felling, consecrated axe to be on the safe side and checked if the old bible he had strapped to his left arm was still in position. The book in question was the old St. Boniface bible whose binding was full of notches acquired when Boniface had been slain by pagans and protectively held the book in front of him. It was the holiest relic in all of Marienkamp.

The flank under Nordendi's command was also in trouble as the kraken attacked more and more of his men and hurled them through the air. The spears some of the men threw at the monster hit their target, but couldn't stop it. The stones they flung at it also instantly bounced off its elastic skin. The dreadful curses straight from the underworld of Hels uttered by Ursula riding on it, paralysed them with fear and robbed them of the will to fight.

Abbot Whyfried closed his eyes, gathered his mental strength and cried out to his brothers to neutralise the witch's chant with their own hymns. Despite the chaotic circumstances the brothers of Marienkamp managed to strike up their songs of praise, thus forcing Ursula's curse back and the Frisians gathered renewed courage. The Chauci unleashed their fury at the Draugr who were wielding their rusty swords, clubs and daggers. The furious Brother Tennus swirled his precious pouch with consecrated ashes above his head like a catapult. The contents spread over the ranks of the undead and rendered them temporarily immobile thereby easing the conditions for the Frisians and procuring them a badly needed reprieve to remove their wounded from the battle field.

Radbod spotted the abbot and calmly approached him "Wouldn't you rather hide behind the walls of your friary, monk? I can see right through your pious disguise of innocence. I could back then and I still can now." Radbod whirled his sword around in a semi-circle and stopped abruptly. Warm blood splattered onto the sand. His smile was grim: "Go and gorge yourself for the last time, you pathetic little monk. Get pissed on your wine, whore around with the nuns, the usual..." Wynfried squared his shoulders: "I don't care about your ridiculing me. Your time is over. You are no longer relevant."

Radbod smiled derisively while his body was trembling with barely restraint rage before breaking out in a guffaw echoing over the battle field that could be heard right across the dyke and the sea. "Tahahaha! You Frisians! My proud, pigheaded Frisians! You fought so valiantly and you're still fighting! Good on you!" The fighting was dying down as the skeletons retreated behind their rotten shields at a signal and the Draugr also collectively stepped back. During the ensuing brief truce everyone listened to Radbod: "Why do we fight each other?! Together we could crush the yoke of hypocrisy once and for all! We could force the Church back to Rome to cower in cold grottoes while we celebrate! They are weak! Just look at them!" He pointed to Wynfried who truly looked like a clown beside him. Radbod laughed: "Our gods rule the seas! We rule the coast! We built the dykes with blood, sweat and our very lives, not the Church! She only came crawling when everything was done and ever since she has been sucking us dry like the parasite it is!

I don't hold a grudge against you, brothers! Your blood is also mine! Don't ever let us forget who we really are and always will be: the people who subdued the sea, the people of the coast, the most obstinate bastards this side of the globe. So who is with me? You will have to decide here and now because otherwise you will inevitably die. What do you say, my brothers? What do you say?!" Apart from the anguished cries of the wounded and the dead, his address was followed by steely silence. The undead didn't move and Ursula's kraken also hovered silently with Hinnerk in its tentacle. The Chauci chief Tjarko's arm had been injured in the battle with Düll and he was bandaging the wound with a piece of cloth. He looked into his compatriots' eyes and saw *sympathy for Radbod?* "I don't believe it..." he hissed.

Radbod had won. He could feel it. Ursula smiled: "It's working!" In order to deal the deathblow to the men's morale Radbod exclaimed: "I saw it earlier: right this moment the ashmen are raiding your villages. The villages you left unprotected to fight this futile battle for the Church and to die for her benefices. Together we can destroy them before worse things happen!" The reactions to Radbod's speech varied. Tjarko was furious. Wynfried demonstratively straightened himself and folded his hands in prayer. The monks followed his example. Nordendi couldn't suppress an appreciative grin: "Not bad, you sly fox!" One of the Frisians muttered: "There's something in what he says. Going to church every Sunday to listen to their drivel... I'd rather spend more time with the little ones." "My thoughts exactly," another agreed. "The Church is just as much on the take as the robber barons. Why do we tolerate the ecclesiastical robbers when we chase off the secular ones?" "They're very clever. We don't have to make donations, but we end up in hell if we don't. They know exactly how to get rich. I guess Radbod is right..." The general silence and murmuring was abruptly broken by blood-spitting laughter. Radbod's eyes widened in disbelief. The laughter was surging and swelling while Attena rose behind the old king's back. His blood now mingled with sand, Behrend's stout legs were pretty shaky as Radbod noticed immediately. The Bear no longer posed a threat to him. But Attena kept on laughing and Friedhelm Nordendi soon joined in as if Radbod had just cracked a joke. The Hauptlinger from Norden had always been a man who loved to laugh, but now he gradually infected everybody else. Nobody said a word while the laughter rose to a crescendo like a massive wave.

Radbod was inwardly raging. His white iris turned red. "What are you laughing about?! Your lands will burn, your families slain! What's so funny about that, you fools?!!"

Attena was spitting blood. He no longer had the strength to walk, let alone fight. He simply stood there: "What's so funny is that you don't understand your own people." "What?!" Friedhelm added: "Tohoho, Behrend is right. You want to liberate us from the Church, from the Franks..." "I do. Isn't that your desire, too? Or do you like grovelling for those hypocrites?! I don't believe that for even a second!" Tjarko panted: "But we're not grovelling at all. The Church is here and preaches, true. But we don't care. We are still free. The monks built the abbey themselves and trade with us. We are still free men." "Their influence is gradual and creeps up on you!" Radbod roared and Attena nodded: "That may be so, but at the moment we exist peacefully together." He looked at Whyfried: "When the sermon annoys me, I smack the priest right in the kisser. But when he talks to me sensibly, if he's a reasonable man, I let him be. I can't be arsed getting involved in other people's delusions." Friedhelm continued: "We do defend our freedom, but no longer just in open battle. If someone like the guys from Oldenburg or the ashmen attacks us, we fight back. But we also fight those who want to force us into changing. Anyone who comes to us as a guest and a friend, who helps building the dykes, we offer a place in our midst regardless of their faith. That's our way. Nobody knows what the future holds. And you don't either, Radbod." Tjarko said: "The current peace cost us dearly and we won't have it interfered with, no matter how noble your intentions, Radbod. We teach our children not to be fooled. If you want to sermonize, do by all means, but don't come to us and force us to do things we don't want to do. Every war destroys more than it helps. Right now I don't see the necessity." The last king lowered his sword. Abashed, he fell silent while Düll exclaimed: "Rubbish! You're not going to listen to their claptrap, are you Raddi?! They're only trying to save their skin because we're winning! We can finally clear the decks. It's what we've been waiting for the last 300 years! Should all our sacrifices have been for nothing?!" Radbod nodded slowly: "Düll is right. You've no idea how long your peace will last. How quickly your tolerance can mean you'll lose everything!! You're leaving too much to chance! You've succumbed to an illusion of peace until it's too late!" Attena laughed: "Tush! That's life. It's full of ups and downs! But a putrid carcass like you wouldn't understand. About the ups and downs!" Attena's bloody laughter once again infected the Frisians and the Chauci and they joined in.

Bathed in sweat and blood they developed a grim determination; no longer afraid of death. Ursula licked her lips. Still dangling from the kraken's tentacle, his head as read as a beetroot, Hinnerk shouted: "Ha! You're too late! We won't surrender!" The kraken witch grinned spitefully: "Pretty mouthy for someone who's at my mercy... Besides, strength has always been the law. When we beat Charles Martel near Cologne, the Frisians were united, mentally and physically. You're only sugar-coating your mental defeat." Radbod chimed in: "I know exactly who is responsible for filling your heads with those lies!" His wrathful look captured Abbot Wynfried who armed himself with his axe and bible. "I shall prove to you who is right here! I shall free you from those lies. I shall remind you of your heritage!" Radbod stormed at the abbot and struck. When his stainless Frisian seax Durjawer grazed the St. Boniface bible, sparks emitted from the book and Wynfried thought his arm would break. He wielded his consecrated axe and Radbod retreated from it. The king mocked him: "Thou shalt not kill? You are still the same old hypocrites." The abbot wheezed: "Your vision has no future!" "There's more life in my world than in your dead god!" Radbod retorted.

Radbod renewed his attack and Wynfried could do nothing but block him. The Boniface bible received more blows. Just before the final hit, Friedhelm Nordendi intervened and averted the hit. "Tohoho! Not so fast, Raddi." The king grimaced with amusement: "Oh! It's you! I thought you knew better than to challenge me?" Nordendi shrugged his shoulders: "I'm no smarter than most..." They fought each other amidst the battle that had resumed all around them. Attena collapsed onto the sand again and kept on bleeding. Düll and his Draugr reinforcement troops stopped the Chauci's advance on the right-hand Frisian flank while Ursula's kraken agitated Nordendi's ranks on the left flank. The undead gained more ground. The tide had turned. The warriors were additionally burdened with the knowledge that their families back home were now endangered.

Jens's confidence melted as rapidly as an icicle inside the jaws of a fire-spitting dragon the longer he ran across fields and meadows with the sack on his back. Here behind the dyke everything was calm and peaceful as if there was nothing wrong with the world. As if there were no battles, no ashmen, no screams of agony, no suffering. He saw two cabbage white butterflies silently fluttering and heard bees buzzing in the buckwheat. His desire to go home to Greetsiel and Taalke was so great, it made his legs feel like lead. His body longed to give into the panic and flee. But he had to go to Ochtersum. At least this once he wanted to do something worthwhile, without calculating and analysing the profits. Just once in his crappy, boring life he wanted to hold his head up high, armed with nothing but the knowledge to have done something good and selfless. It was crazy, not quite comprehensible, but Jens smiled with tears in his eyes, aching leg muscles, cold sweat on his forehead and the sack on his shoulders.

Rörik took a deep breath and a grin flitted over his otherwise grim face when he and his band of 80 men espied the settlement of Ochtersum. The village was all tranquil, unsuspecting and ready to be slaughtered. Following Radbod's orders they had moored their vessels east and west of the battlefield. Radbod's plan was for his main army to tie up the Frisians while the ashmen attacked the hinterland. They were to spread terror and confusion in their usual manner and eventually attack the Frisian's main body from the back. It was a good plan because it meant maximum pickings at the least possible risk for the ashmen. The intoxicating feeling of invincibility was shared by Rörik and all his men. Only the old, women and children had remained; the risk was minimal. Even if some of them should have escaped to the relative safety behind the walls of Esens or another fortification there would still be enough people left to have some fun. Rörik Klakssons men were gasping for fire, plunder and rape. Their Nordic eyes were aflame with adrenalin and greed. They were already fighting over their future spoils and wondering how many girls they would catch to have their way with. Some preferred to capture a few boys to employ them as slaves working the fields back home on the farm. Causing terror and fear was a truly sublime feeling; a feeling of absolute control. They were the masters of life and death, fortune and misfortune. Godlike.

Klaksson wistfully remembered his Jutish homeland and how he had been evicted. As an aspiring fief holder, a thane, he had needed to acquire more land and taken out any rivals standing in his way in the process. His father, Klak, wasn't allowed to support him officially because as a thane of the queen Margarethe he was bound to protect the peace. But he secretly sent him arms and men. Margarete, the ice queen, wanted to have a man called Jörgenssen the Red eliminated as he defended the Thingordnung, the ancient public and tribunal assemblies which limited her power. Rörik's ambitions played right into her hands and Klak proposed that she use his son for her purposes. She agreed and unofficially supported Rörik to get rid of Jörgenssen. Knut Jörgenssen had been allied with Störtebeker and his high standing with the common folk increasingly irritated the rulers and the thanes. Rörik acted with particular brutality to beat the confidence out of the people. Numerous lootings by Rörik decimated Jörgenssen's strength. Subsequently Rörik was occasionally described as "Grendel the Monster" or "the Beast of Randers". Rörik's men and those of the Red Knut fought each other in bloody battle in the dense forest of Aulum. Initially it went well for Rörik whose men fought with the frenzy of berserkers thanks to a reddish brew mixed with poisonous mushrooms. They did serious damage to the enemy lines who were cowering behind their shield wall.

But then Red Knut's warriors unexpectedly and forcefully stormed forward like one body led by a roaring Knut. It was as if they had transferred the enemy's rage onto them themselves and now used it against them. Blows were exchanged, shields were bursting, timber split and iron bent. In the end Knut challenged Rörik to a one-to-one combat. The ashmen was a fine fighter, but Knut's eyes were ablaze with righteous indignation. Daunted, Rörik fled from the battle scene and soon his entire bunch followed. His reign of terror ended as quickly as it had begun and his formerly loyal companions betrayed him with the same enthusiasm with which they had previously cheered him. He would presumably have lost even more men had Knut not ceased his pursuit. Rörik gathered Jörgenssen had held back in order to consolidate his victory and as not to divide his army. All of Rörik's previous conquests collapsed like a sandcastle as news of his defeat at Aulum spread. His army of a thousand shrank to a handful of men and only Karl Ole Brand remained truly loyal. Among other things because he looked back on a long friendship with Rörik's father Klak. Now they could no longer remain in Jutland and, with Margarethe's assistance, Klak helped them to abscond on three longboats. Ever since Rörik had survived by raiding coastal settlements and trading ships, but he still remembered the time when he was young, when Klak, his father, had ruled over parts of Frisia as his fiefdom. In the battle of Norden they had finally been disposed by the Frisians. Rörik now wanted to claim his inheritance.

Certain of success and laughing the ashmen marched towards the village. From afar they could already see people scurrying around in a panic and hear screaming children and women fleeing. Rörik grabbed his axe and his men swarmed out, lusting for blood, slaves and gold. "May Odin grant us a rich harvest! For Odin! Attack!" Rörik yelled and his men, starved by all those months at sea and fear, greedily charged. They had a lot to catch up on.

When they arrived, none of the Frisians was outside any longer. The rest had fled to the south, into the moors and woods. The others presumably waited behind closed doors with cudgels and knives. Rörik shouted: "Burn down the huts!" Moments later torches landed on the thatched roofs. Although they were still wet, they burned brightly and hot. Soon the ashmen were positioned in front of every house to await the residents who would surely have to escape the flames. One of the Vikings grinned: "Let them roast for a bit until they're well done, hey?!" The smoke increasingly obscured visibility and the whole of Ochtersum was quickly swallowed up by the fumes. Rörik became impatient. Nothing was happening. "Right! Just get them out!" He kicked one of the doors to be greeted by embers and smoke. When his eyes adjusted he saw nobody inside.

All he could hear were screams of pain and they came from his own men. One of them had been slain when a clay ball hit his helmet. The dent had cracked his skull. Rörik growled: "What's going on here?!" His men were scattered around the village and now two more of them were killed by the clay missiles. Eventually one of the ashmen right beside him was hit and there was a loud PLONK! when a fist-sized ball dented the man's helmet. Howling in agony, the ashman tried to take off his helmet, but couldn't and

Rörik ended the agony with a quick blow of his axe. Then he cried: "Give the signal to regroup. This is a fucking a trap!" One of his men blew the bugle and the ashmen reassembled in a shiltron, their shields raised. At this stage the clay balls were flung at them from all directions, albeit irregularly and not very accurately. "They can't see a thing either. Hold yourself ready. They are going to attack as soon as they run out of ammunition!" After a while everything quietened down and Rörik thought he could detect shapes in the smoke. "They are coming!" he warned his men as Okko emerged from the fumes. Clad in chain mail, iron helmet, with seax and shield he confronted the ashmen who were hiding behind their formation of shields, axes and lances. "I am Okko Wiards! Surrender and leave. You are surrounded! Go!" Rörik considered and then stepped out from behind the shields. "What is this, hey? Where are the women and the old ones, Frisian? Are they the ones who are pelting us with stones?" Okko spit and replied: "You will meet nothing but your death here." Rörik laughed: "We are off to Valhalla so! That's alright, too. Come on and show us what you're made of. All I can see so far is nothing but one Frisian." Okko sounded his own bugle and Frisian warriors only lightly armed with axes, clubs and spears emerged from all sides. Most of the younger and better equipped warriors were with Attena. Okko's defence had to rely on the older men and younger boys.

The women had taken up position at the outskirts of the village and were throwing the clay balls to the best of their abilities. Now, however, they feared for their sons and grandfathers who dared to confront the well-armed ashmen. It was an unequal battle and the schiltron was impenetrable. The ashmen skilfully aimed their lances over their heads while protecting themselves behind the round and kite shields. Okko was fighting Rörik himself. Nobody else in Ochtersum could have taken him on. Rörik possessed the strength and dexterity of an experienced fighter, but he didn't have Okko's patience. After their first exchange of blows Rörik smiled: "Not bad for a Frisian peasant. This is not your first time to wield a sword I take it?" Okko replied: "I hope it shall be the last time!" The Viking glared at him: "I can safely promise you that!" Rörik produced a vial, swallowed the pale red liquid it held and flailed at Okko's shield with tremendous force. He hit him so badly that Okko crached into the wall of one of the houses which collapsed in on itself. Rörik guffawed and looked back to see his schiltron intact. After having repelled Okko's desperate attack, nothing would stand in his way anymore.

Okko emerged from the debris spitting blood. Rörik shot him a look of appreciation; his forehead pulsating with strength: "Tougher than I thought after all. Don't make it too easy for me. I want to have the feeling that I worked for this land, ha, ha, ha!" Okko swallowed hard and mentally prepared himself for his defeat. He grimly sang a song from his youth in Stedingen: "We shit on the high and mighty lords..." He grinned and flung himself at Rörik.

Jens arrived too late. Ochtersum had already been consumed by the swirling embers and black smoke of the burning huts. With aching lungs he fell to his knees and gasped for air. The smell of burned timber was just as prevalent as the sounds of a nearby battle. When Jens ran to the village he tripped over someone in the brush and rolled down a little slope. When he looked up he saw a trembling spear in front of his nose. A woman was crouching over him: "Friend or foe?" Jens stuttered: " F... f... friend, I should hope." She looked firmly into his eyes and he didn't flinch. Then she pulled him up. Two more women with primitive spears and clay balls in their girdles eyed him intensively. "Our men are fighting," the first one said and Jens nodded. "I can hear them. I have come from the beach and it's not much better there." Her grim determination faltered. "I just hope that they'll all return safely," she sobbed and her friends comforted her. A girl had come out of her hiding place and offered Jens his rucksack. He accepted it with a smile. The battle sounds grew louder, as did the curses and muffled screams of the wounded. The woman wiped the tears from her eyes and flashed Jens a tired smile: "You don't look like a fighter." Jens clenched his fists and composed himself. "You are right. I'm a merchant with an order to deliver."

He ran into the smoke. Injured Frisians passed him while others gathered and risked a renewed attacked against the schiltron. An elderly man with grey, shoulder-length hair and a bleeding shoulder wound shook his head when he spotted Jens: "It's impossible!

Impossible to get through. It's madness!" His legs trembling, Jens approached the main source of noise and peeped around the corner of one of the still intact houses. Just a few yards away a brutal battle was raging against the impenetrable shield wall the Norsemen were so infamous for. The ground was littered with dead Frisians.

Jens quickly retreated behind the wall again and searched for the entrance into the house. Once inside, his knees shaking, he climbed up a ladder to the roof and searched for support amongst the timbers. He was caught by a cloud of smoke and had to cough so hard, he nearly lost his rucksack. He barely managed to catch it with his little finger, which cracked alarmingly. Jens swallowed the pain and looked down at the battle. Small groups of Frisians were attacking from all sides in waves, but their losses were immense. Meanwhile the ashmen dragged their exhausted or injured fighters into the inner circle of their ring. A bit further afar he saw Okko battling with Rörik.

Jens took a deep breath, which made him cough again, and took the container from his rucksack: a small, round clay vase with two handles, the lid fastened with iron clamps. "By God, I hope this will work, Saltpeter, my man," Jens mumbled and took aim. He was no seasoned shot like other Frisians who learned clay-ball throwing in their spare time and to defend their homeland. He was more the clumsy type who would hit himself in the face with the ball if that was even possible. In the Tedeschi tongue he shouted: "Out of the way! Here comes a stink bomb! Out of the way, Frisians!" Okko saw Jens taking aim and quickly cottoned on. "Get back!!" he also screamed in Tedeschi. His fellow countrymen heard him and withdrew while the confused ashmen watched their suddenly fleeing enemies. Jens flung the container and it wobbled through the air and landed – miraculously – smack bang in the middle of the schiltron. He couldn't believe his luck. Or the fact that he'd plummeted from the roof back into the house. At the very same moment the clay jar burst and distributed such a god-awful stench that the close by Norsemen had to throw up and tried to get away from the source. Rörik forgot about Okko and barked: "What's going on?!" The schiltron broke apart. The stink was too overpowering.

A cloud of disgusting, foul and greasy soup gushed over the centre of the formation. Puking, choking and with tears in their eyes they scattered. Okko roared: "Now! Altogether now!!" He bashed away at the irritated Rörik whose peculiar strength had deserted him by now. The remaining Frisians stormed at the ashmen again, isolated them and together they beat them down. Their well-targeted clay balls eliminated even the enemies in heavy armour. Some of the ashmen tried to build a small shield wall, but their tears and chocking prevented them. Rörik cursed: "What is all this crap?!" Okko parried his blow and forcefully pushed him back: "I told you we shit on the lords!"

Okko mentally thanked Jens Janssen for the miracle, broke through Rörik's defence and slashed his sword arm. The Viking broke out in a cold sweat and he looked like someone who had been prepared for anything but being wounded. He tripped and fell. Smoke and stinking fumes crept up his nostrils. Rörik struggled onto his feet and limped away. He fled southwards in the direction of the Ghastly Moors with his men following close behind. The skirmish of Ochtersum was over. Okko helped to slay the rest of the ashmen or chase them off.

Afterwards they brought the women back from their hiding places and treated the casualties. They also recovered the unconscious Jens Janssen from the house and carried him to the women to see to the bump on his head. The girl from earlier on smiled broadly: "I gave him the bag! That was me!" Her mother laughed and cried at the same time, as much overcome by the loss of her father during the battle as the joy about the others' survival. Okko also had his injuries seen to and growled: "I wish not so many would have had to die. I wish I had been able to defeat them on my own." The mother shook her head. "You did everything you could, Okko. We all did. This is my native land as well and it was our own decision. How much longer are we supposed to run? Is there any place in this world they can't reach?" Okko shook his head: "You are right. There really is no such place. Neither in Stedingen nor anywhere else." They had survived and were infinitely grateful. Now they had to pray that the others would be just as lucky.

Chapter 8

With Combined Strength

Ole Brand attacked the small mixed Chauci/Frisian settlement of Thunum which was guarded by a small fortress. Many families from the surrounding farms entrenched themselves behind the narrow passageways and the walls of the wooden motte-and-bailey on top of the mound while the ashmen pillaged and plundered the village. Brand ordered his men to start a big fire around the tower so the wind would blow the fumes right into it and smoke out the Frisians and Chauci just like smoking salmon.

Powerless the thus imprisoned people were coughing while watching their houses going up in smoke through watery eyes. Soon the invaders were roasting a freshly killed pig on the open flames and drank all the beer and mead they could lay their hands on. Brand did nothing to stop them. Complacently he swilled another bottle of expensive Burgundy while most of the liquid dribbled from his mouth. Ole slurped and burped heartily enough for the earth to shake had it not been securely anchored to the ground. "Do you think the smoked eels are ready, hey?" he roared in the direction of the two men who kept stoking the fire. "Not yet, Captain Brand. They need a little longer before they're done!" Ponderously Ole got up from his stool while his men roasted the pig and indulged themselves. Ole was an impressive chap with broad shoulders and no less broad stomach and head to match. Whatever he lacked in height, he easily compensated for with his presence and violence. In Rörik's gang he was the man for the dirty jobs, the one who kept the men together, and in charge of the worst atrocities. Ole gave them what they needed. Meat, mead, wrenches and the occasional fight. Rörik was as rough as any of them, but he lacked the direct contact to his followers; the experience of handling at times quite obstinate fellows. As the son of Klak, the thane, he had always been slightly arrogant. On Klak's advice Ole Brand therefore functioned as his advisor and right-hand man.

While Rörik had still more or less been soiling his nappies blundering through the coniferous forests of Jutland with its occasional fjords, Ole had already attacked Frankish villages in Gaul and plundered them. This siege was ridiculously easy by comparison. The Frisians had left hardly any able-bodied men behind. There would be no battle. Ole hated an easy victory without any blood being spilled. It wasn't earned.

The adrenalin couldn't properly flow. The squealing of an animal was nothing compared to the wailing and death rattle of actual people. Ole loved the battle; craved it. He drunkenly staggered through the burning village of Thunum, looking westwards where Rörik presumably experienced a similar fate. Right now they weren't much more than henchmen in Radbod's plan to re-conquer East-Frisia. Pawns in a game of chess without any say in the matter. Ancient sorcery and heathen rituals kept the king alive and he commanded an army of dead soldiers. Ole asked himself how long their alliance of convenience would last. As far as he could see it would dissolve right after the Frisians' defeat; just like an iron chain rotted by the salty breeze, because Rörik longed for land and his father's lost Frisian estates were ideal. There would be many more battles for Ole to look forward to...

In Tjarko's absence, Hauke was the leader of the Chauci. They were watching the events at Thunum from a small forest south of the village. At first Hauke had been extremely disappointed that he wasn't allowed to fight against Radbod by his father's side. As far as he had been concerned they should have combined all their available forces against Radbod to walk away victorious instead of dividing their strength.

But now that he saw the misery with his own eyes, he berated himself as a hot-headed idiot. Thunum was burning and its people had buried themselves in the little fortress, unable to oppose the invaders. Besides, the term fortress was a little over-ambitious because it was actually nothing but a wooden tower on a mound surrounded by man-high walls. From his position Hauke saw four armed men on top of the tower, their javelins ready in case the ashmen should dare to break down the gate. But, as so often, the Vikings didn't have any siege equipment and, for the time being, settled for lighting fires all around the fortress. The wind drove the fumes towards the people inside. Other than that, mostly loud caterwauling, celebrating a hysterical lust for life, could be heard from Thunum, in stark contrast to the terrified besieged inside the keep.

"What shall we do now, Hauke?" one of the Chauci warriors beside him asked. They were all wearing falcon masks, so Hauke had no idea which of them had posed the question. The Chauci were extremely tradition-conscious and in their heads the old gods as well as the Christian god co-existed peacefully. Outsiders rarely understood the concept, but it worked as a perfect symbiosis for the Chauci. The young man frowned and considered the situation. The ashmen had advanced quickly with their shields, spears and axes, clad in chain mail and pointed iron helmets with smudged runes. They had also brought a number of crossbows.

At first Hauke had intended to confront them in open battle, but then decided against it and advised his people to seek shelter in the fortress. This is how the ashmen had been able to take Thunum without resistance and were now celebrating their easy victory. Hauke and the falcon warriors had taken up position behind a small earthen mound, an abandoned dyke, near the forest where they were lying in wait. Hauke mentally calculated his resources. He commanded thirty Chauci soldiers against roughly eighty ashmen. Each of his warriors owned a falcon that served him as scout or hunting bird as required. Now a whole flock of them were perched on the branches above them. These falcons had been specially trained and been the Chauci's chosen tribe animals since time immemorial. Before the dykes had been built and prey had been scarce, the men had gone hunting with them in the moorlands. The Chauci were also accomplished archers and as such had the advantage of a larger range than the Norsemen who relied on their javelins and an occasional crossbow. "I've got it!" Hauke eventually exclaimed and instructed his men who were glad to finally see some action.

"A flock of birds, Captain Ole!" reported a gangly fellow with a moustache. Ole's head was throbbing from all the mead: "And? Scared they might shit on your head or what?" Ole hated messages like these; they were totally irrelevant. What did he care about those damned birds? "They've been circling right above us and the village for quite some time." "So, let them, you nitwit. Leave them to it until they puke." "Well, we think it's strange…" "Would you ever shut up?! There's nothing strange about those birds. Presumably crows or gulls or whatever looking for food. And now keep your trap shut!" He noticed how his men sceptically eyed the sky now and then until he looked up himself.

About thirty birds were flying round and round in circles above their heads. Although his warriors were a hard-boiled bunch, they were also seafarers with the typical respect for omens and grim portents. They lived dangerously and death was their constant companion. For that reason they also celebrated so enthusiastically and unrestrained, always aware that a brutal demise could be their fate anytime. Their superstitions didn't weaken their muscles, but affected their confidence and thus those all important fractions of seconds that decided the outcome of close combat.

A motivated man fought with just that crucial bit more strength and forcefulness which determined life or death regardless of how well trained he was. So what did those damned birds want and why did they keep flying like that? Reminiscent of crows circling the battlefield, just waiting to descend upon the corpses to peck the flesh from the bloody bones.

The ashmen fought against anything and anyone as long as they could see what they were up against and they drew blood when they attacked with their spears. Just in case, some of them checked their protective runes to see if they were still legible. Others quickly prayed to Odin, Njörd and Freyja. As soon as the thought had entered Ole's head, one of them shouted: "It's Freyja's revenge, the patron saint of the Frisians! She wants to jinx us!" Ole quickly identified the man, approached him with firm strides and hit him so forcefully that he crashed into a wheelbarrow. Ole yelled: "You moron! This is no witchcraft, you fools! We are Norsemen. Odin and Thor's warriors! The likes of us don't whimper at every little fart! Or do we?! Get a grip! Someone's trying to take the piss. And he's succeeding because you're dumb enough to fall for it! It's nothing!" Undecided, the men looked at each other, then they squinted as if they had just woken up from a bad dream. Some even laughed cautiously upon realising that they'd been on the point of acting like panicking fishwives. Brand hissed: "To much mead, hey?! Fucking good-for-nothings!"

While the falcons were circling over Thunum, "Woodpecker" Kea in Werdum was busy calming down the worried women. In the Hauptlinger's large main building they arranged beds and facilities for the wounded they expected. Everyone knew that the battles would incur losses. They prayed much and fervently. Even the feisty Kea had a tough time maintaining her usually sunny and optimistic disposition, to cheer up and encourage the women. The very fact that she didn't have a husband or brother amongst the fighters made her feel connected to all the Chauci, many of whom she had brought into the world. Her duties as Harugari had always included providing spiritual and moral support for the diminished tribe. She knew all their minor ailments and embarrassing secrets which, on closer examination, turned out not be worth worrying about.

For Woodpecker they were like a bunch of children who looked up to her as a big sister or mother. As such it was impossible not to feel close to them, even the grumpy ones like Hauke, the son of Hauptlinger Tjarko, for instance. Kea loved teasing him and quite often became lewd in the process. She had great fun watching him lose his usual composure and blush deeply when she suggestively whispered phrases like: "I like strong, thick.... trees!" into his ear. At this stage it had become something of a running joke. Despite his grim nature, Hauke was wild at heart, not happy to be in the same place for too long. What he enjoyed most was roaming through the wilderness with his falcon and training on his own.

Sure enough, he sustained many an injury this way which Kea subsequently tended to. As the son of the Hauptlinger he took life very seriously. Therefore Kea always strived to help him relax and loosen up. A young man like that wasn't meant to wander around with deep worry lines on his forehead like a grey-bearded wizard. Kea looked towards the west when she heard the familiar croaking of a falcon. She briefly exclaimed when the bird landed on a fence in front of her, flapping its wings. She recognised the animal by the pattern of its plumage: "You are Hauke's bird, aren't you? Hübke. Did something happen?" The falcon cawed and bobbed its tail feathers up and down. Ursula saw a note fastened to its talon, hastily took it off and unfolded it. Immediately the bird flew back to its owner.

The writing was scrawly and not very legible, but she recognised Hauke's characteristic loops, a bit girlish, which she had taught him. The message was short and succinct: her skills as a Harugari priestess were urgently required. Kea didn't hesitate. She instantly made for her hut, built on stilts like a chicken coop, which smelled strongly of herbs and was extremely untidy. There she grabbed a sack and filled it with various ingredients: bunches of dried herbs, preserved roots and pouches of crumbled dust. Then she gathered a few cooking utensils and frantically started the preparations for the requested ritual. An old woman inquisitively peeped into the room: "Are you alright, child? Did you get a message? From Tjarko or Hauke?"

Kea's head appeared amongst the clutter, pointed nose first. She was sweating: "Hehehe – everything is fine, Lumke. I just have to help our boys out there. They need a bit of assistance..." The crone stated resolutely: "Well, make room so! I'm also fed up just sitting around waiting for everything to be over!" Kea hesitated: "D... do you actually know what you're doing with this stuff here?" The old woman scuttled into the far too crammed and rather haphazardly arranged hut. "I've seen a lot in my time, girl, and all you're doing is cooking something, am I right?" Affronted, Kea turned up her nose: "It takes a little more than that... But you could help by taking the big cauldron outside and making a fire with dried wood mixed with devil's twine. The cauldron has to be half-full with icecold water. I'll also need fresh nettle leaves..." The woman nodded: "Do you want to make a green soup?" "Not exactly, hehehe." "Okay, we do it." "We?" Kea echoed bewildered. "Sure, Woodpecker! Or do you think the others enjoy fretting?" Kea smiled gratefully and assembled the rest of what was needed with hands drenched in sweat. Every second could save a life. Perhaps the life that would make a difference!

The thought renewed the young, long-nosed woman's hope like a gust of wind after the calm. She would contribute to the fight in her own way: for Tjarko, Hauke and all the men out there who were risking their lives to save hers. In her view it was the least she could do. Werdum reawakened, grimly determined to survive, when the children eagerly started collecting nettles.

Hinnerk was grinding his teeth and tensed his arm muscles to free himself from the kraken tentacle, but the grip around his chest only intensified. He panted. An amused Ursula giggled while the creature was busy grabbing Frisian warriors and flinging them around as a child would wooden dolls. Now and again a monk attempted to direct a prayer at them and an extremely fine beam of light hit the kraken, singeing its skin which was far more used to the depths of the ocean. But every time Ursula promptly counteracted the effect with a strong counter-spell. Her scythe-wand glowed in the same green as her eyes when one of its bolts hurtled towards the monk. The friar tried to fend it off and folded his hands in prayer, but the bolt was stronger and catapulted him into the air. He was dead before he even hit the ground and his corpse smoked and sizzled with sparks.

Ursula reacted with manic laughter: "HAHAHAHA! Oh, I've waited for this forever! Wonderful! The feeling of revenge!! Ha!" Hinnerk was still dangling from the kraken's tentacle: "Why don't you toss me away as well?! At least I won't have to listen to your stupid cackling anymore!" Ursula grinned: "Still so young and yet so tired of living? You should count yourself lucky that I kind of like you. You remind me of Radbod, hehehe. A younger version of him." "I'm nothing even remotely like that arsehole!" The kraken witch chuckled: "Yes, yes, that's exactly what I mean, hehehe..." Hinnerk saw the nomcrab with Leevke in the magic bubble traipsing behind the kraken. Occasionally Ursula dipped her scythe into the sphere and thus constantly renewed the floating water plateau supporting her kraken. Because of his precarious position Hinnerk could barely follow how the battle was progressing. The tentacle was shaking him about too much and his head felt all woozy. Meanwhile Radbod was crossing swords with Friedhelm Nordendi who relied more on his skill than his strength and was therefore, in his own way, more dangerous than the clumsy Attena. The Hauptlinger from Norden even managed to break through Radbod's defences and injure the old king's leg. Nordendi chuckled: "Tohoho, I can see right through your strategy, king." "Remarkable! Now I now why they call you the laughing death. But I've got no time for such diversions! Ursula! Fog spirit!" Radbod's voice reached the kraken witch and again Ursula wielded her wand. Once more Radbod's shape dissolved into mist as it had done in the fight against Abbo. Instinctively Nordendi drew back to reconsider his situation: "This is new." Radbod's glowing eyes with the crown hovering above them were separated from his sword. "Rather old, actually." Even Nordendi couldn't anticipate Radbod's attacks and was right away put on the defensive. What was there to attack after all? Radbod no longer possessed a firm shape and escaped him like the wind itself.

Hinnerk, on the other hand, had to use Ursula briefly being diverted to his advantage and did the only thing he could do while in the grip of the kraken: "Kiss my arse!" he yelled. The kraken uttered a primeval scream as its skin, so sensitive to fire, was scalded by the hot beam of the magic shield Hinnerk had concealed in his left hand from the kraken's tentacle. The beast released Hinnerk who rolled over in the sand while Ursula tried to control the kraken again. Lux Maris, however, was still embedded in its skin and the creature got extremely upset, wildly flapping its tentacles. After having flung some skeletons aside, it retreated back into the sea, following its instincts.

One of its eight arms hit the nomcrab which tumbled over repeatedly before landing on its back, helplessly thrashing around. Hinnerk ran to it and hit the sphere imprisoning Leevke with Pakhaou's magical blade. The ensuing bang also knocked the nomcrab and Hinnerk off their feet. When Hinnerk got back up, his ears ringing, Leeve was lying on the sand and the nomcrab hastily retreated into the ocean. Hinnerk brandished his Frisian dagger while Ursula forced the kraken back into obedience. She was trembling with rage, eyes torn wide open, teeth bared.

"Turn that off right now or I shall cause you pain the likes of it you've never imagined!" Fuming and sizzling, Lux Maris burned itself even more deeply into the kraken's tentacle. Hinnerk was glad that the kraken witch hadn't thought about using the same spell to turn off the magic light he had used to implore it. She was far too angry and irate. "What do I get in return," he asked. Ursula pointed to Leevke: "She shall be free to go, to die or flee with her friends." "You expect me to believe that?" The kraken witch leapt down from her tortured beast and caressed its head. Her gesture somewhat calmed the creature, but its tentacles were still thrashing about. "I shall also return this shield as long as you end its torture." All Hinnerk wanted was to save

Leevke and he shouted: "Leevke! Wake up. We've got to get out of here!" The girl didn't stir. She was beyond the here and now, in her own little world...

Leevke was snoozing in the warm sand, listening to the rhythmic and reassuring sounds of the sea surrounding her. A crab scuttled over her left leg and tickled her with its claws. She giggled, sleepily turned to her side and snored. The girl felt languid and tired and had no intention of getting up. All she wanted was to stay there and do nothing.

The beach was beautifully peaceful, snug and calm. Until she heard muffled, pounding noises as if somebody were speaking to her through several layers of cloth, that was. With a little imagination she could hear her name. Her peace disturbed, Leevke rolled onto her back and stared at the white clouds in the blue sky above her. She arduously sat up and scanned her surroundings through tired eyes to see a beach with wonderful yellow sand and seashells. A palm tree on her left swayed in the wind and provided some shade. The blazing sun was high and stagnant in the sky. It wasn't hot, just pleasantly warm. In the distance she caught sight of the titanic archway veiled behind the mist; the very floodgate she had swam trough in a previous dream. The roaring waves streaming through the floodgate created an evenly droning, whooshing, strangely soothing sound in the background.Behind it, however, beyond the floodgate and the sea, the teeth-reinforced gorge gaped wide open; a vortex that sucked in the water and devoured it. Leevke had apparently managed to save herself on the small island. She got up, brushed herself down and turned around to face a light purple coloured crystal, broken in several places and twice as tall as she was. Startled, she staggered back and landed on her backside at the edge of the island. She gazed into the ocean and could see right through the crystal clear water, utterly without any particles, down to the endless black abyss. It was frightening how far one could look into the immaculately clear water, nearly as if it were translucent. At an unfathomable depth the ocean got ever darker and finally totally black, without ground. The North Sea was a shallow puddle by comparison. It seemed like a hole that would swallow her up forever. Scared as she was, she broke out in goose bumps.

Whimpering and shivering, Leevke threw herself back onto the safe, warm sand and crawled away from the edge drenched in the cold sweat of fear. She was shocked beyond measure by the infinite vastness of the endless depths and whispered: "There's nothing... No ground...!" Leevke was aware that she was completely alone on a tiny island in an infinite ocean. The sea hardly moved; only swashed shallow waves against the island. The purple crystal's opalescence was reflected in the sunlight like an amethyst. Leevke slowly scrambled towards it and had a closer look. She thought she had spotted something inside the crystal. The longer she stared, the more clearly she recognised swirling and wafting silhouettes. A melted face? Leevke shied away and turned her back to the crystal. Her thoughts were confused. She felt as if she were in a dream without the strength to focus. Yet it also seemed real: she could touch the yellow sand and let it trickle through her fingers. Some of the grains stuck to her hand. The voice that had woken her had stopped by now. Who would call her after all? Leevke had a name on the tip of her tongue and her mouth formed the words, but her brain refused to obey her.

All alone on a tiny island in an endless ocean with a sinister crystal. That was all she could see; all she had. Leevke sobbed and pulled up her legs. "I know nothing... I'm nothing..." she wept without knowing why she had said that. "Does that surprise you?" asked a young, male voice. Leevke lifted her head to see the little crab from earlier squatting in front of her, looking at her through its telescope eyes. Leevke asked: "A... are you talking to me?" Without moving its tiny mouth the crab replied: "No, I'm talking to the palm tree! Really?! Of course I'm talking to you and I said it's hardly surprising that you don't know anything. How could you?!" "W... why? What kind of a place is this? I don't remember anything. Please tell me what all this means, Mr Crab!" The crab crawled onto her knee and was now at eye-level with her: "I'm sorry that I have to be so direct, but you're stuck here. You're being held by pretty strong forces. Invincible forces." "What forces? Whose?" I can't tell you, little one. I can only move things a little; I can't fix them." "What? Why?" The crab hummed and hawed: "I'm just a guest. This shape is the most I can manifest and even that only under certain conditions. But I do want to help you. In my own way." Leevke wiped the tears from her face: "It's okay. Thank you." "Don't thank me too soon. I don't understand all the details myself. Right now, at any rate, we're both prisoners here." "But I don't see any chains?" The crab nipped Leevke with its claw. "Ouch!" "Sorry! It's a reflex." The creature scuttled back and forth in front of her, snapping its claws, and explained: "Believe me, the worst prisons don't have cute things like chains..." "Really?" "The sea all around you will drag you down and swallow up if you try to get away." "Oh! Do you mean the gorge behind the floodgate?" "No, no, not that old thing. That's not important right now. I mean the abyss underneath the island that scared you. Its weight will crush you, inch by inch, and smother your thoughts for all eternity. You'll be depressed and lethargic." Leevke nodded like a patient student. "That's how it felt! What's the story with that crystal there? What's inside it?" The crab hesitated for a moment as if it was thinking: "That crystal is the island's anchor. The island itself is only a reflection of your influence in these waters. It only exists since you are here. Just like me..." Leevke pointed to herself: "So I own this watery desert?" The crab's clicking noises sounded like laughter: "Not the sea, silly! Only this island. Not exactly a large kingdom." "It has its limits, I agree." The crab hesitated again: "I like you, little one. That's why I shall tell you what you have to do now. No, that's wrong, cosmologically wrong. Paradoxes and discord. What? Not there yet? Never mind." It seemed temporarily confused before clearing its throat: "Let me put it another way: "I'll just prattle on and you decide if you want to risk it or not. Exactly. It's the only way to do it. Always these restrictions! Old mummy!" Leevke commented: "You're strange, Mr Crab." She quickly reflected: there was no reason to trust the creature, yet there wasn't one not to trust it either. There was nobody else around. She had no alternatives anyway. "Prattle on so, Mr Crab." "I say just one word: diving." "What? Didn't you say that the sea would swallow me?!" Once more the crab hummed and hawed: "At the moment only your consciousness is truly awake. Your powers are still asleep. Figuratively speaking. You may be able to induce one or two trifles, but those are reactions linked to your subconsciousness without the power to manipulate." Leevke's head was spinning: "Oh, dear! That sounds complicated..." "Sorry, but I can't put it in more simple terms. What you lack is control over your skills; the conscious and therefore controlled guidance of the powers given to you!" Leevke helplessly shrugged her shoulders and the crab energetically nipped her foot, making her jump. It gave out to her: "That's exactly what I mean. You're still not taking any responsibility for yourself. But you have to. Otherwise you'll be stuck here forever and never get back! There's a whole other world out there you want to see again, I take it?" Leevke massaged her aching foot and nodded slowly: "Right! Then you have to free your paralysed mind from its chains. But that only works if you give it all you've got to get out of the cosy prison of your island. And I mean ALL YOU'VE GOT! Until your head explodes. That way you will make the ocean boil and be able to command your power as you wish. Not before that. You have to be prepared to die!" The girl got up and looked down into the depths of the sea: "I don't know. I'm supposed to go down there voluntarily?" "Either that or your basic programme takes over completely: pure reflexes to external stimuli... I wish you luck, little one. There's nothing more I can do for you. I need to rest." The crab dug itself into the sand and disappeared.

Leevke was alone again; the endless ocean stretching out all around her. She certainly didn't want to be sucked down into it, but had to face it if she ever wanted to get away from here. Back to real life... "Someone called me! Someone needs me." Leevke clenched her fists. She positioned herself beside the crystal and ran towards the sea. And stopped at the edge of the island. She didn't have the courage to take that last, all-important plunge. The warm sand, the cosy peace; did she really want to give it all up? She tried a second time and a third time, but always shied back at the last moment. Tears started welling up in her eyes: "I can't do it! Damn it! I'm scared. Scared! I don't want to die. Somebody help me! Please..." Leevke slumped down. She crouched right in front of the crystal and looked deeply into it. But she still couldn't see anything concrete; it was still nothing but a purple crystal with a dubious, wafting inner life. Some of her features were mirrored in the quartz where she saw a girl close to collapsing – herself. Unable to help herself; dependant on others. A miserable sight. She snivelled and slowly got up. Something inside her now started a fierce rebellion and made her angry: "No, I don't want to stay like this! There's more! I know it! There's more!" She nodded at her mirror image with its strangely red glowing eyes, turned around and ran towards the sea. And jumped. The water was ice-cold and an underground suction instantly pulled at her feet. Like a stone she quickly sank deeper as if the water offered next to no resistance. It quickly became darker. Desperation and panic filled her head and her heart. The feeling of yielding to the depths and letting go pounded in her brain. A sly, cynical female voice mumbled from all around her: "Let go. Let yourself fall. Release yourself. Eternal reeeest..." But she most definitely didn't want to be pulled into the depths and lose control! She recognised the voice as her own. "Who are you?" she asked while sliding down further. A loud, animal-like screech answered her through her own throat. The hairs on the back of Leevke's head stood up as she sensed a danger that could wash her away. It was like dealing with a monster lurking for her in the darkness. The water was raging; powerful currents tearing at her arms and legs like whips and chains. Yet she remained remarkably calm and pushed herself up with her feet to get back to the surface. The action temporarily slowed her sinking, but then the swirling water pulled her down all the more violently. Icy cold made the water freeze in lumps. Something rose up from the depths; as gigantic as the gorge, but even stiffer and more hate-filled. Leevke used her arms to get back to the surface. The creature from the depths of darkness came closer, shrieking and hissing. But Leevke ignored it. Instead she had a sudden flash of insight: "I am needed!" With that thought Leevke commanded herself to stop. She was no longer sinking although she hadn't yet reached the ground: there was no ground!

Inspired by her success, she now ordered herself to rise. The water surrounding her appeared to be seething and raging. Now the black monster underneath her didn't advance any further; just tugged and cursed without effect. Leevke intensified her thoughts: "Rise to the surface!" The sea formed an underwater tornado with Leevke in the middle. On top of the endless ocean the water already started to ripple. Leevke concentrated solely on the one thought: "Rise! Rise! Rise!!" She felt as if a valve had exploded somewhere inside her head when she shot up from the depths like an arrow. The beast howled and screeched and sank back. Its power had been crushed and Leevke now took charge of the sea. With enormous speed she catapulted herself closer and closer to the surface. "I'm coming back grandpa and nan!" She laughed: "Hinni! I remember! I'm coming back!" She made it to the surface. High waves broke against the island. The crab eyed her attentively and giggled: "Took her time, didn't she? It's starting so. And they call me crazy."

When his falcon returned, Hauke saw that the note the bird had carried was gone: "Did you find Kea, Hübke!" The falcon cawed to confirm this was the case and greedily swallowed the worm its master rewarded him with. Meanwhile, in far away Werdum, the women had carried the bronze cauldron with the runes to the middle of the village and lit a fire under it. Kea gradually added the ingredients while mumbling ancient Chauci incantations. The rising steam and the trance she was in made her eyes grow darker and her feather-cape flutter. The wind was veering in a westerly direction. The vapours from the cauldron condensed into green clouds and the women and children kept a respectable distance. Bit by bit the green clouds merged with the grey ones over the village and made them larger. Kea raised her arms and moved her fingers as if she were playing a harp. The green cloud was travelling with the wind towards Thunum.

Harugari Kea "Woodpecker" casting her spell

Just half an hour later this green-black cloud appeared to the east of Thunum where it hovered quite low as if a secret load was pulling it down. Every bird and animal instinctively fled from the vapours it drizzled. Not so the ashmen under Ole Brand's command. Too preoccupied with the circling birds, they didn't even notice at first. Hauke and the Chauci, who had been waiting for the arrival of the cloud they had requested, their weapons ready, sent their falcons back into the forest to rest. The ashmen laughed at the flight of the ominous birds and believed themselves to be safe now. Until they were embraced by the cloud. Soon they were yelping and cursing as the drizzle seeped through their rivets, their chainmail coifs, cloth and wool, making them terribly itchy.

Now they were all frantically busy scratching themselves. Some even threw away their swords and shields to take off their itchy clothes. "Keep your armour on, you wankers!" Ole roared, but to no avail. The itching got worse the more the men scratched themselves.

Raging, Ole realised that the green cloud above them was not of natural origin. Hauke gave the signal to attack. Unlike the Frisians, the Chauci didn't use a bugle to underline the effect of the ghostly attack. Instead they croaked like a flock of falcons.

But just like the Frisians, the Chauci warriors had adjusted their fighting methods to the marshy landscape and preferably used missiles like spears against their mostly more heavily armoured enemies from Oldenburg. They abhorred open combat and no longer had the numbers for it anymore. So they primarily laid in ambush and approached silently and ghostlike under the cover of night and fog.

Resembling falcons descending from the silent sky, they ran crouching into the village where they took up position behind walls, carts and fences and peeped around the corners. Hauke croaked like a bar-tailed godwit and his men rained their arrows purposefully on the partly half-naked ashmen who stumbled through the village in a panic. Amidst the screaming and wails of pain, the Chauci fired two more volleys of missiles. Ole called his men to order and managed to create a rudimentary shield wall. "We're being attacked! Come on!" His men staggered around like drunks. Some were scratching like mad and wheezed angrily. Those who recognised the Chauci couldn't believe their eyes and yelled about "Demons!" and "Bird-men!" Whenever several ashmen gathered together, the Chauci quickly hid against the protective walls again and fired from different spots. The masked Chauki didn't wear heavy armour the way their enemy did, but more weatherproof gear. The burning, itchy drizzle therefore didn't upset them as much. Furthermore, they had learnt to endure pain and itching without complaining; of paramount importance when lying in ambush. The ashmen counted on spreading terror, but their tactic was now useless seeing that they were on the defensive. Screams, buzzing arrows and stifling roars filled the air. A giant of an ashman spotted Hauke and stormed at him, threatening to smite him with his warhammer. But Hauke escaped the mighty blow and drove his dagger into his enemy's throat. The giant growled, spitting blood, and fell down dead. Hauke's arm was burning and felt numb. He was dizzy.

At some stage, now fighting for their very lives, the opponents forgot about the itching. None of the Chauci talked anymore. Their falcons circled the battlefield and occasionally plunged at one of the ashmen to aim their claws at their eyes. The curses of warriors drunk with rage echoed through the air as the Chauci came closer to Ole's large shield wall. With his throwing axe Ole split the head of an unfortunate Chauci warrior and the man's mask came off. "They're no fucking demons at all!" he cursed. "They're just ordinary shitheads! Haha! Look!" Roughly half the ashmen had already died in the fracas, but the rest of Brand's forces were gathered behind their round shields, safe from the Chauci's arrows. Hauke and his men, having run out of arrows, stepped closer towards the enemy. Five of the Chauci had been killed in action and after losing thirty of theirs, the ashmen now only marginally outnumbered Hauke's troops. Ole laughed: "Bahaha! I am Ole Brand. I don't believe you're demons or ghosts! Your plan was pretty guileful! Are your wenches like that, too? Never mind! We'll find out for ourselves soon enough, won't we men?!" The ashmen laughed nastily.

Hauke was sorely tempted to storm forward and slaughter the foul-mouthed Viking, but the man beside him held him back. Ole smirked: "What's up? Are you scared? Do you rather watch other men mounting your whores? Is that it?!"

The cloud lost its shape and Kea in Werdum collapsed with exhaustion. The women rushed over and gave her some water. Kea's heart was pounding, her breathing shallow and she moaned: "No, Hauke... Don't... Don't let him... tease you."

Hauke took a deep breath while the Norsemen laughed maliciously and vividly gestured what they intended to do with their future prey. But Woodpecker's taunts over the years had made Hauke more or less immune to insults. He would ignore the provocation and be a real leader. He was ready. He raised his arm and said: "I am Hauke, son of Tjarko, ashman. We are a tribe on hunters and a hunter doesn't hate his prey. Instead he is grateful after he has slain the animal. Be thanked therefore." The Chauci whistled and their falcons came rushing down again in a huge single flock to peck out the ashmen's eyes. The shield wall fell apart, the Chauci attacked and the slaughter began. Shields burst like plywood when they were hit by the axes, blood splashed everywhere over the clay soil and only seconds later every fighter seemed to be covered in it. Hauke himself confronted Ole Brand who was busy bashing one of the Chauci's head while roaring with laughter. His victim's simple leather helmet offered no protection against the brutal blows. When the man's blood sloshed over his face, Brand grinned as if he were standing in a refreshing rain shower after a prolonged drought. "Bahaha, you little bastard! You haven't even stuck your prick into someone's twat yet and think you can beat me?" Hauke didn't even listen. He avoided Brand's powerful strokes, rolled away and managed to partly slit Ole's chain mail with his dagger. The experienced fighter roughly grabbed Hauke by the leg and kicked him so fiercely that the youth's ribs cracked. "Don't think for one minute that I'll spare you because you're just a boy! I've killed much younger lads than you!!" Black dots dancing in front of his eyes, Hauke hissed: "How brave!" With those words, he mobilised all his remaining strength and rammed his dagger right into Ole Brand's foot. Hauke jumped up and saw Ole brandishing his axe. There was no escape.

Life is strange, he thought. One moment you laugh and coldly stare death in the face and the next all you want to do is live, live, live for eternity. Ole's axe came swishing down... but at the last moment the Norseman staggered back, roared, and used his weapon to fend off the flock of screeching falcons now pecking at him. His ribs hurting, Hauke watched as Ole hit many a bird with his axe and feathers and blood swirled through the air. The dead animals piled up around the warrior, but the rest of the falcons didn't give up. Hauke's own falcon, Hübke, had led the attack and scratched Ole's eyes out during the very first onslaught. Robbed of their leader, the ashmen's resistance collapsed just like their shield wall. Ole screamed and cursed in Norse dialect: a blind, wounded and rabid animal foaming from the mouth. Hauke felt neither joy, satisfaction nor hate. Silently he picked up his bow from the ground, inserted his last arrow and shot. The arrow hit Ole right between the eyes. He abruptly stopped moving and fell down dead. The falcons flew away.

Complete and utter chaos reigned among the ashmen and the twenty that were left took to their heels. Thunum had been successfully defended. The remainig eleven Chauci were too weak to give chase. In the next few hours two more of them would die from their wounds, but they could leave this earth with a smile: their homeland had been saved.

There was no jubilation or exultation. Too many had died. Hauke also felt empty and burned out; not just from his injuries. Never before had he killed a human being; just Fenna, Gobolds and other forms of lowlife. The killing had affected his hitherto carefree heart and the thought of his home and cheerful, cheeky Kea made him tremble and weep. His Chauki brothers embraced and hugged him. They felt the same. It had been the narrowest of escapes.

There were, however, shouts of joy from the tower as the children, old people and women ran out of it. Sadly the smoke fumes had also claimed its victims among them. Three of the old people and an already sick child had choked to death. But the people's gratitude was still overwhelming and they effusively thanked their saviours. Thunum's four armed warriors - three young lads and a bearded veteran from Rüstringen – mounted the remaining horses and galloped after the escaping Norsemen to kill them with their lances. Everybody wanted well rid of them in case they started roaming the area, threatening children and cattle. The Thunum warriors made good use of their wrath and afterwards it was doubtful if any of the ashmen had managed to escape...

The people of Thunum tended to the Chauci in the ravaged main building where they arranged provisional accommodation for them when a messenger on horseback approached the village from the west: an old man, bathed in blood, but with a confident smile on his chapped lips: "Ochtersum has been successfully defended! A stink bomb turned the tide! This calls for a celebration!" Hauke hated to put a damper on his happiness: "That's good news, indeed. But how is our main army doing near Esens?" "I haven't heard." Hauke nodded: "Then we're not going to celebrate for the time being. We haven't won yet." The old man looked abashed now. Hauke felt sorry to have crushed his euphoria and hopes for a cold beer, but even their victories in Thunum and Ochtersum were meaningless if Esens should fall and Radbod win after all. They had only eliminated the advance party.

Hauke hoped that his father was doing well. He turned to the remaining Chauci who had gathered around him again. The villagers themselves cheered and thanked them over and over for their help. Then they took everything out of the hiding places the ashmen hadn't already found. Hauke felt lousy, but had to admit that the people's gratitude and kindness came just at the right time. Before all this he would have laughed at the thought, but now he wanted nothing more than hug his father and Kea, hold them tight and never let them go. He also thought tenderly about Mayla from Wangeroog, the energetic girl of the same age with the long brown pigtail. The reason he had fought with Hinnerk Wiards. But he didn't even want to fight Hinnerk anymore. All his rage had vanished and he laughed despite his broken ribs, enjoyed each breath he took, even though it hurt a lot. Nothing in the world was worth more than this painfully clear moment when all the previous difficulties in his life now seemed stupid and childish. He would fight for Mayla, in his own way. He was sick and tired of embarrassment. Life was too precious.

While the Frisian's and Chauci's enemies had been defeated in Ochtersum and Thunum, the battle at the dyke was raging all the more violently. On the Frisian army's right-hand flank the grimly determined Chauci warriors, under the command of Hauptlinger Tjarko, fought the Drauger, those bizarre creatures which may once have been drowned and now answered to Njörd. Captain Düll, whose wounds healed in just moments, was now pushing the Chauci back and Tjarko had to face him directly. Nobody else was able to take him on. The Chauci had always been more skirmishers than warriors. They fought in rough formations like the Cherusci under General Arminius long ago. Suddenly a young novice from Marienkamp pushed himself forward swinging a thurible emanating white smoke and shouted at Düll: "Hey there, you monster. Your time's up!" Düll bubbled with amusement and briefly let go off Tjarko: "Oh, really? Is that so, you little vermin?" His left tentacles shot forward and grabbed the novice, choking him until the young man croaked. He still tried to swing his incense burner, but lost control over it and fell onto the sand with a thud. Njörd's champion laughed: "You want to purify me, boy?! That won't be necessary. I am completely pure. Pure of ridiculous sentimentality!" He wielded his axe and tried to strike Tjarko's spear. The Hauptlinger had thrown himself protectively in front of the novice and severed the krakenman's tentacles with his spearhead. Roaring with rage, Düll kept striking him with his axe while Tjarko pushed the monk out of the way. The axe ripped up the Hauptlinger's dyke wool reinforced armour and sliced his belly open.

Tjarko furiously lunged one last time at Düll who tried to intercept the spear with his tentacles – forgetting they had just been cut off. Tjarko's seax neatly hit the mail coif of Düll's helmet and smashed the rusty chains, the iron, the slime and the flesh underneath.

Gurgling like a drowning man, Düll fell to the ground and jerked while steaming black blood squirted from his throat. Holding his belly, Tjarko went onto his knees and the novice limped over to him. He threw back his hood: it was Brother Witzelt. Three Chauci falcon warriors ran through the Draugr and the skeletons to protect their leader. Witzelt sobbed: "The wound ist d... deep. W... we have to take you to the abbey, Lord..." Tjarko shook his head: "It's too late... Pah! You young people: you rush headlong into disaster without thinking. There are so many past burdens in this world, so much anger and rage..." He spit out some blood and smiled: "But perhaps... perhaps just that is our great hope? You children who know nothing of the old sins and never should know, hehe..." He patted the novice's head: "Don't worry. Please tell my boy not to grieve. And also tell Kea. Tell everyone at home." One of the Chauci warriors took off his helmet and knelt down beside the Hauptlinger: "Master Tjarko... we shall fight to the last man!" "Well said, my brothers. To die amidst one's friends and family is the only meaningful death." Witzelt broke out in tears and sobbed. All around them the enraged Chauci drove back the Draugr who were lost without Düll.

Tjarko was now dying. The world with all its sounds and colours faded into the distance and everything became quiet and grey. He saw himself at the beach with Hauke and the boy's long deceased mother, playing catch and romping about in the sand. But what where they doing here? Didn't they know that this was a battle field? Why didn't they run for safety?

Tjarko watched his alter ego lifting the young Hauke onto his shoulders and running into the waves with the boy, roaring and laughing. Now he knew: this was the past; the safety of more peaceful times. A beautiful, sunny day; seagulls screeching high above, fishing boats from Benswersiel sailing on the ocean. Tjarko forgot about Radbod, Ursula and the undead. Soon he also didn't remember Esens, Thunum, Werdum or the Wangerland. The Chauci, too, gradually left his memory. Just once Kea briefly appeared as a frightened young girl who had learned to laugh again – and never wanted to stop ever since.

His thoughts turned leaden and heavy and all he could still see in the end was this beach with his family. The worried, inquisitive, open look on a boy's face... Then everything went black and Hauptlinger Tjarko died.

Two of the Chauci warriors carefully lifted him up and carried his corpse from the battlefield. The third Chauci, who had knelt beside him, put his arm around Witzelt's shoulder. Words were unnecessary; he didn't blame him for Tjarko's death. Witzelt sobbed gratefully; then the blood froze in his veins. His mouth gaping wide open, he witnessed how Düll's dead body got up and recreated his two-fingered tentacle from a fetid black substance. The Chauci warrior noticed, turned around and was killed as two tentacle tips, hard as iron, plunged into his mouth and eyes before his dying body was flung away like a broken toy. Now Düll's head took shape again: this time without a helmet and anything but human. He resembled a one-eyed octopus. Where his face should have been there was now nothing but that one staring eye without an iris and dozens of tentacles twitched around his mouth, constantly oozing slime onto his plated armour. Even without a helmet his voice was deep and clangorous: "Njörd has chosen me as his champion! I am immortal and your ludicrous god of pain can not stop me! Neither can the Frisians or the Chauci! I am a god!! Begone, worms!" Witzelt crawled back and caught Düll's attention: "I have to thank you, vermin. Only by dying could I be truly revived! Now your life is over!" Witzelt managed to grab his thurible, swung it by its chain and fliung the smoking jar at Düll's head: "Here only one life is over!" Düll coughed and screamed as the vessel exploded. His kraken head disappeared behind hot, sizzling white fumes. His screams became higher and increasingly piercing accompanied by ugly crackling and squelching sounds. When the vapour had vanished in the cold wind, he stomped towards Witzelt. The captain's half-melted face revealed traces of his human skull. Witzelt scrambled away from him while Düll melted like wax. Shortly before reaching the novice, he collapsed onto the sand.

The relieved Witzelt uttered a quick, heartfelt prayer and took a deep breath. His research in the abbey's archives had been successful after all – the mixture he had hurriedly blessed had dispelled Njörd's influence through smoke purification. Blubbering, Düll's body dissolved into a black pulp in front of his eyes revealing the skeleton and skull of the once human being. The novice swallowed hard when he realised that he had killed a person. Christian or pagan, it didn't matter. He didn't like it. Despite Düll's demise, his Draugr and skeletons kept on fighting.

Ursula had lifted Leevke's unconscious body with a kraken tentacle before Hinnerk could reach her. The creature endured the pain and drifted in the tide while Ursula stood before Leevke, her scythe-wand at her feet: "I shall crush this delicate body if you don't stop that glow right this instant, boy! I'm serious. Even with a broken spine the girl is still useful to me, but is that enough for you?! Is a cripple enough for you?" Ursula's grin was disgusting and Hinnerk crunched his teeth. Furious, he rammed the dagger and Pakhaou into the sand: "Kiss my arse!" The shield stopped glowing. Ursula grimaced and moaned with the same relief as the kraken, as if they had shared the agony. Hinnerk extended his hand: "Leevke and the shield. Give them back." Ursula shrugged her shoulders: "Later, okay? It's inconvenient at the moment. I've got a pain in my back, you know?" "Bitch! Witch! Traitor!" Ursula waved him away: "I've heard it all before. Even worse, boy. You can't shock me anymore, believe me." She gazed at the crackling shield burned into the kraken's tentacle: "That will take a while to heal... If I was really as evil as you think I would have torn every limb from your body long ago. But I care about my fellow men and fellow kraken." Hinnerk pulled his blades out of the sand again: "Well, if not this way...!" Ursula raised Leevke and tightened her grip on the girl's body. Hinnerk paused again and cursed. He felt utterly helpless and Ursula nodded sympathetically: "Perhaps now you can guess how we felt all those years. How we suffered." She looked over at the dyke where Radbod, in his spectre shape, was killing Nordendi right now. "The third Hauptlinger is dead. The battle is over. You lost." Hinnerk was trembling inside and out when she passed him as if he presented no danger to her. But he actually did. Nothing physical, nothing tangible stopped Hinnerk from jumping forward and killing the witch. Nothing but the worry about Leevke, which Ursula exploited to the last while feasting on his reticence. It was driving him mad. Was he so easily influenced, freedom so easily forgotten through feelings alone. Was it worth it? Hinnerk gazed over at Leevke – and got a shock. She had opened her eyes and quietly but firmly told the kraken: "Let me down. Go back."

The beast whimpered like an enormous dog which didn't know which master to listen to. Trembling, it deposited Leevke on the sand. Ursula turned around: "What in the name of...? What are you doing?!!" Leevke checked the shield burned into the kraken's skin without reacting to Ursula or Hinnerk: "That looks nasty. Wait a moment." The shallow seawater around her spread out like a fan and slid up the kraken's injured tentacle, enclosing the wound and the shield. Leevke closed her eyes and golden rays projected from her hands onto the water, making it radiate in light golden hues. The kraken whimpered again when the burned flesh became unstuck from the metal and fell into the water. Then the gaping wound closed and healed in next to no time.

Leevke made the golden water recede and said: "That's that. You can go back now. This is no place for you." The kraken hesitated before disappearing into the ocean. Ursula was raging: "How... How dare you, you slut!?!" Leevke seemed removed from the world, as if half-asleep and not consciously aware of the danger. "I helped him. This is not his world. He has to go home." "I have known this creature for more than 300 years! Who are you to send it away?" "Me? I am the Mistress of the Sea." Ursula was totally taken aback by the girl's calm reply: "Oh, really? And don't you think Njörd has some say in the matter?!" "He is irrelevant. His influence is tied to those who believe in him." "I see! And your influence isn't!" Leevke cocked her head as if listening to an inner voice: "I... I don't know... It's all been so long ago. Or at least that what it feels like." She noticed Hinnerk and for several seconds she stared at him as if he were a ghost. One could see the confidence of her dreamlike trance crumbling and being replaced by relieved laughter: "Hi... Hinni?! You came? Because of me?" Hinnerk cleared his throat and turned red as a tomato: "Of course. As if I would leave you with that deranged bitch over there!" Ursula swung her scythe around: "How touching. And useful!" She raised the crackling, flashing scythe-wand against Hinnerk. But Leevke just as quickly produced a stream of water with the shield riding on it towards him. He rolled over on his side and wielded Lux Maris just in the nick of time to divert Ursula's magic energies. But the impact was still forceful enough to make him slide through the sand.

Ursula eventually gave up and Leevke quietly scolded her: "That wasn't very nice." "Puh, I can't stand brats like you. You haven't a clue about the world, its lies and brutal cruelty. A world that makes you compliant with its hypocritical smiles! It's all ahead of you, little Leevke. Just wait. The day will come when you'll be able to see further than now. And you will learn that some cruelty and violence is necessary just in order to survive!" She fired a thunderbolt at Leevke and it hit the girl full on. She landed in the shallow water with a splash and Hinnerk angrily stormed at Ursula with his dagger drawn. She didn't even bother to look at him: "Too predictable..." Four undead now emerged from the sand, grabbed his arms and legs and threw him down in front of Ursula's feet. "Mistress of the Sea. Bahaha. Tush. Don't make me laugh! What... What's happening?!"The water was seething, boiling and foaming.

A deep, muffled booming sound seized the entire coast and the waves rose and fell the way they did during the worst hurricane. Ursula frowned and espied Leevke in the waves with her arms and legs stretched out. The kraken witch made bolts of lightning rain down on her from her scythe and from the sky, but Leevke was protected by the waves which diverted the voltage into the vastness of the ocean where they dispersed without harm. Her voice echoed from the sea: "Take care of Radbod, Hinni. I'll take over Ursula." As soon as she had said it, a hand-shaped wave grabbed the skeletons surrounding Hinnerk and tore them into the water. Free again, Hinnerk asked: "A... Are you sure?" Leevke sounded as if she found it difficult to speak: "Please. I... can't guarantee anything... Go!" Hinnerk ran off, used Pakhaou and Lux Maris to cut his way through the undead who seemed irritated by the fact that one of their enemies was bursting forth through the back of their own ranks.

They were screeching while trying to capture him. Ursula let him go and walked along the beach: "You appear to have your powers well under control now?" Leeve pushed her body through the waves up to the shore. Her movements were tense as if she was wrestling with herself. Her golden eyes quickly changed to red and white several times: "You... hurt me... Stop... Or else..." "Or else what? Do you think I'm scared of you?" Spit drooled from Leevke's open mouth and she was panting. Ursula twirled her wand: "Alright so. You are exhausted. Let me calm you with one of my best sayings." She rammed the wand into the ground and grinned broadly: "Fire cauldron show yourself, show yourself to us. Fire cauldron show yourself, sooth our thoughts just thus!" A billowing field of air formed above Ursula and developed into a circle of fire. In this fire floated a large cauldron elaborately decorated with runes. The fire gathered inside and gently glided in and out of it; like snakes, sensually and languidly. The flames were slowly pulsating to the rhythm of a beating heart from yellow to red. Any of the Frisians who looked at it froze and lowered their weapons. Let themselves be slain by the undead without resistance.

Hypnotised, Leevke herself stared into the lambent flames and Ursula's voice purred: "That's better. You know the cauldron, don't you? I used it to make you sleep before, Mistress of the Sea, hehehe..." She approached Leevke with the cauldron hovering behind her. "You don't have to be conscious to serve me. I'll simply let you sleep for eternity until your friend and all the others have gone. Sleeeeep..." Leevkes eyes turned golden again. Her eyelids became heavy until she finally dozed off....

Radbod in his fog spectre shape threw Nordendi down and pierced him through his right shoulder joint. Nordendi gritted his teeth while the king triumphantly towered over him: "Well fought, warrior from Norden, but your stance was futile. Do you now recognise the power the old gods and our traditions bestow on me? And what is it you have got by comparison?" Friedhelm smiled grimly: "Colour in my face!" "Just you mock me! But take a good look at your divine ministers." With his seax he pointed to Abbot Wynfried who was standing on his own with an axe and a bible. "They're praying to a dying god who has turned suffering into a cult. The god of pain! How much livelier is that? How much livelier is it to have original sin drummed into you, that you can't escape from your whole life long, only through grovelling subservience and ruefulness?! The empty promise of paradise? Pah! No wonder that crap produces nothing but hypocrites! Because deep down they don't believe in it themselves! Their own bodies refuse to accept that pathetic babble. I, on the other hand, respect spirited action and don't bother about collective guilt and original sin! I respect what out ancestors have bequeathed us, to protect us: our community and our way of life! But they treat our forefathers' wisdom with contempt! Through their bonds and lies!" Wynfried nodded: "It is true that much suffering has been inflicted in the name of the cross. To the Frisians and the Chauci as well. But they are not half as weak as you presume! They practice their own kind of resistance against us. They live their lives..."

Radbod's nebulous shape was trembling: "Their resistance is not enough!" The abbot believed that the conflict may perhaps be resolved without further bloodshed and now deployed his verbal dexterity: "So, what values do you represent, King Radbod? Decades of vendettas, feud and the forgiveness of sins through wergild?" "Oh, and indulgences are a different kettle of fish, I take it?" "They are controversial, I agree! But we are more concerned with repentance. Repentance for one's evil deeds. It's the only way to overcome evil. That's what my brothers and I believe in. That's what we teach: man's reform!" Radbod's nebulous shape with its glowing eyes approached the abbot; hovered around him like a spectre: "Oh, yes. You are so peaceful, considerate and reasonable, aren't you? Lies! All lies! Hypocritical bullshit, deception and traps. Where was your remorseful protest when thousands of pagans were butchered; the proceeds of their disenfranchised lands used to erect your monuments of terror?" "Nowadays the churches offer sanctuary from enemies..." "They are the centres from which you practice your oppression! From their pulpits you preach your doctrine of servitude and bondage. Hammer it into enfeebled hearts like nails into a coffin!" "They're just messages..." "And it's just a coincidence that the Frankish hordes are right behind you, prepared to torture anyone who disagrees with you?! Just so you can claim that the secular is not your concern. We are deeply repentant. Forgive them, Lord! Forgive, forgive, forgive!" Radbod attacked with Durjawer and Wynfried repelled the blows with the St. Boniface bible while trying to hit Radbod's crown with the consecrated axe. He didn't succeed. The king of the Frisian was only toying with him. Was far more superior in his fighting skills. And morally?

They separated and the abbot listed the advantages of adhering to the Church while the fog ghost circled around him: "We no longer have feuds! No quarrels and bloodshed. We manage our holdings better than before. Our yields have more than doubled and the economy is booming! Everyone's prospering! The ashmen attacks have decreased through our unity with the one God, with the Church. We have never lived as peacefully!" Radbod chuckled: "Sure, sure, but are you content now? Is the Church peacefully resting in blessed harmony? Or are there already – wonders will never cease – new enemies? Within and on the outside?! Who will the Church direct its next crusades against? The Saracens, the Prussians, the Wends or the Rus? When will your thirst for war end? When will the beast be sated? I shall tell you when: never! Even if you owned the whole world and the sky was plastered with crosses, you would still find excuses to evangelize. With guilt, love and torches. You've always been like that and you always will be. You will pretend, you will murder and afterwards you will repent. Nothing will change. Your cross is responsible for a mountain of corpses. And that mountain is getting bigger all the time. But you repent. How merciful. How peaceable. You stand for decay, for death and deception!" Wynfried silently reflected on Radbod's words. The king laughed: "Hohoho! What's up, priest of the cross? Don't know what to say? Do you suspect I may be right?! That your beloved world is falling apart? That's what it feels like when the truth penetrates your heart. Bit by bit! Relentlessly!" Wynfried lowered his gaze and prayed. He needed divine inspiration, a sign that could save him and his faith because his reason and his intellect could no longer withstand Radbod. He had no counter-arguments. What could he possibly say when everything he had learnt all his life had to yield to the truth. That the Church he had faithfully served his entire life was based on ancient sins it could never cast off. Indeed it even increased those sins by not making amends and restoring all the conquered lands to its rightful owners. Pure hypocrisy. Radbod's rage may be excessive, but not unfounded. It was completely understandable. Abbot Wynfried could no longer deny it. The king had won after all – on every level. God himself remained resolutely silent as if to confirm that this was indeed the truth.

Chapter 9

Sword and Shield

Hinni directed Lux Maris' beam at Radbod's fog spectre after breaking through the enemy ranks: "Kiss my arse!" The king of the Frisians growled: he couldn't maintain his ghostly form under the hot, glaring beam and returned to his previous shape. Abbot Wynfried was standing behind him, motionless and confused with a desperate, helpless expression. Radbod raised his blade and laughed: "You! Put that thing away, boy! It's tickling me!" The light didn't affect him; it only annoyed him a little. Hinnerk charged at him and they crossed swords. Radbod was never in danger during their fight, even when Hinnerk executed a three-in-one blow. He also tried the wave-stroke, rolled down the dyke and used every other technique he knew. Only the tiletop warbler wasn't suitable in the situation. Panting and bathed in sweat, Hinnerk eventually had to stop. Radbod smiled, pointed to the beach where Ursula was hypnotising Leevke with the fire cauldron. "Seems like everything is under control again. You fought well. Reckless and extravagant, but worthy of a true Frisian." Hinnerk wheezed and had to cough. The ribs the tentacle had cracked were exacting their toll: "Why don't you just leave us be...?" Radbod nodded: "You don't just let yourself be. That's why I'm here in the first place. You are confused. All of you." A voice Hinnerk had no longer expected, and which instantly rekindled all his hopes, echoed from the dyke across the battle field: "Go home, Radbod! Hinni, you come to me!" "Uncle Abbo?!" Elated, Hinnerk ran to him and they hugged: "Did you lot think I was gone forever?" Brother Saltpeter behind him said: "I brought him out of his coma a little sooner than usual." Hinnerk laughed and handed his uncle the sword from Satan's Bog. Abbo twirled it around: "Looks good." "I borrowed it," Hinnerk admitted and the warrior from the Ghastly Moors smiled: "So did I! But now I have to see to that King of Wrath. Our duel was rudely interrupted." Radbod panted and the two men circled each other like wolves again. "Did they free you after all, Abbo? I more or less expected it. You were nearly too strong for the soulkraken. I only noticed now." "It's the only way to convince people around here." Radbod spread his arms with a grin: "Why? I even convinced the abbot over there. He's not saying anything now, is he?" Abbo said: "I've made my decision. Life is far from perfect, but it's enough for me. Just because it is full of pain and suffering doesn't give us the right to pass our ancient feuds onto the innocent, the children. Let it go." NEVER!" They jumped at each other and crossed blades with incredible speed. Radbod nodded with appreciation: "Oho! You've learnt a thing or two." Abbo smirked: "On Bant you used the fog to avoid an honest fight. Have you forgotten already?" Hinnerk raised Lux Maris while Radbod exclaimed: "Don't worry. I won't this time. So you say that this has to end at some stage, Abbo? Alright then: what about the crusades? Wherever I look, everything is in flames at the borders of the Western World and also within, thanks to the Inquisition." Abbo leapt back and admitted: "I took the cross because I thought it would absolve me from my faults and sins. Erase my memory." He smirked: "What a delusion! I only made even more mistakes. This time in the name of righteousness and love." Abbo extended his hand to Radbod: "Sometimes, old king, it is better to let go. The hatred will destroy itself. We have to put our trust in our young people." Radbod actually fell silent and Wynfried lifted his head, feeling utterly helpless and deserted by God. At that moment Düll rose once more from the blubbering mass of his skeletal body and formed a black slime out of which emerged a monster with jerking tentacles. Seeing this, Brother Witzelt despaired and silently begged his brothers for help. But Düll and Njörd's voice boomed so loud that even Ursula froze: "DESTROY THEM, RADBOD, AS AGREED! THERE LIES KNOW NO BOUNDS! NOTHING BUT A TOTAL VICTORY IS OF ANY USE TO US! DESTROY THEM ALL! NOBODY UNDERSTANDS WHO WE ARE AND WHAT WE HAD TO SUFFER! AVENGE THE DEAD! AVENGE ALDGISL, WHO WAS BETRAYED! AVENGE POPPO, WHO TOOK A LAST STAND! NOW YOU ARE THE LAST KING, RADBOD! PROVE YOURSELF WORTHY OF THE HONOUR AND FINALLY CRUSH THEM!" Radbod overcame his doubts and crouched down with his arms folded: "The time for discussion is over! Njörd, forefathers, fairies and Albans! Grant me the strength I need! Doniawera! DONIAWERA!" A black bolt of lightning shot from the grey, overcast sky, hit Radbod and enveloped him. The dyke and the sand exploded into dirt and crumbs. His eyes turned completely red with piercing, hate-filled black dots surveying his surroundings. His lips stretched into a wolfish sneer, his white hair crackled with electricity and two scourging, clawed tentacles with poisonous, dripping, steely points shot from his shoulders.

Abbo mocked: "No more tricks, hey?" Radbod's voice sounded bestial: "This is no trick! This is who I truly am!" Hinnerk threw Abbo the shield: "Perhaps it will help!" Abbo nodded: "Stay back, everybody. This is going to be ugly." Radbod's laughter boomed: "Wohoho! Come on then! Show me your godless strength!" Then he attacked Abbo, using his tentacles as additional weapons. Abbo defended himself with the glowing shield which disturbed Radbod more than earlier now and the king protected

his eyes with his tentacles. The first exchange of blows already showed that his speed and strength had increased immensely. Hinnerk growled: "What is that?" Brother Saltpeter had walked up the dyke leaning on his stick and was now also watching the fight. He told Hinnerk: "That's an avatar: one elected by the gods."
"But Abbo can defeat him, can't he?" Saltpeter sighed and glanced down at Abbot Wynfried, who was still standing there, stunned and disconnected from what was happening. "Without God's help, I fear your uncle is fighting a losing battle." Hinnerk gripped his Frisian dagger. He wouldn't stand by and watch Radbod murdering his best friend. He'd rather make one last attempt to end the misery. One way or the other!

Leevke desperately tried to stay awake, but the constant, slowly pulsating glow of the fire cauldron rendered her incapable of resistance. Ursula giggled and pointed to the open sea: "You can come out again now. It appears the little one is fully under our control again..." Timidly and cautiously the nomcrab scrambled out of the water, the bracket for Leevke's prison sphere still attached to its back. The runes etched into its armour lit up when Ursula directed her wand at them. She looked satisfied: "Everything's still in working order. Excellent." But then the kraken witch's face contorted with pain when she sensed Radbod's fog spectre being broken by Lux Maris' beam. Shortly after, however, a black thunderbolt sped through the sky and filled the man she loved with the god Njörd's tremendous power. She smiled reverently while Leevke struggled to keep her eyes open. She didn't want to fall asleep, but her limbs felt like lead and every thought was pure torture. She tried to remember why she was standing here, but the fire cauldron's crackling flames deterred her every attempt and constantly distracted her with their mystical flickering.
Then Düll's blubbering, black corpse arose as well and formed a creature that couldn't as yet assume a firm shape. Two or three tentacles aimlessly thrashed about, eyes emerged and vanished again, phantom-like mouths with fangs grabbed at the Chauci and the Frisians who stayed well clear of the growing monster. A whimpering Brother Witzelt crawled away, searching for his incense thurible, unable to turn around to behold the monster he had helped to create.
Ursula, on the other hand, realised what was happening: "So Düll has actually died and

entered Hel's realm in exchange for this monster: a Grendel from Njörd's depths. It's suffering; it doesn't belong here..." She smiled bitterly: "Faithful and devoted to the last, hey, Düll? Let's just hope Hel doesn't torture you too much. Farewell..." She did actually feel for Radbod's only consciously remaining friend who had condemned himself this way. His soul would have been welcomed in Valhalla; instead he had sacrificed it to Hel in exchange for a creature of the underworld, the realm of the shadows. A being from even more ancient stock than the Draugr, trolls and kraken. Grendels lived in dank caves far beneath the mountains. Where black lakes didn't reflect any sunlight and no pebbles had disturbed their surface for thousands of years. Time had no meaning in this place. Life and death were equally stagnant.

A scaly. four-fingered claw emerged from the darkness, bathed in deathly cold moisture and dried blood, with webbing between its sharp talons. Gills sprouted from the small shoulders supporting the neckless, hemispheric head with its slit-like, yellow eye without an eyelid. On the Grendel creature's back was a ripped fin, covered in shiny, silvery, fingernail-sized scales. Its jaw, a gaping, nearly vertical flap extending from the neck to the belly of its barrel-shaped body, was studded with triangular fangs protruding over the edges. Although the creature's arms and legs were muscular, they were thin compared to its body and the joints swollen and projecting. The Grendel walked in a crouching manner and was actually less than six feet tall. The Draugr greeted its arrival with convulsing sighs and moans. It wheezed through its gills like a monstrous bull...

"Grendel – Njörd"

Abbo clenched his teeth, ignored the ugly wound above his chest and brusquely shoved Hinnerk aside: "Stay away from the battle!" His voice didn't tolerate any backchat. Radbod's kraken tentacles blocked all of Abbo's blows that would have hit him under ordinary circumstance. Abbo's fighting skills were superior, but that wasn't the issue here. This was about who possessed the greater power. And that was Radbod in his new shape. Abbot Wynfried and Brother Saltpeter could do nothing but watch. Wynfried, his face totally devoid of expression, said not a word while Saltpeter commented: "We are faced with extraordinary circumstances we never expected during our contemplative existence in the abbey. A Grendel. Unbelievable! But the old sins will inevitably catch up with us sooner or later. That is the reason I joined the monastery: to leave all that ancient mess behind and dedicate myself specifically to what actually helps. But now I realise that my efforts were ridiculous; ridiculously small to combat that incredible madness. Look at it, young Wynfried: a monster from the heathen world is descending upon us. As if Radbod wasn't enough. But perhaps we deserve it. Now we are the anvil the hammer smites." The abbot gritted his teeth and wrangled with his conscience like never before. As a young, observant and frequently intellectually brilliant man he had been summoned to East Frisia from the legendary monastery of St. Gallen. Right from the start he had researched the local history and enjoyed the liberties the Frisians were entitled to.

He smiled wearily: "A constant give and take... Abbo is wiser than the lot of us together." Brother Saltpeter watched Abbot Wynfried approaching Radbod and Abbo:

"What are you doing, you silly boy?" "I'm going." "I can see that! But... Why? He'll kill you!" Wynfried didn't stop: "Look after the abbey, Brother. You're genial enough for the job." "I'm eccentric!" "Exactly." A smile on his lips, the abbot stepped between Radbod and Abbo. The latter yelled: "Get out of my way!!" He tried to push the foolish monk to the side, but Wynfried's bible flared up and threw Abbo back. Then he raised his axe to strike Radbod. The king just grinned: "So you want to die fighting, monk? Say hello to your foul carcass of a saviour when you enter the hell you believe in!" With those words the king pierced the abbot's breast with his seax. Wynfried didn't even try to defend himself.

He slumped, but still stood there and smiled softly while the blood trickled from his mouth. Oppressive silence spread all around when Radbod laughed and turned the seax inside his enemy's chest to make him scream. Radbod's red eyes were glowing, but Abbot Wyndried simply stared at him. The monk's penetrating, pitying expression baffled Radbod and an unknown, indefinable fear crept up his spine.

Grendel, the monster roared with laughter: "BAHAHA! IT'S OVER!! THEY HAVE BEEN DEFEATED!! VICTORY IS OURS!! OURS, RADBOD!! WE DID IT!" The Frisians and Chauci stopped fighting, as did the undead at Radbod's command. The king slowly shook his head: "Something is wrong here. It doesn't feel like a victory. What did you do, priest?! What curse did you utter?! Talk, you bastard!" The abbot's words were a mere whisper, but still as emphatic as a slap in the face: "The curse is gone, Radbod. Liudger's spell is hereby revoked. My blood seals the deal. You are free. Bant will no longer imprison you. You have won." Radbod felt it as much as Ursula who was busy heaving Leevke into the new protective sphere. The kraken witch moaned, then laughed like never before: "It's... it's gone... The pressure is gone. Hehehe! Free! Free at last..." Radbod stumbled back and forth as if a massive weight had been lifted. His eyes wide open, he asked: "But why?!" The abbot explained wisely: "Because everything has to come to an end. So something new can be created. Just like Abbo said." Radbod's lips were trembling as his eyes changed from red to white and his skin rejuvenated itself. His seax extended, he said hoarsely: "That... changes nothing! My revenge has been carved in stone, in sand and blood!!" The abbot fell to his knees and collapsed. Brother Saltpeter rushed over to him: "You stupid fool!"

Wynfrieds eyes closed as he whispered: "I am sorry. Grant me one last wish..." "What?" "Don't make me into a martyr..." The abbot of Marienkamp died; the monks grieved his loss. Radbod looked even more confused while Grendel howled: "NOW WE ONLY HAVE TO KILL THE REST, RADBOD! THEN NOTHING WILL STOP US! THE MAINLAND WILL SURRENDER! EVERYONE WILL BE LIBERATED! EVERYONE WILL LIVE A MORE JUST AND ORDERED LIFE!"

Radbod's felt like he had been choked. He wanted to laugh and cry and cheer, but couldn't utter a sound. Ominous silence prevailed. He looked around and saw the just as bewildered, disappointed and downright distraught faces of his fellow countrymen. Abbo and Hinnerk gathered the little strength they had left, unwilling to give up. But the remaining army of Frisians, Chauci and monks had no choice but to surrender. Their hopes of victory had been crushed. They were left without divine assistance, without the moral support of a higher power and without a Hauptlinger. Radbod's voice was shaking when he shouted: "You are on your own now!" Nordendi coughed up some blood: "Tell us something we don't know, Raddi." The king paused and Grendel raged among the Chauci and Frisians who were fighting the beast. He flung the screaming men into his jaws and devoured them noisily. Brother Witzelt had taken cover behind a corpse. His legs pulled up and hugging himself, he prayed while blood and sand rained down on him and the yelling and screaming around him rose to a mad crescendo. The Frisians' weapons couldn't penetrate Grendel's scaly armour.

Njörd had possessed him and was exacting his bloody justice.

Ursula felt satisfied. Their combined strength had induced the abbot to relent and now there was nothing keeping them on Bant. They were free again. The victory a certainty; the path to the new Magna Frisia delivered from all obstacles. Grendel-Njörd was smashing the last remnants of resistance and she had safely locked Leevke up in the sphere again. The fire cauldron had once again done an excellent job. She was about to send it back to its ghostly realm when Leevke opened her eyes. They were completely white.

Shaking, Leevke was lying on the beach on the island. Her island. The sky and the sea were raging; screeching in her ears. She whimpered "It's too loud. It hurts!" The purple crystal behind her glowed erratically and aggressively; the palm tree swayed heavily in the howling wind. In front of her the crab dug itself out of the sand and she asked it: "Oh, Mr Crab! What's going on? Why am I here again?! I was already gone, wasn't I?" The crustacean clicked its pincers: "You let yourself be caught off guard, you nitwit! The beast has regained control!" "But I got away from it?!" "Well, that's old hat by now. You should have fought harder!" "I'm too scared to. It's so hot when I get angry. It burns." "That's why the beast has risen once more. Worse than ever!" "I can dive again!" The crab pinched her nose: "Not now! Can't you see what's happening? You've got to wait until it's over. In this storm you'll sink like a rock. It won't be defeated that easily again. We'll have to think of something else... For the time being we can only wait." Leevke sobbed: "Please, don't leave me here alone!" "Child, I'm already risking everything within my power, which, with all due respect, exists on the atomic level. Everything has to be planned and... Hang in there. It will pass like everything else..." The crab buried itself in the sand again and left Leevke on her own after all. The sea was raging, whipping the waves into the sky and back into the depths. The island rose and sank with the movements, but she didn't fall off. Apparently the famous centrifugal forces didn't apply here. Nonetheless, Leevke clawed her hands into the sand and saw the gaping jaw beyond the floodgate. Whatever was happening to her? She gazed into the endless, black depths of the ocean. And held her breath. The beast was staring at her through white eyes.

A perfect, oversized human hand formed itself out of the water and burst Ursula's sphere like a soap bubble. Startled, the kraken witch drew back. The water hand grabbed the still wide-eyed Leevke and gently put her down on the beach. Ursula snarled: "Damned beast! Do I have to intensify the fire cauldron after all?!" She ordered the magic cauldron to hypnotise Leevke more forcefully. But the girl didn't react to the flickering flames. Instead she created a water fist that punched Ursula into the stomach and made her fall. The witch got up again: "Let's do it differently so! Fire cauldron! Let the fire rain! Let the fire spew scorching rain!" The cauldron came closer and shot a dozen sizzling flames at the girl. With a casual wave of her hand, Leevke created a water shield and the flames evaporated. The fire cauldron was shaking and vibrating as Ursula commanded all its destructive powers, willing to kill Leevke. She didn't need her anymore and her death wouldn't be a major loss now.

Besides, Ursula didn't want to share her man with anyone. Holding the scythe wand with both hands she muttered heathen curses and the cauldron vented its rage. Like a volcano it erupted, shooting scorching hot, hissing balls of fire at Leevke. Her water shield shrieked like hot metal being chilled by cold water. Another water hand shot up, grabbed the cauldron. It screeched horribly and immense steam bent it until the runes on its surface flickered and died, leaving nothing but a heap of smoking lead crashing to the ground and startling the nomcrab. Ursula sank to her knees. Her forehead was covered in beads of sweat: "This... this enormous power, where does it come from?! What are you really, girl?! What are you?!" Leevke couldn't hear her. Her face remained devoid of expression apart from an animalistic grin reminiscent of a hunter targeting her prey. Ursula felt an icy cold creeping up her spine. She didn't even notice a thin water hand sneaking up on her from behind and snatching the little kraken from her head. "No!" The hand flung the creature into the sea. Ursula picked up her scythe and stormed at Leevke. The runes blazed in bright yellow. Just before she reached the stoic Leevke, a water tentacle brought her down. Spitting, she landed just inches away from Leevke's toes in the shallow water. The water arm entwined her like the tentacle had done to Leevke previously. It lifted the kraken witch and tossed her to and fro. Ursula growled angrily: "Let me down, you cunt!" Leevke didn't hear her because she wasn't actually there. The water tentacle pushed Ursula's spine until it broke like a twig. For a fraction of a second Ursula felt nothing; just weightless. But then the pain exploded in her brain and she screamed.

Radbod heard her and let go of Abbo and Hinnerk. "Ursula... My little Ursula...? Düll! Where are you, Düll?! You were supposed to mind her!" His claws soaked in blood, Grendel-Njörd stomped over to him while some of the skeletons collapsed as if somebody had cut the invisible strings keeping them upright. "DÜLL IS GONE. ONLY NJÖRD IS HERE!" "We have to stop... I need to think. Something has changed!" The monster wheezed heavily: " NOTHING HAS CHANGED! THEY ARE CHRISTIANS AND THEY HAVE TO DIE. THEIR STENCH IS OVERPOWERING, BUT THOSE WHO WANT TO SURRENDER SHALL KNEEL BEFORE ME!" Whatever the abbot had done to him, all his anger and hatred gradually left Radbod like an evil curse. As if something that had hitherto covered all his thoughts and feelings had fallen off him. With a shudder he recognised the truth and it made his knees tremble. Memories of the true events, previously hidden by a mental block, now returned; his mind cleared.

He, the king of the Frisians and defender of the old faith had been used by his own gods to further their aims. Like a pawn in a game of chess, they had built him up and nourished his wrath. Radbod remembered the dark cave underneath Bant where, fuelled by anger and the thirst for revenge, he had made a pact with Njörd. From then on it had no longer concerned the welfare of his Frisians, no, it had been all about the old gods and most of all Njörd's battle against the god of the Christians. Now Düll was gone; the spell broken – Liudger's and also Njörd's curse. Radbod looked around him and made a decision: "No. It's over. I no longer feel anger. It has to end here. It no longer makes sense." Grendel took a few steps back: "YOU SPEAK LIKE A MAD MAN, RADBOD! YOU HAVE BEEN BEWITCHED!!" "No, I am cursed no longer." Radbod now resembled that man in his mid-thirties again he had been before his banishment. Grendel-Njörd roared: "YOU BETRAY ME? WHAT GIVES YOU THE RIGHT?!" The laws of the old days. The laws that recognised the volatile state of this world. That knew of a race shaken by the tides, by storms and waves. Tossed back and forth by the sea and the earth. It is the right of the people who don't let themselves be dictated to and show the due respect for the powers nobody can escape: the eternal play of life and death. Our time is over, Ruler of the Sea. It is no longer up to us what the Frisians want to remember. They no longer need us. They are going their own way now. So be it." Grendel seized him brutally. Radbods tentacles dissolved into black slime while his pagan strength left him. Njörd himself was revoking it: "YOU ARE NOT ENTITLED TO THE POWER, LAST KING! YOU ARE WEAK! AS WEAK AS THE CROSS!" "All men are weak. But you will never understand that. Because you are a god." Grendel opened his jaws to devour him. One last time Radbod glanced at Ursula who was lying with a broken back on the beach, whimpering with pain. Their eyes briefly met. "Little greasenoodle. My heart. Farewell." Ursula screamed, but her voice was drowned out.

Suddenly the entire northern coast was choked by the swirling boom of a gigantic approaching wave, five times as high as the dyke. Her arms stretched out, her eyes white, Leevke was standing on the shore and grinned. She was awaiting the high tide with open arms.

The Frisians, Chauci, monks, Abbo, Hinnerk, Nordendi, Attena and the freshly arrived reinforcements from Ochtersum and Thunum put down their weapons. Okko, Jens, Hauke and everyone saw the shadow of the thundering water above them obscuring the sky. Everybody instantly knew there was no escape. Jens spotted Hinnerk and stumbled down the dyke towards him. He clutched the boy and shook him: "What are you doing?! Can't you see that Leevke needs you?! RUN! RUN TO HER!!" Hinnerk gulped and Abbo pushed him gently: "Go! It's the only thing that might still save us..." Hinnerk nodded and ran off, past the baffled undead, who didn't know if they should now obey Radbod or Njörd. Their loyalties basically lay with the Frisian king and nobody else. Water and arms tried to stop Hinnerk's progress. He avoided them, jumped threw them and over them. Against the massive roaring of the sea he screamed: "Leevke! It is me! Stop it! You are killing us all!" Leevke didn't react. "Please, Leevke! Do you want to kill us?!" He stopped in front of her and stretched out his hand. A water tentacle seized him the way it had previously done Ursula. Only his fingertip touched the little hairs on Leevke's cheek; a tiny, delicate moment of contact. Then Hinnerk was violently pulled up. The gigantic wave now darkened the entire sky and even Grendel-Njörd paused...

Trembling, Leevke was crouching on the beach with her legs pulled up when she felt the warmth on her cheek. Somebody was there. Out there she wasn't alone, not like here. She got up and walked to the edge of the island. "I've had enough. I don't want to be alone anymore. I was on my own long enough. It's dangerous out there, but... but at least I'll no longer be ALONE!" She jumped into the thundering floods of the white-eyed beast. Icy cold clutched her heart and pulled her into the depths. She braced herself against it. "Not yet. Not yet! Not! Yet!" Her soul was burning; her golden eyes glowed bright as the sun. The beast screamed.

The gigantic wave sloshed back into the open sea. The devastating water mountain now only drizzled onto the people like a warm late summer rain and receded into the ocean. Exhausted, Hinnerk fell into the sand while Leevke toppled over and passed out. Grendel-Njörd was stunned: "Her over there... she can be of use to me! Those powers... Beyond my own! But first of all..." He returned his attention to Radbod. Brother Witzelt – beside himself and in tears – swung his now only faintly smoking thurible around his head: "But first of all you'll swallow this!" He hurled the container into the monster's face where it burst. The vapours irritated the beast long enough for Radbod to mobilise his remaining strength and free himself. Everyone's eyes were on him – he sensed it immediately. Where they looking at him... full of hope? Radbod grinned broadly: "Nothing has changed! Good!" He rammed his stainless seax forcefully into Grendel's jaws and pulled himself onto the creature's shoulders from where he dislodged the blade again and pierced the monster's eye with it. "TREASON! TRRRRREASON!" Grendel-Njörd screeched, reeled, and thrashed around wildly while Radbod jumped off and stepped back. His blade was buried in the eye. A vitriolic, green acid spluttered from the creature's eye and jaws. Bubbling and howling it dissolved in its own acid. Radbod took a deep breath: "One's own poison is always the strongest. I hope you can escape Hel, old friend..." All that was left was a reeking, fuming pulp. Radbod addressed Brother Witzelt: "Thank you, boy. May I ask why?" The novice swallowed hard and crossed himself. He seemed more collected: "Because the alternative would have been even more terrible." Radbod nodded slowly and instructed his undead to withdraw. The Draugr moaned indignantly and he said: "No backchat. Go back to your master. Tell him that Radbod of Bant no longer serves him nor any other vanr. You can either leave in peace or be killed by my entourage!" The skeletons collectively aimed their weapons at the Draugr whereupon the grumbling drowned ones went back to the sea where they had come from and where they would remain until somebody would deliver them from their suffering at last.

Friedhelm Nordendi and Abbo, supporting Attena, approached Radbod who was pacing up and down in the bloody sand with his arms crossed behind his back. The old king proclaimed to the Frisians and Chauci: "Much blood was shed today and I did it to liberate you! But it was I who needed liberating. My anger and wrath had blinded me. All I could think of was revenge and this here is the result of my blind... stupid rage! No weregild and no feud can ever atone for this. This monk of the cross over there, this Wynfried, released me from Liudger's curse and I want to honour his sacrifice. As a man, not as a servant of some god. It was a heroic deed." He spread his arms wide as if he wanted to embrace all of Frisia. "This is my homeland. It always was and always will be. Should you ever need me, I will return. For you. Against anyone trying to enslave you, be it with chains, cudgels or dishonest, one-sided righteousness! I'll be alert and will come when you call me. But no sooner. Show me that you need me and I'll be there. You are free to do what you like. Our laws have survived generations of proud Frisians and Chauci to the present day and beyond. Because it is this flat, cold land, buffeted by storms, which brings forth a certain breed of people, people who are true to themselves and who always feel closer to their neighbour than some far away power or gold. You fought well and the casualties didn't die in vain. Honour and fame will be theirs for all eternity. As long as the heart of Frisia is beating." Abbo stepped forward and handed him Pakhaou: "There. Take it. Perhaps you'll have more use for it." Radbod held it in his hands and smiled: "It is too heavy in my hands. As always. It's better off with you. Keep it." Abbo took it back. The Frisians and Chauci leaned on their comrades, their swords and spears, too exhausted to stand unaided, but, and that was crucial, they were standing upright.

Snorting with rage, Hauke stormed from the dyke and fired an arrow at Radbod as well as anything he could offer in the line of insults. He wounded the king's arm, but Radbod didn't react; as if his body was numb. "You pig! You murdered my father. You will die for that, I swear! I, Hauke, Tjarko's son!" Hauke's blows pelted down on Radbod like a hailstorm, but the king only brushed them off. With his hand. "Come on! Fight!!" Hauke roared in tears while Radbod studied him through sad eyes: "You can be proud of your father, Tjarko's son. A man who defends house and home is the most courageous and noble of all. His forefathers will anticipate his arrival in their halls with pride and deep respect." Hauke collapsed weeping; sank to his knees: "Damn it. God damn it." Radbod let him be and addressed the army again: "Those seeking revenge, come to Bant. I shall expect them. The others I advise to look after each other. I have... seen movements on Frisia's borders. And unrest in the interior that has been brewing for a long time. You know better than I what that could be. So be on your guard. This test was just the beginning. It's not over yet. Not for any of us. I shall go now. Farewell." With those words Radbod turned away. His cape was fluttering in the strong coastal gale. The wind was howling and wailing, drowning all other sounds. Nobody stirred. Radbod walked to the strand where Hinnerk had helped Leevke who had woken up by now and smiled, exhausted but content. Without another word, Radbod went past both of them to Ursula and lifted her broken body. With chapped, sandy lips she asked: "Are we going home?" He replied: "Yes, my heart. We are going home." He looked back at Hinnerk and Leevke and silently nodded to them. Hinnerk returned the gesture: from soldier to soldier.

Both were now reunited with their girlfriends. Radbod walked into the sea with Ursula, towards Bant.

Then he heard the Frisians and Chauci sing behind him:

"Come the flood, come the flood, come the floo-hoo-hoo-hood,
We hold each other, each other we ho-hold...
Come the foe, come the foe, come the fo-ho-ho-hoe,
We hold each other, each other we ho-hold even more.
Come the storm, come the storm, come the sto-ho-ho-horm,
Let the feud, let the feud, le-het it re-he-hest..."

The battle of Osterbense was over; Radbod's invasion repelled. The losses had been great, but so was the gratitude of the surviving men who were all overcome by the feeling of having done the only right thing, the only right thing that echoed far beyond life and death through all of Altera: the feeling of being free, the sensation of having a tight hold on life with nothing obstructing one's actions and thoughts.

Nordendi was the first to cheer and even if all the men were drained and jaded, they joined in. The fear and tension discharged itself in one enormous exclamation until Attena got up and, covered in blood, announced: "Well, well, that kick in the arse hit home, wouldn't you say, men?! Bwahaha! Oh shit, my fucking spleen!" Laughter sounded from everywhere and they rushed to tend to the wounded Hauptlinger and other warriors. Admittedly, they were only covering up the loss of their friends with their laughter and hearty slaps on each other's backs and many of them just crouched in the grass, weeping, while the women from the baggage train rushed over and distributed generous measures of small beer and schnapps to console sons, brothers and fathers.

The dyke was filled with the sound of jubilation, wailing, devotional chants and great excitement as friends believed dead embraced each other with tears of joy in their eyes, glad to have survived. Radbod's invasion had been fended off and they were still standing on the dyke. Not he, a god or anyone else. "Better dead than a slave!" roared some drunken groups on top of their voices every now and then. Many a man collapsed eventually and snored loudly. Friends carried them home.

.Frisians and Chauci fraternised, gesticulating wildly. Some of them hollered and cheered like men possessed and bashed swords, axes and spears against their shields until their arms were burning. The deafening noise nearly made Jens pass out cold. But he still enjoyed the spectacle in the company of Okko, Abbo and Brother Saltpeter who was reassuring the young Witzelt and praised him for his deeds. Hinnerk returned to them with Leevke in his arms and Jens shouted: "Is she alright?" "Yep! She's just a little tired," Hinnerk answered and smiled. "You are still alive, Jens?" "Ask me again! I still can't believe it! Hahaha." Leevke slowly regained consciousness. "What happened?" she asked. "Why is it so loud?" Jens explained: "You beat them all. A giant wave came! It was incredible? D... don't you remember?" Leevke slowly shook her head: "No, I don't. Is it over?" Hinnerk smiled: "Absolutely! Radbod and Ursula are gone and Abbo is back! Everything is alright again. Wait, I'll carry you!" He put Leevke over his shoulders with strong arms and trudged towards the beach. When she saw the nomcrab squatting there, Leevke said: "Go home." The animal cheeped and scrambled into the sea. Hinnerk joked: "Are you aware that this is the second time I found you on the beach?" "Yeah, I'm good at getting stranded. But you're also very good at rescuing me." She tightly wrapped her arms around Hinnerk's chest and enjoyed the fresh breeze and its warmth.

Chapter 10

A celebration

Right after the battle the wounded had to be cared for, the men had to rest and all the damages incurred during the fighting assessed. Thunum and Ochtersum as well as the holdings the ashmen had laid waste to on their track had been the worst hit. Families returned to destroyed, burned-out homes. For the duration of the reconstruction works they were housed on the surrounding farms and with relatives. In some cases, however, this lead to complaints as some of the more affluent farmers felt they were treated unfairly because the Hauptlinger settled them with more refugees than the other, less well off landowners.

But in the end they gave in, especially since Friedhelm Nordendi left them in no doubt that he wouldn't hesitate to forcefully make room for those in need. They brought the half-dead Behrend Attena to Esens where they treated him with herb poultices and bitter healing potions from Marienkamp. Something he didn't appreciate and he openly voiced his displeasure: "Just let me guzzle some strong liqueur and I'll be as right as rain! Bwahaha! Ouch! Watch out!" But the robust Deel-Deern from Esens showed no mercy to the Bear who couldn't really ward off her treatment. "Silence! Rest or your guts will spatter everywhere, you obstinate idiot! The sutures have to heal! REST!"

"Yes, yes. What a woman!"

The list of casualties was long; among it Tjarko, the Hauptlinger of the Chauci, and Abbot Wynfried of Marienkamp. Their corpses were embalmed; the traditional funeral pyres prepared for each of them. It was late in the evening when the sparks were flying from the flames in Werdum and Tjarko vanished in the fire along with his weapons, shield and armour according to the ancient Chauci ritual, accompanied by the great wailing of the Chauci keeners. Kea also burst into tears and Hauke hugged the Harugari who had been his companion from childhood on and had helped to rear him. Now she was the one in need of comforting. Hereafter the Chauci warriors proclaimed Hauke as their new leader. The young man accepted, but presently admitted that he would need their help as he was a yet inexperienced. The Chauci rewarded him for his honesty with a chorus of : "HAIL! HAIL! HAIL!" and Kea already teased him again: "Is somebody retreating into his shell, hey? Hey?" "I'm not, you little goose!" "Oho!" Then she whispered: "I love you. And Tjarko is proud of you!" The young man firmly clasped the woman to his chest. He was not ashamed of his tears.

Jens as well as Leevke and Abbo returned to the Wiards' farm with Okko and Hinnerk. Hilde wept tears of joy that her husband and son had come home in one piece and fussed about them so much that Okko and Hinnerk quickly felt embarrassed. At first Leevke seemed jaded, but she noticeably perked up when Hinnerk's siblings swarmed around her.

Soon she was laughing again, explored the farm, talked to the geese and the pigs or eagerly – if remarkably clumsy – helped with the cooking and treating of the injuries. Particularly in Hinnerk's case she made every effort to heal his wounds with a special herbal brew and poultice of her own devising.

She did, however, use nettles instead of silver ragwort and the result of her misinterpretation could be heard as far as the Jakob's neighbouring holding. Tears in his eyes, Hinnerk asked: "Why don't you just make some healing water?" For a moment she didn't seem to understand what he meant, then she smiled: "Oh, yes! Totally forgot..." "How could you forget? Everybody is already talking about the great wave, but not everyone understands it was you yet... And it's hard to believe, I agree." Leevke laughed: "I can hardly believe it myself! And I don't remember either. It's strange. It feels like I'm... as if I'm missing something. But I do remember that you woke me!" She manoeuvred her body closer to Hinnerk's. The boy blushed and his throat felt suddenly parched. Leevke took his hand and added: "Thank you... Oh!" She flinched. Their touch had produced an electric discharge. Hinnerk smiled: "I'd do it again anytime. You are my girlfriend... Aren't you?" Leevke licked her hurting finger. "I am. Sure I am." Her reply didn't take just one but several loads off his mind and he couldn't stop grinning.

Over supper in the cosy, warm kitchen, Eiko, Hinnerk's brother, younger by two years, asked: "Was there really a kraken?!" "Do you not believe us?" Hinnerk replied gruffly. "Undead, Draugr, a witch and a one-eyed monster. They were all there." Jens smiled faintly: "And yet it is unbelievable when we talk about it over a leisurely meal. Sounds like a fairytale." Abbo stopped him with a wave of his hand: "Worse. We are dealing with the legacy of problems others pushed aside for the younger generation to tackle. Because they didn't have the guts to put an end to those problems when they became apparent. Complacency and fear created this misery. It was foreseeable that it would get so out of hand." Jens agreed: "We certainly had the guts to put an end to it. Do you think we have permanently got rid of the problem?" Abbo pushed his plate away and looked deep into Jens' eyes: "Thinking like that lays the foundation for the next wave of unsolved problems, Mr Janssen. I'm sorry, but if we believe that everything is alright and events like that will never repeat itself just because we think we know what to look out for, we become blind to the real danger which only has to take a different shape... Radbod won't return, true. But another threat can still sweep us away." He gazed into the round: "We have to stay on our guard, friends, to honour the dead and life all the more." The former crusader sighed: "Because I do indeed fear that Radbod's warning to us wasn't due to his hurt pride. He was serious about the threats to Frisia. If from within or without, there is a tumour growing." Okko nodded: "Ever since the great flood twenty years ago nothing is the way it used to be. From that time on the Hauptlinger have become ever more powerful. They behave more like feudal lords than our equals." Okko folded his arms across his chest: "Unfortunately that's a bitter necessity. Otherwise the agents of the realm would have overrun us long ago and sold out to the Hanseatic League." Abbo countered: "I don't mean to diminish your achievements, Okko. It was necessary, yes, but will they surrender their power again? And when exactly? So far nothing has changed." Jens drank from his goblet of blackberry juice: "Well, they certainly won't resign their posts now after the news of the battle has done the rounds. There will be much tension, mistrust and caution on the side of all those who have something to lose... Not good for trade, that. Not good." Hinnerk pondered: "And I thought that war and crises were positive for the merchants?" Jens disagreed: "That's naive. It only applies to those who've already found their market niche, Hinni. For small fry like me it's potentially lethal. By the way, could I interest you in some beans?" Hilde smiled at Okko and he rolled his eyes: "I'm sure we could do with a barrel..." Jens said: "Why do I get the feeling that you pity me?" "Because we do," Hinnerk chuckled. Leevke handed Jens her bowl: "Poor Jens. Don't be sad. Come. Eat. There you go." "I'm not a dog, damn it!" Klütje barked and begged for his share of mutton. Hinnerk gave him a bone and they retired for the night.

The next day a messenger on horseback from Esens arrived on the farm with the news that Attena was organising a great feast...

Jens sipped some mead from his drinking horn and glanced across the assembled guests in Esens. "Ah, there's pointy nose!" He had spotted the Woodpecker strolling over the market on Hauke's side. Jens was in the tavern of one of the innkeepers who would sell all his beverages today. Esens was crammed with convivial people; the square full of benches, kegs and tables. Chauci and Frisians were laughing, chatting, eating and drinking and some of them grandiosely told the children stories about the battle. About Attena's fight with Radbod, Grendel and the appearance of the great wave that so miraculously swashed back into the sea before it could do major harm. Jens enjoyed the loud merriment and rustic high spirits. Still early in the evening, he was already slightly tipsy while he was talking to the local people and merchants. He also walked over to Attena who was covered in bandages. Beside him sat the mischievous Nordendi and the two men's laughter boomed across the square. The Hauptlinger kept flinging insults at each other, which was interpreted as a sign of a blossoming friendship. Attena, the younger of the two, had more or less grown up under Nordendi's constant influence and it was said that was the only reason the Bear of Esens had remained at least marginally sociable.

Meanwhile Abbo and Hinnerk walked to their room in the local tavern. The place was overcrowded with guests, travellers and onlookers who had heard of the battle and wanted to find out more. Hinnerk knocked on the door: "Leevke? Are you coming? We want to join the feast." Instead of an answer they only heard a loud banging and screams. After much clatter and clanking Hinnerk and Abbo decided to break the door down. They rushed into the room to see Leevke half buried under a mountain of pots, blankets and clothes. The wardrobe had toppled over and the girl now peeped sadly out from under the mess, a pair of underpants partly covering her head. "I wanted to dress up." Hinnerk and Abbo asked dumbfounded and simultaneously: "And this happened?" "I'm sorry. I've never... never..." "What?" "I've never seen such fine shirts!" Abbo and Hinnerk looked at each other while Leevke tried to stuff the things back into the wardrobe and kept slipping. "Leave it, little one," Abbo said. "I'll look after it. You kids just go and have a look at the festivities. Those who put work above life, don't have one, am I right?" Hinnerk helped Leevke back up on her feet. She was holding a sheet in front of her completely naked body. Hinnerk's heart skipped a beat: "W... wha... wha...?!" Abbo quickly dragged him from the room and smiled at Leevke. "Put on something nice." Leevke gulped and turned as red as a beetroot.

Outside Hinnerk was gasping for air: "Tha... thank you, uncle Abbo. I got a terrible fright. Sh... she was..." Abbo smirked: "Did you at least get a good look?" Hinnerk stared at him with wide open eyes, then he lowered his gaze: "N... not really." Abbo slapped him on the back: "Give it time. She likes you. It's obvious." Hinnerk said nothing. His heart was beating like mad. Leevke appeared in a knee-length, blue shirt, with a shell buckle, over her usual clothes. Hinnerk took her hand: "You look great..." "Really? You do, too..." Leevke beamed so relieved that Hinnerk forgot his hand was all sweaty. Abbo pushed them forward and together they went to the market square.

They bumped into Jens and Leevke asked: "What are you going to do now, Mr Jens?" "Just Jens will do, Leevke. Wellll, I had planned on sailing to Greetsiel on my Lobscouse tomorrow. My business is there and I urgently need to attend to a number of things. I've got to pay the rent regardless of the invasion of the undead. Besides, Taalke is bound to be extremely worried." "Taalke? Is she nice?" Jens smiled: "She sure is. I think you would get on splendidly. She likes animals a lot." "So do I!" "Exactly." Jens handed Hinnerk a mead-filled drinking horn and Hinnerk took a large gulp. He said: "By the way, me and Abbo have already talked to the new Abbot of Marienkamp, Abbot Saltpeterus!" Jens grimaced sceptically and Hinnerk laughed: "That's what I thought at first as well. But he is the most experienced monk in the monastery and the brothers have lost half their men. It will take them a while to get over that. But this young Brother Witzelt is said to be a busy bee. He's instilling new hope in the older monks with his boisterous way. He advised us to consult Bishop Hungerus Frisus in Emden. Apparently he might be able to help us with regards to Leevke." The girl nodded determinedly: "I want to know where this power comes from and stuff like that." Jens chuckled: "Stuff like that? How quaint. Frisus is indeed meant to be a man of reason: a logician and sceptic." Hinnerk swallowed more mead: "Tastes pretty good. I could get used to it." Jens clinked horns with him: "Cheers! I dare say you'll have to tonight! Will we go to the dance floor?" They went to the innkeeper's serving counter where the people around it were already dancing enthusiastically. A puppeteer had set up a stall and was re-enacting the battle. Leevke curiously scanned the scene and was overwhelmed by the many people laughing, drinking and eating in such a confined space. Some men and women had brought their instruments: the sound of their flutes, hummels, lutes and harps provided a genial and merry background noise.

After all the madness of the past few days, this feast felt like heaven on earth. Children were scurrying about, nibbling on bread and meat skewers, Attena started some moronic drinking song and Klütje was romping around with the other dogs, fighting over a few bones belching men dropped from their plates. Hinnerk and Leevke were delighted when they saw Muddy Joost whose filthy feet made him look like he had come straight from the mudflats, which he presumably had. He sat down beside them and, after they had exchanged greetings, explained the reason for his presence: "Your grandparents asked me to tell you that they are fine, but very worried about you, Leevke. But they also understand if you stay away for another while to figure out where you came from. They love you more than anything in the world and said to tell you never to lose hope, no matter what happens." Leevke was deeply touched and smiled: "Tell them that I love them, too, and that I will come back. They are not my real grandparents, but they were there for me. That alone counts. Will you tell them that, Joost?" He nodded and laughed: "I will, of course. Gerd the Grumbler also asked for you. He said you should never go with strangers or hang around dark alleys." Leevke shrugged her shoulders: "I don't know any Alis..." Joost grinned and turned to Hinnerk: "And I'm to tell you, boy, to look after both of you. That means you as well." Hinnerk raised his drinking horn: "I shall do! Here's to you, Muddy Jost. Cheers! Don't let the mud shrimps get you! Hahaha!" After those words and having taken a bow, Muddy Joost was about to leave again. When Hinnerk asked him if he didn't want to stay and celebrate with them, he replied: "Oh, I don't really like big gatherings, you know. Too chaotic for my liking. And too loud." "Says the man who's not afraid of giant mud shrimps!" Joost said: "At least I can gauge what they might do. I can't do that when it comes to people. Well, look after yourselves. I'll see you." Joost was a mudflats guide through and through. He loved the wide open spaces of the mudflats and the sea. Leevke understood and turned her attention back to Hinnerk and Jens. Jens said: "You've downed three horns full already. How did you manage that in such a short time, Brother Hinnarkus?" "Dunno, buft it wassnnt sso disficult. Chweers!" Leevke, who was also drinking the sweet honey wine, felt only very slightly fuzzy. A fat monk jumped onto one of the tables and roared: "Let's party 'til we drop! God bless you all! Three cheers to drink!" The narrow table collapsed under his weight. The laughter and jubilation lasted for another half hour. The grief had been dispersed; the relief was tangible.

This night belonged to the living and Leevke regained her trust in the future. Ever since Driftwood Theo's raid on Kleene Wacht she had never felt really safe and secure. But now, here among all these people, she could breathe freely again for the first time. She wasn't alone with her worries and she had found honest, true friends. The world wasn't so terrible and dreary after all. She celebrated until the small hours with Hinnerk and Jens. They bawled songs on the top of their voice, laughed about things that weren't funny and danced on the tables and the floor, rolled around on the hay bales.

That night Leevke laughed more than ever before and clapped at every opportunity. She stayed remarkably sober as the whole place around her got completely plastered. Including Hinnerk, who had to throw up at least three times. That night would later enter the annals of history as the Great Piss-up of Esens. But Leevke felt as if the mists had lifted to finally make room for the morning. May it stay that way.

The great piss-up in the early hours

End of Act 1
The Last King

The Next Act of Frisian Freedom!

ACT II – Dense Fog, Deep Moors

Firedevils, Spies, Assassins!

Political Intrigues and Feuds!

Upstaalsboom – Thing!

The Likedeeler Take Action!

Leevke Discovers More About Her Past!

The Meeting with Bishop Frisus!

Introducing Salvatorus, the Inquisitor!

The All-decisive Battle for Frisia's Independence!

Mercenaries Armies from Oldenburg!

The Hanseatic League Intervenes!

Frisian Freedom – The Saga Continues…

Available Soon

A Few More Bits

Alteran Proverbs:

"Even lying down, we stand more upright than anyone else."
Old Frisian Saying

"There are a thousand reasons for giving up, but only one to go on. And that one counts."

"And in the end a horse shits on your head."
Conclusion of Brother Saltpeters: "Life – A Synopsis"

"Better to get off your high horse before you fall!"
A Peasant from Emsland

"Once we build a house, the master has us oust!"
Rhyme from Lüneburg

Why not try stout ale with honey wine? Honeybeer!!

𝔄utograph ℭard

This Copy of

Frisian Freedom, Act I – The Last King

belongs to:

_____

Altera thanks you!
May you never run out of mead,
your larder always be full to the brim,
and may no harm ever come to you!

Signed: GBF a.k.a. The Doyen